Lady of the Tournament

J.A. Stein

J.A. Stein Publishing

Print ISBN: 979-8-9864908-2-3

Ebook ISBN: 979-8-9864908-3-0

Book Cover by Venom Co.

Map by J.A. Stein

Edited by Gail Delaney

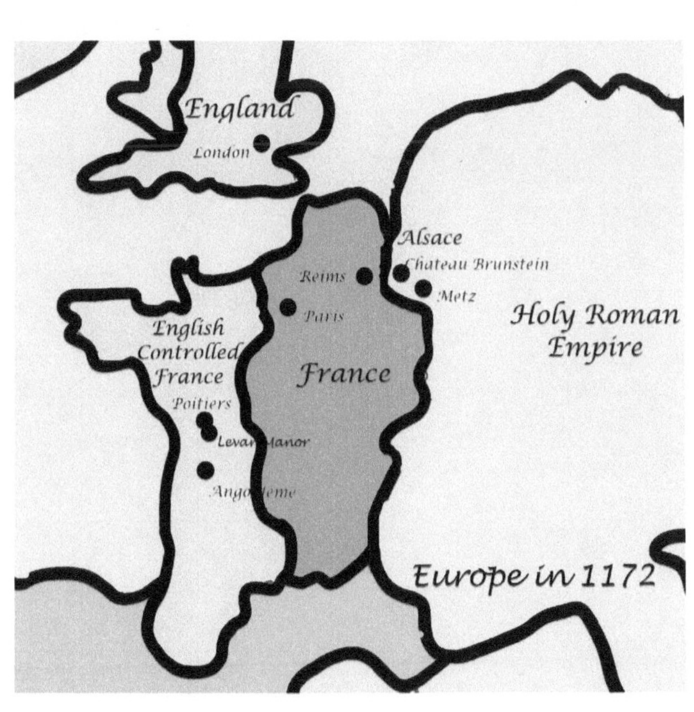

England
London
Alsace
Château Brunstein
Reims
Metz
Paris
Holy Roman Empire
English Controlled France
France
Poitiers
Levant Manor
Angoulême
Europe in 1172

Prologue

May 1199

Eleanor de Levan froze in her tracks, certain she had seen a ghost. She furrowed her brow, assuring herself he was just her imagination. When she looked back, he would be gone again. Slowly she turned. A finger of terror rushed through her veins as if the spring day had suddenly turned back to the bitter cold of winter. She hadn't imagined it. And he was no ghost.

The man's black eyes held steadily on her as he reclined in his chair. Despite the busy jostle of people milling through the market, the two souls faced off, sizing each other up like a bear meeting a wolf. Eleanor knew she was blocking the street; people were bumping into her. Still, she held her ground, a stick caught in the river, immobile, as the current flowed oblivious around it.

Montag.

Impossible.

There was the same shape of the nose, the curve of the chin, and most of all, the unmistakable brown-black eyes. He was clearly a knight, judging by his armor and sword, and built like Montag. The man's lips curled into the faintest of smiles lacking in joy. It was almost . . . cruel.

It was enough to break the spell. The man was not Montag.

Eleanor blinked rapidly as her fear turned to curiosity. Now that she had decided he was not her dead uncle, she noted the grey in his hair, the deep lines on his face. He was old, though from what she could tell from his toothy half-smile and burly build, he had aged well. His skin had a light tan to it, oddly dark for this time of year. In his fingers was a long pipe that swirled smoke around him like a shroud of mist. She caught the scent of it on the air, the exotic aroma all at once tempting and repulsive.

No, even if her Uncle Montag was not dead, this man was too old to be him.

Seemingly as entranced with her as she was him, the man continued to watch her, barely blinking. He raised the pipe to his lips as he inhaled the fragrant smoke. Eleanor steeled herself and took a step toward him, preparing to introduce herself. She could be the brave one. She had nothing to fear, not here in this public market. She had to know who he was and why he looked like her uncle.

"There you are!" Alec appeared at her side, catching her arm and steering her down the street a bit more forcefully than usual. Eleanor stumbled a step, catching herself and stiffening in protest, but a firm squeeze on her arm silenced her. "Don't look back," he whispered under his breath.

In confusion she followed Alec. "Did you see him? I thought for sure . . ."

"That it was Montag? I know . . . me too at first."

"Who is he?"

Alec sighed, glancing around them with an alertness far surpassing his normal caution. His gaze darted to the windows of the buildings around them, tension spreading from him to Eleanor through his gentle touch on her arm. Her brave, fearless knight was scared.

"Eleanor, do you remember after we rescued our son from Brunstein? You wondered what Montag had meant when he said he protected your mother from 'a hell you could only imagine?' Well, I think it was that man."

"Alec, who is he?"

Alec's gaze settled on his wife's face. From his sweating palms and the way his eyes flicked from her lips to her eyes to the ground, she understood this knowledge had been hard to come by. There was an aura of guilt around him: he had never intended on sharing what he knew. When he finally met her eye, that muscle in his jaw worked furiously.

She laid a hand on his arm, imploring.

Finally, Alec resigned himself and exhaled through his nose. "Eleanor . . . that man is your grandfather."

Chapter 1

27 Years Prior

May 2, 1172

Tournament of Obernai, Alsace

L ady Igraine's cheeks hurt from smiling. She debated for a moment which pain was greater; was it really her cheeks or was it her head, in general, that hurt? Though her painstakingly curated beauty glowed for the crowd, her mind could not silence the screams of her inner self, the self that willed her body to be anywhere but on display. For truly, she longed to be curled in a ball in a deep, dark cave where no one could find her. Where no one would talk to her. Where she could unscrew her perfect smile, collapse in exhaustion, and cry.

But the Lady of the Tournament never cried. And she certainly had no business in a cave.

Another knight rode past her as she sat among the other noblewomen. He singled her out with a lustful smile and offered to win the tournament for her, in her honor. She kept smiling and nodded politely. He was what, the twelfth today? For a moment her smile became genuine as she chuckled to herself. She'd watched this man before, weeks ago in Paris. He was a horrible jouster and could barely stay on his horse. He would not win today. At least there was potential for some entertainment if he were to fall.

For a moment, Igraine's smile faltered as she caught sight of her brother across the long fenced tournament arena, the list. He watched her with narrowed eyes. She sat a little straighter and looked away. She could not give him any reason to find fault in her. Cold looks from her brother were the norm, and today was no different. He expected a show from his "dear" sister. It was her duty after all. She was a trophy for display, fit to be judged by every noble she met so that Lord Montag could take the bids by which he would choose her husband. Not literal bids of course, though he would choose a man with extraordinary land holdings and wealth. She'd noticed him talking to the Count of Bologne earlier. The man was almost double her age and battle-hardened. She'd yet to speak to him, but the other ladies whispered of how he had kidnapped his first wife from a nunnery. Rumor was, that marriage had been annulled and now he was on the hunt for a second wealthy wife. To steal or to steal from? Was there even a difference if a woman's value was her property?

The wind blew a piece of Igraine's wavy blond hair across her face, and she absently tucked it away. If her elaborate braids were undone, her hair would hang well below her waist. It was the one trait of which she was proud. She'd been told her mother was a blond like herself. She had no memory of the woman she had killed with her birth. She wished her brother would talk about her, but she'd learned long ago that she was never to speak her mother's name in Chateau Brunstein. From what others told Igraine, she was the image of her mother. Perhaps that was why family tensions ran so deep. She was a painful reminder of the woman that had come before her.

"Look, my lady," her friend Lady Alenor of Tielo whispered from her side, grasping her arm. "Your brother jousts."

The ladies held their breath as Montag and his comrades galloped down the list against the wall of charging knights. Even with his helmet covering the upper part of his face, she recognized the concentration in his mouth, the smooth control of his formidable body as he rode like he was one with his horse. The two lines of horses and men clashed together with a screech of metal and wood, screams and growls: the full chaos of a melee. Some knights fell instantly, shuffling out of the arena to nurse their wounds. Others fought on foot, dancing to avoid the horses that spun next to them, wary that a single hoof could equate death. Within minutes, it was all over, the victors named. Montag was among them, towering a head above his peers. The crowd cheered its approval as the ladies politely clapped.

Lady Alenor beamed and leaned toward Igraine and whispered in her ear, "You need to invite me for dinner again sometime."

Igraine frowned slightly. Alenor's family had visited in early spring; Lord Tielo and Montag had some business to discuss. That was when the young, pretty Alenor met Montag and instantly succumbed to his smooth charms. The picture of her fair, petite form dwarfed by Montag's dark-featured height had led to various indecent, unmerited whispers among the household that Igraine had quickly stifled. Innocent Alenor had remained ignorant of the talk, while Montag for once had taken notice of the lady. In the ensuing months, the two of them had tested Igraine's patience with an elaborate game of cat and mouse across several duchies.

Igraine whispered back urgently, "I told you he's not all he seems, Alenor."

"He's *everything* he seems, I bet." Alenor giggled.

Igraine fought the urge to roll her eyes and instead refocused on the tourney. Her twelfth knight, the bad rider, had landed on his backside in the first charge of the melee. He walked past, smacking the mud off his clothes.

"Well, now, who is this?" Alenor asked. Her tone belied her curiosity.

Igraine turned in the direction Alenor looked and saw a knight enter whom she had never seen before. Over his mail shirt he wore a dark blue tunic with three bright yellow disks emblazoned down his chest in a vertical line. His bay horse was huge, and yet he looked proportionate on it, which meant he must be tall, perhaps even taller than her massive brother. He had a dark brown leather hauberk buckled over his mail shirt that looked a bit worse for wear, as if it had seen several battles in its lifetime. His boots looked even more worn. Like the other knights, he had a metal helmet with a nosepiece down the front that hid his features except for a mouth drawn in a thin line of concentration. Even with all his bulky armor on, Igraine knew he was a formidable man. But could he joust?

A second group of knights lined up for the next melee. The ladies watched intently now, as did the rest of the crowd, all curious of the newcomer.

"Where's the herald?" an elderly lord asked from his seat a few people away. He looked around anxiously for one of the lanky men who announced the knights, and once he spotted him, flagged him over. "Do your job, man! Who is that? Is he even a knight?"

The herald looked pale, but he kept his chin high and answered quickly. "Sir Enric de Levan d'Aquitaine, my lord. Fresh from Jerusalem," he added as if that explained everything. And in many ways it did. Igraine narrowed her eyes at the new knight. So he was battle-made, eh? The eastern-made knights were rare, and when they arrived back to the shores of Europe, one could never be sure how they would perform. Some were so fearsome in tourneys they had been banned from them. They could not control their blood rage in the artificial setting anymore. Others simply were boring, failing in the tasks given whether from lack of motivation or lack of skill, Igraine did not know. Which category would this knight fall into?

They watched as he charged his horse into a gallop with an invisible cue, lance steady in his arm. The first man he rode against fell, then a second, as he turned his horse in the chaotic arena for a second charge. Unable to ride further, he took to his sword, crippling the other knights until he was the last man on a horse. The crowd cheered for him louder than any other thus far, even her brother. They had expected nothing and instead, Enric had tied with Montag, the most consistent champion the sport had yet seen.

As Enric cantered past the stands, he took off his helmet in a salute to the crowd, raking in their cheers. Igraine chuckled. "Modest, isn't he?" she said to Alenor. Her friend was too busy cheering to hear her though. As Enric cantered level with Igraine, he looked right at her. For an instant, their eyes locked. Her clapping hands stilled as she stared, her smile frozen on her face, a pleasant shiver running down her spine to her toes. Then he was past her, and the moment was over. She shook her head to clear it, unnerved at her body's reaction.

"Now, that is a gorgeous piece of masculinity," Alenor breathed from her side.

Recovering her senses, she replied back, "You'd probably be better off pursuing him than my brother."

"Nay." Alenor shook her head. "He's poor. Handsome, but poor. Those crusader knights don't seem to come back with much but religion and a lot of scars."

"Since when is wealth everything?"

"Igraine, wealth has always been everything," Alenor said, looking at her with a smirk and raised eyebrows, her long eyelashes fluttering.

The remaining contest would be between Lord Montag and Sir Enric. The lord of the manor ordered them to joust yet another round, and the knights readied themselves at the ends of the list. Igraine watched as Montag aligned himself with Enric.

She clapped politely but stole a worried glance at her brother. Fury furrowed his brow. Quickly he pulled the laces of his gauntlets tight again. There was no mistaking the force with which he shoved his helmet onto his head. His black horse skittered sideways, nervous at the sharpness emanating from his rider. After a kick, the horse was back in the list. Montag charged, but the horse was nervous. He was not steady as he had been in the first melee, and it was Montag's fault, not that anyone would ever dare tell him that. Montag's lance missed Enric completely as Enric's lance splintered onto Montag's shield, throwing the man back in the saddle with a force like a horse's kick.

The crowd gasped.

Montag straightened and pulled his horse up, staring down at the unblemished lance. As the crowd cheered Enric's name, Igraine grimaced. Her brother would be unbearable tonight. He threw his helmet at his squire, shouting something. This was the kind of familiar scene she wished Alenor would watch, but Alenor's attention was instead focused on Enric, like the rest of the crowd.

Enric took an impromptu victory lap around the list again, his broken lance raised in tribute. All but Montag and his allies cheered; nobles even leaped to their feet. Igraine clapped politely but stayed in her seat. Her brother had not lost a tourney in years. She dared not support the victor in any way. Thank heavens this Sir Enric had not offered to win the tourney for her. She could not imagine if she had been expected to "reward" him. With her brother as the consistent tourney champion, she had never had to worry about evading the attention of the knights that pledged their wins to her. Their wins never existed! This was the first since Montag had put her on display that he had not taken the title and by such, protected her virtue and purity. It was a game he played to make her even more valuable to potential suitors.

But today he had failed. She would reward no one, as usual, but her fearsome brother was no longer her grand "protector."

She would have to tread carefully around him tonight.

Nervously, Igraine followed Alenor and the rest of the dispersing crowd back into the castle on the hill behind them. She looped her arm into her friend's, her frown etched into her brow.

"Stop frowning, Igraine, you'll get wrinkles," Alenor teased, trying to cheer her up. Playfully she poked at the crease between Igraine's eyes that was indeed forming as Igraine aged into her twenties. Though only a few years her junior, Alenor's innocence made her seem so much younger at times.

"He's going to be intolerable tonight. You know that."

"Montag?" Alenor smiled with a mischievous look in her eye and shook her head. "I'll cheer him up, Igraine. Besides, it's not your fault he lost. How could he possibly blame you?"

Igraine shook her head. Alenor didn't know her brother. No one did, other than those who lived with him.

Sure enough, by the time they arrived at the great hall for the feast, Montag still looked like bottled fury and his squire sported a black eye. Igraine didn't ask questions but merely poured him a tall mug of ale as he took his seat by her, then one for herself. They didn't speak. Igraine caught Alenor's glance from across the hall where she sat with her family, eyes inquiring if she could come over. Igraine shook her head, willing her friend to wait a bit. The tension at the table was already palpable. The dull screams in Igraine's head started again as Montag's vile friends joined their table. They were rude, unpleasant company, which made it even more difficult for Igraine to bite her tongue.

Sir Rothulfus Lezay sat down next to her and burped loudly. Igraine wrinkled her nose. The man always smelled of onions. It was beyond the standard male body odor. The stench exuded from his pores like he slept in the garden and ate rotten scraps with the pigs. She sidled closer to her brother.

"I'm half starved. Where's the food?" Lord Godfrey de Fougères asked, plunking down across from them as he looked around the hall, rubbing his belly. He was the most tolerable of all Montag's *friends*. He was polite and hygienic. And also happily married with heirs secured. Igraine suspected Montag kept Fougères around not so much because they had things in common but due to his extensive wealth in Brittany.

"Here it comes now," answered Sir Jean of Thuringia, a lanky knight with squinty eyes that seemed too small for his face. He didn't joust, but he was absolutely lethal with a club or mace. He, at least, celebrated a victory today. "And dessert with it," he sneered, eyeing the pretty maid who carried the tray.

Igraine wished she could warn the girl, but she dared not say anything. The poor thing barely set down the food and Sir Jean had her on his lap, kissing her sloppily. She pushed away from him in disgust, and he released her, laughing. The girl ran out of the hall as all four men, including Montag, roared with laughter.

Igraine frowned and sipped her ale, waiting as the men took their food first. When their plates were heaping, she took what was left for herself. She always was fed well, but she never took first helpings before they did. The choice cuts were for the men, a simple fact. Today's feast was plentiful, and the pheasant wing she bit into was roasted perfectly. She momentarily closed her eyes with pleasure.

Jean watched her, sneering. "Montag, when are you going to let a man give your little sister that kind of pleasure? Poor thing has to get it from a pheasant wing now."

Montag normally would stop such talk, but today he smiled instead. "Actually, just so happens there are plans in the making."

Igraine nearly choked on the pheasant. She looked at her brother.

Montag continued, enjoying her discomfort, "Yes, my dear sister, you have your first offer of marriage. Congratulations."

"Who?" Igraine croaked out.

"Sir Jean here."

Igraine felt her stomach churn. Surely, he must be joking. There was no way he would have waited until she was twenty-two to marry her to a cheap fool like Sir Jean de Thuringia.

Montag's face twisted into a smile at her reaction, and they all burst out laughing.

Igraine frowned. "You are joking, aren't you?"

"I must say, I'm a bit offended at your reaction," Jean said, but he still smiled his rotten-toothed grin. "Fine man like me, and I can't even get a smile."

"Are you joking?" Igraine asked again, narrowing her eyes at her brother.

Montag smiled, but it did not reach his eyes. "Actually, I've had three offers so far. Unfortunately, not Sir Jean."

"And the others?"

"You'll find out soon enough."

The men laughed harder, knowing they had a secret that was eating her alive. And perhaps it would.

"Have I no say in my future, brother?" Igraine asked, the pheasant wing uneaten in her hand.

Montag's smirk turned to a glare. "You are a woman."

Igraine threw down the remnants of her dinner and rose, glaring. "I'm going to get some air."

Her brother would scream at her later for causing a scene, but she knew in order to prevent a greater scene she needed to get out of the hall. Now.

The balmy summer evening enveloped her as she left the inner bailey to walk the battlement wall around the castle. Here and there were guards keeping watch over the peaceful countryside of Brie, but otherwise the walls were quiet. It was always her favorite place to be alone to think. Visible, lest no one sully her reputation for purity, yet isolated from the revelry and lewd behaviors of the hall below. She looked to the night sky strewn with gorgeous sparkling stars. They could occupy her attention for hours.

Igraine took her time, watching those pinpricks of light until her heart stopped pounding and peace overcame her. Time was wasted on worry. If her brother wanted to marry her off to some stranger, that would be her fate. Why ruin this moment? She crossed her arms and leaned against the wall behind her, closing her eyes to steel away the tears. When she opened them again, she felt stronger. She sighed and stepped back toward the stair that led down to the hall. As she reached the landing, she moved aside to allow a knight to pass as he rose to the wall.

They both froze, eyes locked as they had for a mere second earlier in the day.

Igraine took a breath and remembered her manners. She nodded. "Sir Enric," she said politely.

"My lady," he replied with a slight bow. His voice was deep and musical. It reminded her of a wooded forest, deep and strong. He smelled like one too, she noted as the wind shifted. Pine and something spicy, like he had rolled in an herb garden deep in the woods.

She willed her feet to descend the steps like they were supposed to, like she had been doing before this man had frozen her in place. But they would not obey. Her eyes still locked with his dark brown ones. Suddenly aware that he must think her an idiot, she rushed, "Congratulations on your victory today, sir. You gave my brother quite the challenge."

"Ah, you're the Lady Igraine." Understanding lit his features. He'd obviously heard about her, but his expression didn't belie what he'd heard. "Your brother is an excellent knight."

"He is," she agreed awkwardly. Finally, she managed to break from his gaze and glanced down at the stairs. "Well, I better get back." She turned and made her way down the steps, her fingers gracefully tracing the wall as she descended. She heard footsteps follow her and looked up in surprise as Enric descended after her.

"I thought you were going up?" she asked, hesitating.

"Just realized I forgot to give my squire instructions for the morning."

"Oh," Igraine answered dumbly, then spun and hurried down the steps a bit faster. Like a fool, she stepped on the hem of her gown and tripped, her body threatening to tumble head-first down the rest of the flight.

"My lady!" Enric caught her upper arm gently and steadied her. His touch sent a shock through her. She froze, gasping. He immediately released her once she had her feet again, taking a step away from her, as if he too had been shocked. He shook his head as if trying to shake confusion from it.

Igraine smoothed her skirt with her sweaty palms, flushed with heat, her heart pounding harder than it had when she had left the hall in anger. Never had a man had this effect on her. Here she was, the Lady of the Tournament, known for her beauty, eloquence, and gracefulness, and she couldn't even make it down a flight of steps.

"Igraine!" echoed her brother's voice as he exited the hall and came to the landing at the foot of the stairwell. "Where have you been?" He took in her flushed, wide-eyed features and Enric's stiff stance only a handsbreadth away from her and reddened in fury. In two strides, he had Igraine's wrist in his hand, possessively pulling her down the last few steps and behind him. His glare at Enric could have melted ice.

Enric ignored the look and calmly descended to the flat landing. "Sir Montag," he said politely in recognition.

Montag glowered more. "*Lord*. Lord Montag," he corrected. "What have you done to my sister?"

"Nothing!" Igraine said quickly. Montag turned like a snake striking and slapped her.

Before Igraine could process what was happening, Enric had grabbed Montag's arm and spun him around to face the wall, pinning him there with his arm twisted painfully behind him. His deep voice murmured next to her brother's ear, "I don't care if she is your sister. That is no way to treat a lady."

Montag turned purple in rage.

Enric continued, "I swore an oath to protect the defenseless. I intend to keep it. Lay a hand on her again, and you'll have me to deal with."

"You have no idea who I am," Montag snarled.

"Oh, I know exactly who you are, Lord *Elfric* le Brun."

Igraine gasped. Hardly anyone knew her brother's real name. He'd been called Montag since childhood, taking the moniker of their home in Les Montagnes of Alsace. How had Enric learned his hated childhood name of Elfric? And Le Brun — they didn't use that anymore.

Enric continued, "I know what your family has done. I got to know your father rather well in Jerusalem." There was the hard glint of a warrior's gaze in Enric's eyes as he hissed the words. Igraine knew that look of masked pain all too well. "Leave the lady alone," Enric insisted, twisting Montag's arm tighter behind his back. "Agreed?"

Montag growled in fury but whispered, "Fine."

"I can't hear you."

"I'll leave her alone!" Montag bellowed.

Enric let him go. "We'll meet again," he warned, that warrior glint still glistening in his eyes. "For what it's worth, nothing happened between me and your sister. She sings your praises." With a quick glance at Igraine, Enric turned on his heel and stalked out of the vestibule toward the main castle entryway. Montag rubbed his shoulder and ignored her completely, returning back to the hall.

Still reeling with shock, Igraine slid down to sit on the wooden steps that led from the battlement. No one had ever stood up for her against her brother. Joined on his side, teasing and bullying her, yes. But stood against him? Never! She touched her arm where Enric had caught her. He'd steadied her with such a gentle touch, a touch that belied his strength. Her heart pounded again as she thought of the steady look in his eyes. He knew her father, whom she and Montag had not seen in years, and possibly their family secret. Who was this man?

Chapter 2

The ride back to Chateau Brunstein the next day was a solemn one. Montag was not speaking to Igraine. Really, he wasn't speaking to anyone except Sir Lezay, who was the only one still jovial on the ride. He was loudly, poorly, singing rude songs that made even the squire flinch and turn his nose up in disgust. Igraine focused on counting her horse's footsteps in an effort to drown him out.

"*Legs to the sky-y, that look in her eye, a face like a dove,*" Lezay sang and chuckled, "*hehe . . . fits like a glo-ve . . .*" The note was so off-key Lezay coughed on it as his voice cracked.

"Thank God," the squire mumbled under his breath.

Lezay, unfortunately, succeeded in clearing his vocal cords again and continued. Igraine's frown deepened, and the squire looked like he wanted to cry.

"Lezay, sing the old ballad of The Foolhardy Bride," Montag requested. Igraine smirked a little. So even he was tired of Lezay's songs, was he?

Lezay frowned a bit. "That's not a very fun one, Montag."

"Just sing it if you want to sing so bad."

"Oh all right." Lezay opened his mouth to start, but Montag cut him off.

"But first, a dedication to my dear sister. May her fate steer her far from any such terrible adventures." Montag nodded at Lezay to proceed.

Lezay took a deep breath, and in a much steadier voice than his crude songs had shown him to possess, began,

"Forty years ago today a knight was settlin' in.
He dreamt of a lass, complexion glass, ivory pretty skin.
By day he wakes, to steal his fate
And hunt the castle she be within!
The knight knocks twice, then thrice
He busts the great door in!
There in the hall, against the wall,
Luck gives him the lady of his dreams.
He knows she is to be his own,
Tis love, tis lust, Come with him she must!
He drops to a knee, respectfully pleads
And the foolhardy lady declines.
The knight takes her by hand, wills her by force
Sword drawn, fist made, desperation in voice.
And still the lady declines; he minds.
Her fair blood splatters the floor."

Igraine heard the squire's quick intake of breath as her stomach turned. There was no doubt this request was her brother's way of speaking to her. He was still angry. They rode in silence for a bit, even Lezay quiet now.

"Shame, to run a lass through." Lezay finally broke from his thoughts. "Seems a waste."

"Any woman that disobedient is a waste of resources," Montag grumbled.

Igraine bit off a retort, knowing it would only get her in trouble. Inwardly she fumed.

The squire didn't do as well in holding his disgust. "So the knight comes to steal a woman, and because she doesn't want to be taken, suddenly *she's* the one that gets killed? He should be the one that gets run through!"

Igraine's eyes went wide at the boy's boldness. He was young, barely sporting a trace of a beard, but you'd think enough black eyes by now would have taught him something about the man he worked for. Igraine caught the telltale vein in Montag's forehead popping out but for now, her brother didn't explode.

"You're ignorant," Montag said smoothly. "You've yet to learn the curses women may bring upon us, the burden they are to us. Those that do not obey are worse."

"Curses? Burden?" the squire questioned. "Did not our mothers bear us from their wombs? Care for us and bless us with their love? We are the burden to them!"

It was the wrong thing to say. Igraine winced for the boy before Montag had even balled his fist. As it was, the boy was just out of Montag's reach, and seeing how angry he'd made his master, he paled and trotted his horse on a few steps. Montag pursued his jaw tight in rage.

"I'm sorry! I'm sorry! You're right! I won't question you again!" The boy cantered on a few more steps, glancing over his shoulder.

"You won't speak again!" Montag bellowed and kicked his horse up toward the squire boy.

The squire believed him. He kicked his horse into a gallop and took off down the road. Montag was in hot pursuit and on the faster horse. Lezay let out a whoop of joy and took off after them, leaving Igraine alone in their dust with a fidgety mount who also wanted to run with its friends.

She sighed, her brow furrowed in concern for the boy. Run as fast as the squire might, Montag was on the fastest horse they owned. The boy on his rouncey didn't stand a chance. She allowed her increasingly impatient mount to settle into a gentle canter and patted the mare's neck. If there was one credit she had to give her brother, it was that he had taught her to ride, and made sure she had a good horse. As with everything he did, there was an ulterior motive. Their travels to tourneys took them all over Europe and the fastest way to get there was to travel light and on horseback, not by foot or by wagon.

Igraine saw the three riders crest the next hill. They had almost caught the boy. She had to catch up. She let her horse pick up a bit more speed and reveled in the power beneath her. For this moment, she was free as a bird! Free as the wind itself! She felt the power of control and movement beneath her and let it consume her. Suddenly she realized she actually was free. She was alone, with her brother and Lezay distracted. She could turn back to the town and leave Montag forever. Her horse sensed her hesitation and slowed until they were standing still on the road, watching the horizon.

She had always firmly believed in her duty to her family. They were a well-off family, with respectable old bloodlines. As Alenor said, wealth is everything, right? She had every physical thing she could want or need: good food, clothes, horses, even jewelry. Her heart pounded. She knew that sentiment was off. She knew there was more than wealth. Power, of course. Her family had that too. They controlled the majority of Les Vosges mountains, including the roads and a trade route to the far East with its valuable spices and relics from the Holy Land. That was power. But Igraine herself never tasted any of that. That was for the men. What else was there? Suddenly the word came into her mind in a flood so loud it drowned out all the other thoughts that swirled in her mind. Love.

The reins slipped through her hands, slick from the sweat of her palms.

Love.

Now where did that crazy idea come from?

All she'd known were relationships of power and alliances and duty. Her family never spoke of love. She supposed she was largely ignorant of it. But surely, as the troubadours at the tourneys back in Aquitaine sang of it, it must exist.

A shout from up ahead on the road caught her attention, and she shook her head to clear it.

"Igraine!" Lezay shouted to her. "You better come quick. Boy might need some of your doctoring."

The moment lost, Igraine refocused and urged her horse back into a gallop, pushing all thoughts aside for now.

She caught up to Lezay and they looked down into the next hollow, where the young squire was curled in the grass in a ball. Montag stood over him, arms folded.

"Good lord, Lezay, what did he do to him?"

Lezay just chewed his cheek in silence and rode down ahead of her.

Igraine dismounted next to the men and glared at her brother. The squire was still curled in a ball, whimpering. He flinched when she touched his shoulder. He held his right arm tight to his chest, and she noticed the wrist was at an awkward angle, already swelling. "May I see?" she asked gently.

The boy shook his head. "Broken," he whispered.

"Bloody weakling," Montag said under his breath.

"What happened to his wrist?" Igraine stood with her hands on her hips, fighting the fury within her.

"Fell off his horse," Montag said.

Igraine raised her eyebrows at him and looked to Lezay, who still sat on his horse.

"Didn't see," Lezay shrugged.

Igraine sighed. She reached down a hand to help the boy up. "Come. We have to get you to the healer at home. There's nothing I can do for you here." The boy reluctantly got to his feet, paling and swaying into her. "On your horse, lad," she said gently.

The squire gritted his teeth and remounted. Igraine took off her belt and looped it around the boy's neck as a sling. Then she remounted herself and without a word, rode forward to lead the way home. Montag rode up next to her, his frown lines deep.

"Will Madame Brigitte fix him?" he asked.

"She'll help," Igraine said quietly. She glanced back to make sure the boy was out of earshot. "The boy will never regain the same strength in that arm. And his sword arm no less! Montag, what were you thinking?"

"He fell!"

"I don't care if he fell. Even *if* he *did* fall off his horse, it was *you* who pushed him to that point. He's the son of a count, Montag. You're going to have some explaining to do."

"He fell," Montag growled at her and gave her a look that warned if she didn't silence herself she would be next. Igraine looked away from him and cantered on ahead. They were only a few miles from Chateau Brunstein. She heard her brother ride up next to her. His tone low, Montag said, "You should have been more careful, Igraine. What if someone had seen you with Enric?"

"I only saw him in passing. And so what if someone did see?"

"It looked like more than a passing glance," Montag insisted.

Igraine was quiet. At least that much was true. Still, she did not understand what had happened between her and Enric. "It was a moment, nothing more."

"Just make sure it doesn't happen again. We leave for Reims next week. Rumor is he'll be there, too. This time I will smash him to dirt." Montag looked sideways at her to gauge her reaction, but there was none. With a smirk he cantered on over the ridge, he and Lezay again zooming past Igraine and the squire's irritated horses, making them spook. The squire struggled to ride with one arm and despite the pain, he was managing as well as could be expected. Igraine slowed her horse to a walk, falling in beside him. Neither of them had to say a word. The horses quieted.

The castle loomed tall in a valley, barely visible from the road that wove through the forested hills that edged

Les Vosges mountains. It was a massive stone keep, built into the very rock itself. The sheer wall surrounding it rose four stories high, with narrow slits allowing lookouts and crossbowmen to protect the valley below. Behind the castle stood a cliff that seemed to rise almost straight into the sky, the valley beyond sloping at a sharp angle to the gentle ridge of the forested hilltop. Brunstein was built to withstand attack, for the Le Brun family had not gained its wealth from passive diplomacy.

The four riders dismounted in the courtyard below the great wall. A wooden stable sat off to their right, tucked along a small creek. Immediately, grooms emerged from the stable to take their horses. Igraine pulled off her riding gloves and gently patted her mare's neck, murmuring a thank you to the groom as he led the horse away. He gave her a quick smile and went about his work. Igraine was the only one in the family that thanked the staff at Chateau Brunstein, and they appreciated her for it. Outward affection toward or from the staff was one thing Montag deemed unnecessary, but Igraine knew her groom would show his loyalty by putting an extra shine on her horse the next time she rode out.

"Come on, Hans," Igraine said to the young squire. "Let's get you to Madame Brigitte." Hurt servants weren't economical servants, she had long argued. She had won. All these years later, Montag left her to it.

The squire followed her into the keep, his arm still hanging against his chest with the sling. His wrist was grotesquely swollen now, a rainbow of shades of blue and black.

Madame Brigitte beamed when she saw Igraine. "Ah, welcome back child!" She bustled from her space at the great table in the kitchen where she was cutting vegetables in preparation for dinner. She embraced Igraine quickly, smiling. It was grey-haired Brigitte who had nursed Igraine as a babe, and even now she treated her like an adopted daughter.

"Hello, Madame," Igraine answered. After a brief return of the embrace, she directed Brigitte's attention to the young Hans. The older woman's eyes went wide.

"What happened, lad?" Madame Brigitte asked.

"Fell," Hans mumbled, avoiding her eyes.

Brigitte shook her head and gently took the boy's arm from the sling. Worry clouded her eyes.

"Can you fix it?" Hans asked. "I don't care if it hurts, just get it straight again." He was brave, but so were all boys in training to be warriors.

Brigitte looked the boy in the eye. "I need to get the swelling down first. Then I will see what I can do."

Hans nodded grimly.

Brigitte looked around for a kitchen maid and caught one just as she walked into the great kitchen. "Greta, I need cold water. Quickly girl!" The girl ducked back outside, buckets in each hand. Brigitte laid the boy's wrist on the table, gently palpating it. She took a jar of leeches from a shelf and strategically placed them on Hans's arm. He watched her, fascinated. Igraine looked away and sat instead on a chair by the hearth, where a tiny fire smoked.

"What was he mad about this time, lad?" Brigitte quietly asked Hans.

"He lost. And then he was angry at Lady Igraine, and I should have closed my mouth but he and Lezay just got on my nerves and I lost my tongue."

"He lost?" Brigitte asked in surprise, still placing leeches.

"To Sir Enric de Levan d'Aquitaine," Igraine said from her spot by the hearth, not looking up from the smoke of the fire that rose in pale swirls. Even as she said his name her heart pounded again, and she cursed herself as a fool.

"Levan?" Madame Brigitte furrowed her brow. "I don't know the name."

"He's a knight-errant. From Jerusalem." Igraine looked up. "He said he knows my father. He knows Montag's birth name."

Brigitte took a sharp breath. "Well, that is something. And he actually bested your brother in the tourney? In the sword competition?"

"No, in the joust."

"The joust!" Brigitte checked herself. She corked the glass jar of leeches and set it back on the shelf. She looked at Hans. "You are a fool boy, to test him on a day he lost in the joust."

Hans looked miserable as he leaned his head on his good arm, watching the leeches wiggle on his grotesque wrist.

The maid returned with the buckets, and Madame Brigitte took Hans's arm, leeches and all, and set it in the cold water. "Let that sit an hour or so, lad," she ordered. To Igraine she said, "You'd better get cleaned and changed for dinner, my lady. You know he won't be happy if you show up all travel-dirty. You think he wants hot food tonight?" It was still warm outside, and Brigitte was loath to build up a cooking fire.

Igraine rose, slightly stiff from sitting still after the long day of riding. "You know he will." She looked apologetically at the older woman, who merely nodded grimly.

"Hot pork and beans it is then," Madame Brigitte mumbled.

Igraine smiled and took her leave. This dance around her brother was so ingrained in all of them it was second nature. She'd never questioned it. Enric's reaction to Montag's mere slap of her face was starting to make her question now though. Why did they give him this power over them? Why did their world revolve around *him*? She would have to think hard and observe quietly if she was to figure that one out. She desperately wanted to do so before the tourney at Reims, particularly if Enric would be there again.

Chapter 3

May 14, 1172

Reims, France

"A stunning victory!" Alenor breathed from Igraine's right.

Igraine could only purse her lips. She wondered who Montag would bruise this time now that Sir Enric had bested him yet again in the joust. Montag threw his helmet at the newest squire he had acquired. Hans had been sent back to his family to "heal," though Igraine knew the brave young man would never have full use of his arm again, and thus would never be a knight. His future was over before it started. This new squire had some big shoes to fill and so far, he struggled greatly.

Igraine's attention snapped back to Enric as he took his victory lap around the list. His gaze locked onto her for the second time that day, the first being as soon as they had entered the tourney field at Reims. That gaze made her blush red, and a funny feeling fluttered in her gut. She glanced down at her hands, breaking the gaze before anyone would notice, but she felt his eyes linger on her as he cantered past. She had to get a handle on herself or last week would repeat.

Alenor nudged her. "Igraine?" She smiled at her knowingly and nudged her again. "Igraine I saw that. You *like* him."

Igraine looked at her friend, shaking her head as her pulse pounded. "No!"

"You do!"

"No! Alenor, stop it."

"Why, what's so wrong with that? You're allowed a sweet, courtly romance before you're married off. He's gorgeous, beyond a doubt. What's there to lose?"

Everything. Igraine frowned.

As if reading her mind, Alenor quieted. "Igraine, you are allowed happiness. We are young; our lives are only beginning." Igraine focused on her hands. "You're worried about your brother, aren't you?"

Igraine gave a barely perceptible nod.

Alenor sighed. "Come with me." She took Igraine's hand and led her away from the stands, away from the crowd of spectators. They circled around to the back of the castle of Reims near the knights' tent encampment, where only a few squires could be seen, all busy untacking horses or polishing equipment. Alenor stopped on the edge of the field, under a huge oak tree. There, she plopped down on the grass and leaned back, patting the ground beside her. "Come on, Lady Igraine. No one will hear us out here." Alenor looked around then added quietly, "This is my favorite spot in all of Reims."

And a good spot it was. The setting sun shone golden on the tops of the tents, their multi-colored fabric like a rainbow in the field before them, pennants flying in the light breeze. The castle loomed beyond the field, white-grey stone walls a contrast to the bright blue sky.

Igraine sighed and sat down next to Alenor, leaning her head back against the tree and watching the leaves flutter above their heads.

"Now, my friend," Alenor began. "Tell me all about this brother of yours. I don't understand, you know I don't, but before I seduce him into marrying me I should know what I'm up against."

"Alenor, just don't marry him. As much as I would love you as a sister, don't marry him."

"But why?"

"He's an obstinate pig. He's cruel." *He broke Hans' arm. He's slapped me many times. He locked me in the dungeon when I was little as a joke.* The words kept spinning in Igraine's head, but they did not leave her tongue. It was as hard to separate herself from her loyalty to her brother as it was to separate her blood from his.

Alenor mistook her silence as the end of the list. "Igraine, he is a warrior. They all can be fierce at times. He has only ever been kind to me."

"That is what he wants you to see, don't you understand?" Igraine asked with desperation. She pulled grass from the ground in handfuls, throwing it down absently. Catching herself, she folded her hands in her lap, her knuckles turning white.

"And what do I want people to see? What do *you* want people to see?" Alenor pushed back. "We all put on a face in public, another in private. You most of all. The Lady of the Tournament." Alenor scoffed. "She's the epitome of beauty, every woman wants to be her. She smiles, she offers kind words, and every man wants her. Yet what is the truth? Igraine, you are alone. You let *no one* in. Your smiles are not from joy but from . . . I don't even know what. Perhaps Montag is the same; he plays the part of the rugged knight, and when he can let his guard down he becomes a softer man."

"He and I are *not* the same!"

"Igraine, I want you to be happy. But to find happiness you need to live a little."

"Don't you understand?! I can't! I can't . . ." Igraine jumped to her feet and paced under the tree, her arms crossed. "I am his *property*, Alenor. If I don't do what he says, he will hand me off to the worst husband he can find. Or never let me marry at all perhaps. I'm twenty-two now! I'm *old*! I don't know what he's waiting for. I—" She threw her hands in the air, speechless in frustration. "And you . . . you have no idea what he's like away from the public."

"Stop," Alenor said sharply.

Igraine covered her face in her hands, trembling with emotion.

Alenor rose and gently took her friend by the arms. "What will he do to you if you don't obey?"

Igraine shook her head.

"Does he beat you?"

"No. Just slaps me sometimes."

Alenor frowned. "Does he lock you up?"

"Sometimes."

"He hasn't . . . like there's nothing . . . incestuous?"

"Heavens no!"

"Then what's so bad? We're women, Igraine. Our men, fathers, brothers, husbands have a right to manage us."

Igraine looked at her friend as if she were a stranger. Alenor truly was naïve. Igraine could not make her understand what it was like to have to second guess every single action she took, every word she spoke, all day long. To Igraine, Montag was a manageable menace. But what about Hans, whose career as a knight was now over before it ever started? What about the others who had come before Hans, servants who had disappeared over the years? Igraine had only suspicions, not proof, but wasn't the fact that she even suspected her brother of such cruelty bad enough? No, Alenor could never understand, not without living it.

Igraine took the other woman's hand and held it gently, looking her in the eye. "Alenor, I love you as my sister. If you are going to pursue my brother, do it with my full warning. Unless you give him good reason to keep you around, he will break your heart or worse. He's almost double your age. You aren't his first flirtation. Be careful."

"I will," Alenor promised. "And let me tell you something as well, Igraine. If you don't want to be miserable forever, you need to figure out what you want. Do you want to be the perfect bride to a man you don't know? Or do you want to know what love feels like before you do your duty for your family?"

The ladies stared at each other a moment, then their fingers released, and they wordlessly went back to the castle where the evening's festivities were beginning. They went their separate ways, each acutely aware of the other's warning.

Igraine saw her brother and his friends already seated at one of the massive tables mid-way through the hall. Already their hands and mouths were full of the feast presented by the lord and lady of Reims. Igraine took her seat at her brother's side and helped herself. The men continued their conversation without acknowledging her. She sat in silence a long while, ignoring Lezay and Jean's crude banter, then absently let her gaze wander the hall.

Enric's eyes locked on hers. She looked away. A minute later she glanced up again, and still he watched her. He turned slightly toward the entryway and inclined his head. She hesitated, then nodded at him. He excused himself from the conversation around him and slipped from the hall.

Igraine was invisible in the group of Montag's friends who were busy talking about horses and women. The conversation was getting hard to follow as the men spoke of the two interchangeably. She downed the last of her delicious wine, a semi-dry red made in neighboring Burgundy, then filled the goblet again part-way and drained that, too. Setting the cup down, she worked her way from the hall, eyeing the crowd for those who may recognize her, and made it to the grand entry without much ado. It took her a moment to find the way to the battlement wall. This time it was a narrow spiral stone staircase built into the walls of the castle itself. As she emerged from the stuffy revelry below, the cool air of the night brushed her skin to goosebumps. She wasn't cold, for really the night was still rather warm. The cause was rather the man standing there, leaning against the stone, watching her.

Every time she saw Enric, she got a better look at him. He was tall, with straight, dark brown hair that was haphazardly cut just short enough that he didn't need to tie it back. His broad, muscular chest stretched the fabric of his linen shirt and the blue tunic he wore over it. His thick forearms were folded across his chest in a relaxed, confident posture. He smiled, lighting up the chiseled lines of his face, and she felt dizzy. She wiped her palms on her skirts and steeled her shoulders. She had to figure out what it was about this man that led her to make such a fool of herself. Cautiously, she approached him, and together they turned to look over the wall to the village below. A few warm lights shone in some of the windows of the cottages, and the spires of the cathedral jutted up against the stars sparkling in a cloudless sky.

Igraine let the silence carry, afraid to break the peace of the moment as much as she was afraid she would say something foolish.

Enric ventured first. "I hope I was not out of place with my actions last week, my lady."

Igraine stiffened a little, surprised. "Why did you do it? No one has ever stepped in to defend me before."

"I've never seen a man hit a woman like that. I'm afraid I lost a bit of control. Has he been kinder to you since, or have I made things worse between you?"

Enric was observant, she had to give him credit for that. Igraine frowned. "He hasn't laid a hand on me since then, but to everyone else he's been a terror." Quickly she added, "That's just how Montag is. He has a temper."

"And why is it your responsibility to manage it?"

Igraine blinked. "Who else would?"

"Montag himself?" Enric offered.

Igraine looked away.

"Forgive me, I don't know you well enough to make these assumptions. Really, I don't know you at all." He leaned his hip against the stone of the wall and folded his arms in front of him. "I'd like to."

Igraine did not face him. She did not need to. The tingle of his stare already brushed over her as if Enric touched her with a feather. She wanted to step away from it, to laugh, and yet there was something so enticing about it, so exotic, that she was afraid to move. Subconsciously she played with the loose gravel in the stonework. She shouldn't even be here, up on the wall with a man. She swallowed the lump in her throat, grateful for the darkness that hid her blush.

"What do you want to know?" she finally ventured.

Enric still studied her with a relentless gaze. "Has anyone actually succeeded in winning a tournament for you?"

The question softened the mood, and she laughed. "No."

Enric smiled at her amusement. "I heard that rumor. Do you know how the other knights describe you?"

She shook her head.

"The most beautiful, pure angel . . . guarded by the great beast of a brother who protects her virtues until God deems a man worthy to claim the victory and her heart."

"Ha!"

"The stories about you abound in Aquitaine, Lady Igraine. I do not lie."

Still Igraine laughed. "Angel? Really?"

"That part is true as far as I can tell," Enric said quietly.

Igraine ignored his comment. "Lord, I haven't laughed like that in ages." Her cheeks hurt from smiling, but for once she relished the pain. The smile was real. "So now that you've defeated my brother, and twice now no less, does that mean God has found you worthy of me?"

Enric smiled, and Igraine made the mistake of looking him in the eye. He was so handsome he took her breath away. "I think I should worry more about whether *you* think I'm worthy."

"Good answer. Though many would say that's blasphemy."

"And do you think I'm worthy?"

"Ha! I don't know you, Sir Enric."

"Good answer," he admitted. "You know what the stories didn't mention?"

She shook her head.

"Your confidence."

Igraine raised her eyebrows. "I fell down the steps when I last saw you. How on earth do you get the impression I am confident?"

"How you act around your brother. His friends. You have this invisible shield around you when you're with them and at first, I thought it was just because Montag is enough of a bully to make sure everyone knows to keep their hands off you. But I've watched you the last two tourneys — he really doesn't do anything to protect you. At least that I see. No comments, no hovering around you. I think your walls are your own, despite the flirtatious smiles you bestow upon all your suitors as they pledge their hearts to you. It takes confidence to do that, to stand your ground. Honestly, I think that's why you're so gorgeous."

"You think I'm gorgeous?" Igraine's heart picked up.

"That's a statement of fact, not an opinion."

An awkward silence hung in the air.

"You said last week that you know my father," Igraine changed the subject. "How?"

Enric frowned. "There are many knights in Jerusalem." That pained look came into Enric's eyes again, and he did not elaborate. Igraine did not need him to. She knew what her father was like. It was why she understood Montag as easily as she did. As if reading her thoughts, Enric asked himself, "I wonder how you broke out of that mold?"

"How do you know I did?"

"Your brother's squire — the last one, not this new one that's here today — told me everyone at your manor loves you. He said it's well known amongst the household that you're the nice one."

She shrugged. "I suppose. Wait, why were you asking about me in the first place?" Igraine's nerves prickled.

"Not you, exactly. I just like to know all I can about my enemies."

"Enemies!"

Enric shrugged. "You slipped into the category by association."

"And that makes me an enemy?"

"I'm trying to figure that out. You won't say a word against your brother, though he obviously treats you like you're one of the serfs. I'd say you're a typical naïve maiden, ignorant of all that goes on around you, but I can't shake the impression you're hiding a brilliant mind behind that placid mask, in which case you know exactly what happens in your domain. I'm not sure I really understand you. And thus I can't categorize you."

All of those goosebumps and butterflies evaporated. He was as conniving as the next man, and she was making a fool of her family by allowing herself to speak so freely with him. Her walls clicked back into place as she straightened her spine and turned on her heel without a word. She felt, rather than saw, Enric follow her.

"I'll make it down fine on my own feet this time, thank you." She waved him off and started down the stairs.

Enric didn't say a word, but he stopped in the middle of the spiral staircase.

Igraine took four more steps, then suddenly stopped and pulled her long skirts out of the way as she spun back to him, closing the distance between them one stair at a time. "*Enemies!* So all week I've been thinking you defended me, impressed by your chivalric honor, but really you were just *looking* for a chance to pin and bully my brother." Her voice had dropped to a hiss, and if she could shoot daggers with her eyes, she would. "Leave us all alone. Go back to Aquitaine." She was level on the stairs with him now. She took the final step onto the same stair he had stopped on, so close to him now that her skirts touched his legs. Igraine saw the desire flash in Enric's eyes, and for a brief moment, her anger faltered.

Very, very slowly Enric lifted his hand and cupped her cheek. Igraine froze, staring at the intensity of his eyes, not sure if she should run from it or melt into it. She should pull away. She should run away! Enric's other hand caught her wrist, caressing it slightly before he let his hand slide down to lace his fingers into hers. She watched his head tilt, and fire raced through her body. He was going to kiss her.

"Enemy," she whispered.

"Never to you," Enric whispered back, his breath now fluttering against her lips. "I might regret it, but you will never be my enemy, Lady Igraine."

Just as their lips were about to meet, the sound of heavy feet echoed from the stairs below them. Igraine pulled away and rushed down the stairs, past one of the guards of Reims on his way to change shifts. Her heart pounded so loudly she couldn't think, and instead of entering the great hall, she went out to the tent encampment where she, Montag, and the squire shared a massive canvas tent decorated with the family colors. She threw herself into her bed on the ground and buried her face in her hands.

She wanted to see him again. She was afraid to see him again. How was she to play her part with this conflict raging inside her?

"My lady?" Lezay's voice drifted from beyond the tent flap.

"He's still up at the manor, Lezay," she said in a rough voice. "Go look for him there."

"I was looking for you." Uninvited, he entered the tent.

Igraine quickly jumped back up to her feet and wiped her eyes. She pushed messy wisps of hair out of her face. It was dark in the tent, and she could only make out Lezay's shadowy outline. "What do you want?" she asked, not bothering to disguise her grouchy mood.

"Well, you see your brother has won the company of your friend Alenor tonight, and I just wanted to make sure you weren't . . . lonely."

Igraine didn't like how he was standing in front of the tent opening. "I'm just fine, Lezay. I'm sure you can go find some company of your own."

"I'm sure I can." He did not move.

"Go," Igraine said simply and gestured toward the tent doorway.

"But you're sad. You're lonely."

"Go!" She was not going to spend her night chatting with Onion Man. She could smell him across the tent.

"You're lonely," Lezay insisted, and took a step toward her. A beam of moonlight shone across his face and revealed the blatant lust etched there.

Suddenly, Igraine understood and cursed herself for not recognizing it sooner. Her eyes flashed with fury. "Lezay, get out of this tent right now. You so much as lay a finger on me, and you'll have not only my brother to deal with, but me."

"Your brother said I could."

"What?" Igraine asked in shock.

"He said, because you were talking to Enric again, that you must be lonely and I should take care of you. I don't care if you're not pure before our wedding, so long as wrecking that purity is my fault."

"You! You're the one who made an offer of marriage?"

"Leuwenstein is a beautiful castle . . . you'll love it."

"Lezay, *get out*!"

"I love it when you're all fiery, Igraine."

"It's *Lady* Igraine to you, you cow! Now leave!"

Lezay took another step toward her, and Igraine quickly made to step around him toward the tent flap. He caught her with one arm, pulling her in front of him again. That single beam of moonlight showed all his ugliness. Igraine wrinkled her nose in disgust.

"Lezay, get your hands off of me, or I will castrate you right here and now." She was not afraid, only angry. She was familiar with fending off over-dedicated suitors. Yet usually, they did not get as close as Lezay now was.

"With what?" he taunted.

Igraine deftly pulled his dagger from his own belt and held the blade to his groin. He stilled, then dropped her arm. "Get out," Igraine again said, ice in her tone.

Lezay took a step back. "Can I have my dagger back?"

"Tomorrow. I intend to sleep with it under my pillow tonight."

"Aw, love. Think of me. Sleep well." He blew her a kiss and backed out of the tent, chuckling to himself.

Igraine cursed under her breath, spinning the handle of the blade deftly in her hand. She couldn't handle any more men tonight! What was going on? Surely, the planets were out of alignment or something. And her brother — that hypocritical . . . Suddenly she remembered Alenor. Was Lezay telling the truth? Had Montag noticed her friend's affections? Alenor had sounded like she would listen to Igraine after their talk. Was her brother forcing her friend into a situation she didn't want to be in? Igraine paced the tent, then burst back out of it. She saw Lezay in the distance, strolling back to the manor.

"Lezay!" She ran after him.

"I knew you'd change your mind." He smiled as she caught up to him.

"Where is my brother? Where is Alenor?"

"Somewhere up there." Lezay smirked as he gestured toward the massive castle. "Probably a cozy corner, or in the cellars by the sweet wine barrels, or an empty stairwell. Where would you like? I'm not usually one for company, but if that's what you want . . ."

Igraine brushed past him. She kept his dagger tight in her hand though.

Lezay continued to babble next to her as she reentered the castle, searching the secret places she knew couples liked to escape into. Not along the outer wall, not in the hall, not under the stairwell.

She apologized to the couple she interrupted there.

Not in the kitchen, the storerooms, or the stables. She took the stairs up to the battlement wall two at a time, doubting they would be there, but hoping from that vantage she could see more of the castle. Breathless and sweating now, she ran smack into Enric at the top of the stairs. He caught her arm to steady her.

"Easy there," he said gently, like he was talking to one of his horses. "What's the rush?"

Lezay emerged from behind Igraine, still completely un-winded and as amused as ever with the evening's proceedings. "Well, if it isn't Sir Enric."

"Good evening, Sir Lezay."

"It is, isn't it?"

Enric looked back to Igraine, who was looking out over the tents below them.

"Looking for someone?" Enric asked.

"She's afraid her brother is raping her best friend," Lezay answered. "She didn't give me time to explain that Alenor was practically begging for it before he led her away."

"Your and Montag's definition of 'begging for it' is a bit different than mine," Igraine said through gritted teeth. Suddenly she saw two figures entwined beneath the oak tree Alenor had shown her earlier that day, only shadows of them visible in the moonlight. Even though they were far away, Igraine knew it was them. Who else would it be?

"I'm too late," she said under her breath. She was too far away to do anything but watch. And it looked like whatever was done was done. The two figures had risen to their feet.

Enric and Lezay came up to stand next to her, following her gaze.

"See, they're kissing still! She's not running away crying. You know, some women actually *like* men," Lezay chided.

Igraine watched silently but had to admit he was probably right. The two figures under the tree looked perfectly happy with each other. She turned away from them and leaned against the wall, rubbing her temples with her fingers. Lezay's dagger was still in her palm.

"What would you have done if he *was* raping her?" Enric asked.

Igraine inwardly groaned. Of all the men at a tourney, why did he always have to be around when she was an idiot? "I don't know. Yelled. Screamed. Thrown something at him."

"Castrated him?" asked Lezay.

"No, I'll save that for you," Igraine said, her voice now laced with fatigue.

"Lady Igraine?" Enric raised his eyebrows in mild alarm as he looked from Lezay to Igraine.

"I'm going to bed." She ignored him and shoved herself away from the wall and made toward the stairs for the second time that night.

"I'll make sure you make it to your tent," Lezay volunteered.

"No," Igraine said quickly and pointed the dagger at him. "You'll stay right here." She noted Enric wanted to follow her as well. "Both of you." She turned on her heel and went back to her tent for a long, restless night.

At some point she heard Montag and the squire both enter the tent and crawl into their makeshift beds. They were still snoring when she gave up on sleep as the dawn's rays brightened the new day. She redid her braids so she would look presentable, then headed off in search of Alenor's family tent. The burgundy and white striped canvas was impossible to miss, easily one of the larger tents on the field. The Duke of Tielo did not travel lightly when he came to tournaments, and he brought his wife, daughter, knighted son, several squires, and young son along with him. Igraine hesitated at the tent, wondering if Alenor would be awake yet. The young son came out, bleary-eyed, intent on relieving himself, and Igraine hastily questioned him.

"Lady Alenor? Is she awake yet?"

"Didn't come back last night," the youth yawned. "Excuse me."

Igraine paled a little and turned to hasten up to the castle. Where was she?

She repeated the search she had made the night before, again ending up on the wall overlooking the village and the tents below the castle. At this time of the morning, only she and a few servants moved around. Alenor was nowhere to be seen. Nor was Enric, not that she was looking for him.

On the verge of giving up, Igraine turned and headed back down to the great hall. She stopped a servant who was clearing away dishes from the night before. "Does the castle have a chapel?"

"Of course, m'lady. Just up the far stair, then take a right. It's in the top of the tower," the man said.

Igraine thanked him and headed that way. With relief, she opened the door to the little white-stone chapel and saw Alenor sitting on one of the benches. It was a pretty room, now gold and pink tinged from the light of the sunrise. A stone altar with a crucifix hanging above it was in the center, with the room's rounded walls of carved stone arching up to a graceful dome over the center of the room. The architecture drew one's eyes heavenward, and that is where Alenor now stared.

Igraine quietly sat next to her. Alenor's cheeks were dry, but her face still seemed conflicted.

"I figured you would be the first to find me," Alenor said, not changing her gaze, but smiling slightly. "I figured you would be the first to know. I hope you're the only one to know, at least for now."

Igraine took her friend's hand. "Are you alright? That's all that matters."

Alenor looked at her, and her face lit up. "I'm wonderful. I'm in love. I know I should be ashamed, but I'm not. I want to marry him, Igraine."

"Does he know that? Does he want to marry you?"

"I don't know." Alenor hesitated. "My father would make him a lucrative offer. I have a huge dowry. That's what he wants, isn't it?"

"It is," Igraine admitted carefully.

"And I want him. What is there to lose?"

Igraine knew her brother hated having his options limited. Hated being tied down. As much as he wanted to find *her* a husband, he rarely talked about taking a wife of his own. If he was seriously going to consider Alenor, it would be a huge step for him.

"This is what you want?" Igraine asked her friend.

"More than anything." The young woman's eyes brimmed with happy tears.

"Then I will talk to him. I will encourage him if I can. Hopefully, he can begin negotiations with your father."

Alenor threw her arms around Igraine's neck. "Thank you," she whispered.

Igraine hugged her back gently. She wanted to be happy for her friend, but years of dealing with her brother's fickle personality left her worried. She prayed he wouldn't break Alenor's heart. And if he did, she hoped he did it while the girl could still escape him.

Chapter 4

By the time the two women left the chapel, the main hall had filled for breakfast with lords, ladies, and knights. It was more casual and less crowded than the night before, yet still the food flowed aplenty. Fresh biscuits and fried eggs and great, thick slabs of bacon sat on pewter serving trays, still steaming from the kitchens. The smell was mouthwatering.

Montag sat with his friends.

"What do I do?" Alenor whispered to Igraine. Igraine hesitated. Lezay and Jean were going to be ruthless in their torment of Alenor unless Montag told them to back down. Would he? Did he care enough about Alenor? There was only one way to find out. Igraine looped her arm into Alenor's and led her to the table.

"Morning, gentlemen. You've met my friend Lady Alenor?" Igraine said boldly. She sat down next to her brother on the wooden bench, leaving space that Alenor could sit between them.

The men looked between each other, then to Montag, waiting to see what he wanted. The telltale vein on Montag's forehead popped out, but he gritted his teeth and rose to his feet, offering Alenor a slight bow. He motioned to the seat beside him and took her fingers as she stepped over the bench, smiling at him with relief on her face. The other men resumed their conversation about the tourney to come this second day of competition.

"Sword, pike, and archery today. Why do we even bother with archery? None but the Welsh ever win. How do they even do it? Did you ever try to pull back one of their bows?" Fougères asked.

"I met a Welsh archer years ago," offered Jean. "He let me shoot his bow. I did manage to pull it back, but I couldn't hit a thing. They're raised with bows from children on up. Not unlike how you jousters are raised on your horses."

"Takes years to perfect your skills, that's for sure," said Fougères.

"How old were you all when you started learning how to ride?" Alenor asked.

Igraine looked down and nudged her under the table. The girl should not have spoken. Alenor only frowned at Igraine, wondering what she'd done wrong.

The men were suddenly quiet, but no reprimand from Montag came as Igraine expected.

Lezay smirked, "Horses or women?"

Jean and Fougères hooted with laughter, and even Montag looked amused. Poor Alenor blushed bright red and looked as if she could melt into her seat.

"Come now, Lezay. We all know you still haven't learned to ride a woman properly," Igraine said, coming to her friend's aid. She would deal with the consequences later.

The laughter grew louder, and even Montag cracked a genuine smile. Lezay stared at Igraine with a hard look, looking conflicted about whether to be amused or angry. "Maybe tonight you can teach me, my *lady*."

Alenor looked bewildered by the turn in the conversation, but Igraine still was calm. She rolled her eyes. The other men were still roaring in laughter.

Lezay continued, emboldened. "In fact, let's make this official. My lady, I will win this tournament for you!" He gave her a mock bow and a huge, yellow-toothed grin.

Igraine blanched for only a moment, thinking fast. Lezay competed in the sword competition today. Who else was likely to enter in her honor, and more importantly, beat him? Old Lord Geoffrey of London was here, and he was always a safe, reliable bet. He had beaten Lezay several times before, and always offered to win his events for Igraine. His attraction to her was purely for chivalric amusement, nothing more, as he was one of the few knights happily married to a gorgeous wife of his own. But his success rate against Lezay was not consistent. She needed a backup plan, a fail-safe in case Geoffrey lost to

Lezay. Igraine sat a little straighter. There was one, but she wasn't sure how he was with a sword.

Her eyes flicked involuntarily across the hall to where Enric had just entered with his squire. He looked as strong as ever. Would he even be interested in pledging his victory to her? He wasn't known to participate in such displays.

Her silence stretched too long, and Lezay looked over his shoulder in the direction Igraine stared. His eyes went round in understanding, and his sneer got nastier. "Let the games begin then," he said under his breath.

"I didn't agree."

"I don't care," Lezay insisted. "Besides, I'm your betrothed."

"One of her *potential* betrothed," Montag corrected. "Don't forget, Lezay, I have not agreed yet. And there will be no trying the merchandise before it's paid for."

Igraine raised an eyebrow at Lezay. So he had lied last night after all.

Lezay merely shrugged.

Alenor by this point was completely overwhelmed with the crude banter, not to mention hurt by Montag's "merchandise" comment, which basically alluded she herself was now worth nothing. Her own family was deeply religious, descended from knights who had fought back in the first crusade over a century earlier. Sensing her friend's discomfort, Igraine tried to change the subject.

"Can you pass the eggs, please?" Igraine asked Lord Fougères.

He obliged.

"Brother, do you compete at all today?"

"Pike," he said simply.

"Best of luck, my Lord," Alenor offered eagerly.

Montag hesitated, looking sideways at the girl. "I will try to win for you." He looked like he was having a tooth extracted, but Alenor beamed through the rest of the meal. When the men stood up to ready themselves for the tourney, Alenor tagged along behind Montag. *At least she now has the sense to keep quiet*, Igraine thought.

"Coming?" Alenor asked as she hovered in Montag's wake.

"I'll meet you later in the stands," Igraine replied.

The group moved on, leaving Igraine alone at the table. She rested her head on her fists, her elbows on the table. The tourney hadn't even started yet, and already she was tired of the games.

"May I?" a deep, musical voice asked from beside her.

Igraine glanced up into Enric's eyes. Instantly, her mind went blank.

Enric sat down next to her anyway, his hip just on the edge of her skirts. He reached for a biscuit, casual.

Igraine watched him through narrowed eyes.

He noted the intensity of the gaze and leaned away from her. "I'm sorry. Would you rather be alone?"

"No. I'm just trying to figure out what's wrong with you."

"Wrong with me?" His eyebrows rose.

"No." She shook her head. This was exactly the problem. "I mean, I'm trying to figure out what it is about you that makes me a complete fool when I'm around you. I'm usually not like this, Sir Enric. I'm eloquent, jovial . . . I can banter with the crudest men and maintain the upper hand in the conversation." She bit her tongue, aware she was even now being too forthcoming. With Enric near, she could barely function. Her carefully designed persona disappeared.

Enric smiled, his handsome features seeming to come alive. Igraine looked away, unable to take it.

"If it makes you feel any better, I feel much the same around you, my lady," Enric admitted. "I have to ignore you during the tourneys, or I'd be knocked right off my horse."

"It doesn't look that way," muttered Igraine, still refusing to look at him.

"Yesterday, I was distracted and looking to see if you were here. I made the mistake of entering the sword competition instead of the joust. Luckily my squire caught my mistake, and I entered both right away. But I hate fighting with a sword, and guess what I have to do today now?"

"Are you any good?"

"Good enough, I suppose. It's not my best event, but I should survive."

Igraine thought of how Lezay would be interminable if he was the undisputed sword champion after offering to win the competition in her honor.

"What do you know about my opponents?" Enric asked, eyeing her sideways.

Igraine finally turned to face him. They might as well be partners in this. "Sir Geoffrey of London is insanely fierce. He likes to attack hard, and he can overwhelm most knights by tiring them. Overhead swings are his specialty. But you're taller than him, so you have that to your advantage. Sir Alfred is also an excellent swordsman. It's all he competes in. He's not a tall man, but he's nimble, quick. Watch your knees; he can play dirty. Watch everything with him really. He's so technical, he'll make your head spin. The knights that have beaten him overwhelmed him in strength. Except for Lord Gawain, who is an even more technical fighter. He's also very strong. His weakness is his endurance. If the fight lasts long enough, he's out. Then there's Lezay . . ." Igraine's voice trailed, and she frowned. "He's just plain brutal. A mix of everything. He fights like a fiend, but he's not as technical as some of the others. Geoffrey has beat him maybe fifty percent of the time, and in those fights they both were worse for wear."

"How was he with the others?"

"They're all inconsistent. Really, if you're any good at all, you stand a chance."

Enric nodded, thinking. "Thank you. That's very useful knowledge." He drank a sip of ale. "Your brother doesn't compete in sword?"

She shook her head. "Pike is his specialty outside of the joust. He's lethal."

"Good thing I didn't mistakenly enter that then today."

"Very."

"Did everything work out last night?" Enric again looked her in the eye.

It was so much easier to talk to him when they talked technical. Igraine sighed. "They both seem fine. Lady Alenor is in love."

"What about you?"

"I'm not in love . . ." Igraine said quickly.

"No . . ." Enric smiled gently. "Are you alright? You were pretty upset last night. And Lezay seemed to be hounding you. I was hesitant to let you go back to your tent alone, but you seemed to have the situation under control."

"Oh . . ." Igraine said blankly. "Well, I didn't sleep much. But yes, I'm fine."

"If he ever bothers you . . ."

"You going to pin him to the wall like you did my brother?" Her lips pulled into an amused smile.

"I could." Enric shrugged.

"Do me a favor." Igraine looked down her eyelashes at him. "Knock him on his backside in the sword arena today."

Enric chuckled. "As you wish. My lady, I will win this tournament for you."

Igraine's smile faltered for only a moment. "Heaven help me if you don't."

Enric covered her hand, which lay casually on the table, with his own. Igraine stared at their hands as his thumb gently caressed her. Abruptly he pulled away and stood, bowing to her. She stared after him as he exited the hall, still just as confused by her body and mind's reaction to him as she was before he sat down.

The sword arena had turned bloody. It was a brutal day, one of the worst Igraine had seen in all her years of watching tournaments. Sir Lezay dealt a particularly hard blow to a knight new to the field and left the man in a heap in the middle of the arena.

"Oh heavens, I can't watch anymore. I think I'm going to be sick," Alenor said at her side, turning her head into Igraine's shoulder.

"It's over. They took him out of the ring now."

"Who's next?"

"Sir Geoffrey versus Sir Enric. Only this round and the final round, and then it's over."

"Thank God."

Igraine agreed. She was ready for the competition to end. All three knights still remaining in the event had promised to win the tournament for her, and each of them had made their declarations public right at the beginning. The only one that Montag had seemed bothered by was Sir Enric. The man was a wild card as to where he would draw the line of chivalric reward, should he win. That question aside, all three men had been battered by multiple rounds of combat. Geoffrey had taken a hard blow to his helmet and still seemed a bit stunned. Enric had a bloody bandage wound tight around a cut to his upper left arm, his broken mail gaping dangerously. Lezay had a bloody nose that he refused to clean up, insisting that the now-dry blood made him more intimidating, which was certainly true. No matter how this fight played out, Igraine was going to be caught in the middle of the aftermath.

Enric's sword clanged off of Geoffrey's helmet, the sound echoing across the field. Geoffrey turned around, blindly looking for Enric, who cut in again, as quick as a snake, hitting him hard across the chest. As Geoffrey doubled over, Enric kneed the man in the chin. Geoffrey fell to his knees in the dirt and raised his hand to yield. In only a minute, the fight was over.

Igraine applauded, breathing a sigh of relief.

"Enric and Lezay," Alenor said from her side. "What will you do if Lezay wins?"

"I'll do nothing if Lezay wins."

"What if Enric wins?" Alenor nudged her, smiling.

"Shh. Nothing is happening. I'm too valuable to my brother."

Alenor hesitated, frowning. "I'm not valuable to him anymore, am I? He barely talked to me today."

"He's focused on the competition, Alenor. I'll talk to him on the way home tomorrow, see what he's thinking. He talks more after the tournaments." Igraine took a deep breath and focused on the sword arena again as the knights entered: Sir Enric Levan d'Aquitaine and Sir Rothulfus Lezay de Leuwenstein.

Swords started swinging as soon as the flag was dropped. Lezay hammered forward with reckless abandon, initially catching Enric off guard. Enric blocked blow after blow, then finally spun out of reach. The two men circled each other like two dogs, hackles raised. Enric feinted left, swung hard, and the sword sang against Lezay's mail. Lezay roared like a beast and hammered a hard blow at Enric's head, which he ducked while simultaneously delivering an upward slash that hit Lezay hard in the right hip. Lezay staggered for a moment, limping noticeably. He charged again. With a series of quick blows, Enric forced him to the ground. Lezay rolled to get up but was slow;

the pain in his hip was too great. Enric was quick to kick his sword away, placing his own blade on Lezay's neck.

Lezay had no choice but to yield.

Enric backed away from the glaring man amidst the cheers of the crowd. His eyes locked on his prize as if the rest of the crowd did not exist.

Igraine's heart hammered.

He knelt before her, his sword in his right hand, point to the ground. His arm looked like it was bleeding again, and he had to be bruised all over. Yet there on one knee, in front of the entire manor and all the attending knights, Enric said simply, "Lady Igraine, in your honor, my victory." He looked into her eyes. "I am yours."

Igraine wasn't sure what to do. This went beyond the chivalric pageantry she was used to. Knights had pledged their victories to her for years, but none had actually succeeded. And no one made a public show of it. She wordlessly took his hand and raised him to his feet. On impulse, she lifted his arm in the air and shouted, "My champion!"

For the crowd, it made the show complete. Their cheers rang out all along the field, all the way back to the manor and the tent city beyond. Igraine blushed, and Enric beamed down at her. She saw the look in his eyes, that same look he'd had on the steps the night before when he'd almost kissed her. She looked away. Not here, not now, her posture said.

"Kiss! Kiss! Kiss!" the crowd chanted.

Igraine looked back at Enric in panic. In one slow motion, he took off his helmet, his sweaty locks of hair falling across his forehead, somehow making him look even more manly. He dropped the helmet at their feet and clasped his calloused hands on either side of her face. Igraine closed her eyes, the crowd disappeared, and the only thing she could feel were those hands. The only things she could hear were her own breath and the pounding of her heart. Then there was a new feeling, now on her lips. Softness, surrounded by rough stubble, with a taste of salty sweat. Unable to remember where she was, she let her arms twine around the solid shoulders in front of her, allowed the mouth to press into her lips harder, willing them into her. Then the mouth was gone, the hands released her face, and there was a crowd of people staring at her as they screamed and cheered. Igraine stared at Enric, who stood silently watching her, just as breathless as she.

The moment lasted a long while, until the crowd grew bored of them and began to filter off. Enric took Igraine's hand, caressing the back of it gently.

"Now what?" she asked, her voice weak.

"I guess we go up to dinner in the manor, like usual."

"You should clean up first."

"You think I stink?"

Igraine raised an eyebrow, and Enric had to laugh.

"Fine, I'll go change. May I see you again tonight?"

Igraine cringed. There it was. "Enric, just so you know . . . I can't . . . I won't . . . my brother would kill me . . . he's already going to be furious."

"Igraine, I'm only asking for time with you. Nothing more."

"Oh." She swallowed her embarrassment with some relief.

"Meet me on the wall? After dinner?"

"Yes."

"Good." He gave her hand a little squeeze. "If he gives you trouble, find me. I'll reassure him of my pure intentions. Understood?"

Igraine nodded, her unspoken fears relieved.

Chapter 5

"What were you thinking?" Montag bellowed. Igraine stood in the tent before him as he paced angrily back and forth. "You kissed him in front of everyone! What's next, Igraine? Are you going to run around the list naked?"

"I hardly think that's a rational conclusion." She stood, hands on her hips. "It was a kiss, Montag! People kiss in public all the time. He won the tourney for me. What was I supposed to do? Don't forget it was your idea to put me on display like this!"

"I never thought you would start showing affection to your 'champions' in public!"

"What *did* you think?" Igraine fumed. "This has gone on for what, six years now? How long did you think the world would wait before they actually wanted a piece of their prize? I've been keeping them at bay with exhaustive banter for years. Didn't you hear Lezay this morning? And he's not the only one who *talks* to me like that. Now one man, with honorable intentions I might add, finally 'wins' me, and you decide to change your mind about your little game."

Montag's slap slashed across her left cheek. She put her hand to her face and glowered at him. "I'm not sure which bothers you more, brother. The truth or your own hypocrisy?"

With a black-eyed glare and red face, Montag looked ready to slap her other cheek. His knuckles flexed.

"Why don't you marry Alenor, Montag?" Igraine plunged ahead. "You claim I'm ruined if I'm despoiled by a simple kiss, but you ruin her without a care. You have no excuse not to marry her, and you know it. She's young, she's rich, and she's in love with you. What more do you want?"

"Remember your place, sister."

Igraine straightened. "I am the Lady of the Tournament. And as such, my place is up in that banquet hall, at my champion's side."

Montag's slap rang true on her other cheek.

Igraine bowed her head, tears stinging her eyes. She flexed her jaw, then wordlessly looked back up at her brother with a glare that matched his own. They were blood, after all. It was not only the men of the family that inherited Le Brun's fury. Before Montag could say another word, she spun on her heel, pushing aside the tent flap and emerging into the twilight. Her hand still to her cheek, she stretched her jaw. He'd left a good one this time. She wished she had a mirror to check how bad the bruising was before she went in public, but what did it matter? She wanted to be with Enric at this point either way. If he noticed, so be it.

She found him quickly in the busy great hall, and he rose from his seat when she stood before him. He bowed slightly, mildly confused.

"I'm yours for the night," she rushed, then closed her eyes, wincing at her choice of words. "I mean, if I may, I would like to eat dinner with you. And then I will go off on my own. Like a normal, respectable lady."

A few of the men around Enric chuckled, but he held up his hand and quieted them.

"Dinner would be lovely, my lady."

Igraine sighed in relief, and gratefully took the seat Enric offered. He brushed a finger over her cheekbone, and she flinched away from the contact. His eyes narrowed in concern, so she hastily breathed, "The wind outside is fierce."

He looked doubtful, but he stepped over the bench and took his place next to her. He nodded at the men around them. "Introductions are in order I believe. This is my squire Pierre." He gestured to a lanky, blond teenager beside him, who smiled and nodded. "My friend Sir Louis of Angoulême and his brother Sir Josse." The tall, slim, auburn-haired man across from Enric nodded. The long-haired man next to him was so obviously a relation, Igraine wondered if they were twins.

The second man complained, "Don't I get to be your friend too, Enric?"

Enric rolled his eyes. "Of course you're my friend, Josse."

"Don't let this lady make you forget it," Josse bantered.

"Here, eat something before they scare you away from the table," Louis shoved a full platter of meat and vegetables in front of Igraine.

She glanced at it, her mouth watering. The aroma of herbal seasoning drifted across the table. "Did you all get your fill?"

"We will. After you." Josse gestured to the plates.

"Oh, here. Do you want me to fill your plates?"

Enric furrowed his brow. "Lady Igraine, just take what you want. We're all grown men. We can help ourselves."

Igraine blushed and then tentatively took a small portion of the food.

"Is that all you're eating?" Louis wondered as he and the others helped themselves to generous portions.

Igraine didn't know what to say. Apparently her brother's rule about women waiting to eat until last didn't apply to these men. She helped herself to more.

The men's conversation was more polite than she was used to. They still talked about the tourney and horses, but they were tactful about it. There was no boasting, just gratitude for their success and respect for not only each other but their other opponents.

"That Lezay . . . Enric, I thought at one point he had you," Louis said.

"I have to learn that move he did. I've never seen that before," Enric thought aloud.

"I know. Some kind of twist, half-thrust," Louis said pensively. "Want to figure it out tomorrow on the way home?"

"For sure. Josse, you and Sir Jean had quite the battle. How's your shoulder?" Enric took a drink.

"Not broken. Glad I don't have to do anything but sit on a horse tomorrow." Josse rubbed the shoulder and winced.

Igraine listened, fascinated.

"Lady Igraine, are you always this quiet?" Louis asked.

"Um . . ."

"The Lady of the Tourney, speechless." Pierre laughed.

"What do you want me to say?"

Louis shrugged. "Whatever you want to say. Who do you think would win if we put Josse against your brother?"

"What weapon?" She raised her eyebrows.

"Hmmm," Louis thought. "Pike?"

"Montag would kill him."

"Oh, that bad huh?" Josse asked.

"That bad. Face him with a sword and you might have a chance."

"Why doesn't he like fighting sword?" Enric asked.

Igraine shrugged. "Personal preference." *And a lot of bad memories.*

"Which horse is faster?" probed Pierre. "Enric's or your brother's?"

Igraine smiled mischievously. "Mine."

The men's eyes went wide in amusement, and they laughed.

She shrugged. "You all have destriers. They're powerful but clunky. My mare is a charger, light and quick. You wouldn't stand a chance."

Enric smiled at her with something akin to pride. She laid her hand on the table next to his. In seconds he had taken it in his own, lacing his fingers into hers. She felt the heat grow in her cheeks and looked away from him.

"So how is Angoulême?" she asked the brothers.

"Grand," said Louis as Josse said, "Terrible."

Josse explained, "I'm the third son, so there's hardly anything for me to do in Angoulême. That's why I spend so much time here at the tourneys. Just hoping to make a little gold, or a reputation, or both. Louis, meanwhile, lives the grand life with a pretty wife and a big manor full of babies."

"You dream of a manor full of babies?" Enric teased.

"Heirs," Louis toasted. "A warrior's retirement plan. You should think of making some yourself, Enric. You're getting old." He couldn't help but smirk a little as he glanced back and forth from Enric to Igraine.

"How old are you?" Igraine asked. She studied Enric. No trace of grey or wrinkles. He had all his teeth from what she could see. Still, there was something wizened about him that made her question his apparent youth.

"Twenty-four," Enric answered.

"You realize my brother has almost a decade on you, and you beat him in his best event?"

"I guess he's the one that's getting old." Enric smirked.

Igraine felt so at ease with them all. She laughed at their jokes. They listened to her stories, asked her advice on how to handle certain knights she'd seen compete. She felt so included, so valued, that she almost forgot her brother was in the same room, a few tables away.

It was dark outside and the hearths were dim when Igraine felt the shadow fall over her. Her table grew quiet, eyes peering curiously at the man behind her. Igraine bowed her head, looking at her hands, which she clasped tightly in her lap.

Enric rose to his feet, graciously nodding to Montag without breaking his steady gaze. "Lord Montag, I thank you for sharing the company of Lady Igraine this evening. Your sister is a true gem."

Montag held out his hand toward Igraine, and she obediently put her own in his, allowing him to guide her to her feet. She kept her head bowed. Montag's jaw twitched as he eyed the table of knights, then he finally returned Enric's courteous nod. Without a word, he led Igraine from the room.

Igraine didn't dare glance back to Enric or the other men, but she overheard them murmuring.

"What is wrong with that man?"

"She didn't even say goodbye."

Chapter 6

As they rode on to Metz, the location of the next tourney, Montag chose not to bring up the previous evening. Lezay, who again traveled with them, was not as tactful.

Montag let his reins drape loosely in his hand, his horse plodding with its head down after the long miles of travel. The rhythm of hoofbeats steadied his mind. The rhythm of the bickering going on next to him, not so much. Soon they would be in Metz, he reminded himself, and Lezay would be lost to the crowd in his preparations for the tournament, while Igraine would be off to her perch in the stands with the other ladies. How many miles? Too many.

"You understand how I can't have my betrothed going around kissing my enemies," Lezay lectured. He'd been going on for over an hour on the virtues of a woman, what he expected of a wife, his rules for his wife, the physical attributes he desired in a wife — complete with details that made Igraine blush — and more. For the most part, she had managed to ignore him and purposefully had her horse lengthen its trot to make Lezay's heavy destrier work to keep up. Thus why Montag's horse was grateful to be plodding, as the two of them had finally reined up their mounts to a more sustainable pace. "So you see, if you wish to wed me, you have a great deal of work to do," Lezay concluded.

Igraine looked like she was ready to snap, and Montag almost wished she would. At least it would provide some amusement to combat Lezay's incessant chatter. She shot Montag a sideways look and then visibly bit her tongue, her lips pursing into a furious frown. Then she pushed her nose into the air and stared straight ahead. Montag smirked. The posture of her back warned the catapult could still release.

Satisfied that his future wife was going to work harder to be a proper woman, Lezay turned his attention to Montag. The respect he had just demanded Igraine preserve apparently did not apply to Alenor, who was already despoiled and free for the mockery. Lezay was relentless, asking all kinds of lewd questions. Before Montag could start answering, Igraine's patience snapped.

"She's my best friend! I don't want to hear any of it! From either of you. Ever! Understood?"

The men went quiet but not without sharing a sneer. Montag waited expectantly, but she restrained herself to silence once again, her anger radiating off of her.

"I want my dagger back by the way," Lezay looked pointedly at her.

Igraine kept her eyes straight ahead. "I'm keeping it."

"Oh, a betrothal present. Well, enjoy it then, my lady."

"Oh shut it, Lezay."

He couldn't handle another hour of listening to this. Montag's voice spoke over them both, "Lezay, I did not agree to let you have her yet. I said I would consider it. I have other offers still on the table."

"Who?" asked Igraine.

"You'll find out eventually."

"What about you and Alenor?" she ventured.

"What about us?"

"She said she has a massive dowry. Isn't that what you want? More land and power? Her father is a duke for goodness sake."

Montag pursed his lips. "I'm considering it."

"Ohhh!" Lezay hooted. "And leaving the good life before you have to?"

"Like you would for my sister?" Montag pointed out. Sometimes he wondered if Lezay was two men trapped in one body. He'd say he wanted Igraine, then say he wanted his freedom to run wild. He'd say he wanted the power of uniting Alsace, then he'd spend all summer on the tournament circuit instead of managing his property. Of course, with family back home to pick up his neglect, there never had been consequences for Lezay. If only Montag had that luxury.

Lezay took the message and went quiet. "Of course," he said. But he didn't look like he meant it.

Igraine steered the conversation back to Alenor. "Montag, the sooner the better now. What if she gets with child?"

The point hit like a lance to the chest, his heart pounding. He needed an heir more than most. He and Igraine were the last of an ancient noble line, as their father had constantly reminded them both. The pressure had been on Montag for over a decade already to reproduce, and now, at thirty-three he was still unwed. And that was perfectly fine. How could he possibly have time to deal with a woman? He had a fief to manage, tournaments to keep his skills honed, and plenty of assignments to put those skills to use. No, a few minutes after a tournament was the extent of his need for a woman. "Let me find you a husband first, then we can worry about me."

"I can wait. Alenor may not be able to. Negotiations alone could take months. And she says she loves you. What more do you want?"

"You've spoken your piece, now it's time to remember your place," growled Montag.

Igraine went quiet and let her horse fall behind the men again.

Lezay started babbling again to Montag, but he wasn't listening. His thoughts were locked on Alenor, just as Igraine had intended. The woman was different, fiery. And if he really did marry off Igraine, she would leave Brunstein, and thus yield her role as manager of the household. Perhaps it would be good to have a woman to replace her. A wife. He pursed his lips. No sense tying himself down until Igraine was out of the picture. There was a man at Metz who may take care of the situation in the very near future.

The very air within the city of Metz tingled with excitement. It was a medium-sized tournament, so knights had traveled a fair distance to congregate. Montag purposefully strode the crowd, glad as usual that he was nearly a head taller than most of the other men. With ease he spotted Lord Matthew of Bologne in his bright red and white tunic and shouldered his way toward the man.

"Ah, Lord Montag!" Matthew exclaimed when he saw him approach. He made a final adjustment to his saddle before turning to Montag, his hands on his hips. Though his beard was long and grey, he was still a fit man, though not nearly as tall as Montag. His friendly smile twinkled in his eyes. "Will you be competing today as well?"

"Aye, my lord," Montag nodded graciously.

Matthew turned to his squire with a side glance. "You'd best tell the heralds I won't be competing with the pike after all." He laughed, but the squire boy hurried away with all seriousness. He glanced over Montag's shoulder. "And did you bring your fair sister along as well?"

"Of course." Montag smiled.

"Excellent. You've considered my offer?"

"I have," Montag's eyes took a knowing glint. "As you know, it's a difficult decision for me. My only sister! And with our father so far away. But I must say, your terms are generous. And I doubt even she could find a reason to protest becoming a countess."

"Then you accept?"

"We accept."

The men clasped arms, Matthew beaming with excitement.

"We'll finalize the details after the tournament then," Matthew said.

"Best of luck to you today, my lord."

"And you, Lord Montag! And you!" Matthew chuckled and practically skipped back to his approaching squire, ten years younger than he had been just minutes before.

Montag watched him go, absently wiping his sweaty palms on his breeches before turning back toward his own squire, who stood ready with his equipment. He hoped he'd made the right choice for Igraine. It was the best deal politically, for sure. Matthew was an Alsatian by birth after all. And economically, the man was one of the richest in their corner of Europe. Igraine might not even complain. Really, it wasn't her he was worried about. It was the man with a fist emblazoned across his tunic standing next to his squire.

"Lord Matthew looked pleased with your conversation," Lezay said, an edge of warning in his tone. He roughly tightened the laces of his leather gauntlets, the tension obvious.

Montag was silent. He focused on taking his helmet from his squire and positioning it securely on his head.

Lezay laid a hand on his shoulder, forcing Montag to look him in the eye. Meaning passed without words.

"You bastard," Lezay hissed.

Montag shrugged his hand off.

"You promised me. You promised me that with Igraine, we would unite Alsace into one of the greatest provinces in the region. You bastard!"

"I didn't promise, Lezay. We theorized. You are no count."

"Who cares if he's a count? What matters is the territory! We are far from Bologne!"

"He has connections to Alsace. It's a good match for her, Lezay. I've made my decision."

"You've made your decision," Lezay growled. Fuming, he turned on his heel and headed toward the arena, his squire jogging after him.

Montag frowned as he made the final touches to his armor. Lezay had a temper few could match. Even if he had to marry Igraine off to an older man for the sake of his wealth and connections, at least he could give her a man with a steadier nature. He glanced in the direction of Matthew, who was animatedly talking to another knight, his head turned toward the ethereal Igraine as she took her place in the stands. Would a man who had stolen his last wife from a nunnery be kinder than Lezay? He doubted it, but at least he was significantly richer. He took his pike from his squire and entered the arena.

The next hours passed in a monotonous blur. Montag tuned out the crowd, focusing only on the opponents before him. It made him quicker, stronger, and more centered than the others; it made him the victor. He was settled into the rhythm of the fight when the crowd let out a loud gasp. It was from the direction of the sword arena. A herald ran into Montag's arena, waving a white flag to call a truce between the two fighters. A pause in the competition could only mean one thing: someone was grievously hurt.

Montag wiped the sweat from his brow as he slowly made his way toward the wooden-fenced sword arena with the rest of the crowd. "Who is it?" he asked no one in particular.

"The Count of Bologne," a squire replied as he edged past, attempting to escape the pressing crowd.

Montag's nerves sparked, and he pushed himself quickly to the rail. There in the middle of the sword arena lay the count, completely unresponsive with his squire and attendees surrounding him, their faces taut with worry. More concerning still was the sight of Lezay leaning against the opposite rail with his helmet under his arm, brow dripping with sweat. His sword leaned casually against the rail next to him. Montag took a deep breath and worked his way around the enclosure, which was being policed by the heralds to keep the crowd out.

When he reached Lezay, he asked in a low voice, "What did you do?"

"Just a regular fight," Lezay replied casually.

"Is he dead?"

"Naw, he's breathing still. Just took a hard blow to the head."

"How hard of a blow to the head?"

"It was an accident."

"Of course it was." Montag gritted his teeth.

A stretcher appeared and the attendants worked to lift Lord Matthew onto it.

Montag searched the crowd, wondering where Igraine was in all the chaos.

"She's with Alenor," Lezay said, reading his gaze. He pointed to the raised stands above the tourney field. The two women sat in shock, hands interlaced, staring at the proceedings below them. "Pity things got put on hold. I was about to win the tournament for her."

Montag only shook his head. He forced himself to walk away, checking the urge to fight that still boiled in him. Now was not the time to lay into Lezay. They could argue later, on the road back to Alsace. For now, he just needed to pray that the count would survive.

Chapter 7

August 27, 1172

On the road to Poitiers, Aquitaine

The first leaves of autumn were just starting to change. Igraine studied them as she walked through the manicured forest path behind the Crown Inn. They'd just spent yet another long day in the saddle on the way to one of the last tournaments of the season. The sun was setting, heightening the changing colors with rays of golden light. She folded her arms and looked up, marveling at the beauty. The leaves danced in the slight breeze like fairies.

"Lovely," said a man's familiar voice.

Igraine frowned and closed her eyes, trying to hold the moment but knowing that it was already gone. She heard the leaves crunch next to her. The smell of onions tainted the otherwise sweet breeze. Igraine sighed.

"I see you caught up to us, Lezay."

"I missed you, my love." His finger traced her upper arm.

Igraine snorted, opening her eyes. "I must say, it was rather nice to travel without your . . . companionship. Quiet. Even peaceful."

"I am glad to hear I excite you so," Lezay cooed.

Igraine sighed. "Does Montag know you've arrived?"

"No, love."

"No?" Usually, Lezay went running to Montag like a loyal dog.

"I wanted to see you first. We need to talk."

The hair on the back of Igraine's neck prickled. She turned to face Lezay, leveling her gaze at him. He had not shaved since the last tournament, and his clothes were smudged with the dust of the road. It certainly did nothing for his appearance. That she could have ignored. The look in his eyes was much more concerning. Suddenly Igraine felt like she was a rabbit caught in a snare. She tried to shake off the feeling, reminding herself this was the same Lezay she'd always known and always kept at bay.

"Talk about what?" She started to head back toward the Inn.

Lezay caught her arm, stopping her. "Your betrothed is a cripple."

"I don't have a betrothed."

"He didn't tell you yet? Montag engaged you to the Count of Bologne."

Igraine couldn't help but gasp.

Lezay continued. "But after a certain accident the other week, the count seems to be a bit . . . forgetful . . . of such arrangements. Not that he would be in any condition to perform his duties as a husband to you."

Igraine furrowed her brow. "What's wrong with him?"

"Seems the healers believe he'll never walk again. Nor speak, though he seems to have the ability to mumble. And drool."

Igraine moved to snatch away her arm, but Lezay held tighter, his fingers now digging into her flesh painfully. "You have a decision to make, Igraine. If you tell your brother you want to marry me, he will agree. You will be spared life married to an invalid."

"Let go of me."

"Admit it, Igraine, you're comfortable with me. We've known each other for years. Why gamble with someone twice your age, who you don't know? Who knows what secrets the dukes and counts hide behind closed doors? You know me. We could build a good life together."

"Aye, Lezay, I know you. Let go."

"Igraine, you know you want to—"

"Let go!" Igraine yanked her arm away, simultaneously drawing Lezay's dagger from her belt. She pointed it at him warily.

"I want that back." Lezay smiled, but he did not approach.

"Does it seem ironic that this dagger spends so much of its time being pointed at its master? That should tell you something, Lezay."

"You wouldn't stand a chance against me with it, love."

"Just like Lord Matthew? Murder in plain sight for all to see." Igraine shook her head. She'd seen it all unfold, known something was different from the moment Lezay set eyes on Matthew that day. "You're right, Lezay; I do know you. Too well. And apparently, my brother does too. Why else would he pick an old man to be my husband over his own best friend?"

She watched the fury cloud Lezay's face, suddenly realizing maybe she was too right, and she had pushed too far. She stepped away from him, toward the inn. It was within eyesight; she could see the lanterns glowing in the settling twilight. Lezay took a step toward her and she bolted, hiking her skirts up over her ankles and letting her long legs carry her. She heard Lezay crashing just a step behind her. His fingers caught the back of her dress and pulled. It was enough to send her flying into the leaves lining the path. The dagger flew from her fingers, landing somewhere ahead of her.

She whirled around and kicked out instinctively, catching Lezay in the jaw as he tried to catch her wrists and pin her. He was thrown back but pinned her skirts with his knees. His weight shifted above her and she screamed, but the sound was quickly cut out by his dirty hand pressing against her mouth.

"Keep quiet, love," he hissed. "I'll let you to your feet if you keep your mouth shut. I intend to finish this conversation. Agreed?"

Igraine nodded.

In a swift movement that took her breath away, Lezay lifted her off the ground and set her on her feet with a speed that left her swaying into him. He kept one arm wrapped around her waist, his other hand gently picking leaves out of her hair. Stunned, Igraine didn't move.

For a long minute, Lezay held her that way. To an outsider it would seem a lover's embrace. To Lezay, it was. To Igraine, it was the snare setting tighter, the realization setting in that she would never get loose.

A man cleared his voice and stopped on the path a few yards away. "Oh, sorry." Igraine heard the leaves crunch as he headed away again. Then there was a pause. "Sir, did you drop your dagger?"

Lezay stiffened. Even with her back to the newcomer, Igraine recognized Enric's voice. She tensed to pull away. Lezay's arm tightened.

"It's mine," Lezay said calmly. He had to step toward the man to receive the dagger, so he turned Igraine with him.

Enric froze in place, recognizing her instantly. "Lady Igraine," he whispered.

"Sir Enric." She hoped he would hear the strain in her voice.

"Sir Enric, I believe you've met my betrothed?" Lezay drawled.

Even in the twilight Igraine could see Enric's eyebrows go up.

When Enric said nothing, Lezay said coldly, "I'll have that dagger back now, sir."

Enric looked between them and slowly shook his head. "I must have mistaken, sir. What I saw was a stick. If you've lost your dagger, though, I will be sure to look for it on my way back to the inn. He made a show of his empty hands. "I heard you competed at Metz. Can you tell me more about the accident there? I'll buy you an ale."

Lezay fumed beside her, but he was left in too awkward of a position to do anything but follow Enric back to the inn. He held Igraine tight to his side until they reached the door, releasing her as soon as they stepped inside to reveal Montag sitting at a big wooden table. Relieved, Igraine ran a hand through her hair, pulling out the last few bits of leaves. Without a word, she sat at the table with the three men and poured herself a brimming cup of ale. Montag shot her a curious glance but was soon distracted by Lezay and Enric's sudden, obviously fake, friendship.

As the men compared notes on what had happened to the Count of Bologne and who they expected to meet at the upcoming tournament at Poitou, Igraine could do no more than frown into her cup of ale.

She tossed and turned that night, dreams touching her consciousness and confusing reality. Neither was reassuring. As usual, the first rays of dawn were a relief. Igraine was one of the first guests to make her way down the stairs into the common area.

Seated at the same table they had left the night before was Enric.

"Didn't you sleep?" she questioned, amazed he was even more of an insomniac than her.

"Enough. I figured you'd be up before the rest. I have something for you." With a glance around, Enric put a dagger on the table between them.

"You did find it! I think Lezay spent an hour last night looking out there for it before he went to bed."

"I believe you have more use for it than he does," Enric said with amusement before his face tuned serious. "Why do I get the impression the men in your life bully you, Lady Igraine?"

"Poor timing. It's I who am the tempest." She couldn't help but hide behind the mask of the Lady of the Tournament. When Enric's concerned expression didn't change, she let the mask fall. "In truth, it has always been the line I walk. I used to navigate it well, but I seem to have been . . . stumbling . . . more. Particularly since I met you."

"Igraine, you can always come to me if things get out of hand. Last night—"

"Last night was handled," she said firmly.

Enric nodded.

Igraine's face softened as she looked into his eyes. "Thank you."

"You're welcome, my lady," Enric said gently. He rose. "I'm going to get on the road. I will see you at the tournament. Safe travels."

"Same to you."

Chapter 8

September 5, 1172

Poitiers, Aquitaine

The remainder of the journey to Poitou was not nearly as peaceful with Lezay along. He constantly questioned Montag about nonsense and randomly sang his out-of-tune songs. Igraine had told Montag nothing of what Lezay had done the night before, and she didn't intend to. From what she could glean from Lezay's chatter as they rode, Igraine began to understand the benefits proposed by a marriage between the Le Brun family and the Lezay family. It would merge the two greatest landholders in all of Alsace, giving them a massive territorial advantage and practically propelling them into a Princedom. Their geography left them largely independent as it was, and such an alliance would only solidify that independence in the eyes of their neighbors.

She had to admit, from a political standpoint, it made sense.

Thankfully, Montag was still dragging his feet over it. A countess in the family made equally good sense, as did the alliance *that* would forge with their neighbors. For every week that the Count of Bologne survived his accident, Montag seemed less inclined to finalize a contract with Lezay. Igraine pondered if her brother really did care for her happiness. Perhaps not, as at best the count was double her age and, as Lezay pointed out, currently a drooling invalid.

By the time their group entered the tournament grounds, Igraine was grateful for the distractions of the crowd. It was larger than most, perhaps a few thousand strong.

"Igraine! Over here!" Alenor shouted from her place in the stands.

Igraine joined her friend and settled in for a day of competition. She screwed on her smile as the typical rhythm of the event settled in. Lezay and Enric both pledged to win for her, which made things rather tense once again. Enric came out as victor, much to her relief, and with a chivalric display of admiration, sans kiss, she congratulated him and the entire crowd was excused to the feast in the great hall.

Alenor pulled her aside as they followed the crowd up to the castle. "Come with me," she whispered. "I need to talk to you alone."

Igraine followed, her curiosity piqued. Alenor led them down an empty alley in the village. Igraine picked up the hem of her skirts to step around a pile of manure.

"Alenor, what is going on? We shouldn't be down here."

"I don't want anyone else to hear." Alenor looked around once more to make sure no one was in earshot. Only the windowless plaster of the houses next to them surrounded them. "Igraine, I don't know what to do. I haven't told anyone."

Instantly Igraine guessed. "Good Lord. You're with child."

Alenor nodded.

"Montag's? So soon? Are you sure?"

"I have to be. I have not cycled since June. We were together in Reims, then Metz, then that little village we saw you at after Metz . . . what was it called?"

"Provins," Igraine said absentmindedly. "But I don't need to know any of that." She held up her hand to pause her friend from disclosing more of her brother's love life. "Have you told anyone?"

Alenor shook her head. "I wanted to be sure. I'm starting to show." She bit her lip, her unvoiced fears evident in her face. "Should I tell him tonight? Where are you traveling to after this? I don't know when I'll see him again."

"We go home to Alsace in a few days."

"So I'll tell him."

"No! Well, you have to, but we have to do it carefully. Alenor, I've warned you he has a temper. Between Enric winning Tournament Champion again today and Lezay badgering him for my hand in marriage . . . you have to be careful not to set him off."

"Won't he be glad to hear it?" Alenor's wide eyes searched Igraine's, full of hope.

Igraine inhaled sharply. "My brother doesn't like being penned in. He likes to have choices. A potential bastard is definitely going to feel like a threat to him."

Alenor's lip trembled and her eyes teared up. "What do I do? I'm such a fool."

"Shh," Igraine whispered and hugged her friend. "I did warn him this was a possibility weeks ago, and he's the one that didn't stop pursuing you. It's his fault, too." *Which was the precise reason he was going to turn into a bull.* She sighed. "Just tell him when you're alone. Definitely don't do it in front of a crowd. And after you tell him, come to me, and I will intervene on your behalf if I need to. Perhaps I'm wrong. Perhaps he is going to be thrilled and marry you this very weekend." She forced a smile.

"That would be lovely," Alenor sniffed into Igraine's shoulder.

Igraine pulled away and wiped her friend's tears. "Go. Go up to the castle and take my place at the banquet table. Tell him I'm not feeling well. Enjoy dinner and get him to go talk with you alone. If you need to find me, I'll be on the wall of the inner bailey. It's quiet there, and I'm not far from the keep. You can do this."

Alenor nodded, straightening her spine and exhaling through pursed lips.

As Igraine watched her walk away, her heart sank. Her night as Lady of the Tournament was only just beginning. The placations and negotiations would begin after dinner. But until then, she had a few hours to walk the bailey wall and hope that a particular knight had the same idea.

He did.

Enric waited for her as she ascended the wooden steps to the corniced stone wall that surrounded the inner stone castle of Poitou. His face lit up when he saw her.

"How long do I have with you?" he asked.

"An hour or two." She stopped in front of him.

"So long? Won't people talk, my lady?"

Adrenaline pumped through Igraine's veins; her fingers trembled as she laid one on his lips, silencing him. Just the feel of his rough scruff of facial hair was too much, and she instantly withdrew it, folding her hands in front of her. Enric didn't move. He just watched her with an amused expression. Gently he took her hand.

It paralyzed her.

"Hasn't anyone ever touched you before?" Enric asked as he wove and unwove his fingers with Igraine's, their hands like dancers of a duet. Igraine didn't answer, just allowed him to caress her palm. His strength gave him a gentle control he had perfect mastery of. He could break her fingers with these hands if he so chose. But instead, they were like the flow of water over the round stones of a brook, soothing her, rolling bits and pieces of her body into place so that together they could form the gentle current that flowed between them.

Every moment they were together, that current pulled stronger. When they were apart, it pulled her thoughts to him. Now unlike at prior tourneys, or even at the inn, Igraine didn't want to speak with him. Her thoughts had used up all the words. She only wanted to feel him, be near him. She pulled him a step closer, taking in his woody scent, letting it overpower her senses as her eyes closed. Enric brushed a strand of hair from her face, letting his fingers linger on the delicate planes of her cheek.

He sighed, and pulled her into his arms, simply holding her there as they looked out over the city as the sun set. Reds and oranges shot across the sky on the tails of long grey-white clouds.

"I have to know. Are you betrothed?" Enric asked.

Igraine frowned. "They talk of it, but nothing is decided."

"Word among the other knights is that things have been undecided for years. Why?"

"My brother is an indecisive man. He waits until everything is perfectly in place, then he acts. That is why he is so good at what he does."

"But he is a warrior. We have to act on instinct, make decisions quickly."

"Oh, and he can. Those kinds of decisions are usually cut or dry. Straightforward outcomes. He can analyze those in fractions of a second. But give him multiple options with multiple outcomes and time to think about each, and he will take that time. And as such, he is hardly ever wrong."

"You have a great deal of respect for your brother."

"He's my blood."

Enric nodded and looked away. "He would forbid this, Igraine. As innocent as this is."

She looked up at him. "If I am going to be locked away for the rest of my life with an old man, give me this one moment of youth."

Igraine leaned up into Enric, her arms twining around his waist as she pressed her head into his chest. He wrapped his strong arms around her shoulders, holding her tight to him. He kissed her forehead. That was as far as he went with her, at least since that first victorious kiss. It was her lips that needed him, wanted him. But again, he refused.

"Don't you want me?" she asked, her lips pressed to the fabric of his linen shirt.

"I want you too much," he answered. "You know that."

Montag stumbled into the tent long after Igraine had gone to bed. He tripped over a saddle, which woke her. He smelled like a barrel of ale.

She lay quiet but not quiet enough.

Montag staggered over to her and plopped down next to her on the bare ground. All chance of sleep lost, she sat up and yawned.

"I take it she talked to you," Igraine whispered.

Montag nodded.

"This is a good thing, Montag. You need an heir."

He nodded again.

"You just need to marry quickly."

He sat immobile.

Igraine held her breath.

"Is she lying to me?"

"I don't think so. She's scared."

"She said she loves me."

"I think she means it."

"Igraine, no one ever means that."

"She wasn't raised like us, brother." Igraine laid a hand on his shoulder.

A shudder ran down Montag's back, and he hid it by crawling over to his trundle bed. "You need to be more discreet," he said as he fumbled with the blankets. "Lezay saw you and Enric."

Igraine stiffened. "What of it?"

Montag was silent, his breathing quieting as he drifted into a drunken sleep. Igraine lay back in her bed, a wrist across her forehead as a thousand thoughts swirled. So what if Lezay had seen? He was not her kin, not her husband, and she had not done anything wrong. The ache in her gut warned that it did matter though. She rolled over, slipping her hand between the blankets to find the dagger that was never far away. Lezay's dagger, which always seemed to point to its master.

Chapter 9

The silhouettes of man and woman seemed small against the backdrop of the cathedral. Montag and Alenor knelt at the altar before the priest, who crossed them both as he sanctified the marriage. Igraine glanced around the small group of family and friends who had assembled for the ceremony. Alenor's mother wept and leaned into the duke, who watched with conflicting emotions. Alenor's older brothers stood with squared shoulders, their silent, unemotional wives at their sides. The youngest brother yawned as the long ceremony dragged to its conclusion. On Montag's side of the aisle there were fewer bodies. Lezay stood at Igraine's side. He must have cleaned himself, for today at least she could tolerate the smell of him. In the row behind them were Sir Jean and Lord Fougères and his wife. It was a modestly good crowd, assembled at the last tournament of the season in Reims for convenience.

And haste.

Only a few weeks had passed since Alenor told Montag that she was with child, and for now she was hiding her condition well. It was a good match. Alenor's family supported it, really they were grateful for it, and Alenor's profession of love allowed for a simple, hasty wedding. Better to let their daughter marry a wealthy lord than to succumb to lust and scandal, after all.

Onions pervaded Igraine's nose. She wrinkled her nose, second-guessing her earlier assumption of Lezay's cleanliness. How could a smell be that persistent? "You'll be up there soon," Lezay whispered. "Perhaps we'll have a baby near the same time as your friend. Cousins! I'm ready to start as soon as you are."

"Shh," Igraine whispered back, refusing to look at him. She felt his finger brush her wrist and swatted his hand away.

"You let *him* touch you," he whispered.

"This is not the time."

Alenor and Montag rose, the blessing in Latin spoken over them both. Then it was over. Igraine's brother was married to her best friend. Alenor beamed as they turned to face their witnesses. She looked gorgeous today, her hair in a wreath of braids and a cream-colored gown flowing around her. A golden circlet rested on her brow. Montag wore a more complicated expression, but he kept gazing at Alenor as if in awe that she was his. Igraine watched them, hope soaring within her. Perhaps Alenor could soften his hardened heart after all.

The newlyweds mingled into the small crowd, hugs and well wishes smothering them.

Lezay leaned over to whisper to Igraine. "I understand Montag reserved a private room in an inn for the night. Will you be all alone?" He moved to catch her fingers again.

Igraine pulled away. "I'm never alone, Lezay." She went up to congratulate her friend.

Her nerves tingled through the afternoon into the evening. She sat through the small feast, the cheap troubadour's songs, and even a few dances, her smile brightly watching Alenor and Montag's happiness. With frequent side glances to the darkness falling beyond the festive room, she checked off the hours until the festivities would be over, excitement building as night set in. In all her years of travel, she'd never had a night unchaperoned by her brother.

Enric was waiting for her on the battlement, as he always did at this time of night during a tournament. Once Montag and Alenor retired, she took her leave. Her skirts and the soft tap-tap of her shoes were the only sounds audible in the alley as she ducked between houses toward the main wall, letting darkness be her ally. Her heart pounded. To witness the beginnings of love, even in a man so cold as her brother, had her longing for a love of her own. And she knew where one was waiting. It was time to tell him how she felt. She lengthened her stride, ducking into an alley that would lead her directly to the stairs of the bailey.

The breath whooshed out of her as her back slammed into the stone wall to her right. Her head cracked painfully against the stone, sending a blinding light through the darkness. Then all went black and her knees buckled. She slouched against the wall. Dazed and disoriented, she blinked rapidly, trying to discern if the darkness was real or if she couldn't see.

"He did tell me to keep an eye out for you," a man said as he crouched on his haunches in front of her. Onions. Lezay. She struggled to pull herself to her feet. He laughed at her, an eerily grating sound. "Igraine, my love. What are you doing sneaking through alleys in the middle of the night?" He caressed her cheek. "You could be hurt out here."

Igraine swallowed, wondering if her voice would work. She croaked out, "Let . . . let me go . . . Lezay."

"Were you going to see *him*, love?"

Igraine groaned, rubbing the back of her head. Her vision was coming back at least. She could make out his silhouette in the dim moonlight.

"Igraine, come with me. Let me show you what real passion is like. We can be wed on the morrow."

She blinked at him, still clutching a hand to her head. She felt nauseous. "You hurt me."

"Oh, you're fine."

"No, Lezay. You hurt me. Why?" She shook her head slowly. "No, it doesn't matter. Montag will have your hide when he hears about this. Mon Dieu, Lezay. You hurt me." She pulled her knees to her chest, skirts pulled tight around them, and put her head between them, willing the earth to stop spinning.

Lezay laid a hand on her shoulder, and she didn't move. Couldn't move. "It was a joke, Igraine."

"A joke?"

"I didn't mean to pull you back so hard, just surprise you."

"Surprise me?"

"You'll be fine."

Igraine lifted her head to glare at his blurry figure, even though she doubted he could see her face. "I shouldn't have to 'be fine' around you, Lezay. You should be protecting me. Not hurting me."

"I'm sorry."

"No, Lezay. If you were sorry, this wouldn't keep happening. Let's get something straight. You are my brother's friend. I loathe you. Do you understand? I hate the way you walk, the way you talk. I hold my breath so I don't have to smell you. I think you are a self-absorbed, cold, disrespectful ass. I will fight to my dying day to avoid marrying you, and I certainly have no desire for any of the other clandestine, shameful arrangements you've proposed to me. And my brother seems to be on my side for a change, so if you move against me like you just have, you move against him. And since you aren't afraid of me, let me remind you he is a very powerful man, who just married into another extremely powerful family. Cross him, and you'll find doors all across Europe slammed in your face. Get it through your head, Lezay . . . *leave me alone*!"

Lezay rose slowly and stepped back from her. He stared for a moment down at her, and Igraine merely sat watching him. If he was going to beat her, let him do it. Let him leave a mark that would show his treachery. Yet he did not advance. He stepped backward, then abruptly turned and left.

Igraine buried her head in her knees and groaned. A wave of relief flooded over her. Perhaps now the man finally understood. She took a deep breath and slowly pulled herself to her feet, leaning on the wall as the world spun again. Enric. Enric was still waiting for her. Could she make it to him?

By the time she made it to the base of the battlement stairs, her strength failed her. She sank onto the bottom step, leaning her head against the railing. That was where Enric found her. She melted into his arms as he scooped her up.

"Igraine, what happened?"

"Brute in the alley."

"Where should I take you? Back to your brother's tent? Where is he?"

She shook her head. No one else would be there. "Take me with you."

"Igraine I can't do that. Where is your brother? I'll take you to him."

"It's his wedding night."

She felt Enric squeeze her a little tighter for a second. Oh, he hadn't heard the news yet?

"Take me with you. I'll leave before dawn."

"I don't want you wandering alone at dawn either."

"Then I'll leave after dawn. Take me with you."

Enric sighed in frustration. "I only have my tent . . ."

"I like tents. I have a tent, too."

"Igraine, did you hit your head?"

"Hurts a lot."

"We're going to your tent. Where is it?"

"I don't want to be alone."

"I won't leave you alone. Where is it?"

She pointed toward the field of tents. "Find my crest, Sir Enric." She closed her eyes and leaned into his chest.

He sighed as he shifted her in his arms, carrying her down the street and out into the meadow where the tents were set. He found Montag's red tent easily and set Igraine on her feet so he could pull the flap aside. She walked to her pallet bed on her own and sank onto it, again holding a hand to her aching head.

"Do you have a candle?"

"In that bag." She pointed.

In a moment Enric had the candle lit and was inspecting Igraine's head.

"You've got a good lump, but I don't think the skin is broken. Who did this?"

"Brute in the alley."

"You don't know who?"

Igraine stayed silent.

Enric shook his head. "You should get some sleep. I'll wait outside in case you need me."

"Stay with me," Igraine said quietly. She patted the pallet next to her.

"Igraine . . . I—"

"I love you, Enric. I've been wanting to tell you. I love you." She looked down at her folded hands.

He knelt before her. Gently he took her face in his hands, drawing her eyes up to his own. "I love you, too, you beautiful flame of a woman." He hesitated, then kissed her gently. She groaned and he instantly released her, as if he had broken her.

"No, please don't stop," Igraine whispered.

Enric shook his head. "You don't understand, Igraine. If I start, I won't be able to stop."

"Then don't."

"No. No, Igraine. Don't tempt me." He rocked back onto his heels, studying her. "If you want this — me — I want to do it right. I will ask your brother for permission to marry you."

"He won't agree. You aren't a count."

"We're going to do this right." He stood and walked to the flap of the tent.

"Don't leave." Her voice was a breathless plea. "Let's just talk."

Enric nodded. "That I can manage. For a bit. Then you should sleep." He stood. "I'm going to sit outside here though, all right? Right outside."

Igraine sighed, watching his shadow as he settled outside the tent, leaving the flap open. She could see the stars twinkling beyond him. She crawled out of her bedroll and into the one closest to the door, Montag's. Curling her knees to her chest, aching head on her arm, she closed her eyes.

"Tell me about Jerusalem."

Enric's sharp intake of breath cut the silence. "What do you want to know?"

"Everything. What was it like?"

The grass rustled beneath Enric as he shifted his weight.

"I've heard the smells are fantastic." Igraine said with a yawn.

"Some smells. The spices . . . and the food . . . the food is so much more interesting than here."

"What kind of spices?"

"Baskets and baskets of colored powders, each with a smell strong enough to burn your nose if you hold it too close. Bright yellow, orange, reds. Salt from the seas dried like little crystals. Black peppercorns that make just about anything taste good."

"Mmm. That is the part of the Holy Land I wish to see."

"The spices?"

"The flavors, the colors. It sounds so much more exciting than our green hills."

"It is exciting," Enric said quietly.

"When did you meet my father?" There was a long silence. Igraine opened her eyes and sat up, frowning. "I thought you said you met him?"

"I did." Enric rubbed the back of his neck. "I was his vassal for a time. He knighted me."

"*He* knighted you? Why didn't you mention it? I didn't know you were so well acquainted." The many questions that rose up in her mind were forced back by the throb that hammered her skull. She winced.

"Well, remember months back when I told you I had enemies in your family? He would be the one. Suffice to say things between us fell apart not long after I was knighted."

"Does Montag know?"

"I have no idea what your brother knows. Sometimes I think he knows everything, other times, nothing. Like tonight, when he should have been watching out for you instead of leaving you unescorted around the town."

"It got me time with you."

"I like you better when you aren't nursing a headache. And when I can trust you to sleep safely. So I can sleep, so I can compete in the morning."

"Sleep then," Igraine cooed as she laid her head back down. She reached for Enric's hand. "If you still want to protect my honor, sleep outside so he can't get in. Sleep . . . sleep . . ." Her words quieted to a whisper, then silence, as her breathing evened out.

Igraine's hand still clenched Enric's. He groaned and laid outside the tent in the grass, only his hand penetrating the security of Igraine's tent.

Montag froze in his tracks. Was the man dead? Drunk? Why else would he be sprawled out in front of Montag's own tent? He strode up to Enric and looked down. He watched his chest rise and fall. Alive then. He kicked him in the ribs. Enric lurched upright to his feet, looking around in bewilderment. A mumble came from inside the tent.

"What the bloody hell is going on here?"

Enric rubbed his face and ran his hand through his dark hair. By the time Montag had glanced inside the tent to see his slumbering, fully clothed sister in his bed, Enric had straightened and was fully awake. "Good morning, Lord Montag."

"What are you doing here?"

"The Lady Igraine was assaulted last night in town. She asked me not to leave her alone, so I slept outside her tent."

"She alright?"

"I think so," Enric shrugged, formality softening. "She has a bad lump on her head though. She wouldn't tell me who did it."

"Igra . . ." Montag pulled aside the tent flap.

"Wait, wait. She didn't sleep well. She rarely does. Leave her be for a bit. I'd like to talk to you, Lord Montag."

"I had a long night myself, Enric. And we have a tournament to prepare for today. What is it?"

"Lady Igraine said you are entertaining offers for her hand in marriage. But nothing is decided. Please, sir, I would like to be considered."

Montag blinked at him. Was the man dumb? Maybe Montag had been wrong about Enric all this time, sensing the threat not because he was an equal but because he was crazy.

Enric rushed, "I love her, Montag. She says she feels the same. And–"

"And how much land do you own? Are you a count? A duke? Do you have connections within a royal court?"

Enric was silent.

"No? Then don't waste my time."

"My Lord –"

"Enric, you are ruining the perfectly good mood I woke up with this morning."

Enric quieted and stepped back. "Please consider it, Lord Montag."

Montag watched the man walk away. Enric rubbed his neck, which surely must be stiff from a long night on the bare ground. Montag frowned and threw open the tent flap. Igraine groaned quietly, curling into herself more, one hand over her eyes as if the dawn light hurt. Montag stepped over her and fumbled in the bag of armor at her feet, beginning to dress himself for the tournament. As he buckled his sword to his waist she blinked her eyes open at him.

"How is Alenor?" she mumbled, voice raspy with sleep. Not *how was your night* or *did you sleep well?* It was *How is Alenor?*

"She's sleeping still, just like you." Montag smirked a little to himself. Thus far, married life offered quite a bit of promise. Alenor was just fine. Perfect really.

Igraine whimpered as she sat up, a hand on a lump Montag hadn't yet seen. She winced.

"Good lord, Igraine. He wasn't exaggerating. What on earth happened?" Montag squatted down and pulled her hand from her head, eyeing the wound for himself. It was the size of an egg, tender, with just a trace of dried blood. "Who did this?"

Igraine was silent. She pushed him away, readying to pull herself to her feet.

"I'll kill him. Enric did this, didn't he?"

Igraine let out a bitter laugh. "Montag, you need to see past your own rivalries. Enric is the only gentleman around, and he of all people would never lay a hand on me." She pulled herself to her feet, wincing in pain, a hand again going to her head.

Montag watched her, his arms folded across his chest. "So who did it then?"

She snorted, which irked him further. "You won't kill him. Unfortunately."

"Whoever hurt you will pay, Igraine. Now who?"

She looked up at him, her eyes narrowed in her anger. "Your pet. Your partner. Your best friend. Sir Rothulfus Lezay."

Montag's eyes went wide. He felt his heart stop, every muscle in his body stilling. "You're sure?" Suddenly his pulse hammered a wave of heat through his body, as if he'd stepped into a blazing hearth.

"He and I had a lengthy conversation about it last night. I'm sure." She turned away from Montag and headed to her own bag, withdrawing a brush that she attempted to tame her hair with. She suddenly stopped and pointed the brush at him. "You'd kill the man who protected me, but you say nothing of what you'll do to Lezay. You realize how duplicitous that is, right?"

Montag stiffened his spine, now glaring at Igraine. She turned away from him. "You should stay here today during the tournament. Rest."

"Fine," she mumbled, viciously running the brush through her hair. "I'm in no mood to be a trophy today."

Montag opened the flap of the tent, hesitating. "I'll deal with Lezay, Igraine. You have my word."

The sound of the brush ripping through her hair was the only sound in the tent. Montag exited, letting the flap fall behind him, slapping his armor into place and tightening buckles. His eyes zeroed in on the black-and-red-clad knight across the field. He covered the distance in no time, his long stride stretching with purpose, anger building every step of the way. When he was only feet away from the man, Lezay turned to face him, a smile lighting his ugly face.

"Morning, Montag. How was the wedding night?" Lezay smirked.

Montag swung his fist into the other man's jaw with enough force to compress meat to bone. Lezay staggered sideways, scrambling for his feet. He turned back to Montag, a hand on his jaw. He spit blood on the ground.

"What was that for?" Lezay shouted.

Montag kept his fists clenched at his sides. "How about you tell me, Lezay?"

Lezay looked bewildered, then his eyes narrowed. He spit blood again, letting his hand fall from jaw to hilt of sword. "She told you, eh?"

Montag's fury rose as the truth was confirmed.

"It was an accident, Montag. I tried to kiss her, and she tripped."

Montag glared, comparing stories in his head.

"It was innocent. She said she was fine."

He stepped up to Lezay, his face inches away. The man's rotten smell filled Montag's nostrils, but he didn't flinch. "You come near her again, Lezay, and I will castrate you myself. Do you understand? No kisses. No games. Don't talk to her. Don't even look at her. If I hear otherwise, I will feed your balls to my hogs the second we return to Alsace. Is that clear?"

Lezay glared back, his eyes only just below Montag's imposing stature.

Montag grabbed the front of Lezay's tunic, shaking him. "I asked you a question," he growled.

"She's all yours, Montag." Montag released him, and Lezay straightened his tunic. "I won't even tell your wife," Lezay mumbled.

Lezay didn't see Montag's second punch coming either, and this one was a well-placed shot to the man's gut. He doubled over, gagging and gasping for air.

Montag spun on his heel and pushed through the gathered spectators before he beat Lezay to a pulp. He rolled his shoulders, bloodlust thrilling his veins. The tournament couldn't begin soon enough.

Chapter 10

May 1199

A lec pulled Eleanor through the back door of a tavern, glancing up and down the street behind them, which thankfully was empty. He pulled the door shut and latched it. Eleanor studied him, one eye slightly squinted with suspicion.

"You still haven't explained why we're running from an old man — my grandfather no less."

Alec leaned against the door at his back. His pulse hammered in his veins as if he was in the center of the arena, a tournament fight swirling around him. Their run through the streets of Poitiers had elicited the same rush. They should be safe now. No one would expect them to come here. Unfortunately, that included Eleanor once she figured out where they were.

"He is not a good man." Alec managed to exhale, closing his eyes for a second. When he opened them, Eleanor had her arms folded across her chest. She wasn't even slightly out of breath. Was he that out of shape from his months of recovery last year? Impossible. He'd been training hard since his injuries at Brunstein the year before. Was it possible that proximity to the fabled Le Brun could elicit such a physical manifestation of fear?

Alec pushed away from the wall and discreetly shook out his hands. It was only stress. And that, he needed to deal with. Le Brun was only human after all. A human that seemed to never die perhaps, but human he was. He was not going to let the superstitious folk tales surrounding the old man add to the already grim truth.

"Start talking, Alec," Eleanor grumbled.

"You know your mother was a beauty — the Lady of the Tournament. You said as much when we first met."

"Yes." Her eyes narrowed with curiosity.

"You know that Montag was once married, with your cousin Raoul as the result."

"Yes. And I knew I was named after Alenor. My mother told me all the time."

"And I think you know your parents loved each other, but did you know that love came at a price?"

Eleanor's eyes narrowed further, her lips turning into a frown.

Alec took a deep breath. "Do you know what happened to your father in Jerusalem? Or your grandfather's name? His reputation?"

She shook her head. "How do you know?"

Alec pursed his lips together, the muscle in his jaw twitching with strain. He had to tell her now, so she wouldn't overreact. Before one of the women walked into this little back room. "Eleanor, I have been searching for information on your family since well before I met you. At first I was looking for information about Lezay, to avenge my father. But I learned there was a depth to Montag that I could not understand. Curiosity got the better of me. After what happened at Brunstein last year, I enlisted the help of a few old allies — they are from far back in my past—" He felt heat rise into his cheeks and swallowed it down. "But they are trustworthy, and one, in particular, could coax out the information I could not, from sources I cannot name—"

"Alec, are we in a brothel?"

He inhaled sharply and nodded. He braced himself for his wife's reaction. *Let her scream, let her fight, just don't let her leave.*

Eleanor looked around the room with greater interest, her expression oddly calm. "And have you been using this establishment for services other than discerning secrets?"

"No!"

"So what did your sources find out about my family?"

Alec breathed a sigh of relief and took Eleanor's hand. "A lot. Come with me. There is someone I want you to meet. And it will be safer to talk . . .there."

Eleanor's fingers laced in his as he guided her through the empty common area and up the staircase. He had trusted that the establishment would be quiet during the middle of the day, and he had been right. Eleanor took in the rooms with an observant gaze, a gaze he had been helping his already talented wife to refine. Was she counting every window and door as he'd taught her? Was she looking for boots under the tapestries, judging the inhabitants on what paraphernalia they left lying about?

At a thin door at the end of the hall, he knocked.

Chapter 11

Christmas 1172

Chateau Brunstein, Alsace

Alenor's shrill scream echoed down the corridor, making the blood in Igraine's veins run cold. The two of them were at it again. There was a crash, then the slam of a door. Igraine pressed back against the wall, eyes lowered, as her brother stalked by. He paid her no mind, and when he was out of sight she burst into action, running to the room the noise had come from, Montag's bedroom.

Alenor was in a heap on the floor by the bed, sides heaving as she sobbed, her arms wrapped around her stomach. Her crimson skirts pooled around her like blood, her beautiful hair, done in a braided wreath for the Christmas celebration, was haphazardly falling from its plaits, the ivy once woven in the strands now giving her the appearance of one that had been dragged through the forest instead of the elven queen she had appeared as hours before. When she saw Igraine, she held up her hand, pushing away from her friend.

"No, go away! Don't you dare say you warned me! I don't want to hear it! Just leave me alone."

Igraine froze. "I wasn't going to say any such thing, Alenor. I just want to know if you are alright." She kept her tone as gentle as possible.

"Of course I'm not alright! That monster is an uncompromising brute!"

"What was it about this time?"

"Ugh!" Alenor groaned, her head in her hands. "I don't even know. I didn't do something right. And then I got mad, and I threw something at him, and he didn't like that." Her eyes had a wild look that made her look like a cornered animal.

"Did he hurt you?" Igraine's eyes locked on Alenor's large belly. She was too far along in her pregnancy for this kind of strain.

"Just slapped me around a little. I'm fine." Her voice quieted. "I really am fine. He could have done worse. I'm in no position to fight him like I used to."

Igraine bit her tongue, knowing too well how turbulent her brother's first few months of marriage had been. Alenor had not taken to the rules of living with Montag as easily as the rest of the household had. She'd fought back, quietly at first, with silent rebellious actions. When that hadn't been enough, they'd gone to full-out brawls, from which both of them were known to sport a few bruises. At one point, they'd seemed to meet a stalemate, and for the first time in Igraine's life, she wondered if her brother had met his match. He was almost . . . happy? Docile for sure, at least when Alenor was around. And the entire manor had breathed a sigh of relief with them. Now that Alenor couldn't match his fury due to her physical limitations, it was escalating again.

"Should we write to your family? Let you stay with your mother until the child comes?"

"Oh, heavens no, Igraine. I can handle him. He'll come around yet tonight, you'll see." She took a deep breath, pushing herself up from the floor, one arm around her belly. She gingerly touched her face, where a red handprint was visible, and pushed her mess of hair from her eyes. She sighed. "At least we got through Christmas. It was a good day, wasn't it?"

Igraine smiled. "It was the best Christmas this castle has ever seen, that's for sure."

"Heathens. I can't believe you haven't celebrated in years. Especially with your father being a crusader for Christ!"

Igraine again bit her tongue, knowing that her father's crusades had nothing to do with Christ. "Let's get you cleaned up. You have to be exhausted."

When Alenor's hair was braided simply down her back and her bruises cooled with snow, Igraine tucked her into bed.

"You think I'm crazy for fighting him, don't you?" Alenor asked quietly.

"It's not the easiest way to manage him."

"But it's working, Igraine. I may have to scream it at him, but he *hears* me. He doesn't have the power over me that he has over you."

Igraine stilled, her heart skipping an uncomfortable beat. She'd known her brother controlled many aspects of her life, but never had she thought her obedience or silence was part of that. It was more . . . survival. And as such, she'd yielded her own power. Hadn't she? "Alenor, you play a dangerous game. You really think you have control of him?"

"I am his *equal!*" Her eyes shown bright with excitement, even passion.

Igraine stared at the woman in the bed in front of her, the woman who was trying to rival a knight. Perhaps it was better to say nothing at all. "Goodnight, sweet sister." She gave the covers a final tuck and turned away before Alenor could see the concern she knew was etched into her brow.

"Igraine, wait." Alenor caught her hand, pulling her back to the bed. "Did *he* send anything?" She smiled conspiratorially. "For Christmas?"

Igraine shook her head. "Not a word. How could he, with this snow?"

"He will, I think. Just wait. He is still traveling, gaining in reputation. I hear he's a popular mercenary. Montag hates it. Just wait." She gave Igraine's hand a squeeze.

Igraine couldn't help but look past her sister-in-law out the window, where flurries still drifted lazily in the wind. Somewhere out there Sir Enric de Levan was trying to win enough prestige and wealth to buy her brother's blessing. So far, the only thing he'd actually succeeded in buying was time. Indeed, months had passed, and still she was without a formal betrothal. Montag claimed he was too busy to worry about betrothals, but he was stalling once again.

Igraine did not mind.

She bid Alenor a final good night and let herself out of the room. Montag passed her in the hallway, and she couldn't help but glare at him. At first, he let her pass, but she heard him hesitate behind her and follow her. She grimaced.

"Igraine . . ."

"Yes, brother?" She smiled sweetly as she turned, knowing that her eyes still flashed with anger.

He hesitated. "How is she?"

Igraine pursed her lips, considering her words carefully. "I think you should go talk to her . . . civilly."

Montag looked at his feet. After a long moment, he sighed. "Seems strange, celebrating Christmas."

"I know."

"Brought up a lot of memories."

Igraine's eyebrows shot up.

"Before you were born, Mother would host Christmas, and hire musicians, and we would dance. You looked a lot like her today."

Igraine stared in shock. It was the first he had ever spoken of their mother.

"I think Alenor will be a good mother."

"I do, too," Igraine whispered.

"Merry Christmas, Igraine," Montag said quietly and turned on his heel down the hall, back to his wife. Igraine was left reeling, watching after him, a hand pressed to her lips as tears brimmed at her eyes. Something was changing in the warrior, and she wasn't sure if she was grateful or terrified.

Chapter 12

"What do you mean you forgot to send for more linen? That is your *responsibility*, woman. Are we to walk around naked? Sleep on bare straw? When you have time in winter to sew, you better sew. And to sew you need fabric." Montag slammed a fist on the table, which made his little wife flinch. He took great comfort in that. Perhaps she would be tamable after all.

The next words out of her mouth erased that hope. "If you knew we needed them, why didn't you order them yourself?" Alenor put her hands on her hips, her belly huge before her, like a giant melon ready to drop.

"How would it look if I, a knight, was to walk into the village and order *linens*? As if I had the time! I'm running an entire estate, not just a castle."

"Not just a castle. Is that what you think? Do you know what goes on here day in and day out? The sheer volume of mouths we have to feed alone — you should be grateful your household isn't starving. They would be if they were left to you!"

Montag glowered at her. He dropped his voice to a dark rumble. "Igraine never complained. I never had to remind her. Are you saying you can't handle what she can?"

Alenor straightened as if slapped. "So that's how it is? You can't help but compare me to your perfect sister. You wish to turn us against each other." She took a step toward Montag. "It won't work. You are what *unites* us." She met him eye to eye, her brazen energy quieting him to stunned silence in a way only she could. Then she was gone, spinning on her heel and striding out of the room faster than her condition should allow. She hesitated at the door, shooting an indignant look over her shoulder. "For what it's worth, Igraine is not the one sick with pregnancy, carrying *your* heir."

She slammed the door behind her.

Montag immediately heard voices in the corridor beyond and sank into his chair, readying for the next onslaught. Sure enough, the door flew open without so much as a knock. Igraine stood there, her face impassive, hands folded in front of her like a cherub readying to pray. He knew that look. She was boiling inside. The fury at Alenor's mistake still roiling, he debated how to test her control. It would be fun to watch her burst.

"Brother." She nodded stiffly. "The linens were my fault. Alenor asked me to take care of it, and I forgot."

Montag snorted. "We both know that's not true. Do you think you're being a good friend, protecting her?"

Igraine glided over and sat in the chair across from him, straight-backed as a princess. She'd make a good princess. If only he could find her the right prince.

"This is her first time managing a castle of this size — any size. You need to be patient with her."

"I've been patient. How hard can it be?"

Igraine gritted her teeth.

Montag leaned toward her. "You aren't the one defending this castle, collecting our tolls on the pilgrim road, or paying our taxes to a king who doesn't bother with us. You aren't playing politics with local lords. You aren't sending out spies to keep an eye on Le Brun."

Igraine remained stoic. "No, I'm not. But your wife is trying her best."

Montag slouched back in frustration. "You never struggled."

Igraine laughed, a merry sound that seemed out of place in the dark room. "Oh, I did. I still do. I just hide it well. If you're honest with yourself, you struggle, too."

That barb dug in. Montag stood. "Out."

Igraine didn't move. "I actually came up here with a request." She held out a fold of parchment. "I'd like to send this to Enric. Feel free to read it. It's innocent enough." She shifted uncomfortably.

Montag took the paper and read the short note, which only inquired on Enric's health. "Why do you care how he's feeling?"

She clenched her hands. "I haven't heard from him all winter. I thought there would be some message by now. He said he was going to contact you."

Montag clenched his jaw.

"I thought perhaps he had, since you haven't said anything about my marriage to Lezay lately . . ."

"I'm considering all options. The Count of Bologne still lives."

"So you're considering Enric?" Her eyes lit with hope.

"No." He felt a bitter satisfaction as the hope faded.

"And has he written? Have you told him you won't consider it? Any news at all if he's alive?"

Montag avoided her eye. "No."

"To which question?"

"Go, Igraine. You have work to do."

"Montag — just tell me."

"Your lover's probably dead by now. That's what happens to mercenaries. Go."

She straightened as if she'd grown another vertebra. He wasn't sure how that was possible. Before he could muse on it, she called his bluff. "He has written, and you've been taking the notes. Haven't you?" Before he could react, she'd leaped to her feet and grabbed a stack of documents from his desk. Thumbing through them as she paced around the room, she managed to find Enric's latest plea. Her eyes grew wide. "This is to *me*."

Montag moved to snatch the parchment, but she was quick, sidestepping away to the hearth. He followed, snatching it from her hand and throwing it into the fire. As they watched it burn, he knew it was too late. She'd read the words her pathetic, sappy lover had written. The ashes fell, the flames dimmed, and she turned to him, a spark of fury in eyes that went almost as black as he'd been told his own could. As he knew their father's could.

"You lied to me." The words ground through her throat like a blade on a whetstone. He watched her twitch with rage, her fingers stretching and clenching like he'd seen warriors do, to relieve tension before a fight.

He grumbled, "I told you—"

Her slap rang across his cheek with such force it left him stunned. He widened his eyes, not sure if he wanted to laugh or throw her across the room. He expected her to cower at her mistake, but her gaze was as furious as ever, her posture erect.

"It is one thing to tell me you are considering others. That you haven't given him an answer. It is another to lie and tell me you have had no word. To leave me thinking that he's dead in the moat of some castle. How dare you? How many messengers have there been?"

Montag, still caught off guard, didn't reply. Igraine stormed to his desk and tore the sheeves of documents apart, scattering them across the room like leaves. A madwoman's brusqueness intrigued him, so he did not interfere. Montag took comfort that there were no more notes from Enric. The rest had been resigned to the fire. But something had caught her eye, and she was reading intently. Too intently.

He walked up to her and plucked the parchment from her hand. It was an invitation to join The Order, signed with their father's name, the seal stamped with the stag of the Le Brun crest. A rock settled in his gut.

"You've been corresponding with him?"

"It's one-sided."

"He wants you to join that . . . that evil group. That doesn't sound one-sided."

"I didn't respond."

"Perhaps you lie. Why is he contacting you?"

Montag threw the invitation down, adding it to the mess of the room. "You need to clean this all up."

"I won't."

"You will."

Igraine took a final handful of parchments and threw them at his face. That shocked his amusement into action, and he grabbed her wrist. With surprising adeptness, she twisted it away from him as if he'd clutched air. He wondered when she'd learned that maneuver.

The Le Brun fire sparked in her eyes, and he was so surprised he couldn't move. So this was Igraine when the mask fell away. She was shaking in rage, fists clenched. "How dare you! How dare you keep all this from me! I will contact Enric somehow. And from now on *your* letters will come through me, including the ones from Father!" Her voice grew hoarse, such was the volume of her shouts. "You want a woman to manage the household? Then you have one. And between Alenor and I *both*, you will hope for escape to a *real* battlefield, not one of your petty games."

Then, like a candle being snuffed out, she quieted. She backed away, her voice now a raspy whisper. "One day you will manage this fortress without me. You will realize what I have done for you, and how your success is not just your own, but mine as well. I *will* marry, brother, and I will leave. You will be here forever. Perhaps with your wife. Though if you continue to push her away, you will be *alone*."

She turned to the door.

"Marry Lezay, if you're so eager to go." He almost regretted this last sarcasm, so far from his true thoughts the words fell. But he would not let her win. He would rile her once more.

She hesitated. "If you wanted me to marry Lezay, I'd already be fat with his heir. I don't know what game you're playing. But I'm done." She disappeared, leaving Montag standing in a mess of a study.

He looked around, surveying the damage, and realized he would be responsible to clean it up. There wasn't a soul in the castle he trusted with the information contained in these papers, save Igraine. Le Brun had a spy, and that spy could well be a commoner pretending illiteracy. He stalked to the hearth and rested his hands on the mantle, staring into the flames. Enric was persistent, a quality he usually admired. But so was Lezay. Enric was still poor, though he promised Igraine the world. He was a fool. No man could rise that far, not if he wished to keep his conscience intact. And Enric was the honorable kind.

No, they were not to be. And if Igraine was so adamant to unite with Alenor to make Brunstein unbearable, then it was time. This year, she would wed. He had to make a decision at last.

He rubbed his forehead and sighed. On sudden impulse, he let out a shout that vibrated through his chest. The birds on the top of the tower roof scattered, their wings whistling through the air. He could almost hear their whisper, "There's a madman in the tower but he's weak, weak, weak."

Chapter 13

February 24, 1173

Chateau Brunstein, Alsace

"Igraine!" Alenor bellowed. "Igraine!"

Igraine tore down the stairs. "What? Are you alright? Is it time?" Her nerves had been on edge for days, as Alenor became increasingly uncomfortable as her delivery drew near.

Alenor waddled down the castle hall. Her belly hung heavy on her tiny frame. She waved Igraine's fear off impatiently, a big smile stretched across her face. "No different than it's been. Madame Brigitte says the cramping could go on for days like this. I hope she's wrong. But you have a message!" She waved the sealed parchment in front of Igraine's face, giggling.

Igraine snatched at it, her lips pursed in amusement. Her eyes widened as she took in the crest. "How did you—"

"His squire dropped it off just now. Told me to make sure it got to you straight away. Which means your man might not be far . . ." Alenor sang the last few notes of her words, then burst into giggles once again. "Well, open it, open it!" Despite her friend's enthusiasm, Igraine did not miss how she rubbed her back in discomfort.

Igraine cut the seal with her fingernail and read hastily. Alenor tried to read over her shoulder.

"Well, what does it say?"

Igraine's voice was a whisper. "He says he misses me and thinks of me often." She skipped a few lines of more personal sentiment, blushing as a smile lit her cheeks. She gasped. "You're right. He's here." she said breathlessly. "He wants to meet me in the old abbey. That's a long ride away."

"But you can go fast, Igraine. Go! My goodness, it's been a long winter. There's a break in the weather. Go before we start touring for the tournament season again in a few months. Who knows when you'll get to see him again."

"You're about to have a baby, Alenor. I can't leave you. Not for that long."

"I have a whole castle full of servants at my call, including your fantastic friend Madame Brigitte. Don't worry about me. Now get out of this castle before your brother gets back from Leuwenstein. I'll make some kind of excuse for you." Alenor herded her toward the door. "Here's your cloak, its freezing out there today. Be careful of the mud, especially by the river. And Igraine . . ."

"Yes?" Igraine froze, breathless and flushed at the madness she was about to undertake, a madness she never would have dared had Alenor not entered the dynamic of life at Brunstein.

"Remember what I told you last year, Igraine. You deserve happiness. Even for a little while." She laid a hand on Igraine's cheek and smiled, albeit a little sadly.

Igraine pulled her into a hug. "I'll be back soon. Tell that baby to wait just one more day."

Alenor laughed, her arm around her middle. "Ha! He will. Now go!"

Igraine pushed out the heavy door, meeting the grooms in the stable. They had her horse ready in record time without question. As Igraine cantered down the road toward the old abbey, some ten miles away, the words of Enric's letter played in her mind.

My Fair Igraine,

Time has not been generous enough to us, and yet these feelings I hold for you feel as ancient as the stones beneath our feet, as natural as the stars that light your eyes. I have not known the passion that now burns within me every waking day. It has been most useful in the tournaments, and the most terrible distraction in common life.

I love you, Igraine. I love you with a love better than the troubadours sing of. It is a lasting love, like that I have seen in my parents, who now are wed some thirty years. I have told them about you, and my mother warns me that what I feel for you is once in a lifetime. I intend to do what I must that we can be together . . . the right way.

Meet me at the old Abbey down by the river, at high noon if you get this letter in time. And if we cannot meet now, I will be back to Brunstein to meet your brother as soon as a few things are finalized.

With my heart,

Enric

Igraine made it in record time, tying her horse next to the black stallion that stood in the overgrown courtyard.

Breathless from running, she stood in the doorway of the abandoned chapel, waiting as her eyes adjusted to the dim light within. Enric leaned on the wall opposite her, staring at her with wide eyes. Even now, a disheveled mess from the fast ride, he seemed in awe of her, his lips silent as his eyes roamed.

In two steps he cleared the distance to her, pressing her back against the wall and putting an arm on either side of her head. Their hearts pounded. She looked into his eyes, pleading. He leaned down and pressed his lips into hers, claiming them as his own. She reached up to grasp his face in both of her small hands, pulling him into her, offering herself, willing to become part of him. Enric picked up her hips and pressed her into the wall, pinning her there with his own. His hands now roamed the rest of her body, finding places to hold her tighter to him.

She gasped.

Enric's lips traveled down her neck. Every nerve came alive, her heart syncing with his. This new urgency reminded her of an animal finally let out of the cage he had been staring out of for months. It was as if she was all he had had to stare at. A primal sound rumbled from somewhere deep inside him as she grasped his haunches in both her hands. She could feel him pressed against her abdomen, and she wasn't intimidated. As long as he was the animal, she was not scared.

She pulled him tighter.

Unfortunately, her urgency had the wrong effect. Enric pulled away from her a bit, letting her feet slide back to the earth, struggling to grasp his breath. She pecked kisses on his cheek, his lips, trying to draw him back into her. He shook his head.

"Give me a moment, woman, or you'll destroy what control I have left."

"Let it go," she whispered, trying to pull him back.

"I told you, I want it properly." He took half a step away from her.

Suddenly embarrassed, she straightened her clothes. "I'm sorry."

"Don't apologize." He caressed her cheek, guiding her to meet his eyes. "You have to understand, you're different.

I don't want anyone to contest what we have. I want you to be protected by what I can offer you before we sever the ties with your family, which you know has to happen, Igraine. I don't like it, but it will have to happen if you choose me."

"Montag will yield."

Enric shook his head. "He won't. I've been asking him all winter. Did he tell you?"

"I found out." She inhaled. "For once I was the Le Brun that lost her temper."

Enric chewed a lip, looking like he was debating scolding her and then thinking better of it. "I'm going to ask him in person — again. My situation is changing. Maybe now he'll see. That is, if you still choose me?"

"I choose you," she whispered, caressing his cheek.

"Then wait with me. For me." Enric kissed her gently on her forehead, then her nose, then ever so gently on her lips. "It will be soon."

"Really? Can you promise me that? You are a knight, Enric. You know how everything can change in an instant."

"My love for you will not change, Igraine. I promise you. I will not rest, and I will wait, until you are mine."

She pressed her lips onto his, rejoicing as he returned the kiss with a breathless passion instead of pushing her away. When her lips were raw, her lungs breathless, she rested her head against his chest. His strong arms held her tight with a possessiveness no other man had ever held her with.

"I'm almost ready, Igraine. I've made a name for myself. I have land in Aquitaine now. I have connections your brother wants. We will make it work."

Igraine pulled him closer and kissed him gently, less urgently, as if they had all day.

She sighed as he pulled away, his arms still tight around her. "What land?"

Enric smiled. "A small manor, south of Poitiers."

"A gift from the duke of Aquitaine?"

"Yes." His excitement emanated from him, and she felt it as her own.

"Congratulations."

He bit his lip. "If you ever need to escape, or perhaps are traveling by Poitiers, it's a straight shot south on the Duke's Highway, until the road ends."

She laughed. "I'll remember that . . . if I ever need to escape."

Their passion now back under control, Enric took her hand and led her back into the crisp air outside the abbey. He guided her on the overgrown path to the river, which sparkled in the sunlight as if it flowed with diamonds.

"Where are you parents, Enric?" He spoke of them often, yet they still had never met.

Enric squeezed her hand. "They remain in Aquitaine. They run a small farm about a day's ride south of my manor, near Angoulême." He hesitated. "I come from noble blood, but I am the first in my family for several generations to be titled."

"So your father is a farmer?"

"Horse breeder actually. Somewhat retired. He only produces a few a year now that I've been away so much. We used to breed, train, and sell dozens in a year. That's how we ended up in Jerusalem, selling horses for the Lord of Angoulême, Louis and Josse's father."

Igraine blinked. "I never knew that, Enric. There is so much more that I don't know, isn't there?"

Enric frowned slightly, the peace in his gaze faltering. "I will tell you all you want to know, but we need more time than these brief moments today. I'm sure you have people waiting for you at Brunstein." He hesitated. "How is your friend Lady Alenor? Did she have her child yet?"

"Any day now. She's handling it quite well." Igraine chuckled to herself. "I think my brother met his match with her. She took a while to understand how things are done, but I have no doubt she'll manage that castle with an iron fist when I'm gone."

Enric squeezed her hand, a mischievous look crossing his face. "And hopefully you are able to remove yourself from that place soon." He stopped walking and pulled her gently to face him. He caressed her cheek. "I really do love you, Igraine." His lips lifted into a smile, his features lighting with such joy that she had no doubt he spoke the truth.

She kissed him, breathed him, pressed herself as close as clothing allowed. "Just don't give up, Enric."

Chapter 14

Igraine's horse walked with an exhausted amble back into the courtyard of Brunstein, nearly an hour after the sun had sunk below the hills. The stars and moon had lit their path. Igraine was still flushed with a glow that bubbled from every fiber of her being. Despite the chill of the evening, she was warm.

"Oh, thank God." Madame Brigitte had thrown open the kitchen door as soon as Igraine dismounted. "Get in here, my lady. Quickly!"

Igraine's pulse picked up, though her feet were slow to her task. "What is it?"

"Lady Alenor has had the child!"

The warm fog that lingered over Igraine suddenly lifted, and she was acutely aware of every sense again. The cold, the scream of a baby from within the castle, and the pulse of pure fear from Madame Brigitte. She frowned in confusion. "How did it come so quickly?" She stepped inside the castle, hanging her cloak as her ears pricked to the intense squalls. "He — she? — sounds healthy."

"He's fine. It's Lady Alenor! She — I did all I can. I told your brother—"

"Montag is home?"

Madame Brigitte avoided her gaze. "Aye, he's home. Arrived not long after you left." She took a deep breath, hurrying with her short steps down the hall, the screams of the child growing louder. "They fought, as usual. Then Alenor went into labor, only it was wrong. All wrong. I gave them a choice, I did. I gave *her* a choice!"

"Madame Brigitte, what are you talking about?" Igraine grabbed the older woman's arm, her eyes wide. She pulled them to a stop, watching Brigitte's eyes well up with tears.

"I tried, I tried! I didn't see another option. She was straining and bleeding, and the baby was suffocating — he was stuck. My hands — my hands were too big to fix it inside her . . . she's so small." She looked at her open hands, still seamed with blood, like they had betrayed her. "I — I didn't know what else to do." She started sobbing uncontrollably, mumbling unintelligible words.

Igraine took off running, bursting into Alenor's room, which was a chaotic mess of bloody sheets, rags, water buckets, and servants desperately trying to tidy it up. Montag stood in the corner, holding his squalling child awkwardly in his arms, the most fearfully blank expression on him Igraine had ever seen. He merely stared at her as she entered the room, doing nothing to quiet the child who bawled at the top of his lungs. Igraine stepped to the bed, where Alenor lay white as a sheet against the mattress. Her shift was red between her legs and at her stomach, where her hands pressed with a desperate strength. Sweat drenched her, and though she was conscious, she did not acknowledge Igraine as she came closer.

"Alenor?" Igraine whispered. There was no response except a blink, and Igraine slowly pried the woman's hands from her shift to examine the damage beneath. As she lifted the hem of the gown to Alenor's middle, she grew wide-eyed for a moment and stared. Abruptly she dropped the shift, turned away, and vomited. Wiping her mouth with the back of her hand, she turned to her brother.

"Madame Brigitte gave you a choice — a choice — and this is what you chose?" Montag only stared at her with that blank look. Every servant left in the room had stilled, watching Igraine. "You bastard . . ." she hissed, emotion writhing from deep within. Still he stared blankly at her. She pointed to a maid. "You, take that baby and clean him and get him quiet. And find a wet nurse. God knows Alenor won't be nursing this child. You . . . get Madame Brigitte in here with a needle and the strongest thread she can find. Hot water! Get me fresh hot water! Everyone else out! Out!" She stepped up to her brother as he lingered. Her voice was iced with disgust. "You need to get out of this room right now, Elfric le Brun, or I will butcher you like you just butchered your wife."

Montag blinked at her, rage building behind his eyes then fading. He obediently left.

Igraine turned back to the mother on the bed, again exposing the wound across her womb and gritting her teeth at the ugliness of it. They had to work fast if she was to have a chance. She cleaned and with Madame Brigitte's help, they sewed Alenor back together. The woman was pale as a ghost and almost as still as one, only murmuring slightly as they worked. As they finished late at night, Igraine sagged against the bed, exhausted, and broke into tears. Madame Brigitte cried with her, and then they fell to their bloodied knees to pray until there was no strength left to beg God for more.

Igraine practically stumbled down the stairs the next day, overcome by exhaustion. She crumbled onto a bench at the kitchen table, far past caring if her brother already sat at the table. Before she could will her hands to pour herself an ale, one appeared in front of her. She looked up in surprise at Montag.

"She looks better today, thanks to you." He didn't smile, but his expression was for once, gentle.

"Is she talking yet?" Igraine straightened, sipping the ale.

"A bit. She knows what happened. Wants to see Raoul."

"Raoul?"

Montag nodded. "At least that was something we agreed on. Months ago." He looked away.

Igraine nodded slightly. "He's healthy?"

"Perfectly."

A million angry questions ran through Igraine's head, but she stayed silent. If Montag was for once stoic, perhaps he would stay that way. She needed him agreeable if Alenor was going to survive. It was going to be a lot of work to nurse her back to health, provided the fever didn't take her this first week.

Igraine sighed, looking around for food. "I'm starving." She suddenly realized that due to her escapade, she hadn't eaten since breakfast the day before.

"Madame Brigitte has some fresh broth by the fire. She took some for Alenor."

"She was hysterical last night. She thought she killed her." Igraine helped herself to the rich, brothy soup. It was lukewarm.

"I know."

Igraine pursed her lips. Of course he knew. That didn't mean he cared.

"Where were you yesterday? You were gone all day." The Old Montag had reawakened, and he glowered at Igraine.

"I went for a ride."

"A ride?"

"Yes."

"To where?"

Igraine glared at him. "Excuse me, I'm going to go back to nursing the wife you just about killed yesterday." She took her food and ale and left him fuming at the table.

Madame Brigitte was already seated at Alenor's bedside, trying to spoon her the broth. She glanced at Igraine. "The fever started."

Igraine felt Alenor's forehead and sighed. "The broth is a good idea. She needs her strength."

"She isn't eating much of it though."

"In time. The fever will ease and her humors will balance. In time."

As the days of bedside care for Alenor stretched into a week, Igraine and Brigitte were exhausted. They slept in her room, nursing her constantly. Little Raoul stayed with them most of the time when he wasn't with his wet nurse or squalling. Alenor asked for him whenever she was conscious, which thankfully was becoming more and more often. Alenor's improving awareness promised life, but her nurses did not relent in their care. The wound was still too grievous.

Igraine woke to a hand on her head. She'd fallen asleep at Alenor's side.

"Igraine, you need to take care of yourself," Alenor mused. She smiled faintly. "Go sleep in your own bed and rest."

"I'm alright."

"No, you aren't. Madame Brigitte went to bed. You need to rest. I think I'll be alright now for a bit."

"You sure? You do sound better."

"I am sure. Go."

Igraine rose on her stiff legs and stretched sleepily. "Fine then."

"Igraine?"

"Hmm?" she asked from the door.

"Can you ask Montag to visit me?"

Igraine blinked at her a few times but then nodded, ducking out.

Chapter 15

Montag sat down on the bed, finally alone with Alenor after days of waiting for the incessant fussing of his sister and the rest of the household to subside. They told him Alenor was doing better, but he could see for himself she was not. Just by touching her hand, he felt the fever lingering in her. She stirred.

As she opened her eyes and focused on him, she flinched. That hurt him. The woman had been raised too soft. She was weak. Thus the reason she had failed to bear their child properly. Gently he lifted her fingertips to his lips and kissed them. He held her gaze as she watched him, flickers of fear in her eyes.

He ignored it, his eyes rotating to the wound he knew stretched across her abdomen. Gently he pulled down the sheet, then worked up the hem of Alenor's shift to expose her stomach. She trembled at his touch and flinched when he ran a finger along the crusty, red wound held closed with stitching worthy of a fine garment. He could smell the infection on her. He covered her again, tucking the blanket's edges around her sides. She exhaled a sigh of relief.

"You won't bear any more children?" he asked. The midwife had already given him this answer, but he needed to hear it from Alenor herself.

She shook her head, tears leaking from the corners of her eyes.

He nodded, chewing his lip. "Are you in much pain?"

Alenor hesitated before carefully nodding. Montag already knew this, too. Surely, the wounds themselves must be excruciating, let alone the infection.

He'd seen battle wounds before. They could linger for weeks, months, festering before healing. But more often the bearer died anyway. He would spare Alenor that pain. Now that she could no longer bear a child, he would need to remarry. Montag studied his wife, who closed her eyes as exhaustion rolled through her.

He would have to have more heirs. And Alenor couldn't provide. She was suffering. Why prolong her death?

He bent to kiss her pale forehead, clammy with her sweat.

"Thank you for our son," he said quietly. At least he could give her that.

Alenor's eyes fluttered open again, etched in pain and fighting the delirium of the fever.

"You won't fight me, will you?" he cooed, brushing the damp hair from her forehead.

Alenor only blinked at him in confusion.

In that confusion he saw her beauty. He saw her trust in the promise that he would not hurt her; he saw her love. His hands had itched to take the pillow from her head, but now he was distracted with a confusion of his own. His father would call him weak. A fool.

In that moment her fingers traced his jaw, so gently. He flinched. "I love you, Montag," she whispered. "We had no choice. You know that. It was for our son. He's such a beautiful boy. Strong, like his father. I think he looks like you." She was right. The boy's dark brown hair held no semblance to the Tielo family's fair locks.

He couldn't do it. He could not kill her.

He let out a shuddering breath and rested his head on her shoulder, touching her as gently as he could. "I am sorry, Alenor. You would have been a good wife."

"Would have been?" Her eyebrows rose but her lips smiled. She was so innocent. So ignorant.

"No one can know you survived. Not even Igraine. Or Madame Brigitte. Swear to me that you will not tell a soul who you are."

"What madness are you talking about?" She shifted herself in the bed, her eyes narrowing as she focused on him. Despite her weakness, her nerves were stirring. She now sensed the danger.

"I need heirs, Alenor. You are done. I will need to remarry. I will let you go quietly to a nunnery if you . . ."

"A nunnery?"

Montag clamped a hand over her mouth and her eyes flashed in fury. He may as well spit it out. Let her know the gravity of the situation. "The alternative is death." Her eyes suddenly went round. Ah, so she did believe him this time. Maybe now she would realize what he was capable of, as he'd been warning her for months. He released her mouth.

"A nunnery?" she breathed again.

"I will ensure you are taken care of until the end of your days. You have to pick a new name for yourself. I'll have you sent on your way tonight."

"I'm in no condition to travel. A *nunnery*? Montag, I am your wife. I love you. And Raoul . . . how could you take my son away from me? He needs a mother!" As her anxiety peaked, Montag watched her body weaken. She was trembling now, the color draining from her face. Perhaps he would end up killing her after all.

He sighed. "Tonight. You go tonight."

Tears spilled from Alenor's eyes as she stared at him. He didn't expect to be affected, but he couldn't help it. He felt sorry for her. And that in turn made him angry. Anger he could manage, so he let it bubble to the surface. As Alenor recognized it, her tears fell faster, and she turned away from him, curling into herself. He thought she would fight as she always did, but she was too weak. Weak.

He rose and left the room, not even bothering to say goodbye to the mother of his child, his wife. He would have to mourn her, and perhaps he wouldn't even have to pretend. He stomped his foot at one of the dogs as it trotted past, leaving it to shy away with its tail between its legs. Weak, weak. There could be none that were weak.

Igraine's blood pounded in her ears as she took the steps two at a time. She burst into the room and froze, staring at the freshly made bed. Empty. It couldn't be true. Alenor had been improving. She'd said it herself.

The creak of the door behind her made her turn, and she stared imploringly at her brother's impassive face. "Oh Montag. I am so sorry for your loss." Tears brimmed and streamed down Igraine's face. She covered her lips with her trembling fingertips. "Where is she?"

"Buried her." He shrugged.

"What? I only slept the night. Why didn't you wake me? Or Brigitte? We need to have a funeral, Montag!"

"I don't want that reek of death in my house."

Igraine stared at him wide-eyed. "Have you no emotion? No grief for your wife?"

He studied his boots.

Igraine wiped her eyes, letting out a shaky breath. "I only left for a few hours. How could this happen? Did you send a messenger to Alenor's family?"

Montag nodded once.

"I hope you explained it gently. She was their only daughter."

Montag exhaled.

"Why didn't you let me say goodbye? You must have known. Montag . . . did you *do* something?" Igraine's mind reeled in shock. "Is she really gone?"

Madame Brigitte entered the room then, pulling Igraine into her motherly arms. "Oh, love. She's really gone. I told him to wait but he wouldn't . . ." She shot an angry glare at Montag.

"What did we do wrong, Madame Brigitte? She was doing better!"

"A last surge before the Lord took her, my dear. She went in peace."

"No, no, no." Igraine put a hand to the wall for support, desperation mixing with her confusion. "She was better. Stronger. Montag, swear to me you didn't kill her. You loved her, right? In your own way. She was your match, right?"

Montag walked away, his expression as blank as the day Alenor had given birth through her stomach instead of the birth canal.

Igraine crumbled into a pile, sobbing not only with grief for a friend but for the brother she once thought she could trust despite his bullying. Madame Brigitte lingered to console her, but Igraine pushed her away as she realized that had she not been with Enric that afternoon, perhaps she could have stopped them all, saved her friend. The guilt shattered her heart, and she lay curled, weak and exhausted, in a corner of Alenor's room long after the sun had set. The trails of dried tears clung to her cheeks.

The door creaked as it opened, and Igraine didn't bother to look up. She stared at the worn boots in front of her. Such big feet. She sighed, tucking her head back into her arm, not caring how unladylike she appeared. She was not getting up. She was not hungry, no matter which servant asked her. She just wanted to be left alone.

"You have to eat," Montag said as he sat next to her with a sigh, setting a bowl of bread and cheese in front of her.

Igraine ignored him, tears dripping from her burning eyes. She mused how it was possible to even have a tear left.

"Raoul could use an aunt."

"He needs his mother." She tucked her head deeper into her arm as the sobs threatened to rip through her once again. She felt Montag's hand on her back, and the surprising show of comfort quieted her. They remained like that a long while, lost in their thoughts, before Igraine remembered her own mother. "Is this how it was when I was born?"

Montag's hand squeezed her shoulder ever so slightly. "Yes."

"Did father cut her open?"

Montag was silent.

Igraine pushed up off the floor, hastily wiping tears. Montag sat with his back to the wall, knees bent in front of him, one arm casually on his knee, the other absently brushing wisps of hair from Igraine's face.

"Brother, tell me what it was like. I want to understand."

Montag let his head fall back against the wall, staring at the ceiling. After a moment he began, "I could hear her screams all through the castle. We all could. The labor lasted for days. The women worried. The men tried to keep out of the castle. I, as a boy, was caught somewhere in between. I was excited for a sibling, worried for Mother, eager to be helpful, anxious to be free to go back to riding and fighting. No one knows what happened in that room except father and the midwife, who to my knowledge is long since dead herself. But at some point the castle went quiet, and you were born. I never saw my mother again."

Igraine leaned against the wall next to him, tucking her skirts around her feet. "Do you blame me for her death?"

Montag shrugged. "No more than I blame Raoul for Alenor's. It's just a fact."

"Father did, though."

Montag nodded slowly. "He did."

Igraine rubbed her temples. "Alenor really did love you, you know. I don't know why." She let out a mirthless chuckle. Montag remained silent, staring at the ceiling.

"Where were you that afternoon, Igraine?"

"I told you."

"If you had been home—"

Igraine abruptly pushed to her feet. "Why do you think I've been up here bawling my eyes out all day, Montag? Don't make it worse. I can't undo the past."

Igraine watched him sit there a minute longer, then turned on her heel. She'd done enough moping for both of them. She wasn't going to get sucked into a whole night of it.

"Igraine . . ."

She froze with her hand on the door.

"How do you know when you've found love?"

She stared at the man on the floor. "It hurts when you lose it," she said quietly. She let the door click shut behind her as she walked away.

Chapter 16

March 15, 1173

Chateau Brunstein, Alsace

The hushed tone of Igraine's voice gave Montag plenty of warning as to who was at the door. "Something happened — you should go," she was whispering. Igraine backed away from the cracked door as Montag approached. He shot her a glare as he wrenched the door open. She scampered toward the stairs. On the other side of the castle threshold was none other than Sir Enric de Levan.

The man before Montag showed no sign of fear. With shoulders square and drawn to full height, they stood eye-to-eye. That ability should have unnerved Montag. He didn't feel much of anything these days though. Expressionless, he stood there in the entryway, neither inviting Enric in nor casting him away. The two men faced off like lions, sizing up each other's ability, taking in every small detail, practically smelling each other for a hint of fear.

Montag was the first to growl. He stood with his arms casually crossed, but every muscle was taut in anticipation. "You cannot have her."

Enric met the challenge, his hand resting lightly on the hilt of his sword, the other palm subconsciously opening toward Montag, pleading, though his voice belied no such weakness. "We both would like your support on this, Lord Montag. I understand what she is to your family. I swear to you to protect her and cherish her always. She will have everything she needs."

Montag's voice dropped an octave. "You dare to assume you can provide for her? You, a common, poor knight, with no land holdings, with no pedigree to connect you to those in power?"

Enric cut him off, "I have enough to keep her in comfort. Wealth isn't everything, Montag."

"Spoken like a romantic fool who has never seen a day of battle in his life."

Enric frowned, checking his anger. "I may be a romantic, but you have no idea what I have seen in this life."

"Tournaments are hardly experience in the ways of the world!"

"I agree," Enric said coldly. "Those who seek their fame there are insulated from the realities of our brutal world. A world that pits lord against lord. Saracen against Christian. A world that tortures the innocent. Where crimes may go unpunished until the life of the perpetrator is obsolete." His eyes gave a curious flash at these last words that did not go unnoticed by Montag.

"You can't have her," Montag again stated. He shifted his stance so now his hand fell to his sword.

Enric continued to meet his gaze. "What I don't understand, Montag, is why? You've been preventing her from marrying for so long . . . years. If you aren't holding out for someone like me who truly loves her and would do everything to make her happy, what are you waiting for? You've had nobility, the wealthy — really any single man in Europe — at her feet for almost a decade. She tells me it's you who stopped the marriage to Lezay—"

"She may still marry Lezay."

"Will she? I'm not so sure." Enric shook his head, then drew himself even taller, meeting Montag's eye. "I will not fight you here and now over her, Montag. I will not need to. She is loyal to you in a way I do not understand, in a way I don't believe you deserve, yet she has the strength in her to break away from you if she chooses. It will devastate her. But I warn you now, she may well do it."

"She knows her place and her duty, you fool. You overestimate your charms."

"If she marries another, I will trust that you did not force her, and she did it of her own volition, her own loyalty to family, as you say. I will not protest it. But until she either marries another or becomes my wife, I will wait for her."

"You are a fool."

Enric smirked. "I could be a good ally to you. Don't make me an enemy."

As Montag's fury grew, Enric backed away from the manor to his waiting horse. His eyes flicked toward the top of the nearest tower, where a pale white hand pressed against the diamond panes of glass. He nodded his head to Igraine, then turned and rode off.

Igraine met Montag at the foot of the stairs, her stomach twisting with anxiety. The fury in his eyes had not faded. Instead of matching it with her own, she wiped her tears and put on the mask of the Lady of the Tournament.

"Brother, please. He speaks the truth. I love him."

"Then you are as much a fool as he."

"He is a good man. You've seen such yourself. Honorable, a tournament champion. He's a hard worker. He'll provide—"

"You dare to ask for your own say in your betrothal? You dare to assume you know more about your prospects than I?" Montag's full fury turned to her. "*I* have shielded you from men more ruthless than you can imagine. *I* have weighed the benefits of wealth versus birth versus ability. I will choose your husband! And it is not that fool downstairs!"

"Then who will you choose?" Igraine questioned in exasperation. She was so tired of asking.

Montag's voice dropped to a hiss. "I will not rush your wedding like you rushed mine." He took a step toward Igraine. "See what your meddling got your friend? See what Alenor's love did for her?"

Igraine shakily knelt before Montag, her hands folded in pleading as tears streamed from her eyes. "Brother, I beg you. Let me choose my husband. Let me choose Enric. Let me have joy."

Montag stared down at her without emotion. "You have a duty to this family, and he does nothing for us. Remember your place, sister." He turned on his heel and strode out of the castle, the heavy oak door slamming behind him.

Igraine let her face fall into her hands, sobbing there on her knees with her skirts a puddle around her. She would do her duty; she always did. But understanding why this hell was necessary would certainly have made it easier to bear.

Chapter 17

May 14, 1173

Chateau Brunstein, Alsace

I graine stopped, every nerve frozen right down to her heart itself as it skipped a beat before stubbornly hammering on in a rising wave. If she had had anything in her hands it would now be on the floor. Her eyes remained open as the edges of her vision narrowed with stars. Their focus: the burly man before her with ruddy brown-grey hair and black eyes. Her father. He was comfortably seated in Montag's chair at the head of the table, a cup of what must surely be wine in his hand, his cool gaze already boring into her soul. Igraine reached out a hand to grasp the edge of the table next to her, lest her feet give out. The contact with the solid surface gave her enough grounding to focus as she fought down her shock.

"Daughter," Lord Raganor le Brun said coolly, bemused at his daughter's reaction.

"Father," Igraine croaked out, straightening her spine. She cleared her throat. "Welcome home."

At that moment, Montag entered the hall and also froze in place, just behind Igraine. He recovered quickly. "Father, we weren't expecting you." He gave Igraine a sideways glance and approached the high table.

"I see you let anyone through our lands these days. I hardly met a soul on the road from the East. Wasn't asked to part with a single coin."

"We've been charging the tolls as usual, father," Montag said as he crossed his arms in front of himself, taking a wide stance before their father. "Have you been receiving the funds we've sent you?"

Raganor looked down on his son with amusement. "They come. Yet without much news. It's like you've forgotten I am your lord."

Igraine took a shaky seat on the bench, still only steps inside the door to the great hall. Who would Raganor be more furious with? Montag for his unannounced marriage? Or herself, for remaining unwed? What had his spies relayed?

Raganor's glare at them both answered everything. He knew. Which meant he still had spies in the castle. Spies with a reach to Jerusalem.

Montag met their father's stare like the man he was. "I would have sent you word, but in order to protect my heir we had to act quickly."

"Heir?" Raganor smirked in amusement. At least that was news to him. "And how soon will I have an heir, son?"

"You already have one," Montag said coolly.

Raganor raised his eyebrows.

"His name is Raoul. His mother was Lady Alenor of Tielo. But that I'm sure you've heard."

"And here I thought you'd continue thumping the chambermaids your whole life. Now you finally managed to breed a real *lady*. Congratulations."

Montag kept his face unreadable.

Raganor turned his wrath on Igraine, glowering at her from the head table. "And I hear you have requested permission to marry? At least you ask, unlike your brother who just takes whatever strumpet he likes."

Montag interjected, "She was the daughter of a duke."

"Silence!" Raganor bellowed, his fury palpable. He turned his gaze back to Igraine. "How dare you assume you may ask for a husband of your choice? Groveling on the ground like a peasant wench. I raised you better! Or has your brother let you go soft in these years I've been away? He's dragged his feet about finding you a proper match, that much is evident. Elfric you fool . . . she's an old maid now. And from her reputation as the tournament beauty, I see no reason for it. Who is the highest bidder?"

Igraine stiffened.

Montag broke his father's gaze, looking down. "Lord Matthew de Bologne."

"The *Count* of Bologne?"

"Yes, sir."

"And *why* is she not wedded?"

"He had an accident in a tourney last summer. He can't walk, Father."

"Did he lose his wealth because of it? His title? No?" Raganor narrowed his eyes. "You are a pathetic excuse for a lord, Elfric. I cannot leave you with the simplest of deeds. If he is the wealthiest bidder, she will marry him! Why must I come all the way from Jerusalem to press this matter into that thick skull of yours? She is to be wed!"

The edges of Igraine's vision were blurring again, and she was grateful that she was already sitting. She dug her nails into the wooden bench, her gaze now on the ground instead of the men before her.

"I had in mind another . . . more suitable –" Montag started to explain.

"Who is more suitable than a count? Are we waiting for a king? She will be barren before she is bred!" Raganor was standing now, towering over Montag from the slightly raised platform. "Collect the fees, patrol the lands, get your sister married off! Are those demands too much for you, you lazy swine? Or has breeding a *lady* taken so much of your energy you feel completely exhausted? Weak, cowardly . . . Where is my new daughter-in-law? I would like to meet her."

"She's dead." Igraine felt the words leave her mouth of their own volition.

"Did I ask you?" Raganor seethed at her. He glared from one of them to the other. "Which one of you killed her?"

Igraine gasped in surprise and looked up. This was a low blow, even for her father. "No one! She died after the ba—"

"I killed her," Montag cut in. His face was set, a furious look Igraine had never seen on him darkening his eyes to the color of their father's. "I chose the child over the mother, and I killed her."

"Montag, you didn't . . ." Igraine whispered.

"I did, Igraine." He kept his eyes locked with Raganor's. "The midwife told me to choose one, and I chose the child."

Igraine's eyes widened with horror.

Montag motioned to Raganor. "He wanted an heir. Well, Father, you've got one now."

Raganor was quiet. "Maybe you do have the balls to be a lord after all. Did you get to keep the dowry?"

"Of course." Montag nodded once.

"You bastards!" Igraine seethed and rose to her feet. "If that was me, dead in childbed, would you feel the same? You would let my husband gut me open to spare an unborn child and then leave me to lay in agony? And then talk about who gets to keep my dowry?"

"I didn't let her lay in agony," Montag said emotionlessly, his eyes still locked with his father's.

"I attended to her! I saw her! It was a week, Montag!"

"It would have been longer."

Igraine's eyes went round at this implication. Her worst fears clicked into place, refreshing every memory of the one night of her life she should not have slept. The silence made sense now. The hasty burial necessary to hide the evidence, not to cleanse the castle. Despite his words, she had not believed him. "You murdered her?"

"Put her out of her misery." He still didn't look at Igraine.

She walked up to him in a few long strides, forcing him to look her in the eye. "She was my best friend you sanglant beast. She loved you, which you never deserved. And I was the one who convinced you both to be married . . ."

"I guess that means you killed her, too," Raganor said with a grin.

Igraine lost all reason. She strode up to her father and slapped him. As her palm stung, her eyes went wide in fear at what she had done. She backed away slowly, clutching her offending hand to her chest like it was broken.

Raganor stalked after her. "Apparently your brother really has given you too much freedom."

"I . . . I . . . I'm so sorry. I was overcome . . ."

"You are a pathetic fool of a woman. You will not be 'overcome' again."

The back of Igraine's legs hit the wooden bench, and she sank heavily onto it. Her father kept coming. Shakily she sank to her knees before him, hands folded in pleading, her back so bowed her forehead touched her knees as she curled on the dirty rush-covered floor before him. Just as she thought the blows would come, a pair of boots stepped in front of her head.

"I'll take care of it." Montag's voice was as low and cold as death itself.

Igraine glanced up to see her brother standing between her and her father.

Raganor made to step around him. "You've had your chance."

Montag put a hand on Raganor's chest. "I'll take care of it," he said again.

Raganor looked at Montag's hand, then his face. "You would dare to lay a hand on me like your sister just did?"

Montag removed his hand. "Burn the flesh, purge the soul."

Raganor's eyes narrowed. "You'll do it? She needs it."

Montag nodded once, and Igraine curled back into her ball, now sobbing.

"Quit your noise, or you'll make it worse for yourself!" Raganor scolded.

But it was Montag's strong hand that pulled her roughly to her feet. It was him that pulled her from the hall and into the lord's chamber, Montag's chamber now, where the great hearth stood like a terror from her childhood memories. Montag slammed the heavy door behind them and bolted it. He didn't look at her.

"Please, Montag. Please don't do this."

He pulled her across the room and roughly forced her into a chair by the fire. He shoved the tip of his sword into the hot coals and left it there. He leaned on the stone mantel with his arms and stared at the fire. Igraine cried silently behind him, trembling. "Better me than him," he finally said.

"We're adults now Montag. We don't have to listen to him."

"Adults? You just acted like a bloody child in there. What did you expect would happen?"

"Is it true you murdered Alenor? Or did you just say that for father's sake?"

Montag didn't answer her.

"Oh God, it is true. How could you?"

"Unlace the back of your dress."

"No."

"You want Father to do this?"

"You deserve it more than me. I'm not the murderer!"

Montag took the sword from the fire, checked its reddening tip, and plunged it back. He undid the toggles of his tunic and pulled it and his linen shirt over his head.

"What are you doing?" Igraine questioned.

"I deserve it more, right?"

"Montag, no. We aren't doing this. Either one of us."

"Pick up the sword, Igraine." His voice didn't leave room to argue.

Tears dripped down her cheeks as she obeyed. She looked at Montag's burn-scarred back, her arm shaking with the sword in hand.

"Just do it. What's one more back there?" He was wrong. There was hardly room for more scars. Already his muscled back was spotted as if pox-marked, only the deep pits and scars were all so much larger than pox-scars.

"I can't," she said in a small voice.

Montag sighed in frustration and took the sword abruptly from her hand. She stepped back in alarm, uncertain of what he was going to do. But instead of coming after her, he took the hot iron and turned it that he could touch his own back with it. He winced only slightly as the smell of seared flesh filled the room. Within moments he was fully dressed again as if nothing had happened.

"Act like you hurt and don't say another damn word until he goes back to Jerusalem, or so help me I *will* burn you next time."

Igraine nodded.

Montag opened the door and stepped aside for the waiting lord to enter, who, satisfied at the stench of burned flesh, gave a grotesque smile to Igraine. She hastily shuffled from the hall, intent on barricading herself in her room, but the shouts from the hall echoed behind her and she ducked into a servant's corridor. She pressed her back against the wall near the side entrance to the hall, listening intently.

"I don't care if you're back," Montag was hissing in a fearsome tone. "I am the lord of Brunstein now. That was our arrangement, and you will stay true to it."

"You are not managing well," Raganor purred.

"We are managing extremely well. The coffers are full, the servants are fed and working hard, our roads are more traveled than ever, and we are without conflict. That is success, Father, not failure. Your bloodthirst cost us deeply, and you know it."

"How dare—"

"You left for Jerusalem to cleanse your soul, Father. Go back and scrub some more, as it is still as black as that shirt on your back."

There was a thwack, and Igraine flinched from her hideaway behind the wall. There was a scuffle, and then she heard Montag's voice, a low, indecipherable hiss. She ventured a glance around the corner and saw that he had Raganor in an arm-lock against the wall. Had the two men been dogs, they would have had hackles raised, teeth bared, growls rumbling from their cores. As it was, they snarled at each other in a height of fury only two blooded men of temper can obtain.

Igraine turned away and hastened to her room. Montag had come of age and staked his claim. He'd protected her, but she knew it was not of brotherly affection but because she was his property to trade now, not their father's. He physically fought the man who had raised them with a literal iron fist because he was the stronger. He held the power.

He was lord.

Chapter 18

I graine did not leave her room until she heard the iron shoes of Raganor's horse on the road back to the East. As she toed cautiously down the stairs, she saw Montag watching the rider fade from a window in the hall, his arms folded across his chest. She hesitated, then softly approached him.

"Will he be back?" she whispered.

"Not in my lifetime," Montag said coldly.

Igraine turned away, continuing down the corridor.

"You owe me," he said.

"Pardon?" Igraine hoped she had misheard.

He didn't repeat himself. Instead he leaned his back against the stone wall and folded his arms across his chest. "I took your punishment. Now marry Lezay like I asked."

Igraine shook her head. "You murdered Alenor. It was your own punishment brother, not that you needed to do it at all." She started walking away.

The devil in Montag raised its ugly head. He had her back to the wall and his hand on her throat before she could form another word. "Remember your place, sister. As lord of this castle, you will marry who I choose for you. And I choose Lezay." He let her go, and she rubbed her neck.

"Why him? Why not the Count of Bologne?" Sarcasm laced her words.

"You'd prefer a drooling cripple to an able-bodied knight?"

"No."

"Then take Lezay. He is going to have properties this family has only ever dreamed of. We will soon control an area as large as a dutchy."

"Why not Enric? Why not gain liaisons in wealthy Aquitaine?"

"You fool, Igraine. Enric is a penniless idiot. What liaisons could you forge in Aquitaine? There is only the one between his legs."

Igraine knew there was nothing she could do except get herself into trouble, so without further word she pushed past Montag and down the hall to the kitchens, where she knew Madame Brigitte had her little nephew in her care.

"We leave for a tourney in the morning!" Montag called after her. "Be prepared to accept your betrothed."

Little Raoul was in a cradle near the fire, fast asleep. She knelt beside him, her fingertips tracing his brown curls and tiny fingers.

"How is he?" she asked Brigitte.

"Sleeps by day, fusses most of the night." Brigitte had deep circles under her eyes. "Healthy set of lungs on him he has. Just like his father."

"Will he be alright without Alenor?"

"Oh, yes, dear. We've a nursemaid for him. He's perfectly healthy, strong."

"Will you protect him?"

Brigitte frowned. "From what, dear?" She studied Igraine's weary look. "From your brother, aye. As best I can. He doesn't much bother with the boy anyway."

"Madame Brigitte, I'm not going to come back."

"Are you finally going to do it then? Marry Lezay as he's been talking about all year?"

Igraine shook her head. Her lower lip trembled and tears threatened to spill from her eyes.

"Oh, Lord, girl. What crazy idea do you have in your head? We've just been rid of your father, now don't go setting off Montag. He's had a rough few days, and his temper is far from cool."

Igraine threw her arms around the maid's neck and hugged her close. For a moment Brigitte didn't know what to do, then she tightened around Igraine in one of the few genuine hugs Igraine had ever received in her life.

"Thank you for everything, Madame Brigitte."

"You really don't intend to come back?"

Igraine shook her head. She pulled out of Brigitte's arms and knelt to kiss her nephew on the forehead. Then without another word, she returned to her room to pack. Conflict raged within as she doubted her decision. Could she fit her whole life in a set of saddlebags? It was time to find out.

Igraine paced, pulling her hair back from her face in fistfuls of blond tangles. With wood-screeching abruptness, she sat down in her chair by the hearth and let the sobs come. She tried to be quiet at first, but the tension within her threatened to burst, and the sound like a tidal wave crashing on the rocks. Her tears fueled it. Her body shook with its power. As she was caught in its storm, for a moment she felt only her pain, not the thoughts that caused the pain. Gradually the wave's power waned, and she leaned back in her chair, her glassy eyes staring unseeingly into the dim embers of the fire before her.

Thought returned.

The problem was not that Montag was following in their father's footsteps. It was not that his iron-willed control of her was unjustified. These things she could live with, separate herself from. It was the moments of aching brotherly love that reminded her of the man he truly was, the boy she'd grown up with. That man, she loved. He was her brother! Her blood. When he acted on her behalf against Raganor, she had sworn she'd do anything for him, for their family. And that made her decision even harder. She would devastate him, shame him . . . shame the whole family. She was failing in her duties as a sister and daughter of their father. She knew the match with Lezay was less than ideal, but if Montag said it was the only way, it was. At least for him.

She was dying inside.

Igraine leaned forward and put her elbows on her knees, her face in her hands. She didn't sob, but tears dripped freely. She didn't bother to wipe them away. If she did this, married Lezay, she would, in a way, die. The last spark of life that she'd protected from the wrath of their father would have to be snuffed out in order for the body to survive. If the body itself could survive.

She raised her eyes to the fire again, her fingers still pressed to her lips. Bodies were stubborn things that refused to quit easily. She'd seen enough injuries at the tourneys, heard enough stories from the battlefield, to know that the corporeal form was a miracle of healing and survival. There had been men, such as the count, who should not have survived more than a few hours, yet they stubbornly clung to life. She was healthy. There would be no accidents on the battlefield to shorten her life. Perhaps the plague, but hidden away in Lezay's mountain fortress, such diseases rarely came with great severity, unlike in the cities. No, with her fortune, Igraine would live long years at Leuwenstein, with childbearing itself as her biggest threat. She shuddered.

Silent. On her back. How often? How long?

That spark had to die. She had to be able to separate mind from body. Then she could do it. She had to be numb.

Wine.

Igraine rose and uncorked a bottle of strong Burgundian port, a deep red, expensive bottle she hid away for special occasions. She didn't bother to pour it into a vessel but took a long swallow from the bottle. Why not break all the rules?

She went back to pacing in front of the fire, the bottle occasionally rising and falling to her lips as her mind smoked in thought.

She pictured her life with Lezay. A beautiful wedding. Lavish gifts. His stench. She would survive the breeding. She'd have to. Long weeks alone in the castle while he was away at tournaments. Really, it was quite a beautiful location, peacefully nestled in the forested hills. He would return, breed. He would leave. She would bear children. Joyful, smiling children. They would play and run through the castle. They would want for nothing. He would return. Would he cherish them, or raise them in as ruthless a manner as her father? Would he cherish Igraine herself? Her head ached with a phantom pain from the night he had thrown her against the wall.

The vision faded, replaced by Enric. Igraine took another long swallow of port, staring again at the fire. A simple wedding. No gifts. His woody scent, soft caress.

The passion in his kiss. His smile as he would offer to win each tournament for her, for of course he would not leave her behind. A small manor, always wanting for something. But children, so many children, with his dark hair and mischievous smile. He would cherish them; there was no question there. He would raise them with love, with joy, and yet still teach them to be strong and independent. And he had sworn to her he would love her all the days of their lives.

It was a fairytale life, the kind the troubadours sang of. It could be hers. It could come true. All she had to do was leave everything behind. Every jewel, every memento of her youth, and even her friends would be cut off from her. It would be a total blank slate, a descent to nothing, to gamble that Enric would be all she needed. Could he be? Together, perhaps, they could work for what they did not have.

Oppression for love? Wealth for poverty? Despair for hope?

Hope.

Slowly, Igraine returned the bottle of port to its place. She ran her hands over the elaborately carved wardrobe that concealed it: her grandmother's. She looked around the room, with its warm fire and comfortable bed. A tapestry hung on the wall, greyed with dust, that belonged to a distant ancestor. Suddenly these material things seemed invaluable. She felt a pull like an invisible string from her heart as Enric's face burned fresh in her mind. She closed her eyes and felt his lips on hers, his whisper of love a breath in her ear.

Her eyes flew open, now steely with the family glare. There was another option, and she was going to take it. That fiery vein that guided her brother ran in her own blood too. It was time she used it. It was time she listened to it, instead of quenching it with doubt.

It was time to leave Brunstein for good.

Chapter 19

June 5, 1173
Poitiers, Aquitaine

Montag sauntered through the crowd in Poitiers, searching for his squire. His horse should have been visible over the heads of the spectators, but it once again was not. The boy would pay, once again, for a poor job. His frustration with training the latest addition to his staff was overshadowed by the man following only steps behind him, complaining incessantly.

"I told you. When we get back to Reims," Montag growled.

"I want a promise this time. I've waited long enough! You either want this deal or not." Lezay spit on the ground, forcing a maid to wrinkle her nose in disgust as she stepped around them.

"You know things were — are — complicated. I've had other offers for her."

"I'm your best friend, Montag." Lezay smirked. "You've known no other offers ever mattered."

"You're not a count, Lezay." Montag looked again for his horse and squire. Mounted, he could get away and get into the business that really mattered, which at this moment was the looming melee. The squire boy was nowhere to be seen.

"I'm wealthier than a count," Lezay pointed out. He grabbed Montag's shoulder, turning the big man to face him.

Montag glared in fury, shrugging off Lezay's hand but knowing he could not strike out.

Lezay met his glare with his own. "You promise her to me now, Montag," he said in a low voice, "I swear I will take her by force from a damn nunnery if I have to. You know it's a good match for her. We both want Alsace united. You've made me wait a year. I will do the church ceremony and everything you want, make it proper. But you better give me your word. And not some long engagement. Next week when we return to Reims."

Montag chewed his cheek. He looked Lezay in the eye, nodding once. He shifted his gaze behind the man, spotting his destrier led by a panicked squire. Without a word he pushed past Lezay to the squire and yanked the reins from the boy's hand. The boy was stammering something as he mounted, but Montag was too furious to hear. He roughly yanked the stallion toward the arena, scattering pedestrians as he rode.

The two sides of the melee had already formed. Anything was fair game here. Lances were blunted, but swords, pikes, maces — any weapons of a knight's choosing — were also allowed. They all would start on their mounts, but from past experience Montag knew the fight would deteriorate quickly from there. Lances only lasted so long, and the shorter weapons were easier used in close quarters, on foot. He shifted the pike strung on a thick cord across his back. His sword was belted to his left side and a dagger to his right hip. He would be ready when he had to dismount from his horse.

Twenty men on each side. They all shifted, sensing the excitement. Lezay appeared, on his own destrier now, and trotted to his place next to Montag. They were silent, as if their previous conversation had never happened. Montag stole a glance to the stands, to the ladies. Igraine sat among them, slightly off from the group. Her stillness contrasted against the cheers and excitement shown by those around her. She scanned the crowd, her eyes lingering on her brother for only a moment, and then she looked on.

She hated him, Montag knew. Yet he knew, too, she would do her duty to the family.

Lezay spat next to him, following Montag's gaze. "Should I offer to win for her? Show my love?"

Montag pushed his helmet down onto his head, ignoring the man. Thankfully, the melee was about to begin. A herald shouted out the rules, which few knights could hear or cared to hear over the snorts of their horses and clink of their mail and dropped the flag.

Chaos erupted, and Montag lost himself in the bloodlust as his horse bolted in a charge toward the opposing side. His lance found its mark and unseated the man he aimed for, and after that point it became useless. Half the men were unseated, some of them crawling out from under the murderous destriers as the riders still in their saddles fought to unseat the others by whatever means necessary. Montag threw what was left of his lance at a fellow knight, catching him in the back, but not unseating him. The man raised his sword and charged, only to meet Montag's brutal blow as he swung his own blade. Montag didn't linger with the stunned knight, but cantered through the mass of bodies, carefully sidestepping the men on his team as his horse bumped into and kicked those in opposition. In the heart of the melee, he was blocked by a wall of men, who worked as a unit to grab his angry destrier by the bridle and pull Montag from the saddle. He swung his sword down on their heads, but their helmets protected them. He fell to the ground with a crash, quickly scrambling to his feet.

In one motion, Montag took his pike from his back and swung it in a wide arc, clearing the space around him from the bloodthirsty opposition. They stepped back, and he smiled coldly. One after another, the men fell away from him, leaving the arena. Some of his own side had exited as well, nursing their wounds. Lezay still fought. An unbidden fury rose in him, and he took out his anger on the opposition with even more ruthlessness.

In a fearfully powerful blow, one intended more for the battlefield than a tournament, Montag knocked a knight to the ground. He hammered the man again. The man raised his hand in submission, pleading, but Montag could not stop, would not stop. Then the man lay still, and Montag straightened. The tournament field was oddly quiet. The other knights stared at him. Montag looked around, his bloodlust still pounding through every nerve in his body.

Lezay appeared at his side, his face wearing an expression of such solemnity that Montag had to blink at him in confusion. Lezay gently laid a hand on Montag's shoulder, looking down at the corpse. "An accident. An accident," he said clearly. Montag realized the words were not for his benefit but the shocked crowd's. "One of the risks of the melee," Lezay continued, and firmly steered Montag away from the body and toward the exit of the list.

Montag shook as his temper came down, realizing now what he had done. The man had yielded! And Montag had killed him. It was a gross error, one that could possibly warrant repercussions from the hosting lord. Montag opened his mouth to speak, started to turn back toward the lord of the manor.

"Shut up, you idiot," Lezay hissed. His grip on Montag's arm tightened. "Act like you're in shock. *It was an accident.*"

Montag shook his head, a thin line forming across his lips. He stayed silent. As they passed beneath the spectator stands, he glanced up to Igraine. She was likely in shock herself. He'd made a sure show of brutality today for her.

Igraine wasn't there.

Montag stopped, pulling back against Lezay.

"Montag . . ." Lezay insisted.

"Where is she?" Montag cut him off, his eyes scanning the crowd. He didn't see his sister anywhere.

Lezay looked up and down the spectators as well, spinning in a circle. Some of the crowd was returning to normal, leaving their seats to head for the village in a somber procession. Others wept. Still others glared and pointed fingers at Montag.

Montag pushed past Lezay, heading in the direction of the stable. Lezay jogged to keep up.

Wordlessly the two knights burst into the stable, scattering busy squires as they strode down the aisle. When they got to the stall where Igraine's charger had been tied, Montag punched the wall. "Damn!"

Lezay stared at the empty stall. "That bitch ran . . ."

The two men exchanged a quick glance and ran out of the stable. For once they located their squires quickly, who obediently were tending to the destriers fresh from the melee. In seconds they were mounted and with a shout to Sir Jean of Thuringia, they galloped off on Montag's lead. For it was he who knew where the woman had run. It was a race to catch her before she sought sanctuary at her destination.

Chapter 20

Bu-bum. Bu-bum. It was hard to differentiate between the pounding of hooves and her panicked heart. Igraine hunched over her horse's neck, hovering over the saddle as the first fat raindrops pelted her back and bare head. The hot breeze blew around her as if it came from beneath and ahead of her all at the same time. As Igraine sat on a thousand pounds of power with a frightened mind of its own, she felt as if she was riding a lightning bolt itself. A crack of thunder urged them faster, hooves flying down the empty road, prints in the dust like scars on an old warrior's arm. She took a shorter grip on the reins as her mare surged in reaction to another crack of lightning. It wouldn't be long now. The storm was upon them.

The mare tossed her head as the raindrops grew to a steady beat. They stung her eyes as she galloped, and it made her angry. Igraine herself could barely see as she squinted into the black storm that now swirled around them. The last bright rays of the beautiful day they had left just minutes ago faded behind a sheet of grey rain. The rain ran into her eyes now and plastered her long hair to her back. She licked her lips and tasted salt in the raindrops that poured down her face. Was it from her sweat or her tears?

She listened to the footfalls of the beast beneath her, shifting her weight just slightly in the saddle when she felt the horse slip on the now-muddy path, helping her rebalance, then urging her on. They could not stop. They could not seek shelter. Shelter no longer existed behind them. There was only refuge in front of them, and if she didn't make it there before her brother, it and all hope of her freedom would disappear.

The lightning cracked closer to her this time, the flash dancing across the tops of the trees they galloped beneath. She gritted her teeth and took hold of the horse's mane, readying for the spook she was sure would come when the sound of that bright flash boomed. Sure enough, it did in mere seconds and shook the air around them. The horse skittered sideways in alarm, throwing her head. Igraine bounced back hard into the saddle, losing her seat for a moment, then recovered. She gave the horse a sharp kick. It took all of Igraine's strength to keep the horse on the path instead of bolting into the woods. She hauled the reins and shouted, "Go!" The horse snorted but obeyed, again settling into the fastest pace the muddy road would allow. Perhaps faster than it would allow, Igraine thought, as she stumbled in a patch of deep mud. She wove her fingers into the mane once more and held on. There was nothing she could do but ride it out, and trust that they would get there in time.

Time, time. Did they have enough time? This was the fastest road, and she was on one of the fastest horses in her family's stable, but would they make it? She glanced over her shoulder. It was impossible to tell if her brother was catching up or not. She was sure he would ride through the storm as well. Fury drove him. For once, she was grateful for the fear that drove her onward. She harnessed it, used it.

"Easy, girl," she soothed as she spotted the bridge up ahead through the downpour. She sat back in the saddle and slowed her seat to a gentle canter, then cued for a walk. The mare, sides heaving with exertion, gladly complied. Gently she coaxed the horse forward over the thick wooden planks. They were slick when wet, especially for a horse with iron shoes, but the horse was well-trained and took careful steps forward. They were halfway across when the lightning flashed again. The mare snorted. "Oh no," Igraine whispered and flinched as the instantaneous crack of thunder split her eardrums. The horse spooked sideways again, only this time there was no barrier of trees to catch them. Her hind legs stepped off the bridge, and after a brief scramble with her front feet, they both slid into the creek. Igraine screamed, holding on with her legs and her hands as they splashed into the water.

Thankfully, the bridge was only a bit higher than the creek, and the water wasn't deep. The horse miraculously stayed upright, and she only floundered for a moment for her footing before she stood still, muscles shaking. The water reached up to Igraine's knees, soaking her skirts even more than the rain already had. She took a breath to steady her heartbeat and glanced her eyes heavenward in a muttering of thanks.

She grumbled at the horse and steered back toward the bank. They scrambled up the bank to the far side, and Igraine shifted her sodden skirts so she could move freely in the saddle again. She sighed, then bumped the mare with her legs back into a trot. "Sorry, Sterra, but we need to get there, rain or shine. It would help if we take the road from now on."

Suddenly Igraine heard a shout behind her, from beyond the bridge. "No, no, no," she whispered to herself. "Heh!" she shouted at her mount and kicked hard, pushing back into a breakneck gallop. The mare slid on her haunches down the next hill, and still she didn't slow. They were behind them. They had found her. Now there was only speed to get her the last few miles to freedom.

To Enric.

Her heart pounded as the muscles of her legs and abs burned from the exertion of the furious ride. She had never been to this part of Aquitaine, but Enric had told her to follow this road to the end, and there would be his manor.

She hoped it had a moat. And a drawbridge.

The rain slowed just enough that she could make out three figures riding hard after her. It still felt like she was riding through a waterfall. Her fatiguing horse again scrambled in the mud, losing precious seconds. She gasped as she spotted a huge tree across the road ahead, with no way around it. She gritted her teeth and rose in the saddle, locking her legs against the horse's sides, throwing her reins forward, willing her to take the obstacle. If they didn't, it would be the end of them both.

As if sensing her urgency, Sterra lifted from the ground in a powerful leap that almost left Igraine behind. But her grip held her firm as hooves again found ground and for once held true, falling back into their pounding rhythm. She glanced behind her again as the other riders wrestled with their mounts, then forced them into the thick brush around the tree. The time she had lost at the bridge had been regained.

Another flash of lightning illuminated the hills beyond the road. Silhouetted against the black clouds was a small stone keep. That had to be it. God help her if Enric wasn't home.

She urged Sterra faster, hope burning bright in her chest. Almost there. Igraine pounded up the last stretch of road, screaming his name. She could only pray someone would hear her over the din of the storm. She bellowed louder, and her horse screamed with her, his attention not so much for her cause but his own as he spotted other horses in the paddocks around the manor stable. The sound got someone's attention, and the great door of the keep groaned open, showing the light of the torches within. Sir Enric de Levan stood framed in the light, his face in shadows, but the sword in his hand silhouetted. His posture softened as she pounded the last few steps up to him. Her horse slid to a stop in front of the thick oak entryway, and Igraine leaped from Sterra's back, stumbling as her wet skirts caught on the saddle. With one arm Enric swept them clear, and she threw her arms around him, a sob catching in her throat.

She held him hard and said, "They're coming!" He gently pushed her away and stepped in front of her. They were already here.

Enric held his sword at the ready as the three riders slid to a stop in front of the manor. They did not dismount.

"Gentlemen, you have no business here," Enric said coolly in his deep voice.

Montag spat at Enric's feet. "Give her back, and we'll be on our way."

Igraine shivered behind Enric, her hand resting on his hip, needing to feel him, hoping to convey to him every ounce of strength she could share. Her brother looked even more formidable than usual. The rain had plastered his hair and his clothes to his solid frame, which did nothing to assuage the fury that radiated from his posture.

Lezay and Jean looked almost as angry. No one wanted to be tearing through the countryside in a storm after a woman.

Enric straightened his shoulders, pulling himself to his full, towering height. "No," he said simply, leveling his gaze with Montag, meeting the challenge.

"She's not yours," Montag hissed.

"If this wild escape is any indication, she's not yours either," Enric pointed out, his tone level.

The men glared at each other for a moment. With the advantage of three to one, it had to be a tempting fight for Montag. Igraine pulled her dagger from her belt, readying herself for the attack.

As Montag stepped his horse closer, Enric shook his head. "Think about that twice, Montag." He motioned toward the keep with his sword. Montag followed his gaze and checked himself, shock registering on his face. His horse stepped back. Enric continued, "I invited my friends over for a little visit."

Igraine followed Enric's gesture and her eyes widened. There in the slits in the stone wall of the keep were arrows, all aimed at her brother and his friends. *How?* The fear of the archers was no laughing matter, and that fear was enough to check her brother's rage.

"You make her a whore," Montag spit at Enric, turning his horse. Brazenly, he offered his back to the archers as he conferred with Lezay and Jean.

Enric and Igraine watched with blades ready as the men spoke quietly.

Then Lezay's voice rose over the others. "You yield too quickly! She needs to come back with us."

"Are you going to take on a tower full of archers?" Montag hissed, his words barely audible. He glanced over his shoulder at the couple. "I'm not dying for her."

Jean motioned the other two men away from the manor. "Montag, you need to get back to the melee. You will need to defend yourself. We can return tomorrow and negotiate for Igraine."

"Did she know?" Lezay spat, his voice burning with anger.

Enric glanced down at Igraine, his eyes questioning. She furrowed her brow in confusion, wondering what Lezay meant.

"You have no choice, Montag," Jean again pointed out. "You have to go back. Deal with her later. She won't get far."

Montag gave Igraine one more cold glare. Then the three men rode back into the remnants of the storm.

Enric took Igraine's arm, keeping his eyes locked on the knights riding away. Gently he pulled her behind him into the keep. His squire appeared and slipped past them out the door, sword drawn. Igraine saw the boy take her horse's reins and run to the stable, the horse trotting eagerly alongside. Then Enric pushed the big door closed behind them. In the quiet away from the raging storm, Igraine caught her breath. She leaned against the door, lungs gasping for air, looking wide-eyed at Enric. Her clothes dripped on the floor. She was soaked to the bone, yet hot from exertion. Her hair had fallen from its pins and hung in a tangled plaster around her back and chest.

Enric studied her, his body still taut, then suddenly smiled. Igraine threw herself into his arms, pressing her lips into his. He met her with a deep passion that tingled with more fire than the storm outside. He pushed her sopping hair out of her face, his strong hands gentle in a caress of her jaw.

"Lady Igraine, does this mean you will be mine?" He searched her eyes.

"Yes, Enric. If you will still have me, I am yours," Igraine breathed.

Enric crushed his lips to hers again, the stubble of his beard rubbing her face. But she did not care. She was safe. She was free.

She pulled away suddenly, aware of an audience.

"Lady Igraine, meet my household." Enric gestured to the haphazard assembly that had gathered at the foot of the stairs, all with sticks and arrows in hand.

"How . . ." Igraine questioned, then realized what Enric had done. "Archers . . ."

Some of the household smiled and held up their arrows.

Enric beamed at her. "I hoped you would come. We all agreed to be as prepared as we could be. Bows may be in short supply here but arrows we can make in plenty."

Igraine was too nervous to smile back. Actual archers would have made her feel considerably safer. "He will be back, Enric. With more men. This is not over for him."

Enric nodded, his face serious again. "I know, my love. But by that time you will be my wife, and we will have told half the kingdom. There will be nothing more he can do then, short of murder, and despite his cruelties, I don't think your brother is that desperate. Now, let me introduce you to Margarite, and she will get you some dry clothes."

Igraine let herself be steered by Enric's solid arms and told herself she would be safe. Still, she could not quell the fear deep in her gut. She'd awoken a beast in her brother she hadn't known existed. Enric didn't know what he was capable of. The brutal murder at the tournament proved even Montag himself didn't know what he was capable of, and that was the most terrifying thought of all.

She pulled back, emotions still thrumming through her veins. "Margarite will have to wait. He's going to come back, Enric. What are we going to do?"

She glanced at the wooden door. Though sturdy, the manor was a weak defense compared to the layers of stone walls, giant portcullis, and full garrison that defended Brunstein. Enric's entire household was at risk. The storm outside was coming down from the height of its fury, which only added to Igraine's worry. When the rain stopped, would the attack begin?

Tenderly, Enric pulled her lips to his. She leaned into him. He held her tighter, her head against his chest with his strong arms around her.

"Igraine, we can do this together. I told you that the moment you walked through this door. With everything I am, I will protect you. You will never have to return to him. And we will make sure everyone knows it, and by that you will have the world's protection as well."

She spoke her last fear against his chest, "What if something happens to you?"

"Nothing is going to happen to me. But if it does, then you do what you did when you made your escape, and you work out the solution. You are smart, Igraine. Don't waste time on worry. Form the contingencies, then move on and take what you get. He's only human, Igraine. He is no more than you or I."

She exhaled a shaky breath. "He killed a man in Poitou, Enric."

"He's killed many, Igraine," Enric said, his tone level. "He's a warrior. It's unfortunate that you had to see it this time."

Igraine exhaled, steadying herself. "When can we do it? Where?"

Enric's eyebrows went up. "Get married?" A smile crept onto his face. "When do you want to?"

"The sooner the better." She was too anxious to be joyful. Practicality necessitated urgency now. Enric was either serious or he wasn't. She narrowed her eyes at him, daring him to come up with an excuse.

"If you'd like, we could leave for Angoulême today . . . as soon as you change into dry clothes. That is where my family lives. And Sir Josse and Sir Louis. We could stay with them, and they would be excellent witnesses."

"How long of a ride?"

"Two days leisurely. One day fast."

"Can we make it by morning?"

Enric smiled at her as if wondering what he had gotten himself into. "If we stop talking so much."

She nodded her head, the wheels turning. "Good." Suddenly a smile lit her features, the smile that had made her famous as the Lady of the Tournament. "I'm tired of sleeping without you, Sir Enric. No more excuses after tomorrow!" With that she pulled away from him, leaving him longing. "You should pack your armor. There's a tournament in Angoulême in a few days."

Igraine passed a middle-aged maid as she rounded the corner, the woman jumping out of her way in surprise. Igraine paused out of sight, the sound of whispers pricking her ears.

"I hope you know what you've gotten into, Sir Levan," the maid was whispering urgently. "She may be pretty, but that woman is fire itself, and you're already dancing in the flames."

Enric's laugh echoed through the entire manor.

Chapter 21

June 6, 1173

Angoulême

Igraine waited in the stairwell of Castle Angoulême, pacing in a borrowed gown. She had known it would take Enric a while to find a priest, but the wait was interminable. Exhaustion from the all-night ride warred with her excitement, leaving her yawning as she paced around the upper corridor. Perhaps it was good that she was too tired to think. She was about to make the biggest decision of her life, and every fiber of her upbringing told her it was the wrong one. She questioned if she shouldn't wait, rest, and think. With a shake of her head she dismissed that idea. She'd had an entire winter to think. She'd made this decision as soon as they'd left Brunstein.

Right or wrong, it was made.

Lady Mary of Angoulême, Sir Louis's wife, laughed as she appeared, a bouquet of flowers in her hand.

"Rest easy. He's back, Lady Igraine." She smiled, handing over the blooms before stepping back to admire her handiwork. She had braided Igraine's blond hair into an elaborate twist that trailed down her back. A borrowed golden circlet settled on her forehead. The long silk chiffon sleeves of the cream-colored gown fluttered from Igraine's elbows like an angel's wings. Igraine had protested against wearing such a rare, expensive fabric, but Mary had insisted it was a worthy occasion.

"It's settled then?" Igraine felt the breath whoosh out of her in relief.

"Yes. Good thing we got you ready." Lady Mary tucked a few absent strands of hair back into Igraine's plait. "The dress looks better on you than it ever did on me," she murmured.

"I'm sure—"

"Lady Igraine, you don't have to be so modest. We all know you're the Lady of the Tournament." Mary squeezed her fingers in assurance. "I like you just the same."

"You are too kind. We woke you in the middle of the night, and you've supplied us with all this—" She gestured to the gown. "How can I ever repay you?"

"Sir Enric is a good friend to my husband. Treat him well, and that is all we need in return." She smiled. "Now let's get you to your groom! He brought a few people you should meet."

She heard the flurry of enthusiasm before they even reached the foyer. Igraine peered around a corner, watching surreptitiously as two grey-haired people fluttered around Enric. The woman fussed with Enric's unruly hair and straightened his tunic, the blue Levan crest bright across his chest. The man smiled and watched with amusement, his arms crossed. His enormous build left no doubt in Igraine's mind. She was watching the Levans.

Sir Levan was as tall as his son, with bowed legs that looked like they were permanently wrapped around a horse. His grey hair lay askew on his head, his face weathered from years outside. Lady Levan was small in comparison to her husband and son. It was amazing that she had born the giant man she was currently kissing on the cheek. Her grey hair was pulled back in a tight chignon, not a hair out of place. Neither of them was dressed in rich fabrics or carried embellishments like regular nobility. Really, if it wasn't for their regal stature, Igraine would have passed them on the street as commoners.

Igraine stepped around the corner.

Every eye in the room locked on her as she came into view. A few mouths dropped open. Igraine hesitated, then plunged ahead, her shoulders squared like the lady she was. She must look like a queen compared to the lower nobility before her. She shot a glance at Enric, wondering if it was too much, but the bright smile of appreciation and love he was giving her erased all worry.

"I see why she is the Lady of the Tournament," Sir Levan muttered to his wife.

Lady Levan elbowed him, then strode up to Igraine, taking her hands in her own weathered palms. "It is such a pleasure to finally meet you, my lady." She bowed gracefully.

Igraine tensed in panic. No noblewoman should be bowing to her. When the older woman straightened, Igraine dipped her knee almost to the ground. "It is my honor to meet you, Lady Levan." The elder woman flushed pink in appreciation, pulling Igraine to her feet. She laid a gentle hand on her cheek. "You are a sweet one; this I know already." She smiled. As she glanced from Enric to Igraine she became overwhelmed with emotion. "I thought this day would never come. Finally. Enric, get this woman to the church!" She patted Igraine's hand. "We will talk later. I heard Louis has a grand feast planned for you two."

Enric smiled and offered Igraine his arm. "Are you ready, my lady?"

Igraine took a deep breath and allowed herself a smile, despite the nerves.

"Any last doubts?" he whispered in her ear as they walked arm in arm with their small procession to the little chapel.

"Lots of them," she admitted.

"Any worthy of turning around?"

"No." She squeezed his arm.

Enric again leaned into her ear. "I, uh, apologize in advance if the priest is a little short with us. Josse had to — insinuate — some things to his brother to get him to agree to perform the ceremony. No one else would, without your family present."

Igraine's eyes went wide. "He insinuated what?"

Josse appeared at Igraine's side. "Really, my middle brother isn't such a bad man. He's just a little cranky."

Igraine glanced back to Enric, who had his eyes locked straight ahead and his jaw clenched.

"It'll be fine," Josse assured, then skipped ahead of them, offering his arm to Lady Levan.

The chapel was a small one-room limestone building. The priest was a man of few words who could not look Igraine — or Enric — in the eye. In a short whirlwind of words, Igraine became Enric's wife. The emotion ran strong in both of them as he slid a thin gold band onto her finger. "Forever," Enric whispered, looking her in the eye and squeezing her hand.

"I love you," she whispered back.

Enric couldn't help himself and pulled her into a passionate kiss in front of everyone. Their friends cheered. Enric's parents beamed at them. The priest ducked out of the chapel.

Louis led the way back to his massive castle. He furnished a wedding feast for the small party, during which Igraine came to love her new in-laws and their welcoming demeanor. She didn't eat much, the excitement of the last few days wearing on her nerves. Even though she had chosen this, she was acutely aware that she was a married woman now. Things would be expected of her. Her witty tongue would not protect her innocence anymore.

She took a long sip of her wine, eyeing Enric over the rim. He was watching her, as he had been all night. The lust and love were written all over his face, each indiscernible from the other. Her heart pounded harder. She refilled her glass.

His fingers closed on hers. "I think you've had enough." His voice had a husky note to it.

She closed her eyes to steady herself against the flood of heat that seemed to rush from his hand into hers. His fingers were caressing hers now, pulling away the glass to fill her hand with his own.

"I don't want you in a fog of wine," he whispered. "I want you to be with me for every moment. I will stay true to your desire, Lady Igraine. You will not sleep alone." He kissed her temple lightly, and she had to bite her lip to keep from making a sound. Her fingers trembled.

"Ahem," Josse cleared his throat from across the table. "Louis, I think our newlyweds need to retire. Please tell me you found them a place nice and . . . isolated . . . within the castle?"

Igraine and Enric both blushed with embarrassment as the entire table broke out in laughter. Lady Mary rose from her chair, rolling her eyes. "Come with me, you two. You can leave the wine. I had food and wine sent to your room already." She led the way out of the hall to a chorus of well-wishes, made all the more embarrassing by the presence of Enric's parents. They spent several minutes winding through the castle, Igraine paying far more attention to the caress of Enric's thumb on the back of her hand than to where they were going.

"It's not much, but on such short notice the best I could do was get it cleaned up for you," Lady Mary apologized, pushing open a small door.

Igraine noted the huge, wooden-post bed with crisp white bedding. The floor was swept immaculately, and though there were piles of old furniture and clutter pushed to one side, they were covered in clean drop cloths. A stag-skin rug lay at the foot of the bed. On it sat a carved wooden chest containing clean clothes for both of them. Narrow archer slits were the only windows in the room, and they let in a slight breeze along with the rays of sunset light. Several unlit torches lined the walls in sconces. Enric released Igraine's hand only long enough to light one from a torch in the hall. The room suddenly was flooded with the firelight.

"It's perfect," Igraine breathed.

The lady of the manor beamed and bowed herself out. Now, finally, they were alone.

"Husband?" Igraine smiled. She took a single step toward him.

"Wife?" Enric raised an eyebrow. "Want another glass of wine?"

She shook her head and took another step to him.

"Want to go watch the sunset?"

"We have windows." She took another step.

"Want to go for a ride?"

"Hmm." She took the final step to him, now right under his nose, skirts swelling around his legs. She waited for him to make the last move.

Enric smirked at her, teasing. He waited until she was about to give up with impatience, then suddenly scooped her up in his arms and carried her, his lips already busy on hers. She let out a shriek as he dropped her on the bed but was silenced by his mouth as he knelt over her, forcing her back, covering her. One arm propped his body from crushing her while his hand roamed from her hip to her breast, touching the places he had withheld from for so long.

It wasn't enough.

Igraine pulled him into her, her neck stretching toward him so he could kiss her harder, her hands grasping his hips as she pulled him against her pelvis, which she subconsciously tipped toward him. In one slow movement, Enric grasped her layers of skirts and raised them, exposing her thighs. His hand followed the bare skin up and around until he could grasp her muscular backside. She gasped against his lips, flushing hot.

Enric stepped away, his breath heavy. In one movement, he removed his shirt, dropping it to the floor. Igraine's eyes went wide at the contours of his chest, an artwork of chiseled muscle. Enric offered her his hand, and gently pulled her from the bed. Now on her feet, she ran her hands down that solid chest, tracing every line as if to commit it to memory. When her hands reached the curve of the muscles that led to his groin, he shifted. With a mischievous smile, she circled him, studying him, now performing the same examination of his back, while he stood totally still for her, satiating her curiosity. She stopped when she saw the burn marks that spotted his back like a fawn's hide.

"My God . . ." She let out her voice in a gasp.

"They disgust you?" Enric looked away from her.

"No," she managed to say. Gently she caressed and kissed each one, leaving tears behind on his skin as she went.

When she was finished, she stood in front of him and slowly turned her back to him. She pulled her hair to the side, exposing the laces of her gown. Enric worked them loose from the bottom up, till the fabric split from her body. He kissed her shoulders as he slid the fabric off her to a puddle at her feet, leaving only her shift. He pulled that off one shoulder, then the next, kissing as he went. It fell free, leaving her completely naked.

A few wisps of hair fell back over Igraine's back, but not before Enric caught sight of the smattering of burn scars. He gasped.

She looked at him out of the corner of her eye. "My father branded you, didn't he?" Enric had never elaborated on what had happened between him and her father, but the marks were Raganor's signature.

"Yes." Still he stared at her in shock. "And you? What could you have possibly done to deserve this? His own daughter!"

She shrugged. "Montag's back is the worst. I learned pretty quick." She turned to face him. He swallowed, his eyes roaming up and down her bare body. "But that's all behind us now, right?"

He claimed her mouth again, touching her most intimate places until she threw her head back with a moan.

Igraine's fingers worked at Enric's belt, pushing his breeches over his hips to free what she wanted most from him. It did not intimidate her. Purity was not ignorance to the shape of the male body. The culture of the tourneys had made sure of that. Enric pulled off his boots and stepped out of his breeches. Now there were no barriers between them.

Igraine sat on the edge of the bed, and he covered her, sinking back with her into it. He worked his kiss down her body. When he returned to her lips, she felt the urgency in him now. Her body surged with fire, longing for him.

"I love you, Igraine." He shifted his weight. The pain was brief, the feeling full, and they laid like that for a moment, in shock at their joining. Then Enric moved, and Igraine did her best to follow his dance. It was a dance into ecstasy, the pent-up desire after years of denial leading them both to a most exquisite release.

Chapter 22

T hey lay entwined together, sweat beaded on their brows. After a long while, the sleepy euphoria faded, and Igraine traced the spotted scars of Enric's back. He lay on his stomach, arms pillowing his head. His eyes studied her face as if trying to memorize every detail. She could only imagine what he saw. Her normally immaculate hair was tangled around her. Her lips felt swollen from his kiss. And from his worried touch with a single finger, she knew her slender neck was marred by a faint bruise where perhaps he had kissed her just a little too hard.

"Why you?" she wondered aloud, a finger tracing each scar as if to read them like a map.

He rolled to his side and faced her, propping his head on his elbow. He caught her hand and pressed her fingers to his lips. "I could say the same. You were only a girl, I assume?"

"Yes," Igraine said quietly. "But Montag and I, we are his children. We deserved to be punished. At least some of the time." She blinked away a darker thought. "You are a grown man. You met in Jerusalem?"

"Yes," Enric whispered. He caressed her cheek as they lay facing each other on the bed. "Are you sure you want to know this now? It's not a story I planned to tell on our wedding night. I didn't think you would recognize the scars as Raganor's mark. I could have made up a story — saving someone from a burning house or some heroic thing. I didn't know he hurt you . . . What kind of man would hurt *you*?"

"Raganor is a different kind of beast altogether." She lay back, staring at the ceiling. "My brother banished him back to Jerusalem. He can reign in terror there."

Enric turned her face to his own, frowning. "What do you mean 'Montag banished him'?"

Igraine turned back to the ceiling, unable to meet the intensity of her new husband's eyes. Blue they were. Stark blue that glowed even in the dim light. "He came to Brunstein maybe three weeks ago. Montag made him leave. He has been acting lord for years, but he has claimed the title for good now."

Enric let out a whistle. "Raganor was in Alsace?"

She nodded.

Enric rolled onto his back, then abruptly pushed off the bed, still stark naked. Igraine propped herself on an elbow, watching him with appreciation. He poured himself a glass of wine, turning his back to her. She studied the burn scars, noting they seemed deliberate, almost like a pattern, but pushed the thought from her mind. It was a coincidence. When she and Montag were burned, it was wherever the sword point reached first. Sometimes the area burned was small, sometimes large. It was quick, painful, and done. Burn the flesh to purge the soul.

Enric drained the cup, then set it down on the table with a deliberate click. "I didn't want to talk about this on our wedding night."

"We don't have to," Igraine complied automatically, though she had a million questions.

Enric slowly turned to her. "I think we need to."

Igraine blushed as she stared at her husband's lower half. "Then you need to get at least partially dressed, because that—" she pointed— "is far too distracting."

Enric didn't smile, but he picked his breeches off the floor and pulled them on before settling on the bed next to her. Igraine pulled the linen sheet up over herself, then sat up in the bed, waiting for him to begin. He was so distracted by his thoughts that he didn't even notice her continued nakedness. The gravity of that observation made her palms sweat.

"I first went to Jerusalem in anno 1168. My father is a horse breeder, as you know. My family has old noble blood, particularly on my mother's side, but we have not had land or title for generations. We rented our land from the Lord of Angoulême, which is how I befriended Louis and Josse.

We traded and sold our stock all over the world. Anyway, the Crusaders had been focused on Egypt, and they were in constant need of horses. We took as many as we could afford to ship, and we sold them in Jerusalem. It was the best sale we ever made." Enric smiled, remembering something.

"There was this one horse though, a big stallion. He was a handful. He tested me to my limit, but he was also the most athletic horse I've ever sat on. Well, we tried to sell him, but no one else could ride him. They didn't think he could handle the stress of battle without becoming a bane himself. So I challenged all the knights I could to a tournament. I won. He was faster than their horses, more enduring, and when he listened to me, so steady. Still, no one would buy him. But I did catch the attention of one knight who was looking for a squire."

"My father?"

Enric nodded. "I saw it as my chance to become a titled knight. My father saw it as slavery. He wasn't happy when I told him I was going to stay in Jerusalem as Lord Raganor's squire. But I did. Best and worst decision I've ever made." Enric grew quiet.

Igraine took his hand, giving it a squeeze.

"I have not told anyone what happened in Jerusalem other than the obvious fact that I was knighted."

"You must have been a good squire. You were knighted quickly."

"From training the horses I already had the horsemanship. My father taught me what he knew of weaponry, which was a decent bit; I knew at least something going in. Most importantly, I was strong. Raganor — and his wild manor of squires — taught me how to fight pretty quickly. He runs a brutal training program."

Igraine snorted. "I know."

Enric sighed and ran a hand through his hair. "What I didn't know was that he had an ulterior motive for knighting me. I needed to be ordained for what he had in mind. I was a perfect candidate. Noble blooded, but not so noble that anyone would have the power to come looking for me across the world if I were to disappear." He closed his eyes.

After a long silence, Igraine realized he could not continue; whatever memories he held were playing behind his eyelids. Her heart pounded as her own memories flared to a night when she was only a child, hiding in the wine cellar at Brunstein. She put a trembling hand to her lips. That night had not been an isolated incident, as she had hoped all these years. Raganor had left Brunstein and taken his evil with him to Jerusalem. The horrible truth leaked from her lips.

"And then he drugged you." She closed her eyes, hoping she was wrong, as images from her own past flashed behind her eyes.

When she opened them, Enric was staring at her. "God, tell me he didn't do it to you and your brother, too."

Igraine shook her head vehemently. "Our burns came as punishment."

"Punishment?" His words were a whisper under his breath.

Igraine squeezed his arm, knowing that his own experience had been far different. "For us it was. Much like other fathers take a switch to a child's backside when they are naughty." She hesitated, uncertain of how to reveal what she knew of his ordeal. And that he had not been the only one. "Once, when I was maybe twelve, I saw the ceremony."

He took a sharp breath. "How much of it?"

"How did you survive?"

"Before . . . the man didn't?"

Igraine shook her head. "Enric, when we first met, you said you knew our family secret. How would *you* word it?"

"Your father is involved in some kind of dark order of knighthood. They are the contrast to Christian knights, despite public appearances. And powerful. Men in high positions by title or wealth or geography. More than that. I don't — I can't remember enough."

Igraine nodded slightly. He knew enough for her to talk then. She wove her fingers into his as the words dropped from her like the beginning of a downpour. "We still don't know what kind of organization he's a part of. I stumbled into it innocently. I don't even remember what I was looking for, but I ended up in the cellars. They didn't see me, and I hid, full of curiosity. There was a man — I understand now he was drugged — on what I can only describe as an altar. Other men gathered around. There was a fire. They burned him with a rod, but he didn't seem to mind. Montag found me then. He was just as shocked as I. Keep in mind he's older than me by eleven years, so he was already a knight, already a man. He hid with me, and I remember he told me to go back upstairs. I was going to, but then something with the ceremony changed. It was horrible, Enric." She shuddered at the memory of burning flesh, spurting blood. The screams from that night still echoed in her memory. "The man screamed. Then I screamed."

Enric pulled her into his arms. Her heart pounded like what she had witnessed had happened yesterday, not years ago. Enric's body was tense. What memories must be surfacing within a man who had undergone the ordeal? She was afraid to hurt him further by digging into these dark memories.

"Montag protected me from the wrath of our father. He always did. This time was different. Raganor knew we had witnessed something we could use against him . . . murder. He was scared — of us! It made him lethal, a total fiend to the household." Igraine shuddered, remembering how she had been afraid to leave her room in those days. "In order to protect all of us, Montag came into his own. He fought my father and almost died in the process. Raganor is a practical man and knows he can not kill his only heir. Montag is the one that told Raganor to leave for Jerusalem. To 'seek forgiveness for his sins.'

"We never speak of it, never asked questions. Montag may know more about what we witnessed, but I don't want to. I do know that other people who asked questions ended up dead." Igraine shook her head, thinking of the invitation she'd found in Montag's office. "I had hoped he found God in Jerusalem. I was wrong. Enric, I'm so sorry."

Enric's arms tightened around her.

"How did you survive?" she whispered, thinking back to the horrible memory of the man who had never had a chance to escape.

Enric kissed her forehead. "I've wondered it often myself, as it was pretty obvious that I was the first that had ever gotten off their table. I can only guess that I burned through their drugs quicker than I should have. Maybe someone mixed them wrong. Maybe I'm naturally immune. And after the pain of the burns . . . it was enough to allow me to panic. I fought my way out. I was spooked. I hid until the drugs wore off, then I got on a ship and sailed home. I left my horses and my armor. I came home to my family to start fresh, penniless. At least I kept my title. Competing in tournaments gave me the reputation and respect of a champion."

Igraine studied his face as he pulled back from her, again lost to his thoughts. "Why didn't you tell me? All this time . . . my father was so cruel to you and yet you've been nothing but kind to me. You've had so many opportunities to ruin me, Enric." She laughed, thinking back to when she'd begged him to touch her, and he'd remained respectful. "You missed out on them all."

"I don't understand how anyone could hurt you, Igraine." He kissed her lightly. "And I am too grateful to be alive to waste time on revenge."

Igraine smiled as she nuzzled into his palm. Her face softened as she sighed. "How is it that my father hurt you, yet it is he I defied to love you?"

"I think our paths were fated to cross, Igraine."

"You think?"

"How else would I have survived Jerusalem to marry and love the daughter of my enemy?"

Igraine tilted her face to his and kissed him lightly. "Love her, you say?"

"Yes." He laced his fingers into hers. His face fell as thoughts continued to brew. "Igraine, is he going to come after you? Or will it only be Montag?"

"Montag is threat enough." She shivered.

Enric pulled her in close to him, curling her into his chest as they lay together on the bed. She nestled comfortably into the crook of his arm. After a long, thoughtful silence Enric whispered, "We'll face whatever comes together." He kissed her brow. Igraine closed her eyes, and true to Enric's promise, she did not sleep alone.

Chapter 23

"**I**t's her!"

"She's back!"

"Who's she with?"

"Sir Enric! Sir Enric!"

The crowd picked up the chant as their champion strode among them. Igraine smiled so widely her cheeks hurt and for once, it was real. Her arm looped around her husband's. Enric waved at the crowd, reveling in the attention, then suddenly jumped onto a wagon, giving the crowd of Angoulême a better view of his already towering form. He pulled Igraine up on the wagon next to him, holding her to his side.

"My good people!" Enric shouted. "It is wonderful to be back to tournament with you all! You must forgive my hiatus. You see, I've had quite the adventure to preoccupy me. May I introduce to you my wife? The lovely Lady Igraine . . . de Levan!"

The crowd broke out into a round of applause and laughter as Enric planted a quick kiss on Igraine's lips and lowered them both back to the ground. The crowd dispersed, with well-wishers patting Enric on the back and extending their congratulations.

When the time came for the contest, Enric left Igraine in the stands with a bow and gentlemanly kiss, her scarf tied tightly around his armored bicep.

"You did well to catch that one," a lady nudged Igraine. "Handsome *and* talented."

"He is." She nodded agreement, her eyes lingering on her knight as he made his way toward his squire. Though they had only been married mere days, she felt as if she lived a fairytale. Enric was everything she had hoped for in a husband. Her life with him, despite still being unsettled as guests in a friend's castle in Angoulême, was so different from her cold, calculated existence in Brunstein. She could breathe.

"I'm surprised your brother let you settle for a poorer man," another lady cut in.

Igraine's attention snapped to her, her eyebrows raised. The thin-faced willow of a woman was dwarfed by her high-backed chair. "Forgive me, I don't believe we've met."

The woman glared at Igraine. "Of course we haven't met." Her accent was rich, Germanic, but she did not speak further, instead turning back to the events commencing.

The woman on Igraine's left leaned toward her. "She is Lady Agnes . . . from Hesse. Her father just decided to pursue finding her a suitor. Ridiculously high dowry. They say he won't settle for less than a prince."

Igraine nodded and let her attention return to the competition. Oh how she missed Alenor. Her friend's small talk had always made the time pass quickly, and though the ladies around her were polite, except for Agnes, they were strangers and as such did not include her in their conversations. Ladies Mary and Isabel would have been good company, but they, as tournament hosts, were preoccupied. Igraine watched in silence, accepting occasional congratulations as Enric succeeded in his events. Mercifully, the usual line of suitors vying for her attention was absent. Enric's claim had been made loud and clear, and he reinforced it with his sword.

By the end of the day, he was Tournament Champion.

As she and Enric walked arm-in-arm back to their tent that night, she leaned into his strong shoulder. He winced. She apologized and stepped away, knowing he must be bruised from the many blows he'd taken during the tournament.

"How many tournaments are you going to compete in? I didn't think I would feel a difference, but I do. You are a part of me, and when you hurt, I hurt."

"I will be fine, Igraine. You know this is what I do. And I'm good at it."

"How many?"

Enric chuckled. "This year? As many as I can get myself invited to. I want every knight in all of Europe to know you are mine. I will announce our marriage and pledge my victory to you at every one. We will be traveling quite a bit, my love. I hope your years traveling with your brother have prepared you."

Igraine sighed. "I don't have much choice, do I?"

Enric stopped, gently turning her to face him. He pulled her chin up to look her in the eye. "Igraine, you always have a choice with me. If you say no, we will go home. But know if we go home, we will be short on funding, I will be short on practice, and we leave your brother to spread whatever rumors he wishes. By competing, we gain all of that. We control the rumors. We stay ahead of Montag. And your father for that matter. Isn't that what you want?"

"Yes," she admitted.

He kissed her deeply, then pulled her tight. "Trust me, Igraine. I am good at what I do. You cannot worry about a knight. There would be naught left for anything else. We will live with confidence, and God forbid something does happen, we will deal with it."

They joined the other knights in the castle that night, feasting, dancing, and laughing. Igraine again missed Alenor. How her friend would have loved to be there, gossiping and laughing with her. The thought stilled her for a moment as she took another sip of her wine. Her eyes flicked across the room to Alenor's brother Stephen, who had competed. She quickly glanced away. He was openly staring at her, and it was not a friendly gaze. Did he suspect what her brother had done?

Igraine pretended to turn back to the conversation Enric was having with Josse, but a shiver ran down her spine. She hadn't told Enric what Montag had done to the daughter of one of the most powerful men in Europe. When a man cleared his throat behind her, she swallowed hard, closing her eyes for a moment before slowly turning to face Stephen. His gaze was cold, bubbling fury behind the veil of his eyes. Enric was still deep in conversation, and though he was only feet away, Igraine wondered if he was too far to feel the palpable anger that seethed off the man behind her.

She forced a smile, falling into character. "Sir Stephen, how are you?"

He stared into her eyes, and she felt her smile falter. "We need to talk. Alone."

Igraine glanced at Enric. Still in conversation, he noted Stephen and smiled and nodded at the man. Stephen gave a friendly nod back, his own bright smile plastered on his face until Enric turned away. It faded like the moon slipping behind a cloud as he again focused on Igraine. He nodded toward the end of the hall.

Igraine felt obligated to follow, so with a last glance over her shoulder at Enric, she worked through the crowd after

Stephen. Enric turned to watch her with furrowed brow, but she motioned with a finger that she would be back in a moment. Stephen stepped into the quiet, drafty outer hall. She thought he would stop there, that they could talk, but instead he made a sharp right into a narrow corridor.

"Where are you going?" Igraine protested, after a few steps into the darkness. "What do you want?"

"I want to know the truth of what happened to my sister." Stephen didn't stop walking. The corridor was angled slightly down into the depths below the castle. It bent sharply left and Igraine stopped just beyond the bend, where the last rays of light from the torches in the hall were visible.

"We can talk, but I'm not going any further," she insisted. Her heart hammered in her chest. She should just go back to the party. Footsteps sounded from the corridor behind her, and she spun to face the second Tielo brother, a pimpled teenaged squire. She looked back and forth between the two of them. "What is this?" Every nerve in her body tingled. They were just beyond the bend of the hallway. No one from the hall could see them.

"What did he do to her?" Stephen questioned. He crossed his arms over his chest, but the younger brother's hand hovered near the short dagger on his hip.

"The birth was terrible," Igraine said quietly. "I'm so sorry for your loss. She was my best friend, a true sister. We did all we could." She didn't have to fake the tears that leaked from the corners of her eyes. The emotion was real. She hastily wiped at them as they blurred her vision in the dim torchlight.

"Where is her body then? Why were we not invited to a funeral?" Stephen asked.

"They didn't have a funeral," the teenage Tielo spit out.

Igraine shook her head. "You're right. I . . . I don't know. Montag is . . . set in his ways when it comes to things like that. He had it taken care of before I myself could even say goodbye. I think it helps him grieve . . ."

"What of our grief? My family's closure? Do you know what this has done to my mother?" Stephen hissed.

"You need to speak with my brother about it." Igraine looked at him earnestly, hoping he would understand.

"We have sent a dozen letters with a dozen messengers. The only word my family has received is that Alenor is dead, and the child was a healthy boy. That was months ago. My mother has asked to meet her grandson. We get no reply. My father has asked where she is buried, that he may donate to that church. We get no reply. I have invited Montag to meet me at a tournament of his choosing. I get no reply. To us it seems like he has taken my sister's dowry, used her like a broodmare, and killed her. Am I far off?"

The words stung in their truth, but she could never admit it without incriminating Montag. She wiped her palms on her skirts as she avoided Stephen's eye. "It was a horrible birth . . ."

"Where is your brother?"

"At Brunstein, I imagine. I don't know."

"And you don't know where Alenor is buried?"

"No."

The younger brother groaned in frustration. "Will you at least talk to him? Have him contact us? Let our mother meet her grandson?"

"I . . . I can't . . ." Igraine stammered.

"Right, the Lady of the Tournament is powerless after all. Isn't she?" the younger brother snorted. He turned to Stephen. "Maybe she was too busy planning her own wedding to plan our sister's funeral."

Igraine glared at him. "How dare you . . ."

The younger man continued to taunt, "I bet she didn't even have a real wedding. Certainly didn't bother to invite us, now that our sister is dead. She's probably already halfway along with Enric's bastard."

Igraine continued to glare at the young man, her own Le Brun fury bubbling forth from months of pent-up anguish. She clenched her fists at her sides, gritted her teeth, and fought for the control to silently return to the hall. She moved to sidestep the youngest brother, only to be snatched back. In seconds, Stephen had her by the throat, pressed up against the wall. His hand was firm enough to threaten, not to harm. It scared her nonetheless.

"You don't fool me, Lady Igraine. You are the only one brazen enough to control your brother, and you know what happened to my sister. I want the truth, and I want her body, so my family can have the closure we deserve. And if her death was in any way unnatural, I don't need to warn you that your brother will pay. An eye for an eye . . ."

"A sister for a sister," the younger one smirked.

"I told you all I know." Igraine croaked. Her hands clamped around his, trying to push him away but not standing a chance against the sinewy muscle of the knight. "I left my brother if you must know. I cannot help you." Stephen's fingers began to tighten in threat and her eyes grew wide. She squirmed, trying to knee him, but he kept her skirts pinned in with his knees that she could hardly move.

"What the hell is going on here?" an angry voice sounded from their right. Igraine breathed a sigh of relief as Stephen's fingers instantly disappeared, and she was freed from the wall. Enric stood glowering at the two younger men, glancing back and forth between them as he tried to piece together the inappropriate scene before him. Igraine rubbed her neck and looked away, well aware that her entrapment with Stephen could have just as much looked like a lover's embrace as it did the threat it was. She was the idiot that had followed him down the corridor. Montag had warned her not to be caught alone so many times before; what would Enric do?

The younger brother tried to edge past Enric, but the big man merely had to put out a hand to stop him, and he backed toward his brother. "Explain." Enric glowered at Stephen.

"We needed to talk. We talked. I think we've reached an understanding." Stephen said, shooting Igraine a look laced with their warning. *A sister for a sister.*

"And what understanding is that, exactly?" Enric persisted.

"Enric, it's fine. Let's go. It's late," Igraine gently pushed his chest toward the hall.

Enric held up a hand to her, silencing her without turning his gaze from the Tielos. "I want to have a little something made clear myself. You do not touch my wife. You do not talk to my wife. You assault her again, your lord will know about it. And then I will not be merciful when we meet in combat. Understood?"

The two men were silent a long moment. Stephen then spoke quietly, "I see her ownership has changed after all."

Enric glanced at Igraine, and she was surprised that he was smiling. He twined an arm gently around her shoulders and steered her away from the men. Igraine caught the glance on their confused faces before they were lost to the darkness of the passage. They may not understand Enric's actions, but she did. He had won her, not by price, but because she wanted to be his. He did own her heart, and he knew it. He knew, because she had his as well.

Chapter 24

Montag stomped his foot at one of the dogs as it trotted down the hall, a ham bone in its teeth. The dog flinched to the side, warily eyeing him, then continued on his way, shooting only a glance over its shoulder before ducking around the corner. Montag had noticed the staff had been treating him much the same as the dog, warily eyeing him, gauging his mood, then continuing on with their business as if nothing was amiss. Ignoring him, as if they judged him to be fine.

He was not fine. He was a roiling mess inside.

A baby's scream echoed down the hall, putting Montag's nerves even more on edge. He gritted his teeth as the wails continued. When it did not cease, he turned down the narrow corridor toward the sound, slamming the door open to the room where a wide-eyed nurse was desperately trying to soothe his son. The boy's wide eyes looked at him from over the nurse's shoulder, then he began his screams with renewed force.

"Get. Him. Quiet," Montag growled.

"I'm trying," the young nurse said in a small voice. "He's teething. His poor little mouth hurts him—"

Montag spun on his heel, slamming the door shut behind him, which did little to dampen the little boy's screams. One of his squires jogged down the hall towards him.

"My lord, your big destrier is colicing. What would you like us to do? We've been walking him for hours. He doesn't want to stand anymore."

Montag stopped and rubbed his forehead, where a headache bloomed in full force. "Which one?"

"The black one," the boy said nervously.

Montag had always held a certain detachment from his animals. He bought and sold them often. But this particular horse was an exquisite animal. "Adelbern," he whispered. "Any idea why?"

"No, sir. But the last delivery of hay was less than ideal."

"And why did you feed it if it was bad?" He let the ice lace his tone.

The squire frowned. "You told me not to waste it, my lord. And we didn't have any other. The manor's first cutting hasn't been dried yet. It's been a rainy year."

Montag groaned. That was his fault. He had been told, and in the whirlwind of other tasks he was doing, he'd forgotten to send for new hay so the bad hay could be disposed of. Now his best horse was dying. "Do what you can. Tell the horsemaster the final decision is in his hands. Then burn that moldy hay and send a wagon wherever it needs to go to get more. Today."

"We'll need coin to purchase new hay, my lord."

Montag sighed and pulled his coin purse from his belt. He drew what he figured would be more than enough, then held out the coins. His hand hovered over the squire's open palm. "If I don't get the change back that this order requires, I will cut off your sword hand myself. Do you understand?" The boy nodded, and Montag let the coins drop. The squire ran off at a sprint.

Montag again rubbed his forehead. Ordering things like grain and hay fell under management of the castle. Which fell under the role of the woman of the manor. Of which there was none. Montag let out a long line of expletives as he stalked back to his study, slamming the doors at both the foot and the top of the spiral stairwell. He fell into his chair, his head in his hands, elbows on his knees.

He could not, would not, admit that he missed them. Igraine had betrayed him, abandoned him. He would not grieve for her. She had made her bed, and now whatever happened to her was on her own conscience. Alenor . . . his thoughts wandered, envisioning her on the back of the wagon as it rolled away into the first rays of dawn, her face pained, her eyes locked into his as if he was going to change his mind, order the wagon to stop, allow her to return.

Had she survived, or were his words to his father true, and he had killed her?

A tremble ran through his shoulders. He swallowed, pressing his lips together and squinting his eyes so tight they watered. His shoulders shook again, and he gasped. He pictured his screaming son, his dying destrier, Alenor's expression as she realized he was sending her out of his life, Igraine's expression as she stood behind Enric as if he was her shield.

He pressed to his feet and threw his chair across the room in a shout of rage that echoed back to him. Then he stood in the middle of the room, his shoulders rising and falling with his breath. He cracked each knuckle of his hand in order, then calmly walked over and picked up the chair. It was no worse for the wear. Thank goodness for quality craftsmanship. He set the chair in front of the desk and settled into it. With a deep breath, he slit open the seal of the first letter in a pile of correspondence without noting the crest.

It was a mistake. His head throbbed anew, and he skewered the parchment right through the signature line with his dagger. The metal vibrated over the name Tielo. Montag pushed back away from his desk, backing into a corner, pulling his hair in tufts from his temples. Normally, he would head out on his favorite horse and go for a ride to calm down. But he could not go anywhere near the stables right now, not if they were dealing with the horse. He slid down the wall to his haunches, wrists slack on his knees, and finally let his head fall in defeat.

He fought the shaking of his shoulders until he could no longer, then let the sobs rip from his chest. He prayed no one heard, that whatever spy still lingered in Brunstein would not tell Raganor of his son's weakness. And for once, he prayed that he would one day be strong enough to handle it all on his own. He would have to be. He would be.

This was the last time he would lose control.

Chapter 25

E nric exited the swordsmith's shop with a smile on his face and a small package in his hand. They'd been on the road for months, hopping tournament to tournament. Igraine had hardly been without an escort after the incident with the Tielo family, yet there she was in the middle of an open street in Poitiers, waiting for Enric to get out of the shop. And now that he'd emerged with something far smaller than a sword, she was baffled as to why he was so excited.

Her look must have said it all, for he chuckled and beamed at her as he handed her the package. "Forgive me, ma chère. A belated wedding present. I wish it had been done weeks ago."

"From a swordsmith?" Igraine asked with confusion. She took the cloth-wrapped package and untied it. Her eyes flicked to his as they took in the dagger. It was so like Lezay's that it gave her chills, which she recognized as foolish. She'd purposely left that blade at Levan Manor before they left for Angoulême, sick of the memories it evoked. As she looked closer she noted Enric's crest of three linked disks engraved on the hilt. Partial relief surged. "An odd style to choose," she ventured. She carefully unsheathed it. It felt comfortable in her hand. Balanced, maybe?

"You seemed pretty capable with it before I met you."

Igraine looked at him again, her eyebrows knitted. Why were his eyes still twinkling with mischief? She glanced back at the blade, noticing that there were faint scratches and dents, that though professionally sharpened, told that the dagger had seen use in the past. She frowned, studying the hilt closer. The same interwoven wire handle. The same bronze block for the hand. Only the crest on the end of the hilt was different. "Did you . . . ?"

Enric beamed. "I had it remade for you. I know it isn't much, but you seemed to like it, except for the former owner's crest." He shrugged. "Now it's yours." He hesitated as emotions flashed over her face. "If you don't like it I'll get you a new one . . . your choice. We just have to wait until after the next tournament, after I win a bit more . . ."

Igraine's face broke into a smile. What irony, that she'd stolen the blade from her enemy and now it had Enric's . . . *her* . . . crest embellishing it. She held it to the light to admire it. It actually was rather beautifully made, especially now that it was all polished and resharpened. That blade looked sharp enough for a man to shave with.

Enric seemed relieved. "I know you are already pretty adept with it, but we're going to practice a bit more. I don't want to find you pinned to the wall in a dark corridor ever again."

"Fair enough." She still smiled as she sheathed the dagger and tied its belt to her side. She reached up and kissed Enric. "It's a perfect wedding gift," she whispered against his lips. She pressed her hips into him, and he groaned.

"Come on, woman. We have a lot of riding yet to do today."

"Yes, we do." She winked at him as they remounted their horses. Thankfully, the next destination wasn't too much further. They were on their way to yet another tournament, this time closer to Enric's manor. There were many others on the road that week, as this tournament was one of the largest yet, at the grand Chateau Poitiers. Enric had been looking forward to it for weeks before they were even wed and now, more than ever, he wanted to use this very public event to declare their marriage. The Duke of Aquitaine, Richard, would be there, as would many nobles from surrounding countries. Once everyone at the tournament knew of the marriage, everyone in Europe would know.

Montag would know they were married beyond contest.

The thought settled heavy in the pit of Igraine's stomach. Would he be there? Would there be a confrontation? Would he challenge Enric? Would he try to kidnap her back to Brunstein? Her mind raced as they traveled the last few miles through the winding streets of the city. There were people everywhere. Inns overflowed, and the tent encampment of the visiting knights sprawled across the tournament fields near the castle. The smells of food and humans and manure filled her nose as the noise of hundreds of people surrounded her. This was one of the largest tournaments in the world, a showcase of several nations' talent. Igraine's horse shied sideways as a noisy cart bounced by only a handsbreadth away on the crowded street.

"Let's eat and then we can find a place to set up our camp," Enric practically had to yell to her.

She nodded in agreement. The squire Pierre took their horses and led them toward the tournament stabling area as she and Enric browsed the vendors for food.

Igraine froze and laid a hand on Enric's arm. "Look." She pointed at the lanky man across the street, seated at a table outside a tavern, cup of ale in his hand. "That's Sir Jean of Thuringia. Montag's friend."

Enric nodded but didn't seem bothered. "I expect most of them will be here." He turned to Igraine and winked. "Thus the wedding present, right?"

Igraine smiled slightly, but her nerves were getting the best of her. Had he not seen her brother's rage that night at the Levan manor? The memory still burned hot in Igraine's mind.

"Enric!" Sir Louis shouted as he elbowed his way toward them. "You made it." They shook hands and smiled at each other. Louis turned toward Igraine, nodding politely. "My lady."

"Hello, Sir Louis."

"Enric, they've had such a showing for this tournament they're threatening to turn down new entrants soon. Lady Igraine, may I steal your husband for a moment? I have to go sign him up to kick my bum and become the next world champion."

Enric rolled his eyes. "You have such confidence in me. Though you are right. You don't stand a chance next to me." His smiled faltered as he looked back to Igraine. "Come with us? We can eat later."

Igraine glanced at the lines for food that were getting longer by the minute. The sun was beginning to set, after all. "Go. I'll get food and find the tent. We didn't travel all this way for you to not compete."

Enric glanced back toward Jean, who still sat watching the crowd, nursing his drink. "You sure?"

"I've been to hundreds of tournaments and survived just fine without an escort. Go. I'll catch up to you. You're going to need all the strength some good food can give you." She waved him away with a smile that hopefully looked more confident than she felt. Though she knew her words were true. This was her world, and she knew it well. She wasn't sure why she felt uncomfortable navigating it all of a sudden.

Louis pulled Enric on, and they jogged down the street toward the tournament grounds. Igraine sighed as she watched after them. Smoothing her hands on her skirts, she looked around at the food vendors again, wondering what would be best to feed her knight. Roast pork, sweet apples, savory cakes . . . the smells were making her mouth water. The bright colors of banners and signs surrounded her, and she relaxed a little, working her way deeper into the market and settling into the rhythm of the tournament.

"He's a bit foolhardy, leaving you alone. Don't you think?" The smell of onions overpowered even the market, leaving Igraine's blood to run cold.

She turned to face the man that spoke, hands clenched at her sides. She backed away from him, glaring. The crowd was dense, and people flowed around them like leaves down a rocky brook, paying them no mind. She debated speaking to him, giving him a piece of her mind, a threat to leave her alone, but decided it would come out weak. Instead, she pivoted on her heel and strode down the street toward a meat vendor with a short line. Lezay followed her, hovering behind her in line as she waited. She ignored him, placing her order and keeping her back to him as she received the food. It would have to be enough to feed them for the evening. She wasn't going to wait for other food.

"Why do you pretend to hate me?" Lezay cooed, a step behind her.

"She knows it makes you want her more," a second voice chimed in.

Igraine flinched and looked over her shoulder at Jean. The two men flanked her. She turned straight ahead and picked up her pace, working through the center of town toward the tournament grounds.

"Is my brother here, too?" Igraine finally asked, her eyes darting around. There was no one else she recognized. A babble of different languages chorused around them, showcasing just how internationally uniting this event was. The crowd became sparser as they headed toward the open space between the town center and the tournament ground in the distance: not good. Lezay and Jean didn't answer her, so she shot them another glare over her shoulder. They still followed, mere steps behind. Montag wasn't in sight. "What do you want?"

Still silence. The crowd was too sparse for comfort. She felt for the knife belted at her waist, a present mere hours old. Her fingers closed on it, heart thumping in anticipation. She drew it and spun to face them in a fluid motion, stopping them in their tracks as they backed away from the blade.

"Stop following me or tell me what you want." Igraine clutched the food under her left arm, the dagger at the ready. She kept her feet light, stance spread at the ready, though running was more likely to occur than any further action with the dagger.

"Just checking up on you." Jean eyed her from head to foot, his eyes lingering uncomfortably. Lezay's gaze was locked on her face, his lust barely concealed. He moved his tongue like he was working a piece of steak from his teeth. He probably was. Jean turned to Lezay. "At least we know for sure there's no upcoming bastard. She would have been showing by now. It's been a while since she ran . . ."

Igraine flushed bright red.

Lezay's eyes dropped toward Igraine's flat stomach, the laces of her gown cinched tight up her back. "There's no way he waited . . ." he mused.

Igraine longed to turn away from the men but feared giving them her back. She started backing away.

"Maybe he hasn't done it at all." Jean shrugged. He looked indifferent to it all. "Come on, Lezay. Let her be." He started to walk away.

Igraine took a few more steps backward, but Lezay closed the distance. She readied the dagger. He stepped within range, and she swiped at him in panic.

He caught her wrist, holding it tight, as he looked down into her eyes. "Are you truly his wife?" he asked, his face more serious than she'd ever seen him.

She stopped trying to pull her arm away and instead dropped the package of food on the ground. She held up her left hand, the gold ring on it shining in the sunset light. Lezay's expression fell.

"Now look at the dagger," she said quietly. Lezay's eyes flicked up to it and froze, taking in the crest. The glare that shifted to her eyes confirmed his recognition of the blade. Slowly he released her. She watched the anger simmer, his jaw clenched, but it slowly mixed with something like resignation, defeat. "I am the wife of Sir Enric de Levan, for now and forever. It's over, Lezay." She watched as her words took hold. Sir Jean reappeared and took Lezay by the shoulder, steering him away from Igraine. Lezay shrugged Jean's hand off after a few steps but continued to walk away.

Igraine let out a whoosh of air, feeling her knees weaken. The earth spun a bit as she picked up her bundle, but she breathed deeply and pressed on toward the encampment. It was going to be a long tournament.

Enric waited for her at the tent, pacing steadily back and forth. When he saw her, relief flooded his features. "I didn't know anxiety until I met you, Lady Igraine." He kissed her lightly on the lips. "I'm sorry to have left you in all this chaos. You are quite capable of handling yourself though, aren't you?" He smiled down at her.

Igraine bit her lip as she debated whether to tell him about the encounter with Lezay and Jean. He had to focus on the tournament. Brevity won over. "Lezay and Jean are here."

Enric nodded. "I figured they would be. Montag?"

"I didn't see him."

"Well, it's going to be a long week. Prince Richard, the duke, is here. As are Josse and Louis of Angoulême, as you know. Sir Stephen of Tielo and his older brother Sir Roger." Enric paused, watching her expression. "You tell me if they give you trouble, Igraine."

She nodded.

"The King of France, Louis, is also here as is the Crown Prince of England, Henry. I hear he's a fearless jouster. I haven't seen the whole list of nobility. I've been watching the heralds hang pennants by the minute."

Igraine nudged him. "You aren't nervous are you?"

Enric smiled. "No, not at all. Just excited." His stomach growled. "And hungry."

Igraine handed him the meat.

"You didn't get more?" His eyebrows rose. "I thought you had an eye for some of that fruit."

"I'll go back for more later. You and Pierre eat."

"What about you?"

Igraine shrugged. "I'm not hungry," she lied.

Enric knew her better than that though. "What happened? I know you have plenty of coin on you. Unless someone robbed you—" Igraine started to protest and he cut her off. "You be honest with me, Igraine. That's all I ever ask. What happened?"

She sighed. "Lezay and Jean followed me. I just wanted to get back here to you. I can get more. I'll go back." Her need to placate was instinctual. She waited for Enric to fume or point her on her way at the very least, and yet he still stood staring at her. His lips pursed in a frown, but it was far more sad than angry.

"Come with me." He held out his hand and Igraine took it, his warm fingers squeezing hers gently. He guided her toward the center of the colorful encampment where a scaffold had been erected for the heralds to communicate with the many knights present. Enric took the short stairs with heavy footsteps, Igraine's hand still tightly in his own. A few men stopped and curiously looked at them, and even more gathered as he shouted out across the field, "Listen! Listen everyone!" He yelled in Lange d'Oc, Lange d'Oil, and English. When a curious crowd had gathered around him, he again called out, "I am Sir Enric de Levan d'Aquitaine! Before we commence our tournament on the morn, I need you all to know, that just a few months ago, I married this woman, Lady Igraine of Alsace! Sirs Josse and Louis of Angoulême, with their wives and my parents, are our witnesses." He held Igraine's hand high, as she stared at him, her cheeks red. "And now, with all of you as my witnesses . . ." He turned to Igraine and bowed slightly to her, pressing his lips to her now lowered hand. "My lady, should I have the honor of winning the tournament this week, may I do so in your name?"

Igraine's face lit with the smile of the Lady of the Tournament, and the knights started murmuring amongst themselves. She nodded and pulled his face up to hers to kiss him. The crowd's reaction was mixed. A few cheered. A few rolled their eyes. A few just furrowed their brows in confusion over the early display, probably wondering why Enric was making such a show out of it. But there was one man watching who did not tear his eyes away, as emotionless as he seemed. Lezay. Enric pulled Igraine tight to his side as they descended the scaffold. The two men locked eyes in a wordless standoff. Then they walked right past Lezay, who merely watched them.

When they were again back at their tent, Enric pulled Igraine close and whispered in her ear, "Now they all know you are mine." He kissed her temple. "Let's go get some real food. We have a big day tomorrow."

Chapter 26

October 19, 1173

Chateau Brunstein, Alsace

Lezay threw the tournament roster across Montag's desk, earning a hard glare. "You should have seen them! Parading around together! Kissing in public! And then he won the damn tournament! It was horrible! I wanted to kill him, as did half the knights there I think, it was so sickeningly sweet. And instead he set us on our asses, won the bloody purse, and a new horse, too! The man has to be bloody charmed."

"Calm yourself, Lezay, or get out of my study." Montag settled himself into his chair, slouching back.

"Doesn't this bother you at all? You are the only one that can declare this marriage invalid. You are her farturnal protector . . ."

"Fraternal."

"Whatever. You didn't give permission for the marriage, so technically it could be illegitimate. And since there is not yet a child on the way, the church *might* just grant them the annulment."

"Lezay, I told you before, I don't care anymore. And you shouldn't either. She made her choice. She is dead to me, and she is to you as well. Stay away from her."

"You lied to me." Lezay leaned across Montag's desk, saliva flying from his mouth as he spit the words. His face had turned a deep shade of red. "You told me she would be mine."

Montag was unfazed. "And now she won't be. Get over it."

Lezay slammed a hand down, making the ink pot rattle and a few other trinkets fall to the ground. Montag launched to his feet and gripped the man by the front of his shirt. Like a wolf with hackles raised, he snarled at Lezay. "I told you I want you out of this, and I mean it. I told you I don't want to hear about her, and I mean it. You do not challenge me, do not test me, or you will know just how strong the power of the Le Brun line runs in my veins." He released Lezay, who looked even more red but remained silent as he straightened both his back and his clothes. Montag looked down at him. "Get out, Lezay. Find yourself a wife." He rested his knuckles on his desk, his big frame intimidating.

Lezay turned on his heel, slamming the door behind himself. Montag watched from the window as the man scattered dogs as he strode through the courtyard a few minutes later. A squire held a horse at the ready, and Lezay snatched the reins away and mounted. When Lezay was beyond the gate, Montag turned toward the long roll of the tournament roster, painted with the crests of the victors by order of event. Enric had done well, taking every event he had competed in. Montag threw the roster back across the room, just like Lezay had minutes earlier. He uncorked a bottle of port with his teeth, and after spitting the cork across the room, slouched back into his chair and took a long swallow.

Enric and Igraine, married at last. And they were making a scene of it, that was for certain. No one would contest their marriage. What was the point, with witnesses and a public display of their partnership? Montag took another long swallow. At least there was not yet a child.

The sound of laughter echoed from the courtyard, and he rose to look out at his own son, who chased a puppy around the yard with the strength of a future warrior. Well, at least all the strength an eight-month-old with a fast crawl and a few wobbling steps of walk could manage. When he finally caught it, the puppy gleefully barked and pounced on him, licking his face as the boy fell to the ground giggling, his little arms wrapped around the puppy's wiggling body. His nurse wasn't far behind, ready to scold them both. Montag watched as the boy was pulled to his feet and his clothes dusted off. As soon as his nurse's back was turned, he was back kneeling on the ground, the puppy again licking his face and wagging its tail.

Where did such innocence come from? Such simple joy? Montag tried to think if he had ever even petted the castle dogs, much less wrestled a puppy so gleefully. Likely not. His father was his nurse, and he had not scolded gently. He rolled his shoulders, the thickened skin of his scarred back brushing the fabric of his shirt. He had taken Igraine's punishments as much as he could, saying it was his fault when a gate was left open or something wasn't put away. He couldn't save her from this one, not if Raganor found out. He had wanted her married to a duke or a prince, after all. Word would reach him within the year that Igraine had wed. Would he hold to his promise to stay in Jerusalem? Or would he return back to terrorize them more? Time would tell.

Montag reminded himself not to care.

He turned back to the ledgers and papers on his desk. Acquiring an empire and keeping power over it was an art. Without Igraine or Alenor to manage the castle, he had more than a share of work to do. He would not compete for some time. There was no need. He had his heir. He had his money. And there was far more to make by patrolling that pilgrim route through the Holy Roman Empire than there was playing in tournaments.

He got to work.

Chapter 27

December 1173

Levan Manor, Aquitaine

As the wife of a knight, she'd known what she was getting into. She was the daughter of a knight. She'd lived with Montag long enough to learn how to deal with him going off to fight, wondering if he'd return and what condition he'd return in. Doing the same with a man who shared her bed was another thing entirely.

It was nothing like when he went to tournaments.

In a tournament, though the fight was brutal, it was a controlled atmosphere. There were some loose rules. They wore protection. They blunted lances. And the lord could always step in if things got out of hand, though admittedly Igraine had never seen such interference occur. It didn't need to. Accidents happened, but for the most part the knights didn't *want* to kill each other. In a real battle, they did.

The fair weather of tournament season had come to an end, and now Enric was in search of a different pay.

He was beholden to the Duke of Aquitaine, Richard. The son of the English king had not called upon Enric since his ordination but now, an armed messenger had called him to Poitiers. He was to leave immediately. True, Enric had fought as a mercenary for different lords the prior winter, traveling through Aquitaine and the lower end of France, putting down petty rebellions or settling rivalries for whoever was willing to pay. Due to Montag's confiscation of Enric's letters, Igraine had been mercifully ignorant of the extent of Enric's travails. Even now that she had been informed as part of Enric's attempt to soothe her fears, there was something about Prince Richard's hasty request that set Igraine's nerves on edge. Something was brewing, and it was more than a petty rebellion.

"He didn't say how long you will be away?" she asked Enric as he gathered his armor, checking the mail carefully for any weaknesses in the links. "Or where you're going? Are you going to England?"

"No. He didn't say anything other than to report to Poitiers. And he rode on. I assume he's gone to muster Josse and Louis as well. Maybe they'll know more." Enric set the mail aside and turned his attention to his sword.

Igraine set the whetstone before him.

He shot her a grateful glance and set to work sharpening the blade. "I'm going to miss having someone around that can read my mind."

"I'm going to miss having you around, period." She laid a hand on his shoulder and listened to the rhymical scrape of the metal on stone.

"You are set for the winter. There is plenty of hay, grain, apples. Try not to eat too many of the chickens." He smiled. It was an ongoing joke that he hated eating chicken because he liked eating eggs more.

"What, you think you won't be back until spring?" Igraine wasn't falling for the distraction.

"If I'm not, Gustave knows what to do to get the planting started. I doubt it would take that long though."

"Enric, *I* know how to get the planting started." Igraine stifled a laugh, not wishing to offend him. Running Levan Manor was nothing compared to running a castle like Brunstein. Their household was only about twelve individuals, most of whom maintained their own huts on the grounds. Brunstein had a household of over one hundred, if one counted the guards who came and went to patrol the estate. "I will be fine keeping things going without you. It's you I am going to miss. For you. Not whatever help you provide. Though I must admit, you are probably the most helpful lord I've ever lived with."

Enric set his sword aside and pulled her onto his lap. "Well, compared with the other abominable men you've lived with, I certainly should be." He kissed her.

After a long moment, Igraine pulled back and laid a hand on his cheek. "Be careful. Please."

"Always. And the same goes for you."

Igraine nodded, shifting the belt that sat on her hips. The dagger with the Levan crest showed. They still lived with the fear that Montag, Lezay, or even Raganor would return for Igraine, but the past few months, since their marriage had been made official, things had been quiet. Montag ceased to exist. Or perhaps, in Montag's mind, Igraine ceased to exist.

There was one other thing that was absent, though Igraine wasn't sure if she was grateful, due to the uncertain state of things, or sad. Alenor had conceived quickly — too quickly. Igraine knew Alenor and Montag had not had much time to be together. Yet now, after months of freely loving her husband in a very active manner, there still was no sign that she was with child. It was too early to worry that it would take years. Meanwhile, she looked at some of the household women, and a few of them had a child on the breast and another in the womb.

Enric furrowed his brow. "What's wrong? Your mind is in another place."

"Nothing." She kissed him lightly.

He laid a hand on her womb, and she straightened in surprise. "It will happen in time." Her eyes grew wide, and he laughed. "You aren't the only one that can read minds." He shifted her in his lap, pulling her skirts out of the way that her bare skin was against his legs. "And since I'm going to be away for a while, we certainly don't want to waste any opportunity . . ."

He kissed her as he guided her hand to his groin. She took hold. He groaned against her lips.

"The messenger said I have to hurry—"

She freed him from his breeches. Her lips were still against his as she breathed, "Good. Because I need you. Right. Now."

He took her there in the armory of the castle, seated on a chair, in plain sight of anyone that would have walked past the room. There was an urgency to their coupling she had not felt before, and it both thrilled and worried her. No, this would not be the last time she saw him. She had more faith than that. Still, fear brought on passion, perhaps because it brought on courage. And she was going to need plenty of that in the cold winter months to come.

Chapter 28

May 1199

A dark eye framed with raven-black hair was all Eleanor could see of the woman on the other side of the cracked door. That eye glanced over Alec with recognition, only to linger on Eleanor herself with the same suspicion she felt racing through her veins. After a moment's hesitation, the door opened fully, and the woman stepped aside. She was stunning, with sharp features and a dark tone to her skin that hinted of some kind of far eastern bloodline. Her thin shift did little to hide the ample curve of breast and hip and for once, Eleanor felt doubt surge through her, her feet frozen outside the threshold.

How did Alec know this woman?

Alec pulled Eleanor behind him into the small room, and the woman shut the door behind him.

"Why did you bring her?" the woman asked with a tinge of a Germanic accent, not at all what Eleanor was expecting. She crossed her arms over the chest, her agitation obvious even in the dim light of the small, curtained room.

"She needs to know everything. And she might as well hear it from the source." Alec squeezed Eleanor's hand, but she was too bewildered to return the reassurance.

"You both better start explaining," Eleanor said. She pulled her hand from Alec's grasp.

"Did he follow you here?" the woman asked nervously. She pulled aside the dark curtain that covered a tiny window, glancing through it without placing her body where an onlooker could see. The sunlight streamed in for a brief moment before being extinguished to a dim trim of light around the curtain as she dropped it.

"No. I made sure he couldn't. And I don't want to stay long. Can you tell her what you know of Le Brun?"

The woman turned towards Eleanor. "Le Brun is not a man to be trifled with. I have watched him, only from a distance. But the stories told to me by others, by dark men themselves, paint him even darker."

Eleanor narrowed her eyes at the woman. "Who are you? And why do you know about my grandfather when I do not?" She shot a look at Alec, her trust in him beginning to fade. He met her gaze without hesitation, his lips in a thin line.

"It is better for us both if you do not know my name. I have known Alec for many years. He once helped me, so now when he asked me to make inquiries, I helped him.

My sources do not matter. What matters is the stories they tell about Le Brun."

Eleanor was losing her patience. Alec was going to get an earful when they left *if* this woman ever revealed whatever great secret she was holding in.

Sensing Eleanor's distress, the woman raised her chin and perched on the corner of her bed with all the dignity of a princess. "During the tempestuous years of the revolt of King Henry's son, there was one tournament in France that managed to call in knights from all around the land. That tournament in Paris was not the beginning of Le Brun's treachery, only the crux."

Eleanor listened intently as the mysterious woman told the story of her father's experience in Jerusalem with the illustrious talent of a troubadour. It seemed terrible, but also so distant Eleanor did not yet understand the point to Alec's worry or the involvement of this woman. Then as the woman began to tell of what happened in Paris in 1174, Eleanor began to understand.

Chapter 29

May 15, 1174

Chateau Brunstein, Alsace

Montag rested his elbows on his desk, his hands clasped at his forehead. To an onlooker it would seem as if he was in prayer, but he was far from it. Anger seethed within him, barely contained, as he struggled to cork it. He didn't like being pulled into other people's wars, but as usual, when people wanted money they knocked on his door. He'd shoved more than one messenger back out of his gate in the past few weeks, to the point that said gate was now shut tight to everyone. Thus was the source of his anger, for the inability to send his men in and out of Brunstein at will was an inconvenience for conducting business.

He didn't care who was King of England. As long as whoever that king was, left Alsace to its own doing.

Montag knew things were always far more complicated than that, but a massive upheaval was about to begin. Apparently the issue was that good old King Henry of

England's son, Henry the Young, had become impatient and was attempting to usurp the throne. Already tournaments were being cancelled, the pilgrimages were on hold, and trade was slowing. How long would it last before one king managed to kill off the other?

The knock on the door did nothing to assuage Montag's mood.

"What?" he bellowed.

His squire tentatively opened the heavy door, staying on the other side of the threshold. "My lord, Sir Lezay is downstairs. He says he needs to speak with you."

"Oh, now he decides to pay me a visit?" Montag grumbled. He stalked to his chair and pulled on his thick coat, belting his sword to his hip. Without a word to his squire, he pushed past him down the narrow spiral staircase to the lower levels of the castle. Lezay hadn't been seen since their altercation the past fall. Montag had thoroughly enjoyed the peace and quiet. The man better have news alluding to which King of England had won. Montag was not in the mood for small talk.

Lezay waited in the entry, a sign that he still was not ready to repair their friendship to the level it once was. A year past, he would have been settled into the kitchen, terrorizing the maids and downing a brimming mug of hard cider. Montag stopped a few feet from him and crossed his arms, studying his once-friend. Lezay had lost weight but instead of making him look weak, he looked even more fit and more vicious than ever. Behind the mask of travel dust and scruff, there were dark circles under his eyes.

"What brings you, Lezay?" Montag asked cautiously.

"Have you seen them?" Lezay held up a roll of parchments.

"What are those?"

"Tournament rosters."

"I thought tournaments were on hold. Giant crisis with England if you haven't heard."

"Small tournaments are running. He's winning them all."

"Who?"

Lezay handed Montag the rosters, which when untied revealed that Sir Enric de Levan was indeed winning everything he could compete in. "We need to stop him. We need to meet him at the next tournament. It's an embarrassment. He's been uncontested. Men are almost too afraid to meet him. They say he spent the winter in Normandy, fighting for Richard Plantagenet."

Montag pondered a moment, thumbing through the rosters a second time. Perhaps at a tournament there would be current news on the state of the uprising. As long as said tournament wasn't in English territory, it could be a good distraction. Lord knew he had horses to sell, people to meet, business to attend to beyond Brunstein. He had not competed since the accident that had almost had him banned from Aquitaine. With the passage of time people had likely already forgotten that little mishap. "I agree. What did you have in mind?"

"Paris. Three days' time. I am going. My squire is waiting with the horses. Join me."

A neutral kingdom, where neither they nor Enric were beholden to the lord, and thus could not be subjugated to his bias. Montag nodded in agreement.

Within an hour the two knights and their squires were on the road to Paris. They moved quickly and spoke little until they pulled up to a village inn for the evening. Unsurprisingly, the inn was full. The landlord directed them to a back street, where there was another, much less reputable, locale.

"A brothel?" Montag's squire questioned, paling slightly. He was the newest in the line of squires and came from a rather traditional noble family.

The other three men ignored him and arranged for lodgings and food. As they sat in the common area forcing down a rather thin soup that probably had been simmering on the hearth for a week, Montag eyed Lezay, noting he studied every woman in the establishment as they wandered between the sparse patrons.

"I heard you finally married. Lady Agnes the Hessian?"

"Two months ago. She's lovely. Obedient." He didn't smile, his eyes lingering on a willowy young whore who was currently trying to seduce an old man seated in the corner.

"Congratulations."

A heavyset woman waddled over to their table, her bosom voluptuously exposed. She eyed the men and smiled, revealing a broken tooth. They looked at her blankly, and she shifted her attention to the young squire, who looked horrified. She laughed at his expression and leaned forward. His eyes grew wide at the bosom right before them. Or perhaps it was whatever she whispered in his ear. She laughed again and moved on.

"Lord Montag, if you need me, I will be in the stable for the night," the boy said hastily, and hurried out of the room, leaving what was left of his soup behind.

Lezay and Montag chuckled. Lezay's squire managed to finish his soup before he too bowed out, seeking the sanctuary of their accommodations, which tonight consisted of thin walled rooms the size of broom closets with beds that had seen lord-knows-what. Alone, the two men watched the fire in silence for a while.

"Have you heard from her?" Lezay asked.

"Not a word."

"You're a fool for not having pursued her harder when she escaped."

"Lezay, I'm not arguing this now. We didn't have a choice. I had to answer for killing that man in the tournament, and by then it was too late. They were married before God. They are never going to get an annulment. They made it public. I have been forced to admit, Igraine was smart about it. I didn't think she had it in her."

"Bull of a woman."

"Agreed."

The fire crackled in the hearth next to them. They, as nobility, had been given the best table in the establishment, by the warm fire that chased the evening chill.

Lezay leaned across the table to Montag. "We need to convince Enric to compete in pike, sword, and joust. Convince him he won't take tournament champion without winning three events this time, instead of his usual two."

"Why would he need three?"

"Because we're both going to enter three."

Montag raised his eyebrows.

"You have to do the sword, Montag. I will enter club. Jean is not coming; I can win club. You will win pike. Between the two of us, we are enough of a threat to his reign in sword and joust that he'll question if he can win two events. And if either of us win two events, we take tournament champion. To even stand a chance at challenging us, he'll have to enter a third event. He'll enter pike. We wear him down. Exhaust him. He'll falter . . ."

"He'll fall . . ." Montag finished. He took a long swallow of his ale. "You know I hate sword."

"I know. But you hate Enric more. And you're good at it."

Montag narrowed his eyes at Lezay. "You want him dead."

"Don't you?"

"Killing him won't get you Igraine. You're married now."

"I'm married *for now*." Lezay's eyes flicked toward the willowy whore again, who had given up on the old man and was now clearing empty tables.

Montag studied Lezay again, noting the man's tone. "Not every woman dies in childbirth like Alenor did."

"Hmm" was Lezay's only reply. He downed the last of his ale. "See you at dawn, Montag." He rose and approached the willowy whore who looked at him tentatively before allowing him to steer her up the stairs.

Montag stretched out his legs, leaning back in his chair. A pretty maid approached him, her terror evident in her trembling hands and shaky voice, asking if he needed anything. He asked for more ale, and she ran off with relief to bring him a fresh mug. Finally understanding that he wanted to be left to his own company for the evening, the remaining women occupied themselves playing dice at a table on the far side of the room. Montag stared into the flames. He didn't mind being alone. Ever since Igraine had left, he'd realized he enjoyed the solitude, the independence. At home this reverie was occasionally interrupted by his son, who now was running around the castle, a strong young lad that exhausted his nurses. Here on the road, it was as if he had no past. Unknown to the world, he could be whatever kind of man he wanted to be.

Tonight, he was a widower.

There was a shout from upstairs, and the women glanced up. In the silence that followed they whispered amongst themselves, and when no further noise ensued, they resumed their game. Montag stretched and downed the last of the ale. Tomorrow would be a long day, and then there was the tournament the day after. He would need every bit of rest.

He woke in the dark after a restful night. By the light of a taper, he gathered his things and headed to the stable. The sky was just starting to lighten when he met his squire in the barnyard. The boy learned quicker than most. The horses were already fully tacked. Montag swung into the saddle, patting his horse. Lezay's squire emerged from the stable, two horses saddled and ready. Montag glanced up at the brothel. Lezay better not be late.

On cue, Lezay came out the front door, still buttoning his jacket.

"Good morning," Montag smirked, taking in the man's disheveled appearance. "Did you save any energy to fight?"

"Always enough energy for a fight," Lezay smiled. "Suffice to say my nerves are calmed for a few days."

Suddenly the brothel's madame burst out the front door. "You bastard! Get out of here, and don't you come back! You hear me? Don't you come back!"

Montag's eyebrows rose. "Not a very grateful farewell. Did you forget to pay the girl?"

"Oh, no. I paid her triple her fee." He chuckled. "Shall we?" He kicked his horse forward, the pinks of sunrise stretching across the sky before them.

Paris was as busy as ever. Nearly five hundred knights had been invited to compete from across all of Europe. Some even had come from as far as the Holy Land. The bright colors of different tents and tunics were as varied as the languages that surrounded Montag as they rode into the camp. Heralds directed the crowd from raised platforms erected periodically throughout the city, and then in even greater concentration around the tournament grounds. They made the knight's entrance into the city smooth in what otherwise appeared to be a chaotic mess of humanity.

"You didn't tell me this was such a big event," Montag said to Lezay.

"It's big. A celebration of so-and-so's son's christening."

"So-and-so, huh? We don't even know what we're here for."

"We're here for Enric. The hosting lord can pretend we're here for whatever he wants."

Following the directions of the heralds, the two knights worked their way to the registration tent. Their squires took the horses to the temporary stabling set off from the arena.

"Five events!" a herald shouted as they passed. "Sword! Club! Wrestling! Pike! Joust! He who wins the most events will be tournament champion! The prize is fifty pounds in gold and silver!"

Montag let out a whistle of appreciation. Fifty pounds was a huge prize, enough to change a poor knight's status. Enough to buy land. Enough to buy power.

They continued toward registration, entering the line formed there.

"What do they do with the prize if no one wins more than one event?" a knight in front of them in line turned to ask.

"The hosting lord keeps the prize," Lezay answered. "Which is likely why it's so high this tournament. The prize draws a huge volume of knights, all with varied skill sets. It's unlikely that one man will be best in all events, or even several events. Thus the lord gambles that there will not be one superior champion."

Montag chimed in. "And yet if there is, that man will not have an easy time earning the title. The cost of the prize is worth the entertainment of watching us try."

The knight nodded and turned back toward the registrar. When he approached the desk, he entered only one event.

Lezay motioned Montag ahead of him. Montag took a deep breath and took the staff at the table, striking the symbols of joust, pike, and sword. The registrar wrote down his selections and asked for proof of birth line. Montag showed the crest of his new ring, molded over the winter out of pure, heavy gold. The Le Brun stag was gone, only the diagonal slash across his shield remaining. Montag kept with the family colors in his other heraldry, trusting that his reputation and lineage was well known enough to ease the transition. He was right. The registrar jotted down his name, Lord Montag of Brunstein, and drew the crest without question.

Le Brun was one step closer to being erased.

"Next!"

Lezay stepped up and repeated the process, entering joust, sword, and club as they had discussed. They turned from the registrar, intent on finding some more filling food than the weak soup they'd had the night before. A booth further down sold hot pork, portions big enough to satisfy a man's appetite. Digging into their purchases, they wandered the tournament grounds.

"Do you see him anywhere?" Montag asked, eyeing the crowd just as much as Lezay.

"I don't. But he's here. I feel it."

Montag rolled his eyes.

"There she is." Lezay pointed.

Montag spun around, mouth full of food. There at a booth down the street was Igraine, another noblewoman at her side. They were deep in conversation, shopping through the spices at the vendor. Lezay took a step toward them, and Montag grabbed his arm. Lezay looked at him in confusion, but Montag only shook his head. They watched from a distance.

Eventually, Igraine turned around, her face alight with joy, more radiantly beautiful than ever. Her hand absently rested on an obviously pregnant belly. Her eyes flitted across the crowd, passing over Montag and Lezay where they stood frozen in place. Suddenly her face fell, and she turned her attention back to them, staring at them from across the street. She looked her brother up and down, conflicting emotions flitting across her face. Her companion again drew her attention, oblivious to her distraction. Igraine turned away, glancing briefly over her shoulder before disappearing into the crowd once again.

Lezay let out a low whistle. "At least we know they're here."

Montag was silent. She was happy. So happy! Why did that bother him? Did it bother him? He shook it off, reminding himself how she'd embarrassed the family name. He clapped Lezay on the back. "See you tomorrow. I need to sharpen my damn sword."

Chapter 30

May 22, 1174
Paris, France

"You did what?!" Igraine stared at her husband in shock, fists clenching and unclenching at her sides, her blood turning to ice as fear chilled up her spine.

"It's my next best event. If I want a chance to win tournament champion, I have to win pike as well as my other two events." Enric's expression was apologetic, but cool. He was as confident as ever, perhaps even more so after months of steady victories, not to mention actual combat.

"You don't need to win tournament champion."

"Fifty pounds of gold and silver! That's enough to change our futures, Igraine. For me to give you the life you deserve."

"I'm happy with our life, Enric." She put her hands on her hips, showcasing her burgeoning belly, reminding him.

"I am too, but this is the opportunity of a lifetime."

"It's not worth it. I warned you before, my brother with a pike—"

"Is lethal. Yes, Igraine, I've seen him."

"You didn't see him in Poitou last summer!"

"That was an accident. Don't you have any faith in my abilities?"

Igraine miserably sank onto a bucket outside their tent. Her back ached, she was uncomfortable, and this was not the kind of fun tournament she had envisioned it would be. Montag and Lezay's appearance had changed all of that. "Montag is competing in sword, too, Enric. I told you once he doesn't like it. I never said he wasn't good at it."

Enric sat next to her and wrapped an arm around her. "Igraine, this is what I do. Stop worrying."

Igraine pressed her fingers over her lips. She shook her head after a moment. "I'm asking you not to. Please, Enric. Withdraw. Let's go home. You've done enough this year. Blame it on me; blame it on the child."

Enric let out an exasperated sigh. "Igraine, this is the biggest opportunity I've ever had. I am a knight. I must compete."

As trumpets sounded from the tournament field, Igraine flinched. It was starting. "Then I am not going to watch. I can't. I just can't." She shook her head.

Enric fell to his knees, taking her hands in his own, kissing them. "Give me your blessing my lady, and I will win this tournament for you."

She gave him a stern look. "Be careful, Enric. He is ruthless. They are both out to get you. You know it. Don't turn your back for a second."

Enric rose and kissed her lips. Then he was gone. Igraine stared at her hands, trembling as she sat there in the empty tent camp. After a few minutes, she could gauge by the crowd that the events had started. A mix of cheers and gasps reached her ears. She busied herself reorganizing the equipment inside the tent. Then she mended a shirt. She cleaned her boots. By high noon the tenor of the crowd had increased as the intensity of the events increased. She paced back and forth. She retrieved her embroidery, a project for the baby. It sat idly on the bench; she was far too distracted for its detailed work.

The camp had been empty most of the day. Now knights and squires filtered back to their tents. They had finished, losers. More than a few limped. Others nursed cuts. She was afraid to ask what the status of things was in the competition ring. She paced some more.

Sir Josse of Angoulême limped by, and she rushed up to him. "Are you hurt?"

"Nothing a bit of rest won't fix," he replied. Noting her worry, he smiled gently. "Enric is doing just fine, Lady Igraine."

She breathed a sigh of relief.

"They're getting close to the finals, and he's still going in all three events."

"All three?"

Sir Josse nodded. "Give him credit, my lady. Your husband is a fighter."

Igraine nodded, leaving Josse to hobble on to his own tent to tend to his injuries.

The pacing resumed.

Lost in her thoughts, she didn't hear a knight come up to her.

"You look good with child." He chuckled at her panicked expression as she whirled to face him, her hand going instinctively to her dagger, belted at her side. Lezay smirked, standing just feet away from her with his arms crossed. "I wondered if you were hiding back here. Couldn't stomach your pretty husband losing today?"

"Obviously he must have beaten *you*, or you wouldn't be here." Igraine bristled, regaining her composure.

"Ah, true. But he still has to survive your brother."

Igraine swallowed, making her face expressionless. "What do you want?"

Lezay shrugged. "To congratulate you."

Igraine studied him, slowly resuming her pacing. "Thank you," she said shortly. "Congratulations to you as well. I heard you've been wed."

"Ah, thanks." His smile sent chills down her spine. There was something far colder about him than she remembered. "She'll do for now. Until you're available again."

"Pardon?" She stopped pacing. She must have heard wrong.

Lezay chuckled. He closed the space between them, looking her in the eyes. "When you tire of him, you just say the word, Igraine."

"I don't know what you're talking about, Lezay. He is my husband till death do us part."

He caressed her cheek. "Precisely," he whispered. Abruptly he turned away from her, striding back toward the tournament arena. "The final of the pike competition is about to start. Your husband against Montag."

Igraine hesitated a moment, then quickly followed after him, hiking her skirts up to allow her legs to stretch out, matching him stride for stride. They rounded the corner into the mass of the noisy crowd. The excitement was palpable; the sound drowned out even the pounding of her heart. Lezay nodded his head to the left, and she followed behind him. When they reached the stands, they were able to slip out of the peasantry and find two open spaces among the nobles. Reluctantly, Igraine sat next to Lezay.

Montag and Enric were already in the middle of the fight. It appeared as if Enric was holding his own, but he was struggling. Montag was quick, hard, and ruthless with the weapon. He hammered a blow onto Enric's shoulder that made him shout out, but in a fury of movements Enric had slammed Montag back a few paces.

The fight continued on for a few long minutes more. Igraine's heart pounded, yet she could not tear her eyes away from the scene. She tried to pretend it was any old pair of knights, not the only two men she cared about. Suddenly Montag dealt a heavy blow to Enric's head. Igraine flinched as if she herself had been struck. It appeared as if the helmet had taken the worst of it, but Enric sank to his knees. He yielded.

Lezay let out a roaring cheer as Igraine's heart sank, her palms sweaty with worry. She watched Enric slowly get to his feet, working his way to his squire. The crowd was too thick for her to make her way to him, so she stayed frozen in the stands.

When Lezay calmed down enough to resume his seat, she asked, "Who is left in the other competitions?"

"I won club. A Norseman won the wrestling. Now Montag is champion of pike. He and Enric are both finalists in the sword, and then they have to finish up the joust. It's them and the Prince of England in the joust yet."

"Which prince?"

"Richard."

Igraine nodded. They'd met him in several tournaments in Aquitaine. He was a fierce competitor. Though it was surprising he was here at all with the drama surrounding his family.

"Sword is next."

"They have to give them time to recover."

"Not necessarily." Lezay shrugged.

Igraine frowned at him, then abruptly stood and pushed her way through the crowd. She ducked under the rail, running toward Enric and his squire as they got ready for the next event at the side of the arena. Some members of the crowd noticed her and let out a cheer.

"Lady Igraine! Lady Igraine! The Lady of the Tournament!" they chanted.

Enric looked up, his face bruised and sweaty. It lit up with a beaming smile when he saw her. He stood and swept her into his arms, kissing her. "You came!"

"He fights left-handed!" Igraine said urgently. "It's why he hates the sword. He's not right-handed, yet he'll try to start that way. You have to injure his left arm."

Enric shook his head in surprise. "You're only telling me now?" he muttered.

"How's your head?"

"Hurts. But I'll be fine."

The herald called for them to enter the ring. Igraine checked over Enric's armor, making sure it was solid. He shoved his helmet on his head and drew his sword. With a last sweaty kiss, he stepped into the ring, where Montag was already waiting, watching them with an expressionless stare.

The fight was just as intense as the pike had been. Enric followed Igraine's advice and dealt a heavy blow to Montag's left arm. He bellowed in pain and anger, shooting a glance at Igraine that belied his fury at her betrayal. But left to fight with his weaker arm, Montag could not overcome Enric's skilled attack with the sword. Battered to his knees, he yielded.

Enric ran into Igraine's arms in celebration, picking her up and spinning her with her skirts a whirling flag around them. He pressed his lips hard onto hers. The crowd around them cheered.

There was one last event that would determine if there would be a tournament champion: the joust. The crowd shifted to the even larger arena built around the list, where five rings hung from their post. Enric leaned into Igraine, practically having to shout in her ear over the noisy excitement of the crowd. "We ran the rings all morning between events. Just me, Prince Richard, and Montag in the final. I have a good shot to take tournament champion."

"I want a contact joust!" a spectator shouted.

His friend agreed, "We want a melee!"

"Thank goodness for the rings," Enric muttered. "I don't feel like taking any more injury today." He located his squire and horse. Igraine helped him adjust his armor, checking the mail for any damaged links as she always did.

Just like that, the heralds emerged from convening with the lord. "A contact joust!"

"What?" Enric and Igraine exclaimed. Montag's voice resounded with theirs, and Igraine noted his jaw had dropped open with shock and fury.

Lezay shouted back to the herald, "You wanted this to be a ring competition! If you want it to be a jouster you need to rerun the entire event and let the rest of us compete!" He stood at Montag's side, hands on his hips, looking red with fury.

The rest of the crowd erupted in a series of cheers, complaints, and suggestions. The heralds fought to restore order while again conferring with the lord.

"The top six finishers will compete in a melee!" a herald shouted.

This brought on a whole new flurry of complaints.

Enric shook his head. "That's not fair. It was down to the three of us." He tightened his girth with unnecessary force. His horse snorted in protest, and he apologetically patted it on the neck.

"They just want more entertainment," Igraine said, shaking her head in awe. "And the lord is afraid you or Montag could claim the title of tournament champion. He doesn't want to part with his precious purse. Or maybe he doesn't even have one."

"You're right on that." Enric nodded. He shouted in frustration, then shoved his helmet onto his head.

"Don't compete."

"Igraine, I'm so close."

"It's a melee! No! You are battered enough."

Enric turned to his squire. "Who are the other three knights? Prince Richard, Montag, me, and who?"

"Sir Alfred of London, Sir Henri of Burgundy, and—" he squinted towards the banners being hung in the colors of the competitors. "—Sir Rothulfus Lezay!"

Enric took a sharp breath.

Igraine shook her head, her eyes wide with pleading. "There is no shame in yielding. The two of them together will kill you, Enric. Let's take the purse for the sword competition and *go home*." She had worried all morning. There was no way to tolerate watching Enric take on Montag and Lezay at one time. How could she make Enric understand their hatred? Her betrayal to the family burned bright in Montag's eyes — she saw it. And Lezay — he didn't need to voice aloud he wished her widowed.

The squire shifted his weight impatiently next to them, waiting for instruction. Montag and Lezay looked eager to fight. They expected Enric to compete. They knew how much that fifty-pound purse could change his life. Enric looked thoroughly tempted, the bloodlust from the sword competition still thrumming through his veins. When he looked back at his wife, Igraine let him see the worry in her eyes, her hands protectively around the child she carried inside her.

He hesitated.

She could not force him to withdraw. It was his reputation at stake. His decision. The right decision was the hardest to make.

In a quiet voice she said, "I won't watch."

"Tell the heralds I yield," Enric said firmly.

The squire hesitated, uncertain that he'd heard correctly.

"Go! I yield," Enric insisted.

Igraine breathed a sigh of relief as the boy ran off. She laid a hand on his arm. "Thank you."

Enric twined an arm around her and kissed her forehead. With reins in one hand and Igraine's hand in the other, they left the booing crowd behind them.

Chapter 31

As twilight fell, Montag rubbed his aching shoulder. It wasn't the only part of him that ached, though it was the worst at the moment. The melee had proved to be a brutal affair after all, and that coward Enric had been wise to withdraw when he did. *Of course* only the Prince of England, Richard, could have won such a fight. He and Lezay had not gone easy on the prince, but the other two warriors had seemed to avoid him. The fight was unfairly matched by all accounts, and his battered body was proof.

"I finally see you compete, and it's only to watch you lose." The man's voice made Montag's blood run cold. He whirled around, his hand already on the hilt of his sword.

"What are you doing here, Raganor?" Every nerve in Montag's body tingled, the edge of a great storm brewing.

"Nice to see you, too, my son." Raganor stepped out of the shadows. He looked travel-worn, dirty. There were dark circles under his eyes and a gauntness to his face that had not been extant on his former appearance.

"I told you never to come back."

"I didn't come back . . . to Alsace. You did not specify that all of Europe was part of my banishment. Be more specific if you wish to rule, Montag." He gazed around him in the twilight. "Really I quite enjoy Paris. Pleasant climate. Fantastic wine. Gorgeous women. But Aquitaine seems even more to my liking. I may purchase an estate there if I can befriend the duke. Though that may be rather difficult, seeing that my son spent much of the evening hammering him with a lance."

Montag knew he referred to Prince Richard, Duke of Aquitaine. "What do you want?"

Raganor's black-eyed smile made Montag grip his sword a little tighter. "I wanted to give my daughter a wedding present."

Montag involuntarily flinched.

Raganor chuckled. "You thought I wouldn't find out? Where is she?"

Montag's back stiffened. He held to the hope that Raganor had arrived late enough to the tournament to miss Igraine's embarrassing show of affection. "I haven't spoken to her in months. They are wed before God. There is nothing we can do."

"Oh, there is a lot we can do. Drag her home for one thing." Raganor's voice rasped like a curse. "You cowardly fool. You let her go to him. You told me you had a count! A count wanted her! Yet I heard her name tied to this petty commoner's all the way in Jerusalem! Do you know *who he is?*"

"Leave her alone, Father." Montag took a step toward him, his eyes narrowing. "This does not concern you. No part of our lives concerns you. Go back to the East."

"Or you'll do what, son? Slam me up a wall in front of all your peers? Air our family affairs in front of the entire kingdom? What will you do?"

Montag instinctively glanced around. Raganor was right. There were a few other knights watching them with curiosity. He pulled himself to his full towering height and stepped up to his father. He looked down at him as he glowered, whispering, "If you touch her, Raganor, I will kill you this time. You are done with us. Get out of France, get out of the West entirely. Go dig yourself a cave in the sand in the *Holy* Land and make your peace with God. We are done with you."

Raganor's lips twitched maliciously as he shook his head.

Montag turned on his heel and walked away, his hand clamped on the hilt of his sword.

Lezay found him pacing on the edge of the encampment. He folded his arms and watched.

"What do you want, Lezay?" Montag finally growled.

"Well, I came over to make some crude jokes, but now I'm trying to figure out what has you so aggravated. I know

I'm too exhausted even for company tonight, yet here you are wearing a new jousting path into the grass."

Montag narrowed his eyes and glared at Lezay. "You remember what I told you about my father?"

Lezay's smile faded. "Some things, yes. You've always been pretty vague about him, Montag."

"He's here."

"Oh?"

Montag stopped pacing and whirled on Lezay. "I told him never to come back! I told him to leave us, and to stay in that sand pit for good. Yet he's bloody here!"

Lezay's eyebrows went up. "And why do you care?"

Montag resumed his pacing, shooting Lezay a sideways look. It was enough for the man to comprehend. His eyes went wide.

"Ohh. You still care for the traitorous bitch. You think dear old papa is going after *her*?"

"She's my sister, Lezay. My only sister."

"So . . . go warn her."

"She's a traitorous bitch."

"Montag?"

"What?" he growled.

"Go warn her. Unless you want me to."

"You stay away from her!"

Lezay threw his hands up with obvious frustration. "Look, I'm tired. I'm going to bed. Let me know if you want help. You know where to find me."

Montag ceased pacing and rubbed his jaw. "Wait." He sighed. "Where are they?"

Lezay got a mischievous glint in his eye. *Of course* he knew exactly where Igraine and her husband were. "They were down by the river. Very romantic spot. I only watched a little bit . . ."

"Shut up, Lezay. Take me to them."

Lezay smirked. He led the way through the encampment and down the dirt path toward the river. The sun had set now, and the gentle moonlight glistened off the water. Lezay pointed down another side path. "Not sure if they're done yet. They seemed keen on taking their time."

Montag gritted his teeth. He had no desire to walk in on anything. "Enric!" His voice boomed through the darkness. They heard the faint clink of metal. Enric emerged from the trees, sword drawn. He was as fully dressed as if he had just left the tournament. Perhaps Lezay was exaggerating Igraine's romantic walk? Montag kept his hand on his own sword but did not draw. "We need to talk."

"Talk or fight? I'm never really sure with you, Montag. Especially when you have your sidekick on hand." He eyed Lezay cautiously.

"Is Igraine with you?"

"What do you want?"

Montag smirked. She was there all right. He called over Enric's shoulder. "Igraine! He's here."

Igraine appeared behind Enric within seconds. "What do you mean, he's *here*? You banished him."

Enric held up his arm to stop her. "Igraine . . ."

"Montag, don't joke with me." She ignored Enric and pushed his arm out of the way.

Montag's features softened. "I don't joke. He's here, and he's after you."

"You spoke?"

"Who are we talking about, Igraine?" Enric said quietly.

"My father," she answered without breaking her gaze with Montag.

Enric's sharp intake of breath was audible to them all.

"He's mad?" Igraine questioned.

"Of course. And apparently he is acquainted with your husband. Care to enlighten me as to how?"

"No," Enric said firmly. He sheathed his sword. "Igraine, let's go. We'll ride through the night."

"To where?" she asked.

"Your darling little husband looks a bit panicked, Igraine," Lezay observed.

Igraine glowered at him. She said, "Shut it, Lezay" at the same time Enric said, "Stay out of it."

"Whoa, whoa!" Montag placated. They all quieted, the anger as palpable now as it had been on the front steps of Levan manor that stormy day. "Look, I wanted to warn you. Now I have. But you know you can't run from him."

Montag hesitated, replaying Raganor's words in his mind. "I believe he knows where you live."

"So what do you suggest?" Enric asked.

"He said he's going to try to befriend the Prince of England . . . Richard. We should befriend him first."

Lezay snorted. "Montag, you and I just kicked the manhede out of wee Richard. He's not going to be your friend."

"Good thing I didn't join you in the melee then. Right, Lezay?" Enric interjected coldly.

Igraine pulled Enric's arm. "Come on, let's go."

Enric resisted for a moment, still fuming, then yielded to his wife. Igraine turned over her shoulder and quietly said, "Thank you for the warning, brother."

Montag stood frozen, a mix of worry and anger fighting behind his darkened eyes. "Igraine, why would Father tell me I don't know who Enric is? What don't I know?"

She shook her head and pulled Enric on, but now it was Enric who stood frozen. He paused and turned back to Montag. He pulled from Igraine's grasp and strode right up to the man, meeting him eye-to-eye. Montag narrowed his eyes but didn't flinch.

Enric's voice was a low, bristling threat. "Remember when I asked for Igraine's hand? I told you, you know nothing about what I've been through. Well here's a hint . . ." He took two steps back and pulled off his linen shirt. Montag and Lezay watched in bewilderment.

Igraine gasped and pressed her hands to her mouth. Slowly Enric turned his back on Montag, and the white spots of his burn scars could be seen even in the moonlight.

Montag's back stiffened, remembering what the searing pain of wounds like that felt like. His sword hand trembled by his side. Usual composure lost, he let his eyes go wide. "When?"

Enric turned around and quickly slipped his shirt back over his head. "Jerusalem." He gently took Igraine by the hand and left Montag and Lezay staring after them.

Eventually Montag turned back to Lezay, a thousand thoughts on his mind. Lezay stood still, looking utterly confused.

"Would you like to tell me why our greatest rival just took off his shirt? And why you look like you've seen a bloody ghost because of it?"

Montag shook his head. "I need to find my father."

"I thought the whole point of this moonlight escapade was to *avoid* your father."

"I need to find him. Igraine is in more danger than I thought."

"What are you *talking* about?"

Montag ran a hand through his hair, his face etched with worry. "Igraine's marriage is more than just a shame to the family because she disobeyed, Lezay. She chose one of my father's pets. I can't say more, but I will tell you — Enric should have been dead years ago. I don't know how he's not. And my father is going to do everything in his power to remedy the situation. He's not going to stop until they are both dead."

Chapter 32

Montag found him in the tavern. Raganor's back was toward the corner where only shadows of light danced across his features. No one paid him any mind, though it appeared the tavern matron kept his cup full of ale. Raganor's eyes flicked toward him, their white gleam like a flash of lightning in a black sky.

Holding up a hand to stop Lezay, who had followed him in his search asking a thousand unanswered questions, Montag quietly said, "This is where you leave me. Go wherever it is you're staying."

"I'd like to meet your father." Lezay smirked and moved to push past Montag, even though he did not know which patron the famous Le Brun was.

Montag grasped his arm, his grip firm now. He caught Lezay's eye. "No, you don't. Now get out."

Lezay frowned, frustrated and still confused from the evening's proceedings. "Fine." He shrugged off Montag's arm. With a last look around the room, he turned and left, the heavy door thudding shut behind him.

Montag turned back to the man in the corner, noting that he still watched. He covered the distance across the room in mere strides, weaving between tables as he did so. The tavern was still at least half full, being that it was a tournament night, but the tables around Raganor were empty. Most of the patrons of the tavern gathered closer to the fires, which kept the cool spring air at bay.

"You could have let your friend meet me," Raganor said. "Who is he?"

"None of your concern." Montag sat across from him.

"Ale?" Raganor offered.

Montag let out a humph and shook his head. "What will it take to ensure you return to Jerusalem and stay there? For good?"

Already Raganor's eyes were blackening, the hard glint behind them like metal. "I intend to. As soon as things are — tidied up — here."

"No manors in France then?"

"No, son." Raganor smirked.

Montag leaned back in his chair, considering. "What will it take for you to leave her alone?"

"I should remind you, son, that she is my daughter. I cannot just 'leave her alone.' That would be in violation of my duties as a father."

Montag snorted. "Duties as a father? Raganor, you have twisted and corrupted the meaning of fatherhood into something unrecognizable."

"Ah, and you'd know something about that now, wouldn't you? Now that you're a father yourself, eh, Montag?" Raganor's teeth glinted as he smiled that grin that never reached his eyes.

Montag frowned and tapped a knuckle on the table. He wasn't going to let this man bait him into a fight. Not here. "Have you seen her?"

Raganor weighed his response. "No." He took a sip of ale.

Montag bit his tongue, forcing his face blank. If what he said was true, perhaps he didn't know that Igraine was with child. "What do you want from me to keep it that way? I want you to leave her alone. Leave her husband alone. Him, I'll deal with myself."

"He is mine," Raganor hissed.

Montag didn't flinch. "Oh, I know."

Raganor stilled, a smirk playing at the corner of his lips.

Montag continued, "I hoped you would change your ways over there, but apparently being on holy ground means nothing to you. But here's the thing . . . he knows your little secret, and as much as I hate to admit it, he is a well-traveled, well-connected man. He is a tournament champion for God's sake! You move against him, or Igraine, and everyone will know. He can't just disappear like your crusaders. Not anymore. So you leave him to me, and you return back to your dust bowl."

Raganor leaned forward across the table. "You think I enjoy traveling thousands of miles to interfere with your lives? I have a castle with a harem of beautiful women in a place where the sun always shines and the wine is good. I would rather be there, I assure you, son. But blood calls blood, and when I am told just how much you two children are destroying our family line, I come."

"I am not going to argue about how we are or are not destroying the family line."

"What would you call it then? When I left you last year you were going to marry Igraine to a count! Then I hear she's being paraded around like a trophy by, of all men, Enric de Levan! Even if he had wealth, he does not have the bloodline to mix with our family. I practically gave the man his title."

"I'm sure that's a fascinating tale for another evening, but right now I want to know what you want. You can't touch either of them without revealing yourself, though I would relish the creative ways Enric's lord will think up to kill you. Drawing and quartering? Hanging just seems too . . . civil. Since you're obviously too stubborn to die, what do you want?"

Raganor again leaned into the corner, studying Montag. The metal glint in his eyes still flickered. "You want me gone for good?"

"Out of all of Europe. Your boundary lies beyond the Mediterranean Sea."

Raganor pursed his lips. "A thousand pounds in silver . . . no, make it gold."

"Fine." Montag clenched his fist. It was half the treasury of Brunstein.

Raganor's gaze narrowed. The hair on the back of Montag's neck stood up; the man wasn't done yet. "We never did get to induct you to The Order, son." Raganor's voice was so low it was practically a growl. "If I'm to never come West again, I need to know that someone is upholding our traditions."

Montag felt himself stiffen, though he fought to maintain his indifferent expression. "I have no interest in your traditions."

"Those are my terms, take it or leave it. I cannot stay away without a new inductee to take my place."

"Give me another option. More money? Horses? What do you want?"

"No. I want you to join me."

Montag shook his head, getting to his feet.

"I thought you loved your sister?"

Montag ran a hand through his hair and abruptly sat back down.

"Be honest with me, for once in your life, Father . . ."

"Montag, I am honest to a fault. You know that."

"Then tell me exactly why you are here. What do you have planned for her?"

The grin crept across Raganor's lips. His eyes held the closest thing to a twinkle Montag had ever seen in them. "Well . . . first I plan to kill her common-bred husband. And no, I'm not some novice that would leave the mark on my own back, Montag. No one will know who did it."

"Poison?"

Raganor studied him for a moment then slowly nodded. He took a small vial from a pouch tied to his belt. Watching Montag carefully, he tucked it back away again.

"Then what?" Montag prodded, his features indifferent.

"Igraine returns to Jerusalem with me, where I will find her a suitable husband."

"You don't want to kill her?"

"Kill her? No! Of course not. My only daughter . . ."

"Then what do you want to do to her? Surely you won't let her off that easily." When Raganor was slow to respond, Montag goaded, "You promised me honesty."

Raganor inclined his head. "She will marry one of our Order. He shares many of my . . . philosophies. Particularly when it comes to 'Burn the flesh—'"

"'To purge the soul.'" Montag closed his eyes for a moment, remembering the terror Igraine had shown when he himself had threatened to burn her again. She had sobbed, shaking, begging. And he would merely have tapped her with the iron. These men — this twisted order of theirs — they liked to brand until the flesh stank, until the skin peeled back and the muscle below blistered and cooked. His own back was proof of it. How could she survive it?

Why did she have to?

"I join your Order, and you and your friends swear never to touch her? Or her husband? You leave, you take your poison with you, and we never see or hear from you again?"

"Don't forget my gold, but yes, I will leave after your induction. You, Igraine, and her husband will be untouched."

"Do I need to stipulate that my son is also off limits? Or can you deduce that by your own reasoning?"

"You better be specific, Montag."

Montag stood and leaned over the table. "You don't touch any of my family, you devil. Not my son, not Igraine, not my brother-in-law, not any of my future wives for that matter. Not my great-aunt twice removed if she's still living. Understood?"

"I agree if you agree," Raganor said coolly.

"God help me," Montag said under his breath, anxiously running his hand through his hair again. He'd spent years avoiding what he'd witnessed a decade ago in the cellars of Brunstein. He'd been so disgusted he had cast his own father out, risen to power overnight, and fought to hold it every day since. To protect Igraine, her family, perhaps even Raoul, he would have to lower himself to his father's darkness. There was no noble twist to it, nor could he see another solution that would protect them all. Already he felt the hard malevolence eating at what conscience he had left.

"Fine," he spit. "You have your deal. When and where?"

Raganor's face lit up. "Tomorrow. Chateau Bergfried."

Montag stared at him stiffly for a moment, then turned away.

When he was a few steps away, Raganor called, "Oh, Montag. Bring your friend. If you don't want him to be in the ceremony, perhaps he'd like to join our ranks. He has a look about him . . . I think he'd fit right in."

Igraine felt utterly exhausted as she and Enric left the castle the next morning. They'd managed to speak with Richard and explain the situation. The lead into the conversation had been a diplomatically long one that took until dawn. Only then had they made their way back to their tent, intent on packing and leaving under the eyes of Enric's fellow knights. Igraine hardly noticed the red splashes of color that streaked the sky with the rising dawn. The heavy clouds that threatened a long day of rain were rolling in. She yawned and stumbled a little. Enric caught her elbow, then slipped his arm around her waist.

"Easy, there."

"How are you still awake? You fought a tournament yesterday, and you're as steady as ever, Enric." She squinted into his face, willing her tired eyes to focus. "Though you do have some circles under your eyes . . ."

Enric chuckled. "I went for days in Jerusalem without sleep." His face fell to a frown.

Igraine looked toward the village. "Ironic, how your lack of sleep last night happened for the same reason as before. My father has a way of doing that to people."

"At least our duke is on our side. Raganor will not gain a foothold in Aquitaine." Enric squeezed her hand.

As they entered the knights' encampment, Igraine saw Montag mounting at the far end of the field. He was already prepared to head out, while the rest of the camp dozed.

Their eyes locked despite the distance, and instead of seeing the concerned brother from the night before, she saw a black look of malice. And all of it was focused on her. A chill went down her spine. She froze, pulling Enric to a stop with her. He followed her gaze to the knight across the field, the man who even now jerked his horse around and kicked off into a canter.

"He made another deal," Igraine whispered sadly.

"What do you mean, a deal?"

She could only shake her head. "We won't see him again, Enric. Or my father. He does this, only when he can't see another way to protect me. He takes my punishment at some cost to himself and hates himself for it. Hates me for it. But this is the last time."

"Why would he take your punishment, Igraine? You have *me* now . . . he knows I will protect you."

Igraine looked up at her husband, blinking away tears. "That's the problem, Enric. Whatever deal he's made with the devil this time . . . this time it was to protect *you*." She looked after Montag's fading form as he rode away. She shook her head as the tears streamed. She could tell by that one brief look. This time Montag had done more than burn another scar onto his back or threaten Raganor to exile. This was more than a deal.

This time, Montag had sold his soul.

Chapter 33

T he storm was in full force now, swirling around them as Montag and Lezay trotted up to the main gate of the castle. The rocky cliff that lined their path glistened from the rivulets of water that ran down the hillside. Lightning flashed, framing the massive castle's silhouette against the darkening sky. The wind whipped hard enough to force their sodden cloaks into the air around them, then dropped them with a wet smack against their horses' foamy, panting sides.

Montag set his mouth in a hard line, biting his cheek to steady his nerves with the dull pain. There would be more pain ahead, of that he was certain. And if this was to work, he would be tested as a man as he'd never been before. He would pass, of course. That didn't mean he was looking forward to the ordeal. Or the black marks it would leave on his already battered soul.

Lezay gave Montag a light shove. Montag looked at him, noting the excited glint in his eye. "I finally get to learn all these secrets you've been keeping from me, eh, Montag?" He smiled a rotten grin.

Montag faced the castle. "You may wish you never met me."

"Never! Without you, I would never have met your sister."

Montag jerked his horse sideways, blocking the path in front of Lezay. If there was any part of him that was his father's son, he knew his eyes were black and hard as he glared at his once-friend. "From here out, you never speak to or of her again. You will not touch her or her husband. Do you understand?"

Lezay narrowed his eyes.

"Never, Lezay. This thing you have for her . . . it ends now. Understood? Answer me!"

"Alright! Understood! She's dead to me now." A loud clap of thunder echoed his words.

Montag glared at him a minute more. "You should go back home. You have no reason to be here. You don't need to join this Order. Go be free and live in the light with your wife."

Lezay snorted. "You think I'd turn back now? I just rode all this way."

Montag shook his head. "The journey hasn't even started yet." His face fell in sadness, and he tried to hide it by turning his horse up the hill to the castle.

Lezay hesitated for a minute, then with a sneer rode ahead of him. He seemed eager to join in whatever secrets Montag was privy to. They both knew that they had passed the point of friendship. There had been enough conflict and betrayal for that to be erased. By entering through those massive gates of the castle ahead, whatever ordeal they were about to undergo would forge something stronger than friendship. Secrets were to be shared, deeds done, and with that, they would be leaving bonded as brothers. The old, fragile alliances of friendship were going to be remade into something no conflict could render.

Lezay was eager. Montag tentative. Both knew the alliance being forged was better done together than separately. It was necessary. Montag steeled himself with that thought. To push his father out, this was necessary. And having Lezay along would strengthen his own power, hopefully catching Raganor unaware, which was the only way to weaken him. The rain pelted them as their tired horses leaned into the wind, forcing their way up the mountain. It was necessary.

Igraine shifted uneasily in the saddle, soaked from the rain that cloaked the countryside. With her grey hood pulled down over her face, the fabric of the thick wool caped out around her, she blended well into the scenery. She'd ridden hard, guilt overwhelming all sense, but at the base of the road up the gorge she knew it was already too late. Too many sets of hoofprints. There was nothing she could do, and to bear witness could just as well sign her death. Surely, they would be done soon anyway. The ceremony she had witnessed had been short, and Enric said what he experienced before escaping had been brief. But those were both interrupted ordeals. Who knew what they really did in that cloistered castle? So she waited in the shadows of the trees, hoping her brother would come down from the hill alone.

It was a risk she had to take, for her own closure. Enric had pleaded with her not to go, offered to go in her stead. Her aching, pregnant body had protested of its own accord. But the Le Brun determination persisted. With Enric's past, if any of The Order found him, he'd be dead. No, she was the only one that could try to stop Montag, the only one that knew the secret location he'd gone to.

She had tried to save her brother, one last time, from his fate. She had failed. Now all she could do was thank him and offer him what solace she could.

Her senses pricked at the sound of hooves splashing and sliding on the muddy road. A lone rider on a familiar horse: Montag. She urged her mount out of the trees, waiting in view for him to notice her. After only a few moments, he turned his horse toward her. She withdrew back into the trees, then waited.

Montag rode into the forest and stopped in front of her, the steam of their horses' breath mingling as the two beasts eyed each other, much like their riders.

"I wish you hadn't," Igraine whispered. Her bottom lip trembled.

"It had to be done." Montag's voice was sad, tired. "You didn't lead Enric here, did you?"

"No, of course not." She snorted a laugh. "That would be a death sentence for us all."

"You shouldn't even be here."

"I wanted to make sure you were all right." She forced her eyes up to Montag's. "Are you, brother?"

Montag held her gaze, then looked away. "He wasn't the first. He won't be the last."

Igraine swallowed, lifting a trembling hand to her lips. It was the duty of a knight to kill. They were raised for it, from the age of small children on up. Their lives were designed to make them mentally and physically lethal machines. But the kind of killing that had happened tonight was different, and both she and Montag knew it. This was murder, not defense nor even for some greater gain on a lord's order. It was different. All she could utter through her tears was, "I'm sorry."

Montag looked at her with a weariness he would never have shown another soul. "Make it worth it, Igraine." He gestured to her heavy womb. "Enjoy your life like you should. Live for both of us." The last words were a whisper.

"Montag . . ."

He shook his head. "It's worth it, Igraine." He rode up next to her, knee to knee, that he could cup her cheek in his hand. He let it linger there a moment, looking like there was something else he wanted to add, then shook his head, turning his horse away. The compassionate Montag switched off like the snuff of a candle. His walls crashed back down. "Get out of here before the rest of them leave. Lezay is among them. And don't ever come back here again." He kicked his horse forward without a backward glance, leaving Igraine alone to wrench out a sob.

She knew he was right and didn't linger. As fast as the slippery road would allow, she made it back into Enric's arms, where he held her close and dried her tears and whispered that somehow, he would make it right. She tried to explain that there was nothing he could do, no "making it right." Her family was a broken mess and always had been, the wound of such a barb in her chest that Enric could only soothe, never heal.

Chapter 34

T he tournament in Paris, with its dramatic conclusion, was Enric's last that summer. Igraine had taken the last ride her body could handle while under the duress of pregnancy, and she was grateful when they returned to Levan Manor. Enric jumped into the labor of the farm and started several of his young horses under saddle, while Igraine made the manor keep even more of a home.

She tried not to think too much of the labor to come, though her fears woke her from her dreams. Her best friend Alenor was one of five children, and once told Igraine that childbed came naturally to women — they could do it on instinct as easily as a horse passed manure. Her education obviously had been incomplete.

Igraine did not voice her fears to the other women of the manor. First of all, she was their Lady, and as such felt the need to maintain the visage of fearless control.

They also had a marked sense of positivity about them that both reassured her and reminded her of Alenor. At times that was good, but then memory would surge and the worst-case scenario burned in the back of her mind.

By the middle of August, she was so uncomfortable that she just wanted the babe out.

Nature obliged.

The pain seared through her from the base of her spine to toes. No, worse than that, as her entire frame contracted and bore down, everything pushing toward her core, her womb, in one radiating wave. Igraine gritted her teeth, one arm firmly around her middle. She'd been pacing all day as the discomfort increased. Now, as the sun began to set, there could be no doubt. Her labor had begun. The next hours would decide if she lived or died.

The contraction began to ease, and she breathed with relief, straightening with no small degree of tentativeness as she wondered when the pain would begin again. She rubbed her heavy belly, her other hand on her lower back which still ached. Her pacing resumed.

Enric's unmistakable footsteps sounded on the stairs. His pace seemed relaxed. Didn't he understand her situation? Where was his haste, his worry? As he opened the door to their room she shot him an angry look, which instantly softened when she noted the concern etched into his brow.

"It has begun?" he asked, stepping up to her and brushing hair from her forehead.

Her braids were an embarrassing mess. Even though it was mid-day, she was dressed in only her shift. She didn't care. She curled into Enric's shoulder, wrapping her arms around his middle. His solid strength comforted her. The heat of his body alone seemed to soothe her aching muscles.

"I'm scared," she whispered.

"Don't be." He kissed the top of her head, arms pulling her as tight as her belly would allow.

Her body chose that moment to tighten into another contraction, this one stronger than the last. She curled into Enric, buckling in pain, and let him support her. *It's not that bad. Don't scream. Don't scream.*

She let the groan tear from her, sweat breaking out on her face.

She panted as the pain dissipated, this time her knees a little wobbly. Enric's hands stayed steady on her back and arm, and she slowly was able to straighten, arms clamped around her middle once again.

"I can't do this," she muttered.

To her great frustration, Enric chuckled.

She glared at him.

"I think you're going to have to, my dear." He smiled gently, more amused than intimidated by her angry gaze. "Junior wants to come out." He led her toward the bed. The maids had already pulled back the bedding and readied it for the birthing. Igraine prayed it would not be as bad as Alenor's. As the images of her butchered friend in a pool of blood resurfaced, she pulled away from the bed, away from Enric. Hot tears threatened at the corners of her eyes. She resumed pacing.

Enric sat on the bed himself, watching her. "I sent someone for the midwife in Poitiers. She should be here soon. The maids are in the kitchen, ready as soon as you call them. Madame Gastineau has had five children. She assured me everything is going exactly as it should thus far."

Igraine continued pacing, rubbing at a sore spot that threatened to release into a full wave of pain.

Enric rose and caught her hands, pulling her pacing to a stop. She met his imploring eyes. "How can I help you? I would take this burden from you, but I cannot. Tell me how I can ease it."

Igraine gave him a grateful smile and sighed. "You being here helps." She shrugged. "I just think of Alenor — Enric, I don't even know how to direct you if you need to make that decision — to save me or the child. I suppose I empathize with my brother for having had to make it. I want, above all else, for this child to survive. It is *you*. I want it to survive. And yet — I want to live, too." She roughly wiped a tear, straightened her spine, and let out a frustrated sound, something between a growl and a groan.

She met Enric's eye. "I suppose I worry about nothing. It is your decision, after all."

Enric watched her in silence a long moment. "It won't come to that, Igraine."

"You don't know that."

"There are thousands of women who birthed thousands of babes without issue. Alenor was the exception."

"And my mother?"

Enric again grew quiet. "I didn't know she passed in childbirth."

Igraine nodded, avoiding his eye. She couldn't voice the words, *It was my fault.*

"So you have a right to be nervous. I will not leave your side. And I will do everything in my power to make sure you *both* survive. If we have to make decisions, you will make them with me. Though I must warn you, I will not let you go easily."

Igraine felt his sincerity and took comfort in it. Still, the stories of the women that came before her surfaced. The women laughed about men that tried to witness births and fainted. Or vomited. Or were so distracting they had to be pulled out of the room by no-nonsense midwifes trying to get their job done. "No man can stomach a birthing room. Even I know that."

Enric pulled her arms gently, forcing her to face him, meet his eye. "I will not leave you."

When Igraine finally nodded that she understood, she felt the relief wash over her. If he said he would be there, he would be, as long as the labor lasted. Even if the women tried to chase him out. And he would watch over her, make sure everything was done that could be done. If all that was to happen, then maybe she could survive.

A contraction raged through her with such rapid fierceness that she screamed, her knees finally buckling. Her fingernails dug into Enric's forearms as he reached out to catch her. When the moment had passed, leaving her breathless, he lifted her up and placed her on the waiting bed.

With some satisfaction, Igraine noted he now looked a little worried himself. She reached out to caress his cheek.

"Sorry about the fingernails," she cooed. "I can't promise I won't break any fingers the next time around."

Enric placed her hand firmly in his own. "Squeeze away."

People had warned her that the pain of childbirth was the worst a woman would feel in her lifetime. Birthing the child that now rested in Enric's arms had been a temporary pain compared to her emotional strife the past year. And it had been a pain well served. The child was perfect. And Igraine was very much alive.

The first rays of dawn cut through the manor window, illuminating Enric in a halo of warm light. His strong hands were bigger than the child's tiny head. The little girl fussed and murmured, eyes still squinted shut from the indignity of being pulled from her warm nest against her mother's breast. Enric looked upon her with such awe that it brought happy tears to Igraine's eyes. She smiled, overwhelmed with joy, and quickly wiped them away. Perhaps it was the callouses of his hands, or maybe the smell of horses that rose from Enric's tunic, but the little girl's fussing grew louder until she let out an ear-splitting wail.

Enric looked to Igraine in panic.

"Just rock her," she said softly.

The big knight, used to cutting through a man's armor with his sword, gently started to sway as he rocked the baby, whispering to her. Slowly the baby stilled, her big blue eyes locking into his own. He ceased his movement, caught in her stare. She waved her little fists at him, then decided she didn't like being still and started squalling again. When he obliged, she quieted, snuggling into his chest, blinking at him with those big, beautiful eyes.

"She's a fighter, that one," Igraine whispered, pushing herself up on the pillows of the bed. "She tells you exactly what she wants. What did you tell her?"

"That she can't grow big and get a pony unless she sleeps well."

Igraine burst out laughing.

"It's true!"

"I know, I know. She's not even a day old yet, Enric, and you're planning on putting her on a horse."

"She wouldn't be a Levan if we didn't."

"You don't care that she's a girl?"

"Why would I?"

Igraine shrugged and leaned her head back against the bedframe. "I know you wanted an heir."

"In Aquitaine, the women are also our heirs. Look at our former duchess, once Queen of France, now Queen of England. She was the heir of Aquitaine, and she's done remarkably well."

Igraine knew Queen Eleanor's rule was shaky at best. Even now rumors spread that King Henry had taken a mistress and locked the queen away. Her part in her son's revolt had not helped her case. But that wasn't important. What was important was that Enric didn't mind that his new heir was a girl. He obviously adored her.

"What do you want to name her?" Enric's eyes shot up to Igraine. "Luci for my mother? Or Adelheid like your mother? I always thought Sibylla was pretty — but then again, that reminds me too much of Jerusalem . . ."

"Eleanor. Enric, there is no option but Eleanor."

"After Eleanor of Aquitaine? Our queen?"

"In part. Like you said, if she is to be your heir, she should have a good role model to look up to. But also for my friend. Alenor . . . I can't stop thinking about her. I think she would be honored. And perhaps it will get the Tielos to believe I had no part in her death."

"It's a beautiful name." He looked down at the feisty child in his arms. "Eleanor . . ." he whispered. The little girl yawned, then settled into the crook of his arm, fast asleep. "Our very own Eleanor de Levan."

A knock sounded at the door. Before Enric could even shift to open it, it burst open, his parents spilling in with smiles as wide as the horizon. Igraine smiled as Enric handed little Eleanor to his mother, her face alight with joy. His father congratulated them, slapping Enric on the shoulder. It was a beautiful moment, the kind Igraine once thought would never come to her. She gave up a prayer of thanks, eternally grateful for the desperate ride that had pushed her forever into Enric's arms. Eleanor yawned as her grandmother brushed her delicate hand with a fingertip.

This was Igraine's life, her future. And it was worth everything that had been risked.

Chapter 35

September 24, 1174
Poitiers, Aquitaine

There was a final tournament of the season in Poitiers, and curiosity got the best of Montag. He'd heard his sister had had the child, and he had to see for himself. Enric wasn't there to compete; he was networking. It took Montag a while to find Igraine, but she was there, in the market. He watched from a distance.

Montag's frown sank deeper as he watched Igraine pull her shawl tighter around herself. The baby was tucked into the crook of her arm, and Igraine was oblivious to his presence, so focused was she on the child. At least she looked happy. She wandered further into the marketplace outside of the tournament ground, and he followed from a leisurely distance, debating if he should make his presence known or not.

Lezay appeared at his side, his gaze as fixed on Igraine as Montag's. Montag tore his eyes away and spun on his heel. He was increasingly resentful of the man, and yet still he always seemed to appear, like a child teasing another just for the pleasure of aggravating him. Knowing Lezay would follow him instead of Igraine, he headed for the encampment.

"Did you hear what she named the child?"

Montag let out a grunt, hoping Lezay would take the hint and go away.

"Eleanor." Lezay smirked as Montag planted his feet so fast Lezay almost walked into him.

"What?"

"She named the baby girl Eleanor. I hear she spells it with an E though. Don't know what difference that would make."

Montag glared at Lezay. He longed to punch the man but as usual, due to the crowd, he could not. Of course, this is why Lezay had told him now. Montag felt like he himself had taken a blow to his gut. Eleanor? Of all the million names in the world, his vile sister had chosen *Eleanor*? He let out a stream of expletives under his breath as he stormed through the crowd, looking for his lazy swine of a squire. He no longer cared where Lezay went. He needed a horse. Or his pike. It was time to get the tournament started.

Hours later, utterly exhausted and battered, Montag seethed as he again watched the Levans from across the room. Eleanor. Eleanor. Alenor. Someone was talking to him, but he did not hear. He stood abruptly and left the hall, dragging his squire from a table full of peers by the scruff of his neck. The boy knew better than to protest, and Montag only released him when they were in the barn. He threw the boy across the barn aisle, watching the lad scramble to catch his feet. Wordlessly, as Montag finished his cup of ale, the boy got Montag's horse ready to ride.

There was no one thought in Montag's head but a thousand, running as fast as the wind in his face, the thunder of hooves beating loud in the moonlight down the road. He rode until the foam frothed off his horse, the legs of his pants wet from the beast's sweat. Only then did he slow, calculating the value of the charger beneath him and the sizeable cost to replace it. The sum was too great. He let the horse catch its breath, drink water, eat grass, then set off again at a more reasonable pace. Still he arrived at the Abbey Saint Catherine as dawn was cresting Les Vosges in the distance, the river below the ridge sparkling in the pink sunlight.

Red sky. A bad omen.

He wordlessly entered the abbey, ignoring the nuns who intercepted him, protesting. He knew where he was going. And they were not going to stop him. He burst through the door to the nuns' quarters, sending women screaming and grabbing for their veils. Then there she was. Her back was to him as she knelt beside her bed, hands clasped before her in prayer. Her long black veil hid her golden hair, but Montag could imagine it beneath the rough fabric, fine as silk. He shifted his weight anxiously, waiting for her to rise, as the rest of the nuns continued to flurry around him, backing away in terror.

She crossed herself. Then slowly she rose. He watched her shoulders rise and fall as she drew a deep breath, then turned to face him. And there she was. In the habit of a nun, no trace of adornment on her person, and still as beautiful as ever. His heart pounded in his chest for the first time since she had left. At least, the first time that he did not have a man on the other end of a weapon.

Her face was expressionless, though she stared right at him. No smile, no fear, just blank contemplation. For once he was speechless, the urgency of his journey forgotten. It took her to break the silence.

"What do you want?" Alenor asked. It was gentle. Not angry, not indignant.

It brought him to his knees before her.

Her eyes went wide at that. Montag vaguely registered the sisters being ushered out of the chamber, until suddenly he and Alenor were alone in an eerie dawn silence. Still he stared at her from his knees, debating if he should beg her forgiveness or simply bow to her beauty. She held herself nobly, her chin up, back straight. She looked thin, perhaps too thin; it was impossible to tell with the baggy habit.

"How is our son?" Alenor asked stiffly.

Montag blinked himself to awareness again and slowly rose back to his feet. "He grows. Strong boy. He's beginning his training." He bit his lip as he tried to think of something more substantial to tell the mother of his child. "He likes the puppies."

Alenor didn't smile, and Montag noticed her hands go white as she clasped them together. Was she shaking? No, probably not. She studied him a moment, then said, "I haven't broken my silence. What do you want?" Her gaze was beginning to ice over now.

"I . . . I needed to see you."

"You left me here, half dead, over a year ago. Now you want to see me? I don't exist, remember?"

Montag stared at her again. "I have not remarried."

Alenor snorted. "What is that supposed to mean?"

"You can come home."

Alenor's eyebrows shot up her forehead. Montag took a step back, realizing his mistake, hating himself for it. When she spoke again her words came out iced. "You left me in my greatest need. You stole my child. You threatened to kill me. And now because you've been unable to find a suitable replacement for me, you want me back? No, no, no, Montag. You will not. For *I* have remarried. I am a bride of Christ now; I am Sister Mary, the mute who showed up butchered like a cow years ago. This is my home now, these women my family, and God help you if you force me from this place." Montag noted the iron in her spine and the way her hands fisted at her sides, and he withdrew.

He looked her up and down a last time, then turned away for what he knew for sure now would be forever. His chest hurt, like a blow to the sternum. He rubbed the spot, curious about it. He stepped toward the door.

"You could have asked for my forgiveness. You could have apologized." Alenor said coldly behind him.

He kept walking, rubbing that spot on his chest. Perhaps he had been bruised in the tournament? There was a crash behind him, something shattering on the wall. The nuns stared as he left the abbey, mounted his horse, and rode home to Alsace. He needed a good port. That's all. Too long a night. Too long a day. It would soon be time to rest.

He looked down at his exhausted horse and again debated its value. There were a few promising prospects at home that likely were just as fast and far younger.

He kicked the horse on.

Chapter 36

May 1199

Eleanor had remained quiet as they exited the brothel late that afternoon. They still had a few hours of daylight, and Alec intended to ride through them and home to Levan Manor before darkness settled. Eleanor kept pace with him as they cantered out of town, her lips in a thin line.

They were a few miles out of town, in a dense cluster of forest, when she reined up. The late afternoon sunlight glowed as it cut through the trees around them, framing them all in patchy golden light. The earthy smell of the forest filled Alec's nose as he inhaled, preparing for the onslaught he knew he deserved.

"You've known all this time?" Her voice was the whisper of a sword blade, cutting the silence of the forest in which not even a bird had dared to chirp. The accusatory tone sent a tingle down his spine, but it wasn't unexpected.

Alec met her gaze with practiced calm, ready to meet the wrath he imagined bubbling under the surface. "I've known a while. I'm not sure what 'all this time' could be defined as—"

"How long, Alec?"

Alec frowned as he ran a hand through his straggly hair, sweeping it out of his eyes. He stared into Eleanor's, willing her calm. The turmoil within her roiled in front of him like a boiling pot. She would not calm easily. "I learned about Montag's strange Order while you were with child. Actually, while I was in Normandy with Lord Otto, while you were giving birth. We were in a tavern on the road. We'd been drinking, and we started talking about the darker side of knighthood, the side that isn't chivalry and faith based. One of the older men said he'd heard rumors of a knight that had sold his soul to that dark side. He mentioned the name Raganor le Brun."

"You didn't know I was a Le Brun?"

Alec shook his head. Eleanor was still full of surprises. "I am surprised you know. Montag and your mother, Igraine, disassociated with him in every way they could. And Montag rose to power a great deal on his own. He put Brunstein on the map. And he never used the name Le Brun. Always Montag of Alsace or Montag of Brunstein or even de les Montagnes. So I did not realize at first that your mother's family name is in fact Le Brun—"

"Until we raided Montag's castle, and you saw the heraldry on the walls. The brown stag, right? Mon Dieu

. . . why didn't you tell me my grandfather was still alive? Did you know?"

Alec worked his jaw as he carefully chose his words. "I had a suspicion that if he was, he would show himself when Montag was dead. Something Lezay said years ago, before you and I met. I suspected Lezay joined The Order as well, but that's another story. He said to Montag, 'The devil from the East will find her if you let him come home'. In reference to finding you, of course." Alec furrowed his brow. "At the time, I thought they were talking about a Moor . . . or a tracker. Not Raganor himself." He stared intently down the road ahead for a minute. "I asked — that woman — to help me piece together the story, which you can see she did rather well. When I saw him today, like Montag's ghost, I knew he had returned."

Eleanor let out her breath, dropping her reins to press her fingers into her temples as if her head ached. She blinked at Alec.

"This unnamed woman . . . she is an old friend, nothing more?"

"I promise you, Eleanor. She is our ally." He hesitated. "For her safety, I am sorry I cannot tell you more. When I can, I promise I will."

"Alec, I'm trying really hard to trust you."

He swallowed, his attention again traveling down the road ahead of them. "I know."

Eleanor was quiet for a while, the sound of their horses' footsteps thudding into the leaf-strewn dirt. "What about Montag's wife? Is Alenor alive? How on earth did you find out she survived childbed?"

"Another story from Lezay. Perhaps only hearsay. No, I don't know if she's still alive."

"Does Raoul know about her?"

"I haven't told him."

"We spent so many hours talking about how our mothers were dead. It bonded us. I doubt he knew." She stared ahead of them, her eyes distant. "And that is a greater tragedy still." Abruptly she turned in the saddle to face Alec, startling her horse. "Why didn't you let me meet my grandfather, Alec? What if he has returned to repair the relationships Montag shattered?"

Alec shook his head incredulously. "Didn't you hear what he did to your parents? To Montag?"

"It was a long time ago. Montag is who kept him away all these years." Confusion etched her brow with deep lines. "If they were such kindred souls, why?"

Alec reached between their horses to take her hand and squeeze it. "There is a part to the story no one else knows yet." He inhaled sharply, biting his lip, wondering how to resume with the most difficult part. How much did Eleanor herself remember?

The silence stretched.

"You already know the end of this story. You lived it."

Eleanor looked away, but not before the pain in her eyes flared. She knew the tale all right. She'd been so young when things fell apart, and some memories left an impression even on a small child. "From the sound of things, Montag is the last person my mother would have entrusted me to. Are you going to tell me how that happened?"

"Eleanor, last year, in Alsace . . . you did what you had to do. You saved my life that night. And our child's. There was no other choice. He left you with none."

She looked warily at the man before her. "Alec . . ."

Alec shifted in the saddle. His voice dropped to a solemn whisper. "I've learned a lot about Montag this past year. He was a lot of things, some terrible. But when it came to you there was one thing I think he really did try to be, just like he was for your mother." Alec hesitated, then spit out, "Protector."

Chapter 37

August 12, 1179
Angoulême

Igraine and Enric watched from their blanket on the grass as five-year old Eleanor raced their friend Sir Josse's sons, one of which was a whole year older than her. Lady Isabel sat with them, laughing. The children's little legs pumped as fast as they could as they raced tree to tree. At the last minute, Eleanor pushed ahead, determination etched on her little face.

"I win!" she squealed and jumped up and down.

The other little boys weren't enthused. "You took a short-cut."

"Did not!"

"Did to!"

"Fine, let's go again, and I'll beat you again," she said, stomping back toward the starting line.

Igraine bit her tongue to avoid rolling her eyes, though Enric was chuckling.

The boys snickered amongst themselves and then took off running in the opposite direction. Eleanor spun around and immediately changed course after them. "Hey! Come back!"

"We don't want to play with girls!" the boys said and disappeared into the courtyard of the manor and out of sight.

"Eleanor!" Enric called, wagging a finger at her for her to come back.

"She's a fireball, isn't she?" Isabel asked as they watched the little girl stomp back to them with her arms crossed, a big pout on her face.

"She's certainly enough to keep us busy, that's for sure," Igraine conceded. The girl now within reach, Igraine reached up to brush her off. "Now, now, Eleanor. A pout is not very becoming for a lady. Come sit with me and Lady Isabel."

"I don't want to sit," Eleanor whined.

"Eleanor," Igraine warned. The girl obeyed, sitting gracefully on the grass next to her mother. She didn't smile, but she didn't whine either.

"I hear you're learning how to ride a pony, Eleanor," Isabel prompted.

Eleanor's face lightened. "Her name is Buttercup."

"That's a great name for a pony. Did you name her yourself?"

Eleanor nodded proudly. "I rode her here all by myself, too!"

Isabel looked at Igraine in surprise. "Did she really?"

Igraine chuckled. "Mostly. Enric had Buttercup on a lead, but Eleanor did ride most of the way." She was proud of the child. She certainly was following in her parents' footsteps.

Enric leaned in toward the women. "I think she rode in the saddle with me about fifty percent of the ride," he whispered. "And most of that she was asleep."

They all laughed, except for Eleanor, who gazed longingly out toward the courtyard where the boys had disappeared. Igraine followed her gaze, then looked to Enric, who shrugged.

"Listen, Eleanor. If you still want to go play with the boys, why don't you go up to them politely and ask again. Apologize for bragging about your victory—"

"But they always rub it in when I lose!"

"Eleanor . . . humility is a virtue. Try it and ask again if they'll play with you. Maybe a different game?"

"Oh, all right. I'll try . . ." She picked herself up and hurried off, half running, half walking, as if she was torn between being a lady and playing like the boys.

Isabel laughed. "She has your spirit in her, Lady Igraine. And Sir Enric's athleticism if I dare say. She looks more like you, Enric, every time I see her."

"She does, doesn't she?" Enric obliged, stretching out on the grass. His confident look made Igraine fall in love with him even more. She smiled to herself, a hand casually on her womb.

Isabel chewed her lip.

"What is it, Lady Isabel?" Igraine asked, noting the woman's frown.

"I shouldn't bring it up, but have you talked to your brother lately?"

Enric sat up part way, propping himself on his elbows.

"We haven't spoken in years." Caution and regret soured Igraine's jovial mood. "Why do you ask?"

"Rumors were spreading at the last tournament. No one has seen him at a tourney in ages. He appears to be a recluse, sending other men at arms to enforce his rules, collect his taxes. I just wondered if you know if that is true or not."

Igraine and Enric shared a confused look. Igraine replied, "No. Well, we haven't seen him either. We assumed with all our moving around, we just avoided his path. Things obviously haven't been well between us in a long time, so I can't say I've been searching him out, either."

"I just wondered." Isabel shrugged and looked away..

Igraine furrowed her brow, still thinking. She was as guilty as Montag for not making contact. The unspoken agreement to avoid each other had left a scar she did not know how to mend. He had given of himself to protect her family, and when last seen, was furious at himself and thus them. Still, he was her brother. How was he? How was little Raoul, who must be so big by now?

Suddenly a child's scream split the air, coming from the direction of the courtyard.

All three of them were on their feet in moments, Enric leading the way a good few strides ahead of the women. Igraine and Isabel halted just inside the courtyard, eyes wide at the sight of Isabel's eldest pinning a screaming Eleanor against the wall with his wooden sword. The little girl's face was streaked with tears, her hair even messier than it had been when they were racing. Enric snatched the wooden sword away in a deft movement. The little boy turned to face him, face going from anger to fear in seconds as he looked up at the towering knight. Enric crossed his arms, the sword still in his hand.

"Care to explain, Young Josse? Why is my daughter pinned against a wall?"

"She wouldn't leave us alone," the boy mumbled.

"What?" Enric prompted, even though he'd heard the boy.

"She wouldn't leave us alone!" Young Josse shouted, tears starting to fall down his own cheeks.

"And you thought it acceptable to chase her with a sword?" Isabel implored, stepping up to Enric's side, her face red with fury and embarrassment. Igraine skirted behind them, scooping the sobbing Eleanor into her arms, checking her little arms and legs for bruises. Enric looked at her imploringly and she looked back to him, nodding once. The little girl was fine, just upset.

Enric turned his attention to the boy again. "Josse, do you know what the code of knighthood entails?"

"Yes."

"Really? What does it say?"

"Protect the defenseless," the boy mumbled.

"Which means we protect women. We protect those weaker than us. You will be a man one day, hopefully a knight like your father. You need to learn that lesson now. Do not hurt girls."

"She's not defenseless," the boy mumbled again, kicking the dirt.

Igraine shot Enric a bewildered look. "What did you say?" she asked.

"Nothin'," the boy insisted.

Enric turned to Eleanor. "Eleanor what happened here?" She turned her face into her mother's shoulder. "Look at me. Why was he picking on you?"

Still she tried to hide, looking away.

Igraine set her down, her lips set in a stern line, suspicion now growing that perhaps it was not only the boys to blame. "Act like a lady and answer your father."

Eleanor met her father's gaze. "I was throwing globs of mud at him. He said I couldn't play because I'm a girl."

"I told you! She started it! She wouldn't stop. She hit Pieter right in the head!" young Josse suddenly burst. The other boy did in fact sport clay on his forehead as proof.

"Eleanor!" Igraine scolded.

"He pushed me!" Eleanor shouted.

"She pushed us first!" the boys insisted.

Enric shook his head and held his hand up for silence, which fell instantly. "Boys, I will leave your mother to discipline you. Eleanor, you come with me. Now."

The little girl hid behind Igraine's skirts, crumbling under the intensity of her father's anger. Igraine kept an arm protectively around her, warning flaring in her veins. Her memory flashed to how she was disciplined as a child, for crimes far less than what Eleanor had committed, and she paled. Her arm wrapped tighter. She didn't want to fight Enric in front of their host, but she would if she had to. She would protect the girl. Her back straightened; she glared at him, like a mama bear protecting her cub.

Enric reached to grab Eleanor's little arm, then stopped as Igraine shifted the girl behind her. He caught her gaze with all the fears and threats it wordlessly conveyed. His face fell in sadness. He cupped her cheek, caressing it. "Trust me," he whispered, his eyes pleading. Slowly she relaxed and allowed him to bend down to pry Eleanor's fingers from her skirts. "Come with me, little one," Enric growled. His tone was hard, but he winked at Igraine when

Eleanor's little back was turned. "Forgive us, Lady Isabel. We will return momentarily."

Lady Isabel now had her oldest by the ear and was leading him into the castle, saying something about, "Wait until your father hears about this!" Pieter followed behind, dragging his feet.

Enric guided Eleanor behind the stable, out of view of the manor household. Igraine followed a bit behind them, still stiff with worry and clenching her hands together until they were white. She readied herself to watch her child be thrashed for the first time. Eleanor's tears were streaming down her face, mucus running down her nose onto her pink lips.

"I'm sorry, papa." She sobbed. "I was—" sniffle "—mad."

To Igraine's surprise, Enric smiled softy and knelt in front of the little girl, using his sleeve to wipe her tears and nose. Eleanor quieted at his gentleness, still sniffling.

"You understand why what you did was wrong, Eleanor?"

"Ladies don't throw mud." She sniffed.

"No one should throw mud. We must do unto others as we would have them do unto us. You wouldn't want someone to throw mud at you, so you don't throw mud at them. Does that make sense?"

Eleanor nodded. Igraine leaned against the side of the barn and let her smile return.

"Now how about you tell me what happened leading up to the mud throwing?" Enric prompted. Still he knelt at the little girl's eye level.

"They were playing sword fight, and I asked if I could play too. Pieter said no, and they ignored me. I tried to join in anyway, and they both . . ." She started to cry again. "They took my sword and said girls can't use swords. And then they broke it!" She was overcome.

"So you threw mud at them?" Enric asked, shooting a bemused glance over his shoulder toward Igraine. Eleanor nodded. "And then Jacques came after you with his wooden sword? And you had none to defend yourself with?" Eleanor nodded again. "I see." Enric rose to his feet, his big hand on the girl's shoulder. "I see only one way to remedy this." Eleanor looked down, her lip trembling. Enric gave her a look of utmost seriousness. "You must make sure no boy ever steals your sword again."

Eleanor's eyes shot up to his, her expression brightening as his lips cracked into a smile. "Really, Papa?"

Enric looked around, locating two sticks, which he broke to an appropriate length. Igraine straightened from her place along the building. "Really, Enric?"

He glanced to her, his eyes alight with joy. "You might as well join us, my lady. I promised you training years ago, and we never quite finished it." He tossed her the stick he held and located yet another from beneath the tree. "Now, here is how it's done . . ." Enric spent the next twenty minutes schooling his pupils behind the barn, showing them how to block and deflect blows, how to sidestep away from an opponent. By the time he was done, Eleanor was in a fit of giggles, and Igraine was at a loss as to how she would ever train the girl to be a respectable lady.

They returned back to the castle, Eleanor running ahead, while Enric's arm twined around Igraine's waist. He leaned into her, kissing her temple. "I had you worried, didn't I?" he whispered.

Igraine nodded slightly. "Discipline in my household went a bit differently."

Enric caressed her back through the fabric of her gown. "I would never, Igraine. I swear to you. She must learn, but never like that."

Igraine nodded. "I know now."

He whispered in her ear again, the bristle of his short beard tickling her, "I love you."

She stopped him, pulling his lips to hers in a lingering kiss. No words were necessary as she looked into his eyes, her fingers caressing his cheeks. She moved his hand to her stomach.

"You are going to have your hands full if this child is anything like your daughter."

Enric furrowed his brow, then suddenly his eyebrows rose. "You're sure?"

She nodded.

"Finally—" He breathed and kissed her with a crushing force.

She laughed when he finally pulled his lips away.

"Come on, you love birds have been married six years already! You don't have to keep showing off," Sir Josse called from the castle doorway. He smiled. "Dinner's ready if you can keep your hands off each other long enough to eat."

Chapter 38

August 23, 1179

Levan Manor, Aquitaine

A few weeks later, shouts drew Igraine out of Levan Manor. It didn't take her long to discover the source, and she picked up her skirts as she strode purposefully towards the paddock.

The fiery chestnut reared into the setting sun, his copper coat shining. Igraine's heart was in her throat, not only in awe of the beauty of the animal, but for fear for the man astride it. As with most of their horses, Enric had won this one. It was the least generous prize he had yet received.

For years now the two souls had been trying to tame one another, with varying degrees of success. When the horse had the mind, he carried Enric down the list and likely would face the fires of battle for him. But then on days like this, with no obvious reason, he was as wild as they came. Dangerous wild.

Enric tried using the stallion for breeding. He tried not breeding him. He tried working him harder, working him less. He changed feed. He gave the horse a pasture mate, which only ended in a massive laceration for the other poor beast. Finally he let him sit for an entire year, thinking maybe the horse only needed time to heal from some unknown injury.

That year was now complete. With the antics being demonstrated, the horse was not only unappreciative, but showcasing his supreme athleticism. And certain lack of injury.

Enric stayed on, yet Igraine judged from the sweat pouring down his face and the look of stoic concentration that it was taking all he had to channel the animal to his will, which was merely to move calmly forward. As the horse's feet returned to the earth, it seemed a shutter had been opened to the animal's mind. For all his prior unruliness, he was the picture of obedience, and Enric trotted around the pen, then cantered. The footfalls fell heavy on the earth yet the picture was as light as if they danced. Enric did a little more, then reined up in front of Igraine.

He patted the chestnut, his face lined in thought.

"I just don't get it. It's all there. But I never know which horse I'll get."

"I don't trust this one." Igraine reached out a hand toward the horse's face, and he snorted at her, whites of his eyes warning. She sighed and withdrew her hand. Before Eleanor was born, Igraine had ridden every horse in their stable herself, just to prove to Enric that she could. He'd been most impressed. Now she was slightly more selective, more careful, but still found it rare to be fearful of one of the animals. This stallion, named Draca, was the exception. "I don't know why you want to sit on his back."

Enric laughed and swung down from the saddle, again patting the stallion on the neck. "I like a challenge."

"You have a wife and children to think about now." She patted a hand on her growing womb, the bump just barely showing.

"Don't worry, this one will get a pony soon, too." He kissed her belly and then her forehead.

Igraine smiled. As he moved to walk away, she caught his fingers. "Enric . . . I mean it. I think you should let this one go."

Enric eyed the ball of muscle he held in his hand by a mere leather strap and nodded. "I know. You've always had a good eye. He just needs a little more time." He squeezed her fingers and pulled away. "The Fougères will be here any minute. Let me get cleaned up. You better check on Eleanor."

"She's supposed to be getting dressed. Though who knows what's really happening." Igraine fell into step with Enric as he headed to the stable. "Are you sure she's not too young, Enric?" Igraine's smile wavered.

"Lord Fougères is a good man. We will wait until she is old enough, have no worries there." He glanced up at

Igraine, then to the child running toward them. He gave the chestnut's reins a firm tug as it pranced a few steps. "The betrothal is meant to protect her."

"Just . . . shouldn't she have a choice? I took my own choice at the cost of my family."

Enric hesitated. "It's better if we make a good choice for her than the options for a bad choice fill that void. This contract will hold over those who would propose more wealth, power . . . but not a match in age or morality."

"Morality! Little Edmond is only six years old! How do we know what kind of man he will be?"

"What do you want me to say, Igraine? Your—" he hesitated, frowning. "Your family has a far reach. I just worry what could happen if these decisions were ever to fall into their hands."

"We have so much time—"

Enric winced. "My love, I am a knight. And though I hope to live to a ripe old age, your warnings do reach me. I am very aware that I am a mortal man."

Igraine inhaled sharply. She knew he was right. She said as much to him before every tournament. He was listening, in his own way. They had to think this way. All of their peers did. But the children were so young.

"Can we at least see if they get along?" she asked.

"They are children."

"Enric. Please?"

Igraine pleaded with wide eyes. Enric sighed in frustration, absently catching Eleanor's hand as she reached to pet the chestnut's nose. Gently he pulled her to his side, away from the horse. "Fine. We will see how the meeting goes."

"Fair enough." Igraine shielded her eyes from the sun and squinted down the road. A dust cloud rose in the distance. "Riders approaching."

"Are they here? Are they here?" Eleanor bounced up and down as Igraine tried to straighten her hair.

"Yes, love. Now remember how we practiced. Today you must act like a lady. Show our guests you are the lady of the manor. Be court—"

"Cour-te-ous and kind and dig . . . dig-ni-fied!" Eleanor beamed at her mother and straightened her back, mimicking Igraine's regal posture. Igraine couldn't resist placing a kiss on the child's forehead.

Enric handed the stallion off to his squire and straightened his clothes. He reeked of sweat and horse, but the Levans knew their guests were going to smell even stronger after their long days on the road. The riders cantered through the trees, slowing as they pulled up in front of the hosts of Levan Manor. The household had gathered behind the family in curiosity and excitement.

Lord Fougères dismounted and handed his horse to a groom, raising his hands in greeting with a beaming smile. "Sir Enric, a pleasure to see you again!" He extended his arm, and Enric readily shook his hand, a cautious smile lighting his features. "Lady Igraine, you are as stunning as ever. Motherhood looks well on you." He bowed gracefully.

Igraine shifted her dress uncomfortably as his eyes locked on her stomach. She wasn't ready to tell everyone about her condition yet, but Fougères was as observant as any of the other men her brother was friends with. He did have the best manners though.

"Welcome," Enric offered. "You've had such a long journey. You must be exhausted."

"Ah, I may not compete in tournaments anymore, Sir Enric, but I'm not old yet." They laughed.

The riders behind Fougères dismounted, dusting off their clothes and handing off their horses. From among them a small boy emerged, chin high as he gave his horse a pat on the nose before stepping forward. "My Lord." He bowed to Enric. "My Lady." He bowed to Igraine. "I am pleased to meet you. Thank you for the invitation to visit your home. I look forward to meeting your daughter." He stood straight-backed as a prince, chin jutted forward in confidence. His curly brown hair stuck out in odd angles, his sun-tanned skin accenting features that hinted the boy would be at least as handsome as his father when grown. He, too, offered his small hand, which Enric shook with a firm grip.

Enric shot Igraine an amused look, and she smiled back. Turning to Edmond she said, "Edmond, let me introduce to you my daughter, Eleanor de Levan. Eleanor, this is our young friend Edmond de Fougères."

Eleanor studied the boy, a frown on her face. He bowed politely, but she did not return the courtesy. "How old are you?"

"Seven, my lady. You?"

"I'm only five. That must be why you're so tall."

Edmond shot a questioning look at his father, uncertain how to react.

Eleanor continued, her gaze still focused on the boy. "I like your horse. When I'm seven I want to ride a big horse like that, too. What's his name?"

"Blaze."

"Yes, fitting name. He does have that marking on his face, doesn't he? I like to be more creative with my horse's name though. My horse has a star on her forehead, but I don't call her star. Her name is Buttercup because she's yellow. Do you want to meet her?"

"Uh . . ." Edmond glanced at his father. "Yes?"

Lord Fougères waved his son forward to follow the little girl that was already striding off toward the stable, her chin high, hands clasped before her. Edmond took a quick step after her to catch up.

Enric hid a smile behind his hand as Fougères chuckled.

"She's a handful, that one, isn't she?"

"Like her mother," Enric admitted.

"Hey!" Igraine laughed. She shook her head. "My Lord, why don't you join us inside for some wine and food, and we'll let Eleanor finish showing Edmond around the manor."

By nightfall, Edmond sat bewildered at his father's side as Eleanor enlightened all of them about their adventures. It sounded like she'd run him around the entire estate a few times without rest.

"I told him to throw a penny in the old well and make a wish, but he wouldn't," she pouted.

"I'm saving my pennies to buy honeyed bread at the next tourney," Edmond protested.

"But he—"

Igraine laid a hand on her daughter's arm. "Eleanor, you weren't down at that old well again, were you?"

Eleanor looked down at her plate, finger pushing around her uneaten food.

"Eleanor. I told you that place is dangerous. Certainly not somewhere to take a guest."

"Sorry," the child mumbled.

"If you're done with your dinner, get along to bed."

"But . . ."

"Eleanor." Enric's commanding voice left no room for protest. The child sighed and made her way up the stairs and out of the hall.

"She's a gem," Fougères said gently.

"Our one and only," Igraine pointed out.

"It is a good match," Fougères nodded. "This is a very good match. We can help each other. The children get along. It is all I could ask for my son."

Igraine's conflicted thoughts rolled through her mind. Too young. *Give her the choice*, one part of her said, countered by *don't let Raganar have a chance to choose for her. Nor Montag. Enric is mortal, and so are you.* She looked up into Enric's eyes. Their conversation continued in that gaze, though no words needed to be spoken. She eventually nodded at him.

Enric smiled. "It is all we could ask for our daughter. It will be good to ally the families."

"She will be your heir?"

"Yes. She is already, unless we have a boy of course." He shot an adoring look at Igraine. "Either way, she will have a considerable dowry. Our estate is ever expanding as you know. I hope after a few more years of tournaments it will be even larger."

"It is plenty. She is worth it. That child has been blessed with your face, Igraine. I will be grateful my son won't have to fight off the other men for her when she is of age."

"What of his prospects?" Enric asked.

"He will have to make his own way," Fougères said. He hesitated, studying his empty plate. "My oldest will inherit my estates. Capable young man. Recently knighted. My second oldest is already taking steps to enter the church.

Then my youngest and the baby are to be decided. Edmond has fight in him. He will be a masterful ally to the king, a smart advisor and leader. I have no doubt he will be very successful on his own path." He looked down proudly at Edmond, who remained quietly at his side. "Already athletic and an excellent rider."

Silence echoed around the table for a moment.

"Lord Fougères, who is he mentoring with?" Igraine asked tentatively. She regretted not asking sooner.

Fougères' lips twitched. "Lord Montag of Brunstein."

Igraine inhaled sharply, her knuckles white as she clenched her cup. There it was. The old alliance. Her fears were not unfounded.

Enric slowly turned to Igraine. "This could be to our advantage."

"To our — Are you mad?" She turned to Fougères. "How could you ever let a child be raised at that place?" She thought back to Hans — and all the others — she had been forced to doctor over the years.

Fougères turned to Edmond, who watched the conversation with rapt attention now. "Edmond, get along to bed now. One of the servants will show you the way." The boy obeyed instantly. Turning to Igraine, Fougères hissed, "Your brother is still the best knight in Europe. If my son is to earn his way in this world by his sword, I would have him learn from the best."

Enric bristled. "Montag has not competed in a tournament in years. He is no longer the best."

Fougères looked Enric up and down in amusement. "He is still the best. Those who compete without worthy competition and win are not necessarily the best." He smiled gently, avoiding their eyes.

The three of them sat in silence a long minute.

Finally, Fougères shook his head. "It's not my place, but I think the two of you — three of you — need to mend the old wounds. By letting them linger the pain only increases." He leaned toward Enric, pointing a finger at the table between them. "Your relationship with Montag does not change our children's futures. My son is going to be a fantastic knight. He is going to be wealthy and offer your daughter a good life. And your daughter is a beauty that would do well to have the protection of a betrothal. This between us . . . this is a good match."

Igraine watched as her husband tempered himself against Fougères' barb. They had discussed this for years already, since Eleanor was practically born, and had always come to the same conclusion. A betrothal was best for Eleanor. "I'll have the contract drawn up tomorrow," Enric offered.

Igraine withered beside him, her thoughts warring once again.

Fougères smiled. He stood and again held out his hand. "My word to you is good. If yours is as well, we need no papers. Our children will be wed before God when they are of age."

Igraine knew that without papers, the betrothal could not be proven. She started to reach to Enric, to protest, then stopped. Perhaps that would give Eleanor a way out if she needed it.

Enric rose and shook Fougères hand. "God will it so."

Igraine rose on shaking knees and crossed herself. May God will that Edmond survived long enough under Montag's care to marry Eleanor. She thought of the brutal training the innocent boy would have to undergo. She was grateful to God for a daughter, that she be raised with kindness and love. She laid a hand to the faint bulge of the child inside her. How would she handle it if a boy was born?

"Sir Enric, who did you mentor under?" Fougères asked as they stepped away from the table.

"My father," Enric said, the words coming without hesitation.

"Humph," Fougères said, his brow furrowed in confusion.

They knew Fougères had never heard of Enric's father — no one had — but it was a far smarter to say that than let Raganor's name taint the air.

Enric twined an arm around Igraine's waist and guided her to their private quarters.

"Fougères is a good match," he whispered, kissing her temple. "A good match."

Igraine could only pray their daughter would one day agree.

Chapter 39

"Montag, my friend, we've missed you." Lord Fougères clapped Montag on the back, beaming. Montag greeted him less enthusiastically, smile forced but polite.

"It's been a long time, Godfrey," Montag admitted. "I'm glad you could come. Is this young Edmond? So big already!" His eyes fell to the seven-year-old boy before him. The boy stood at attention, his sharp dark eyes studying everything around him, particularly Montag. Montag held out his hand to shake the boy's, and the boy instantly took it, his grip as firm as little fingers could allow.

"You're bigger than I thought, too," Edmond said in a small voice, his eyes staring up at Montag.

Fougères chuckled, and even Montag had to smirk a little at that.

"He's been training with me and his brothers, but it's time he learned from a master. He's excited to be here, aren't you, Edmond?" Fougères clapped his hands down on the boy's shoulders.

Montag noted that the child didn't seem intimidated or afraid like so many other, often older, boys were when they first came to Brunstein. That showed potential for something he could work with, beyond just doing Fougères a favor. "You will learn much here." At that moment Raoul entered the hall, eyeing the new boy cautiously. "This is my son, Raoul," Montag gestured.

Raoul, though a year younger, was already taller than Edmond, though lankier.

"Shake hands, boys. You will be training quite a bit together," Montag ordered, watching the interchange.

Fougères looked to Montag in surprise. "You aren't sending him to train with another?"

"I will train him myself." Montag was careful to keep his tone indifferent. Beneath that surface he already bristled with anger at the mere suggestion of Raoul leaving his care.

Fougères studied the boys as they shook hands, both unsmiling. "He's tall. Your blood runs strong." He frowned. "But why not—"

Montag cut him off. "He's training with me." His tone left no room for argument. "I'd like to see what Edmond knows, if you think he's up for it." He was already reaching for two wooden swords, knowing that Fougères wouldn't dare protest.

"Of course. Come now Edmond, show Lord Montag what you've got."

Montag handed the boys two wooden swords, and they faced each other there in the courtyard. Edmond made the first move, coming at Raoul with a fast overhand swing. Raoul quickly blocked it and threw in a low jab that Edmond stepped away from. The two little boys clacked sword to sword in a gridlock that danced them around the courtyard. Occasionally their wooden swords would make contact, forcing a yelp of pain, but the boys didn't stop. Finally, locked in a wrestling match with each other, the exhaustion kicked in and they both ended up sprawled on the ground, panting in a stalemate.

Montag's shadow stepped over them both. Raoul flinched and pulled himself to his feet. Montag glared at the boy still on the ground, then suddenly snatched him up by his hair. Edmond yelped and squirmed. "Lesson one. Do not leave a fight unfinished." He thrust the sword back in Edmond's hand. Raoul was already prepared, his face unfocused through his physical fatigue and the ache of the bruises that had been inflicted. Edmond looked from Montag to Raoul to his sword. Raoul was bold and used that moment to charge Edmond. Edmond swung hard at Raoul's head, knocking the younger boy down with a loud crack. Raoul groaned from the ground, and Edmond hesitated in helping him up, looking to Montag for approval. With a single nod it was granted, and Edmond pulled Raoul back to his feet. Raoul looked at him with respect, tenderly rubbing the lump that was beginning to form on his forehead.

"He will do well here," Montag offered Fougères, who had watched the whole affair with tight-lipped silence. "Let's go eat."

A great feast had been set before the visiting lord. The smell of spices and roasted meat filled the room. Fougères and Montag watched the dynamic at the squire table as Raoul introduced Edmond to the rest of the boys. There was maybe a dozen of them now. Montag had taken to hosting numerous squires at one time now that Igraine was gone. Not only did the multitude help in training, but those that couldn't handle it could be easily replaced. The oldest was now sixteen, soon to be knighted. Montag smirked to himself as he watched the young man, who was watching little Edmond's every move. Simon was smart, with the determination of a mule and the deadly stealth of a tiger. Montag had trained him well, and within a few days the elder squire would be setting Edmond's education in motion.

"We've missed you at tournaments lately," Fougères was saying. Montag snapped his attention back to his friend . . . no, peer. There were no friends. "No one seems to be able to hold against him."

"Who?"

"Sir Enric." Fougères chuckled. "Have you been listening at all?"

"Only some." Montag's eyes went back to the squires. His fist clenched involuntarily.

Fougères leaned back in his chair. "You're planning his training already, aren't you?"

Montag didn't answer.

Fougères sighed and took a long swallow of wine, holding it in his mouth to savor the flavor before swallowing. "I know it's moot to remind you to go easy on him. To remind you he is only six. But that is also why I brought him to you." Fougères glanced at Montag, likely suspecting that he was talking to himself. "My other sons . . . they are proficient. But Edmond is too far down the line to be my heir. He will need to fight for his place, to win in battle and tournament alike. And if this is how he must train, so be it." He quickly drained the rest of the cup and poured another, frowning.

Montag suddenly turned to him. Fougères raised his eyebrows expectantly. "When is the last Enric lost?"

"Past my memory."

"When did he last compete?"

"Maybe a month ago. Why does it matter, Montag?"

"Was my sister there?"

"No. She is with child again. She was at the tournament in Poitou a few months back. That is as far as she travels."

Montag felt the color rise in his cheeks. He should not have asked about her. Enric was to have a second child, likely now a son. He checked himself. Why would that matter? Enric's child had no claim to Brunstein. Raoul was a true and proper heir.

If he was tough enough to handle it.

Montag glanced at Fougères, who was watching him with a knowing gaze. "You are allowed to be happy for her, Montag," Fougères said gently. "They are good people. *She* is happy."

Montag looked away, finishing his own drink and rising from the table. "I will, uh, write to you with the boy's progress."

Fougères nodded sadly. "I have to head out in the morning. Montag—" He hesitated. Shaking his head, he dismissed the thought. "I'll send for him at Christmas. Send word often, for his mother's sake."

Montag nodded, distracted, and then turned and left the hall. The squire boys stood at attention as he passed, like a small army. Edmond mimicked the others. Montag ignored them, bursting out of the hall with doors slamming. He should not have asked about her. He avoided tournaments for this very reason. Why would he invite that information in? He should not have asked.

Chapter 40

"My lady, I know you are not yet healed, but he won't stop. The squire — the grooms — they all said we have to tell you."

Igraine winced and sat higher against the headboard. "What's he doing?"

"He's with Draca, m'lady! And that beast is having one of his days, he is. And Sir Enric — he just won't quit. Never saw him like this, m'lady."

Igraine pulled herself from the covers before he finished, a blanket tight around her shoulders. Her womb ached, yet not more than she could manage. The maid offered her an arm as dizziness overcame her.

It was an unfortunate effect of the illness she'd been battling for weeks, the illness that had resulted in tragedy.

She forced herself down the stairs and into the yard, where Enric had center stage with the big red-haired horse. The maid hadn't exaggerated. Both horse and man were drenched in sweat, each fighting the other in a silent battle of the wills. Enric would apply leg; the horse kicked out. He'd apply more leg; the horse shot sideways in an overreaction. Usually by now the stallion would yield, but not today.

Igraine watched all this with her hands on the fence. She winced as the horse threw a particularly hard buck. Enric held on with an iron grip. Anger bubbled inside her and yet she feared to distract Enric, which right now could prove deadly.

Finally the horse yielded, trotting amicably, his head down, ears flicking back and forth. His mouth chewed the bit with acceptance. Igraine watched in amazement as the entire dynamic instantly changed. The pressure Enric applied became gentle, his words soothing, encouraging. The horse responded in turn by further relaxing, obeying. Igraine slowly worked her way to the field, using the fence to compensate for her weakness. While the horse had yielded, his eye still shone with an angry fire, waiting for Enric to break the fragile agreement they had established so the fight could begin anew.

Igraine watched, fear rising within her.

Thankfully Enric seemed to sense the fragile line he and the horse had negotiated, and ended the session while things were going well. He asked the horse to stop, and the animal obeyed promptly, raising his head to glare at Igraine's presence at the rail of the arena like she was intruding. Enric dismounted, wary of the four hooves that had the power to kill in a single blow. He stroked the horse's neck, the beast blatantly ignoring him. He pulled the tack from the horse's back and whispered to him as he toweled him from a bucket of cool water, washing away the sweat until the copper coat gleamed in the sun. When he led the horse to a nearby field, the horse took off at a full gallop, bucking and kicking toward the other horses, who were safely on the other side of the fence. It was as if he'd never even worked.

Enric wrapped the rope in his hands as he approached Igraine. The sweat that drenched his shirt and his slow gait were evidence that Enric *had* worked.

Her fear turned to rage as she noted how relaxed her husband was. Her hands shook.

"You told me you were done with that horse!"

Enric frowned, focusing on the rope.

"Did you hear me?" Igraine shrieked. "You promised me you'd sell him. Put him to stud. The household got me out of bed to stop you!"

Enric sighed, running a hand through his sweaty hair, still avoiding her eyes. "When we get through this, he'll be worth a fortune."

"Enric, you know that horse is different. There's something wrong with him. I don't want you riding him."

"People have said that about many of the horses I've had. They all turned out to be fantastic. He just needs time."

Igraine gritted her teeth with frustration. "This one is different. If he wasn't different, you would have already made a fortune on him. He is too old, too strong."

Enric gestured toward the horse, now contentedly munching grass. "You just watched him go. He's getting better every day."

Igraine's eyebrows shot up. "He's the most dishonest horse I've ever met. Draca...there is a reason they call the animal a dragon."

"Fine. Next tournament I'll sell him, all right?" Enric threw the rope down beside her, his own anger unmistakable.

Igraine checked her temper, startled by Enric's rare aggression. "I know why you're doing this. You're trying to prove you're in control. It's part of the grieving process. I understand, but this isn't the way."

"What do you know about the grieving process?" Enric shouted. He leaned his hands against the fence between them, glaring at her.

Igraine took a step back as if he had slapped her. "What do I know?"

Enric's face instantly fell. "Igraine, I'm sorry." He looked down and kicked the dirt.

"You are not the only one that lost a child, Enric!"

"I know . . . I just—"

"Mama . . ." Eleanor's little voice cut in. She stood a little bit away, looking from one parent to the other.

Igraine wiped a tear and turned her back to Enric. "Yes, dear?"

"Cook helped me bake something for you. Want to try it?"

"Oh, you're so kind. That sounds delicious." Without a glance back at Enric, Igraine followed the girl, her warm little hand twined in her palm. Igraine moved slow to better balance her accursed, weakened legs.

At dinner that night, the family picked at their food. It wasn't that it didn't taste good. On the contrary, the cook had roasted the pheasant to perfection, adding just the right amount of herbs to make the dish burst with flavor. No, the mood had nothing to do with the food. Eleanor was angry that she had not been allowed to stay out playing with the other children at the manor. Igraine was at her wits end trying to discipline the child toward ladylike behavior, and Enric was no ally, encouraging her with mock swordfights. Then there was the lingering argument over the chestnut horse. Now they all sat at dinner, furious with each other for different reasons.

"Can I play now?" Eleanor whined, pushing her plate away.

"No," Igraine spit impatiently.

"I'm not hungry," Eleanor protested.

"Eat what is on your plate," Enric growled. For good measure he stuffed a large bite of his own food into his mouth. He chewed slowly, as if it was a struggle to get the food down.

Igraine rested an elbow on the table, watching the two of them as they forced themselves to finish their plates of food. Always the competitor, now Eleanor was suddenly interested in her meal, and finished it all, likely just for spite. She again looked to her mother.

"Now can I go play?"

"Go, Eleanor," Igraine said with a wave of her hand.

The child scampered away, only half pretending to carry herself like a lady before she took off running toward the door.

Igraine rolled her eyes, taking a sip of her wine.

"You won't tame her, Igraine," Enric said, his judgmental tone putting her on edge again. "I'm only trying to channel all that energy."

"Like one of your horses?" Igraine snorted.

"Yes, actually." He glared at her.

"And how's that working for you?"

"Fine."

"Hmm." Igraine rubbed her temples. Her head ached, which didn't help her sour mood.

Enric sighed. He took her hand and gently clasped it from across the table. "Do you want to see the doctor again?"

Igraine shook her head. "He has no idea what's wrong. I felt *worse* after he was here last time."

"Then what can I do?"

Igraine looked at him, his concern etched all over a haphazardly bristled face he hadn't shaved since she'd — become ill. His hand squeezed hers, and she felt the love that still brimmed from him, despite the agony they shared. "Don't fight with me." She let out a short laugh. "That's the most exhausting of it all."

Enric brought her fingers to his lips and kissed them. "I know. And I'm sorry for what I said earlier. I wasn't thinking." He took a deep breath and abruptly changed the subject. "Soon the stallion will be ready to sell, like I promised you. He just has to be rideable."

Igraine straightened.

Enric nodded. "I don't expect to have trouble getting my price. But I need to take him to a large market, where there are a lot of arrogant, talented knights like me."

That could mean only one thing. "You want to take him to Blackstone." What little blood she had left in her head drained, yet she could not bring herself to argue with him. It was a rough tournament if one could call it that. A large crowd that often attracted more of the knights-errant and mercenaries: men that fought hard and often dirty. They had little to lose and everything to gain. "You'll sell him quickly there," she had to admit. "Do you have time to get him ready?"

"It's a few weeks away. It will take work, but he will be ready." Enric squeezed her hand. His lips cracked into a smile, his handsome face lighting like that of the man she'd first fell in love with. "I'll buy something a little more reliable, alright?"

"Is Sir Josse going with you?"

"Of course. And Sir Louis."

She let herself breathe a little easier at that. At least he wouldn't be alone. With the mercenaries. "Fine."

Enric looked her up and down, frowning. "I originally wanted to take you along, but we will see how you feel by then."

Igraine pulled her fingers from his so she could sip from her cup again. With a subtle shake of her head she whispered, "Even if I am, I will not go to Blackstone with that rabble."

"Soon, Igraine. Soon I will have you out — with Eleanor — to the tournaments again." He pulled the cup from her hand so he could clasp both of hers again, eagerly leaning toward her. "The atmosphere will bring energy back to your soul again."

Igraine tried to smile, but felt it fade. "Hopefully soon." Perhaps if she hadn't traveled so much in the early pregnancy and put herself to bed like the midwives told her — perhaps then the child would not have come too early to survive. Perhaps then she would not have gotten sick in the first place. It would be some time before she was ready to spend days in the saddle traveling to a tournament. "Enric . . ."

"Hmm?" He squeezed her hands.

"Do you still love me?" She felt a tear slip from her eye.

For a moment he looked stunned, then burst up from the table. She shrank back in alarm. Within seconds he had reseated himself on the bench next to her, his arms twined around her, pulling her into his strong embrace. With his face buried in her hair, he whispered with a gravelly voice, "Of course I love you, Igraine. Forever." He pulled back, both of his palms on her wet cheeks, studying her face. The emotion in his own was so raw Igraine felt a sob shake her shoulders. He kissed her soft and long, then pulled her again back into his arms. The wetness on his cheeks streaked her forehead. They stayed twined together like that a long time, mercifully uninterrupted by Eleanor or servants.

"Do you love me?" he whispered into her hair.

Igraine squeezed him tighter in response, heart pounding. "I love you too much." That was the truth. How could she put into words how she wanted to be with him every waking moment, and yet felt unworthy? She'd failed to give him what he wanted most; their son was buried behind the manor, under the big oak. He'd fit in the palm of Enric's hand, his tiny arms and legs far too premature to ever survive. These things happened sometimes, the women of the manor told her unanimously. But the guilt remained, tarnishing the love she felt she didn't deserve.

Enric's lips were on her own, coaxing without demanding. She stiffened and pulled away, masking herself with the airs of the lady of the tournament. She tried to shove her heart into a cocoon of indifference. He wouldn't let her. His touch burned like fire. His eyes pleaded, refusing to let her hide. As if he read her mind, he said, "We are partners in this, beautiful wife. Together. No matter what. If you love me too much, I am guilty of the same. I can't possibly voice, much less show, what I feel for you . . ." His words trailed as his voice choked up.

Finally, Igraine looked into his eyes and believed him. She pressed closer to him, twining her arms around him, and together they mourned. Together they would heal. Together they would face whatever came.

Chapter 41

October 3, 1179

A road outside of Alsace

Montag felt a chill run up his spine as he noted the rider waiting ahead on the road. The man's grey horse was dark with sweat, steam rising from the beast like a cloud on the unseasonably cold evening. There was just enough light remaining to cast a shadow, lending to the knight's ethereal image, the light haloing him from behind. Montag frowning, knowing there was nothing angelic about the man. He wasn't afraid. The chill in his bones was more from a guttural anger than fear. As he slowed his horse to a walk he knew the same steamy mist would envelop him, rising from his lathered bay stallion. The two men together could face off with equality as they were meant to.

As they stood facing each other, Montag and Lezay each frowned, sizing the other up. Montag was loath to complete their latest assignment for The Order, particularly with Lezay as a partner, but it was a necessary task.

"You got the message then?" Lezay finally asked, his lips pursed to a frown.

"Yes." Montag let out a breath, the air misting from his nostrils in the cold like a dragon's smoke. "Let's get it over with."

The two men turned to the fork in the road and moved on, resting their steaming horses in a walk. After a mile of silence, Lezay cut in, "Agnes is dead."

Montag's eyebrows shot up.

"Childbirth." Lezay didn't look at Montag, but Montag still caught the subtle twitch of his lip.

"I didn't know she was expecting." Montag replied carefully.

"Certainly isn't now." Lezay shrugged. Even for him, it was too casual, and it made the hair on Montag's neck stand on end.

"I'm courting a lovely young lady from Thuringia. She's sweet enough." Now his lips did curl into a twisted smile. Montag stared, that sense of repulsion again tingling up his spine. "You should remarry, you know. You've been a widower too long."

Montag straightened in the saddle. The nerve was struck, just like Lezay had intended. "Mind your own business, Lezay."

"Really? It's not like you were in love, that you're too heartbroken. You're young, Montag! Get yourself some sweet little thing to hold in your hands . . . delicate little flower . . ."

Montag pulled up his horse to face Lezay. "We are not friends, Lezay. We are not going to chatter on this trip. We are going to ride in silence, get this done, and go home."

Lezay's lips stayed in their amused smirk. Montag glared at him, but the man didn't yield, which was a new development. Montag's eyes narrowed further.

"Ah, yes. Now you notice. We are equals again, Montag. The scales are balanced. I'm done with your better-than-thou nonsense." Lezay's eyes narrowed, the smirk darkening to a leer. "Friend or not, you can't shake me now, Montag. We are so much more . . . brother."

The ice in his tone didn't faze Montag. "Maybe so, but that does not mean you have a right to know anything about my life. So we *will* ride in silence."

Lezay had the nerve to chuckle, but he pushed his horse forward into a trot. Montag followed behind, the tension in his back aching, his hands itching to do the easy thing and put a sword in the man's back.

The one consolation Montag held was that when this business was done, they would be near the tournament at Blackstone, and he would get news firsthand for the first time in months. He needed to know if Raganor was keeping his word and staying in the Holy Land. And how was Igraine?

He mused on these questions as he and Lezay rode in silence toward their dark destination. Another induction. They were not getting easier to witness, and Montag was not enjoying having to fill the power void his father had been forced to vacate. It was tedious, negotiating the alliances of such powerful men. Still, he would a thousand times more do the job than let Raganor return. Even if it meant long hours riding next to Lezay, smelling onions and cruelty wafting on the breeze.

They rode alone, without squires. They did for all Order business.

He would need help at Blackstone though, and he had not told Lezay he planned to attend. He'd instructed the squire, Simon, to meet him there. That in itself was a test for the boy, the first he had agreed to knight. Could he travel alone, like a man? Fougères would be there as well, as his eldest son would try his hand in the competition.

The young Fougères was a terrible knight. It was a foolish mistake, a vain mistake, for Fougères to put his eldest up against the mercenaries. *Simon* could best him. Thankfully, the eldest Fougères heir was not Montag's charge, nor the embarrassment his responsibility. The young lad, Edmond, now that boy showed potential. He trained hard. He would not turn out like his older brother. Montag would make sure of that.

Lezay started humming next to him as he rode. Montag winced. He pushed his horse on faster, hoping to finish the business at hand and get to Blackstone.

Chapter 42

Montag was careful to skirt the edges of the crowd at Blackstone, having no desire to confront the Great Sir Enric. Lezay had not overestimated the man's fame if this crowd was any indication. Montag himself was as inconspicuous as the next man, but Enric — it was his name on the lips of the grizzled men. The deep voices rumbled as they spoke quietly amongst themselves, their eyes taken up by Enric, who was centered in the arena, shouting. Fougères trailed along at Montag's side, intently watching the dramatics occurring before them. The mass of men around them created a wall of stinking, dusty-clothed bodies to blend into, and they remained hidden from the knight who demanded center stage.

Enric was trying to sell a horse.

On any other day, that would be a normal occurrence. As knights, they were always eyeing each other's most valuable asset, the rippling flesh of their equine partners.

The amount of work it took to produce a horse strong and schooled enough to be a worthy partner in battle was greater than it took to produce a decent foot soldier out of a peasant. Enric had forged his reputation on the quality of his mounts, and even Montag had to admit it was his skill with the difficult ones that had allowed him to rise through the ranks. Which was why it was odd that Enric sat on a goliath of a destrier, shouting out its attributes, here at the lowly mercenary tournament of Blackstone instead of at some well-to-do lord's castle where people had money to buy quality.

It was only by chance that Montag himself was there. Had it not been for his business with The Order, he would be in his castle. Still, he figured it was a convenient opportunity to test if his skills were intact. He had plenty of pent-up fury to unleash.

"What do you think is wrong with it?" Fougères whispered to Montag, his arms folded across his chest. "He's asking the price of a three-year-old, not a mature destrier. That's unlike him."

Montag studied the horse closer, intrigued. Craning his neck to see over the heads of those in front of him, he caught glimpses. The animal's legs looked clean of defects, straight and solid. Though the hooves were without cracks, they were unshod, which was odd. The horse's body was solid muscle, with conformation through body and limb that promised superior athletic ability. Even after days of travel to the tournament, it certainly wasn't fatigued, its wide eyes attentively taking in the crowd. Enric trotted a small circle, pressing the nervous crowd back. The horse moved as if on wings instead of legs, a fluidity to the gaits that promised above all else, power.

Montag frowned.

"This animal's price will double after I win the tournament today!" Enric shouted to the crowd, a confident smile on his face. "Place your offers now and make him yours!"

Montag found it curious that the rest of the onlookers were murmuring among themselves, yet no one was making a move forward. Fougères' elbow nudged his arm.

"Looks like a mount for you," Fougères said, a twinkle in his eye.

"Humph." Montag eyed the horse a last time, then turned away. "Not this time." He worked back toward the list, adjusting gauntlets along the way. Fougères followed.

"You really have that many prospects that you can't take another?"

"I don't want another."

"He's your brother-in-law. The horse is amazing. You could do so much—"

Montag whirled on Fougères. "Why would I buy anything he has to sell? Hmm?"

Fougères took a step back but shrugged. "He's your brother-in-law?"

"So what?"

Fougères sighed, again trailing Montag as he steamed ahead. "They—" He was abruptly cut off as shouts were heard from where they had come. The big chestnut horse came charging straight toward them, riderless. Instinctively, both knights held out their arms and said "whoa." It stopped a few feet from Montag and snorted. Even Montag had to admit the animal was a work of art. With wary eyes, Montag closed the distance slowly, and the horse remained motionless as he took the dangling reins. Twisting the leather in his hands, man and horse eyed each other.

Enric cleared his throat as he caught up.

Fougères chuckled. "Too much to handle, Sir Enric? You don't look too dirty at least."

"Well, I'm not dirty because I'm not the one that hit the ground. Some Spanish knight threw his squire up on the horse, and the boy couldn't ride a palfrey. I'll take him, Lord Montag. Thank you." He held out his hand for the reins.

Montag passed the reins over wordlessly.

"I'm sure you'll have a buyer before the day is done," Fougères assured.

"I better, or my wife may string me up by my toes." Enric smiled. "How are you, Lord Fougères? The family?"

"Well, quite well, thank you for asking. Edmond is doing exceptionally well under Lord Montag's tutelage, or so I am told."

Montag frowned, his eye still on the big chestnut stallion, who watched them all with alertness, ears flicking back and forth.

"Isn't he, Montag?" Fougères nudged him.

"He's a typical seven-year-old," Montag grumbled. He spun on his heel and walked away.

"Nice to see you, Sir Enric," he heard Fougères say, and then the knight was jogging back to Montag's side. "Montag, that horse is meant for you."

"Since when are you and Enric best friends?" Fougères hesitation made Montag pull up stride. He glared down at Fougères. "What aren't you telling me?"

Fougères scratched his head and looked down. After a moment of debate, he sighed and faced Montag head on. "Our children are betrothed."

"Your children . . ."

"Yes, Montag. It is a good match. Little Eleanor is going to be a beauty, and Edmond is —"

"Edmond? The Edmond you currently have apprenticing in my manor?"

"Yes . . ." Fougères frowned.

"Damn it all to bloody hell and let God's bones rot with the rest of them." Montag turned from Fougères, fighting a strong desire to strike him. No footsteps followed. At least the man was intelligent enough to leave him be.

He clenched and unclenched his fists at his sides. Edmond and Eleanor? How dare Igraine?

He'd avoided tournaments for years, and sure enough, one step into public and boom — there's Enric. Oh, but that was not enough. Montag himself was hosting the future husband of the bastard pixie! Her very name itself was an insult. Igraine had done it for spite.

Instead of heading to the registrar, Montag turned and headed back to the encampment. He was in no mood to compete with Enric nor the traitorous "friend" Fougères pretended to be. *No friends. Peers. Don't forget it.* As usual, his squire was nowhere to be found and must be hunted. He had a strong desire to take each of Simon's fingers one by one and smash them.

"Lord Montag," said squire called from across the field, running to intercept him. "What do you need?" Simon's sharp eyes promised to snap into action at his every whim. Best squire he'd yet had, this one. Good with a sword, pike, and lance. Perhaps he'd leave his fingers intact after all.

Montag stopped and put his hands on his hips, thinking. The young man waited.

Slowly Montag's lips curled upward. Why not take advantage of such an outlet for rage? It was Blackstone after all. "When we get back to Brunstein, we will teach young Edmond a lesson. Until then, I will compete in pike today and only pike." He wanted to beat, maim: anything to release the fury bubbling from within.

"Yes, my lord," Simon nodded, the excitement sparkling in his eyes. When Montag gave no further instruction, the squire jumped into action, already cognizant of the long list of duties Montag would expect of him.

This young man would have made an excellent husband for his young niece.

Montag growled to himself, again doing an about-face in the opposite direction, now back to the registrar he'd been intent on neglecting. How old was Eleanor anyway? It had been years since he'd seen them. Lost in thought, he almost didn't notice the chestnut stallion that was again cantering across the list . . . riderless. He froze in place, watching the horse buck and kick, gaining speed as men tried to intercept and stop it. Curiosity again piqued; he went to the rail of the list and watched.

"Who tried to ride this time?" he asked no one in particular.

"Sir Alberto Milano, my lord," the man next to him answered. Montag gave a sideways glance down to him. He had the burly build of a blacksmith, face streaked with soot. The man's sleeves were rolled up to his elbows despite the chill air, revealing thick forearms. The leather apron around his middle confirmed it: blacksmith.

"Is there a line of men waiting to be bucked off or what?"

"Must be." The blacksmith shrugged.

Someone caught the horse and led it to the end of the list, where another man waited. They watched intently as the man no sooner put his foot in the stirrup than the horse reared up. That man put his feet firmly back on the ground and shook his head. He would pass. The next rider took his place and managed to get a leg over, only to be thrown in the first mighty buck, one that seemed to elevate the horse up above the heads of the men on the ground.

A smile turned up Montag's lips. So this was why the horse was so cheap. He was the child of the devil himself. The list of riders was shorter now, only those with the largest egos waiting to take a go. Some of them managed to last a few steps, but no one made it down the list. The tournament was getting close to starting, and Sir Enric was running out of time.

"Let's see you ride him, Enric!" Montag shouted across the list. Enric turned to face him, meeting his eye for a moment, then took back the reins to his dragon. He patted the horse on the neck, talking to it, letting it settle after the last eventful rider fail.

Then to Montag's surprise, Enric vaulted up onto the great horse with a strength and grace that proved his years of training. The horse fidgeted, then seemed to breathe. Montag leaned forward expectantly. The entire tournament ground seemed to hold its breath as Enric walked, then trotted, then cantered the horse around the list. The horse was tense but obedient. He halted in front of Montag.

"Want to try him?" Enric asked. Montag expected a smirk, but there was none. Just a quiet look of respect, almost pleading. Maybe Igraine really had threatened his toes. Which was odd in and of itself. She was quite the horsewoman — he'd made sure of that — and if she had told Enric to sell, that indicated the depth of her fear. Or was she unwell? Perhaps only wielding a maternal urge. Her second child must be coming due soon. That thought made his chest ache, and he pushed it away.

Montag folded his arms across his chest. "Win the tournament on him, and we'll see."

Enric nodded once and rode away.

"That man is a hell of a horseman," the blacksmith whistled. "Don't see why he doesn't keep that beast for himself."

"His wife won't let him."

"Really?"

"So he says. I can see why. She's got two kids at home. Needs a husband to provide for her."

The blacksmith nodded, rolling his sleeves an unnecessary turn in preparation to head back to his forge. "You know them?"

Montag frowned. "My sister . . ."

The blacksmith seemed oblivious of his tone. "Nice talking to you." He headed back to his workshop.

Montag looked back toward the list, where Enric had ridden back through the crowd and into the encampment. He had to get to the registrar and get ready for the pike competition. By nightfall they could be on the road again, perhaps with a spare destrier in tow.

Chapter 43

Montag gleefully swung his pike down for the final blow, feeling the man before him collapse under the heavy blade. He raised a hand to yield, and Montag pumped both fists into the air. He was still the undefeated champion of the event. He roared out his victory, the men around him closing in to pat him on the back. Fougères fell into step next to him as they exited the list, the bloodlust still pounding through Montag's veins like he was ten years younger.

"Well done, old friend," Fougères slapped him on the back.

"Not old like you."

"Fair enough." Fougères smiled as if Montag's words were not the insult they were. It was one of the endearing qualities of the man. He either was so smart, so thick-skinned, or so stupid that nothing offended him. Montag often flipped back and forth as to which option it was. Regardless, he was steady company.

"How's your boy doing in his debut tournament?" Montag asked.

"He's already withdrawn," Fougères wrinkled his nose in disgust. "To his credit, he drew Enric as his first match in sword. He never had a chance."

"Ouch." Even Montag had to wince at that. Enric's style had only improved since he'd last seen him. His time as a mercenary had taught him new tricks. He was glad not to be competing with the man. He undid the laces of his gauntlets and loosened the mail fastened at his neck. "Well, I'm going to collect my prize and get out of here. Safe travels."

"You're not going to stay for the joust?"

"Maybe one or two runs. We've got a long ride ahead of us. And we know how it'll play out."

Fougères smirked. "You think he'll have it that easy?"

A trumpet blared from the list. The joust was beginning. Montag inclined his head and the men walked over to the rail. Enric and the fiery chestnut charged down the list flawlessly, the horse a mass of muscle that only gained speed as the opponent drew near. Enric's lance impacted the other man's shield, the force throwing him clear to the ground.

Fougères let out a low whistle. "Now that is a horse."

"The horse is only fifty percent of the equation," Montag mumbled.

Fougères' face lit up. "Did I hear you right? I think you just offered up a compliment to Sir Enric!" He laughed at Montag's frown.

Montag pushed away from the rail. "Well, be sure to tell him all about it next time you see him and your son's future wife. I'm going home." He beelined for the encampment.

Fougères waved. "Nice seeing you, old friend!"

Montag rolled his eyes. Thankfully, Simon had once again done his job, and their things were almost completely packed. He'd even fetched Montag's prize, a small gold statue of a horse. With the bowed head of an altar boy offering up incense, he held it out to Montag. Montag took it roughly and hefted it in his hand, impressed that it was heavy enough to be real gold, then threw it in his saddlebag.

In the distance, the crowd let out a collective gasp. They both turned toward it, ears listening. When no further excitement could be determined, they went back to their packing. A while later, Montag glanced up to see a man running toward them at full speed. He furrowed his brow.

Fougères pulled up, gasping for breath. "Lord — Montag — you need — to come." He stood with his hands on his hips. "Dang, I must be getting old."

"What do you want, Fougères? We're about to leave."

"It's Enric. He took a lance."

A cold chill ran down Montag's back. And it was not an image of Enric speared that flashed in his mind but the sobs of his sister ringing in his ears that made his feet follow Fougères' jogging steps back toward the list.

"What do you mean, he took a lance?" Montag growled at Fougères. He picked up his pace all the same. The alarm on his peer's face was unmistakable. Sir Enric de Levan was hurt. Badly.

"It went clean through his mail and broke. I haven't seen a lance do that in years. Not since we started blunting them for tournaments at least."

"Who was the opponent?"

"Some Italian knight. Sir Alberto something?"

"Milano." Montag had fought him with the pike. The man fought hard and dirty. Montag had had great pleasure taking him down. Apparently he had not taken him down hard enough. Or maybe he'd crippled the man enough that he'd been driven to cheat. This *was* Blackstone after all.

They were stopped at the rail of the arena by the thick crowd that had grown. There was a hush over the normally noisy group. Only the buzz of a thousand whispers vibrated through the grounds. In the arena, amidst the settling dust, a man curled on the ground, clutching his chest in agony. His scream cut the air, sending a chill up Montag's spine. There were several knights and heralds gathered around him, and none seemed sure what to do.

"Damn it," Montag exhaled through his teeth. "And how is this my problem?" He shot a sideways glance at Fougères.

"Just thought you should know, since he is your brother-in-law and everything." Fougères shot him a pointed look and turned back to the horrifying scene unfolding in the arena.

"Damn it!" Montag ran a hand through his hair. With a last dirty look at Fougères, he bellowed, "Move, move! Let me through!" His broad shoulders instantly parted the crowd that he stood a head taller than. When he reached the rail, he ducked under and took long strides to the man in the dirt. The knights around Enric parted wordlessly, watching him. He knelt in the dust, making eye contact with Enric. The man could hardly focus, his teeth gritting as spasms of pain coursed through his body.

"Where's the priest?" Montag asked the question he was expected to ask, eyeing the large piece of wooden lance still embedded in the upper right side of Enric's chest, practically in the shoulder.

The knights all looked at each other, then finally one said, "I'll find one."

"Now! We need one now!" Montag bellowed. He tore the fabric of Enric's tunic, revealing the torn mail beneath. The metal rings were embedded with the lance into the skin on one side of the puncture. On the other side, Montag could pull the mail back just enough to reveal the blood oozing in a steady stream. He laid his hand flat to put pressure on it. Enric groaned.

"That's right," he hissed. "No more screaming now that I'm here, you bloody bastard. Show how tough you are."

Enric again groaned through gritted teeth, but he lay still and internalized his pain. "Tell Igraine . . . I'm . . . sorry."

"Tell her yourself," Montag grumbled, looking away from the knight's pleading eyes.

Enric clasped Montag's forearm with surprising strength, and Montag was forced to look him in the eye. "I do love her." The words came out forcefully, though the effort weakened him further. "Don't hurt her. Please . . ."

Montag looked at Enric's panicked face and nodded once. "I may be mad as hell at you both, but I have only ever protected her. Sometimes even from herself," he muttered. As relief flooded Enric's features, he relaxed and looked heavenward. Montag felt the hairs on the back of his neck stand up. He knew that look; the coward was going to try and die on him.

"Priest! We need a priest now!" someone was screaming.

Montag leaned over Enric, urgently now. "Don't you dare, you little scum. You aren't getting out of this life that easily!" With a glance at the lance and back to Enric's face, Montag steeled himself. With one hand holding pressure on Enric's broken chest, he wrapped his strong left hand around the base of the lance.

He hesitated, knowing once he intervened, there would be no turning back.

Montag's eyes flitted around the scene. Enric's eyes were open but glazed. The knights around him were glancing around urgently, as that well-needed priest was seen being dragged across the arena by two knights.

"I told you, we aren't *allowed* to administer last rites to those killed in tournament," the priest was insistently trying to explain.

"This man is a good Christian knight, as good as they come. You want us to keep fighting for the church, you pray for him," the knight on the priest's right arm said harshly.

"Ohh," the priest again tried to pull away. "But if I break the pope's order, what will happen to my parish? I want to help you, to help this poor man, but I'm not allowed!"

"What about human compassion? You preach on that enough, don't you?" the knight on his left arm said.

Montag cut in, "How about this: if you don't pray for this man, I'll shove this broken lance through *your* chest so you have something to pray for!"

The priest paled and stopped struggling. The knights holding him released his arms so he could cross Enric and fold his hands to pray. The Latin words floated on the air for what seemed like an hour but perhaps was only a minute. When the priest again crossed himself and kissed his rosary, the arena was still.

Enric let out another labored groan. His eyes turned back to Montag. He was fighting. He wasn't dead yet. Montag held his gaze.

"I hope you got to the part with the Last Rites," one of the knights said solemnly.

"I started with it," the priest said sadly. "No one ever calls me to this field unless it's for Last Rites." He sighed, looking thoroughly exhausted. He looked at the small gathering of knights as a whole. He shifted uneasily, obviously wanting to go. He glanced at Montag.

Montag waved a bloody hand at him, his eyes still locked with Enric's. "Go."

The priest nodded and shuffled off.

Montag narrowed his eyes at Enric, frowning. The power over life and death thrilled through his veins. He knew his time to make a decision was getting short, or the decision would be made for him by God. He looked at the lance tip. He would have to move quickly. But there was a chance.

With a final glance back at Enric's pained face, Montag gave the lance a sharp jerk. It popped out with a sucking noise, and blood squirted all over his hands. Montag glanced at the needle-sharp tip caked in blood and meat and threw it aside. Enric let out another blood-curdling scream, arching off the ground before laying still, only barely conscious. Montag grabbed the first cloth he could find, Igraine's scarf, her token to her beloved. Hastily

Montag shoved the fabric deep into the wound, plugging it.

"He's going to bleed to death," Fougères whispered, appearing at Montag's side.

Montag gritted his teeth, watching Enric's ashen face, his hand still deep in the man's chest, plugging the scarf into the wound. Already the cloth was saturated. "No, he's not." He glanced around. Four of Enric's pathetic friends stood nearby, watching with hopeless looks. Montag glared at them. "Get over here and pick him up. We need to get to the smith. Now!" The men scrambled to do his bidding. They lifted Enric and did a shuffling run toward the blacksmith, who had burst into action at his forge next to the arena. At least that man had some sense. He knew what Montag would need.

The bellows pumped, the forge blazing hot. A few rods of iron already lay in the coals, their tips red as sunset. The blacksmith cleaned off his worktable with a sweep of his arm, and the knights laid their friend flat on it. Montag caught the smith's eye, his hand still keeping pressure on the wound.

"You know what I must do. It needs to be a fine pointed iron, red-hot. Quickly, on my cue."

The smith nodded, turning the irons in the coals, the billows pumping to turn the flames blue.

"What on Earth are you doing?" one of the knights cut in, brazenly clapping a hand on Montag's shoulder.

Montag's glare made him hastily remove it, but he did not waver in his questioning. "You can't cauterize the wound . . . he's bleeding *inside*!"

The idiocy of men normally amused Montag, but there was no time. "Move." His body trembled with anger, his nerves surging with energy down into his fingertips. He again looked to the blacksmith, who pressed the bellows a last time, checked the iron, and nodded. Montag took a deep breath, studying the wound. He had only seconds to find the source of the bleed and stop it. Blood was already dripping onto the table despite the scarf. With a last glance into the smith's eyes, he removed his hand and the scarf with it. Blood gushed anew, a stream shooting into the air like a miniature fountain before steadying to a thumping pulse.

Montag pressed fingers into the hole, eyeing the damage within. He picked out bits of shattered clavicle as they cut his fingers. Enric groaned. "Better stay unconscious," Montag muttered, his fingers finally finding the source of the bleed, pressing on the tuberous artery. "Iron," he ordered, and the smith placed the rod in his hand.

Montag took the red iron and laid it against the place his hand pressed against. Flesh sizzled; smoke burned his eyes. He felt the heat of the rod against his hand, the burn light but not as much as what he was doing to Enric's insides. Two of the knights holding him turned away, emptying their stomachs outside the blacksmith's shop. Montag handed the rod, now blackening, back to the smith. He dabbed at the wound with a clean cloth, provided by one of the men. The blood no longer filled the wound like a goblet, but the raw tissue oozed.

"Another." He frowned.

A second rod as fine tipped as a dagger was produced. Enric's flesh was charred inside and out as Montag sealed the bleed. Enric stirred on the table, gritting his teeth and moaning, sweat beading on his brow.

Montag stilled, rod in hand, regarding his work. Blood no longer pulsed onto the table. The ugly, gaping wound would host a mess of other problems before — if — it would heal, but bleeding would not be one of them. High on the list was that without a clavicle, Enric would never use his sword arm again. His days as a knight were over.

The smith gently took the rod from Montag's hand, shoving it back into the coals.

"Help me get his mail off?" the knight at Enric's head asked.

Montag blinked at him, surprised he was still there and not emptying his stomach with the rest of his friends. He nodded once.

With some difficulty they managed to pull off Enric's mail and upper layers, for the first time revealing the full extent of the man's injury. His chest was streaked with blood. The knight produced a bucket of water and clean cloth and worked to wipe the blood away. The skin underneath was black and blue in a large circle around the blackened hole. It was more than just the clavicle that was broken. They both sucked in their breath, meeting each other's eyes.

"Do you think he'll make it?" the knight asked.

Montag frowned, tentatively prodding his cauterization. He sighed and shook his head. "I should have let him die on the tournament field. I fear what I've done has given him a much slower, more painful death."

"I wondered that. Did you do it on purpose?"

Montag narrowed his eyes at the man. "Do I know you?"

"No," the man met his eye without hesitation. "But I know about you." The man let the tension out of his shoulders and offered Montag his hand to shake. "I'm Sir Josse of Angoulême. I am the one that witnessed Enric and Igraine's wedding."

Montag glanced at the offered hand, then decided against taking it. Eventually Josse let it fall back to his side, an amused smile twitching at his lips. Montag instead thrust his hands into the water bucket, rubbing off the blood that lined the creases of his knuckles. He dried them on the last clean portion of Enric's bloody, tattered shirt. Then he turned back to face the watching Sir Josse.

"I'm sure you'll figure out how to get his body back to his widow, right, Sir Josse?"

Josse nodded once, frowning.

"At least she'll have a fresh corpse to sob over instead of a maggoty one." He ran a last look over Enric's broken body. The man was starting to tremble, the shock to his system setting in at last. He was a fighter. There was a chance he would make it. A better chance than he'd had ten minutes ago with the gawking crowd that was watching him die. "Better get some blankets for him."

"Lord Montag . . . don't you want to tell Lady Igraine?" Josse ventured. "She might like to see—"

Montag snorted. "No, I don't. I'm sure the story will be more believable if she hears it from someone other than me." He glanced around, spotting the lance tip in the hand of one of the queasy knights. He took it from him, squinting at the foreign-made point. Perhaps Fougères had been mistaken. "Who dealt this lance-blow?"

"Sir Alberto Milano."

Montag nodded. "Excuse me." He left the men staring after him, their shock as evident as Enric's.

Sir Alberto Milano stood at the end of the list, waiting. His smug look of self-assurance told Montag all he needed to know. As an unregulated mercenary tournament, there was no presiding lord, no one to determine rules and enforce them. Dirty play was expected, but even to Montag, this Alberto had taken it past acceptable limits. You didn't use a real lance unless you were on the battlefield with the intent to kill. Perhaps that had been his intent. His order.

"Who else is left to compete?" Montag asked the registrar, leaning across his little table on his knuckles.

The man looked wide-eyed at him and leaned away. "None, my lord. It was the last joust of the day. Sir Enric and Sir Alberto. Sir Alberto is our victor. We only wait to gather the crowd for awards."

"He cheated and you know it. He is not victor. Though he is a murderer."

The registrar opened and closed his mouth like a fish.

"He wants to be victor, he has to joust me. I will be Enric's proxy."

"I don't know . . . I can't . . ."

Montag rolled his eyes at the herald and turned to bellow to Sir Alberto, "I challenge you to a joust! You want to fight with real lances, we run with real lances."

The crowd around them stilled. Alberto smirked and spit toward Montag. Montag bristled and glared at the man, anger bubbling.

"You do not have a horse ready, Sir . . . ?"

"Lord Montag of Brunstein." He saw Milano flinch before a mask of indifference fell. Interesting. "You should remember that name, as it will be one of the last you hear. And you can either spare the time for my squire to ready my destrier, or I will ride his." He motioned toward Enric's chestnut stallion, who anxiously pranced in the hand of Enric's wide-eyed squire.

Alberto hesitated. "That horse is crazy."

"All the better for you then, right?" Montag smirked.

Alberto hesitated, sizing Montag up, a wariness now obvious in his expression. There were too many people watching. He had a reputation to uphold, as Montag well knew. "Fine."

The crowd buzzed like the hum of bees, the news spreading up and down the list. The crowd regathered. Montag turned, looking for his squire, and found him waiting with a fresh lance, un-blunted. They left Alberto to walk to the opposite end of the list, where the chestnut stallion waited.

"It will only take me a moment to get your horse ready, my lord," Simon assured.

"This one is fine." Montag approached the big stallion, stroking his neck.

Enric's squire looked worried, but he handed over the reins. "He's mighty sensitive, my lord," he warned. He glanced anxiously at Montag's squire, as if expecting him to intervene, but he was met only with silence. He stepped back.

Montag vaulted up onto the destrier, feeling the horse's back tense beneath him. He mimicked Enric's pat on the horse's neck, then turned it toward the list. "You mess with me, horse, and you'll be on my dinner table tomorrow," he warned. The stallion seemed to listen. Montag took up the lance.

The flag was waved. The horses charged. The clash and suck of iron and wood and flesh echoed over the silent tournament grounds. Then Sir Alberto lay silent, a spear tip through his heart. His soul was gone before he hit the ground. Montag rode to the end of the list, halting in front of Sir Josse of Angoulême. He drew a coin purse, tossing it to the man.

"Make sure the widow gets the money for her horse," Montag said, then turned away. He knew there was more than Enric's asking price in there, but the show Enric had put on today with the animal had made it worth it. Montag would be feared for years as both horseman and knight. He wouldn't have to compete in these accursed tournaments in order to maintain his reputation.

He smiled as his squire jogged up to him.

The young man had few words and greater actions. "I still have the horses ready to head out. Unless you'd rather stay, my lord."

Montag ran a hand down the fiery stallion's neck. A fine piece of horseflesh. "Let's head out then, shall we?" They could be in Alsace within a few short days. There was much to attend to. Edmond's education for one thing. And more importantly, he needed to dispatch his allies, perhaps even Lezay, to discover what arm Raganor was extending from the Holy Land. Montag was sure of one thing, and it was that Milano had not acted on his own. Was it Raganor that wanted Enric dead, or was there a new enemy?

Chapter 44

"Mama, Mama!" Eleanor burst into the manor, her little legs flying. "There's a group of men outside! Knights!"

"Oh, is your father home, love?" Igraine finished a last stitch on her embroidery and rose, brushing her skirts smooth. She held the back of her chair with a clenched hand as dizziness overcame her, as it still occasionally did, but it passed.

Eleanor shook her head. "No, but they said they're friends."

Igraine frowned, forcing down the prickle of alarm that tingled up her spine. She took Eleanor's hand and followed the girl into the courtyard, where indeed, there was an entourage of knights waiting.

She sighed in relief when she saw the familiar faces. "Sir Josse! Sir Louis! What a pleasant surprise. I thought you were away at tournament."

Josse dismounted and handed his horse to his squire. With a low bow, he tried to meet her eye and smile, but it flickered.

"What's wrong?" she asked, the prickle of alarm returning with ferocity. She noted Enric's squire, Pierre, who avoided her gaze. A few other familiar men surrounded a wagon, including Louis. Her heart pounded and her vision narrowed, eyes locked on the wagon. They rarely traveled with wagons. Too cumbersome.

"My lady, there was an accident. At the tourney at Blackstone."

"An accident." Igraine squeezed Eleanor's hand a bit too hard. She felt the child whimper and released her. "Eleanor, why don't you go run along and play?" Eleanor seemed to sense something was wrong and for once obeyed without question, walking slowly to the stable, her sharp eyes glancing over her shoulder every few steps. When she was out of eyesight, Igraine turned back to Josse. "Where is he?"

"In the wagon, my lady."

Her eyes went wide. "Is he . . . " The world seemed oddly sharp around her, the birds noisily chirping, the sun a little too hot.

"Alive, my lady."

She breathed a sigh of relief, her knees trembling. She held a hand to her heart. She quickly moved toward the wagon.

Josse caught her arm. "Igraine, I want you to steady yourself. He's not well."

"But he's alive! Josse, let me see him." She pulled away.

"Igraine—"

She pushed past him to the cart where Enric lay tucked in a dozen blankets, still trembling with fever despite the warm day. There she froze. How could this ashen-faced skeleton be her husband? She looked to Josse, a hand over her lips as color drained from her face. He was merely studying his boots, so she turned back to the man in the wagon.

"Enric?"

The corpse opened its eyes.

Igraine clambered onto the cart with him, a sob catching in her throat despite all her years of training to hide emotion. She threw an arm over his chest, kissing his forehead, his chapped lips. "Enric," she choked, tears dripping onto his cheeks. She dug into the blankets to find his hand, pulling it to her chest. "What on earth happened?" she breathlessly turned to Josse.

Josse sighed. "He took a lance at the tourney."

"What do you mean he took a lance? They blunt them!"

"This one was tipped." He shifted uncomfortably as Igraine gasped. "The man that did it is dead."

"Dead? How?"

Josse met her eye. "Your brother."

"My brother?" She furrowed her brow in confusion. "He doesn't go to tournaments anymore." He certainly had never set foot at a lowly event like Blackstone.

"He did this time," Louis murmured.

"So was everyone riding with tipped lances?" How could they let that happen? Now one man was dead and Enric . . . she pushed the thought away. Enric's gaze seemed to look past her, though his eyes were open and his breath came steadily.

Josse shook his head. "You don't understand. Montag *challenged* Sir Alberto. *Because* Alberto tipped the lance that did this to Enric." He shrugged. "He challenged him in Enric's honor."

Igraine stilled, her hands caressing Enric's ashen face.

"There's more." Josse shuffled his feet. "He's the one that saved . . . or prolonged at least . . . Enric's life."

"What?" Her eyebrows shot up.

Josse shrugged. "We didn't know what to do. The lance was embedded deep. We knew to pull it out would make Enric bleed to death. Montag came along and pulled it and immediately staunched the bleeding. He cauterized the inside *and* outside of the wound . . . I've never seen someone do that with such adeptness before. He tried to save his life, Igraine."

Igraine rocked back onto her heels, tears streaming anew. "Enric, oh Enric. Why?"

Louis motioned to the squires and the man driving the wagon. "Come away with me a moment." The audience vacated, Igraine took the moment to cry with Josse at her side. When she regained control, she straightened.

Josse cleared his throat, voice choked with emotion. "Fever set in on the road here. I thought he was going to pull through. The wound itself doesn't seem to have damaged organs, by some miracle. We tried to keep it clean. But the fever . . . I am sorry. We tried . . ."

"Oh, Josse, I know. You did well. Thank you so much for bringing him home." She clasped Enric's face in her palm again, staring at him. "Enric?"

But he didn't have the energy to speak. She brushed a tear that glistened at the corner of his eye with her thumb.

"He wants you to know he loves you. He made us promise to tell you a hundred times on the way here. We told him to tell you himself." Josse had to turn away, his lips quivering. He hastily wiped at tears. The other men lingered near the stable.

Enric's lips moved ever so slightly.

"I love you, Enric de Levan. And I always will," Igraine whispered, a smile brushing her lips as she ran a hand through his sweaty hair.

Enric's breathing changed in a heartbeat, the gasps coming ragged and further apart. Igraine put a hand to her lips, her other hand clasping Enric's with all her strength. "Josse!" she let out a frightened squeak. She trembled from head to toe, her eyes unable to pull from the rise and fall of Enric's chest. Josse laid a reassuring hand on her shoulder as Enric took his last. Tears blurred Igraine's vision as she stared now at the vein throbbing in Enric's neck. Thump. Thump. Thump.

A heart's last deafening beat.

A sob ripped through her as she dropped Enric's hand. It no longer belonged to him, but to a corpse, all in that transitional moment. A solitary blink in the vast scale of time. At first, she pulled into Josse, whose strong arms tried to steady her as tears streamed from his own eyes. But she was breaking, breaking somewhere so deep inside that she needed to burst out, get away. Pull away.

She scrambled off the cart, hands pulling her hair, not sure where to run. The pain cut so deep she could barely breathe. She wanted to fall to her knees, pound the earth, run until her legs would not carry her. Run. Run.

"Mama?"

Igraine spun around into the gaze of her child, every emotion she was feeling echoed on the brave little girl's face. She let herself sob, but opened her arms to her daughter, who ran into them. Together they kneeled in the grass and cried. When the well of tears dried up, Igraine pulled herself to her feet, wiping Eleanor's tears.

"As much as it hurts now, Eleanor, your father was a good man. He's in a better place. We'll see him again there, in time."

"But I miss him already."

Igraine sighed. "Me too." Slowly she stood up, exhaustion rolling over her like a wave, making her dizzy. She pressed a hand to her head. "We must be brave, Eleanor. We are Levans, but we are also Le Bruns. We are strong." She swayed slightly. The little girl appeared under her arm to steady her.

She turned toward the party of knights who discreetly spoke among themselves. Their squire Pierre's face was streaked with tears. The others were somber.

"Come . . . come inside." She turned to the manor.

"My lady . . ." Sir Josse protested.

"Come inside! Come eat. You can put your horses in the stables. You've had a long journey; you must be exhausted."

Igraine averted her eyes from the wagon, a blanket drawn over the body of the greatest man she had ever known. She tucked Eleanor into her side and straightened her spine, pulling on her full reserve of the airs of the Lady of the Tournament. With glances to each other, Josse and Louis made their way into the manor. After caring for the horses, the squires followed, their shoulders slumped like a somber funeral procession.

In the solitude of the manor hall, Igraine sat on a bench in front of the hearth. Louis approached her with his eyes cast down, hugged her briefly, and whispered his condolences. One by one each man did the same. Louis turned to Josse, whispering, "I don't want her to feel like she needs to entertain us and put on a brave face. I'll keep the others over here, but you sit with her. I'm sure she has questions. You can answer them better than me."

Josse nodded.

Louis waved the squires to another table, engaging Eleanor along the way, who followed them with unabashed curiosity. Igraine was proud of her. She was playing the role of little hostess instead of wallowing in grief. Time would tell if Eleanor truly understood what had happened, but for now she was putting on a brave face. Igraine used the child's example and faked her own bravery. She had far more years of training, but it was taking all the strength she had to control her emotions when she really felt as though she was gutted.

She poured Josse a cup of ale, asking a maid to get food and start cooking more. She watched Josse drink, her brow creased and her fingers absently fidgeting with her clothes. Josse readily drank half his cup before he again leveled his gaze at her.

"Thank-you for your hospitality, my lady."

"Always, Sir Josse." She did not meet his eye. She didn't want the pity that emanated from him. She took a deep breath, forcing her voice steady. "Another hour more on the road and I would not have been able to say goodbye. Thank you for bringing him home."

"I wish we could have traveled faster." He cleared his throat. "I think he was waiting for you. He talked so much of how you'd never forgive him. Something about the horse, and you didn't want him to go to Blackstone."

Igraine rolled her eyes. "Oh, that horse."

"I told him you understand that he is who he is. Was . . ." He looked away.

They sat in silence awhile, listening to the knights at the other table burst into laughter at something little Eleanor had said. Josse took a small pouch from his belt and passed it across the table to her. "The effects he had on him, my lady. We have his armor as well."

Igraine's hands shook as she withdrew a scrap of fabric, embroidered by her own hand, now stained a shade of rusty pink.

"It staunched the wound. I tried my best to clean it," Josse muttered, looking away.

Igraine closed her eyes, then abruptly dumped the contents of the pouch on the table. A few coins and Enric's ring rolled with a loud clang, drawing a few glances from the other table. She ignored the coins and gently picked up the ring, staring at the pewter crest. Three disks entwined with tendrils of fire.

Igraine stared at the ring in her palm. "A lance . . . where?" He'd taken so many lance hits before and never had more than a few, albeit large, bruises.

"The chest. Right side. It, uh, penetrated the mail. Broke the collar bone and a few ribs."

"How? Was his mail broken?"

"Not that I am aware. My feeling is that Milano did it for spite. Enric made a fool of him earlier in the day. Well, your horse did. Dumped Milano in the dirt like it was nothing. Maybe it was revenge, maybe something else, but he cheated and would have gotten away with it, if it hadn't been for Montag."

Josse reached out a placating hand to quiet her, alarmed at how her stoic countenance was flipping to a seething rage. "Montag wasn't even near the arena when it happened. He . . . long story, but he was done for the day. Packed up. But Lord Fougères caught him after the accident, and he came to the arena. None of us knew what to do, yet he did. Up until a few days ago, I really thought he'd saved Enric's life. But the damn fever . . ."

Igraine let her breath out in a slow whistle. She was quiet a moment, thinking. "He didn't send any message? He just was there for my husband's accident, and now not a word?"

"Your brother handles emotional situations very differently from other men." Josse reached inside his vest to pull another, heavier coin purse from a pocket, which he set before Igraine. "He rode your chestnut stallion in that last joust. This is his payment for it. I have not counted the coins, my lady, but I know it is well over Enric's asking price."

Igraine put a hand to her lips as her tears brimmed her eyes.

"I'm sorry, Lady Igraine."

Igraine shook her head, suddenly exhausted. "Sir Josse, you have done so much. Thank you. And Louis. And the squires. I know it was a long journey. I'm sure it wasn't easy. You and your men stay as long as you wish. Make yourselves at home. Let the cook know if there's anything you need."

"Please, my lady. No need to apologize. We'll speak tomorrow about final arrangements. I will tell his parents when I return to Angoulême. Sir Enrique isn't moving well these days, but I will try to get them up to see you. You and Eleanor have been through so much these past few months. Anything our family can do for yours, you need only ask."

"Yes," Igraine replied stiffly. She moved to replace the coins in the pouch and hesitated. "What do I owe you?"

"Nothing, my lady."

"Surely . . ."

Josse held up a hand. "Nothing." He replaced the coins for her, knotting the string top and handing it to her. "*You* let *me* know if you need more later."

Igraine stiffly nodded, taking the pouch. Enric's ring she slipped on her thumb. Then before her legs or voice could betray her, she withdrew to her chamber where she could let the veil fall and her heart break. She fell into her bed, their bed, and screamed into a pillow, praying the sound did not carry through the small manor. When her cries were spent, her ribs aching from her sobs, she let the tears run until her face was raw. In the morning she would start putting the pieces back together. She had to, for the sake of the little girl who had stepped into her role as lady of the manor by entertaining their guests in the darkest hour they had yet seen.

Chapter 45

Montag smirked as he rounded the corner, the sounds of the battle in the corridor ahead echoing through the entire castle. Finally, Simon and the other squires were educating cocky little Edmond. A traditional initiation. It was sure to be an interesting show. He leaned a shoulder against the wall, arms crossed, taking in the scene. As he watched, his brow furrowed. Instead of seeing Simon beating Edmond with the help of the other squires, Montag saw Edmond and Raoul back-to-back, fighting off only four others. Their small swords slashed desperately. The older boys had only their fists.

A third boy came running down the corridor, sword in hand, and knocked Simon right on the head with the hilt of it. Simon yelped in pain and swung wildly at the child half his age, who shot sideways and hit someone else with the sword. There was blood in the hall now, and the three young boys seemed determined to defend themselves against the older ones at all costs. Montag frowned. His policy was to let all fights finish out and not interfere, but it was also very impractical to send a battered child home to noble parents. He certainly didn't want the inconvenience of sending a dead one back. It would be a political nightmare. Half these boys were the children of counts and dukes.

Three of the older boys had stepped back in defeat, limping away and nursing bloody wounds. Simon, dagger outstretched, was now surrounded by the three little pages, who collectively weren't much more than his age. But they had small swords, and he only had a short blade. He seemed nervous. Montag remained against the wall, waiting to see how it played out. Edmond stepped in first, parrying a flurry of attacks that drew Simon's attention. That left him open for Raoul to jump on his back, pulling his hair, while the third young squire kicked his knees. Simon fell hard onto his knees, throat exposed to the blade of Edmond's sword. His Adams apple bobbed as he swallowed, eyes leveling at Montag with shaded emotion.

Edmond also looked to Montag, little chest heaving as he panted. His sharp eyes met Montag's bravely. Raoul gave Simon's hair a rough tug, exposing his neck even more, a fiendish gleam in his eyes. Montag straightened from the wall, beginning a slow clap. All seven of the boys looked worried, Simon most of all. As Montag approached, those that could stepped back, leaving Edmond, Raoul, and Simon together in the middle of the corridor. Raoul lowered his eyes as Montag approached, finally releasing Simon's hair and stepping back to the wall of the corridor with the rest. Montag held out his hand for Edmond's sword, which he reluctantly handed over. Montag could tell by his posture he was still ready to fight. He laid a hand on the boy's shoulder, turning him away. That was as much reward as he ever mustered. Edmond seemed satisfied.

Now Simon remained kneeling before him, bloody, bruised, and worst of all, humiliated. His eyes were locked on the toes of Montag's boots. Montag felt the fury within him bubble.

"You were given the task of teaching a seven-year-old a lesson. Tell me how you have failed so miserably that a little boy could bring you to your knees? Tell me!" Montag's spittle flew through the air as he screamed in Simon's face. "I was to make you a knight — a man. To tell your parents you are ready to go off and fight wars for a king with real men, men that won't stay their hand when their blade is at your neck. Men that will take great pleasure in hacking you limb from limb. Do you think you are ready for that? *Do you*?" Montag struck Simon across the jaw with his fist, sending the young man almost to the floor before he recovered. To Simon's credit, he didn't cry out; he didn't show any emotion at all. After a while he spit out the blood from his mouth, staring straight ahead past Montag.

Montag paced before him, twirling Edmond's little sword in the air before him. "What am I to do? Cancel your ordination? Your mother will be most disappointed."

"Don't cancel," Simon said quietly.

"What?"

"Today was a mistake. It will never happen again."

"A seven-year-old brought you to your knees."

"There were three of them. I didn't expect them to have swords."

Montag struck again with the speed of a snake, hissing through his teeth with fury. "They will *always* have friends. *That* is your first mistake. And *you* must *always* have your sword. That is your second. Fool."

Simon glared, again spitting blood.

Montag resumed pacing. The squire was bold, loyal. Montag actually did want to knight him but under the circumstances, he didn't deserve it. He had to prove himself once again.

Montag turned to the rest of the boys, half of them still nursing some ugly wounds. He sighed. "Get down to Madame Brigitte." The lot of them scurried off. "Raoul!" His son turned back to him. "Remember you serve your lord before your friends." The boy nodded once, slowly. Montag trusted he would remember, and he would test that later. For now alliances were allowable. He waved Raoul away, and the boy bolted down the corridor after the others.

Once more Montag turned to Simon. He rolled his eyes in disgust. "Get up." The young man rose to his feet. Montag looked down his nose at him, utilizing the full intimidating advantage of his height. "How on earth are you going to prove yourself now? We have what, two weeks before the ceremony is supposed to take place? You have lost not only my respect, but that of your young peers, who outwitted your daft brain."

The muscle in Simon's jaw worked. He looked down, lips in a thin line. Was he biting his tongue? How quaint. Simon glanced up from his lowered eyes, the cocky fury bubbling in his tone of voice. "You want me to kill the boy?"

Montag straightened with surprise. "My friend's son and niece's betrothed? I think not." He smirked. "You want to though, don't you?"

Simon nodded, jaw clenched.

Montag folded his arms across his broad chest. The boy likely *would* kill Edmond if he had the chance. Fury was good. But only when controlled. He needed to put that fury to work. "Perhaps in time you will take your revenge on Edmond. But not when you are a man and he is a boy. There is nothing to be gained in killing a child. You would lose the respect of your peers, if not be drawn and quartered yourself. No, you will have to wait until he becomes a man."

Simon spit blood out of his mouth again, wiping the back of his hand across a split lip. "I'll do whatever you want," he said casually, his voice bristling.

Montag sized him up. There was one thing he needed done, and to complete the task before the ceremony in two weeks would take immense stamina and bravery, particularly if the young man was to do it alone. It was perfect. "Here's what I want you to do. Saddle the chestnut I purchased at Blackstone. Ride to the Levan Manor in Aquitaine. Find out if Sir Enric de Levan is dead. To prove you were there, I want you to leave that horse and steal my sister's bay mare. I'll recognize it; don't try to fool me. You should be able to return in time for the ceremony."

Montag watched Simon calculate the mileage. He was familiar with the journey, at least to Poitiers. They usually took a solid two weeks to travel that far, but now he had to ride double the distance in that time. It was going to make for some very long days in the saddle. Wisely, the boy didn't complain.

"Can the horses handle that?"

"The chestnut will make it. *If* you can ride him." Montag smirked as Simon swallowed. "Go easy on Igraine's charger. It's a fine horse, and I want it sound. Understood?" Part of Montag's challenge was if the boy could time his distances right. He would have to make the trip to Aquitaine much faster than the return trip to Brunstein.

Simon's brow furrowed. "I can ride the chestnut harder?"

Montag grew impatient, his hands clenching. "Ride the thing into the ground if you must. But bring me back word of Enric and the mare. Before your ordination! If I have to explain to your parents why you aren't here for your ceremony, you *will not* be knighted at all!" Still Simon shifted his weight, calculating. Montag put his hands on his hips. "If I were you I would be running to pack my bag and get on the road."

"What if the charger isn't there?"

"Then I suggest you bring me a letter from Lady Igraine herself."

The boy was satisfied with that. He nodded to Montag, then quick-stepped down the hall, breaking into a run as he rounded the corner. He had a long ride ahead of him. If he could survive the chestnut long enough to make it.

Footsteps sounded behind Montag, and he turned. On seeing who it was, he frowned.

"Apparently I need to clarify to my household that you are not allowed to freely roam my castle."

"As if they could stop me," Lezay smiled. He looked around at the blood that splattered the hall. "What happened?"

"My squires got into a little fight. Why are you here?" Montag growled. He strode off toward the great hall, his stomach rumbling after the afternoon's excitement.

"Wanted to see if you had any news of Igraine."

"I will in two weeks. Come back then," Montag spat, then checked himself. "Why would you care anyway? We're past this nonsense."

"Her husband is dead. My wife is dead."

Lezay picked at lint on his tunic, which would have been comical in other circumstances since the tunic itself was stained and filthy.

Montag hesitated, then opened the door into his tower study, leading Lezay in the upward spiral to the very top of Brunstein. There was an unfinished conversation that needed to occur in private. Food would once again have to wait. He shut the top door behind them with a loud bang.

"What the hell did you do to your wife?" he seethed, turning on Lezay with fists clenched.

"Why would you care? It's nothing you haven't done yourself."

"You know nothing about what I've done!"

"Or haven't done . . ." Lezay smirked.

Montag looked at him incredulously. "Alenor died in childbirth."

"Right." His dark eyes twinkled.

Danger tickled in the back of Montag's mind. Lezay couldn't possibly know Alenor had survived, could he? He rapidly seized control of the conversation. "Lezay, you have no children! How does that look?"

"I am a most unfortunate widower."

Montag ran a hand through his hair. This man was impossible. "You are not going after my sister again. Find another new wife. Igraine is taken."

"Word is Enric's dead."

"Says who?"

"Fougères." He shrugged.

"Fougères knows no more than I do. He was with me."

"Sounds like it was pretty bad."

Montag sighed. "It was. But his friends took him home. My squire will be back in two weeks with confirmation if Enric is dead or not."

"If he is, I want to marry her, Montag. You owe me. You know the alliance between our two families is even more important now. A child out of her—"

"No, Lezay. Find a new wife. What happened to the girl from Thuringia?"

"Lanky Jean put an end to that. Don't know why." Lezay picked at his teeth with a fingernail. "Let me ride down, talk to her. I understand her pain."

Montag snorted. He knew for certain that whatever it was that Igraine felt for Enric, it was nothing like whatever Lezay felt toward his dead wife. "For the last time, Lezay, stay away from her."

The foul man before him smirked. "Didn't you want something from me?"

Montag cursed under his breath. "I'm not bargaining for it. You either tell me, or I'll find the answer elsewhere."

Lezay playing with a small gold statue of a horse on Montag's desk — the same statue Montag had won at Blackstone. When Montag snatched it away, Lezay met his eyes with a cool self-satisfaction.

"I'll tell you for free. You'll owe me later. Your suspicions are correct. Milano spent the past year in Jerusalem. Under the hire of the great Lord Raganor."

Montag withered and sat on a corner of his desk. Raganor had broken his word. Though in his mind, he wouldn't see it that way. Already Montag could see the hole in their bargain as brightly as if it was laced with the fire of hell. Raganor had agreed not to touch them. He hadn't. Raganor had hired someone else to do the dirty work. The fury bubbling in Montag's chest mixed with the misery that — as his father had tried to teach him — he'd failed to make a complete agreement.

"Still don't want me to marry your sister? If his reach is that long, she's going to need protection."

The words came quietly. "I'm not convinced you are safer than Raganor."

"My, what a compliment."

Montag gritted his teeth, his fingers aching to throw a punch and yet too distracted to act, his thoughts looping around that *Raganor had broken his word.*

"He has to be punished," Lezay said as his eyes twinkled.

Montag regretting letting the man learn him well enough that he could read his mind. For he was right, there was one more card Montag could yet play that would make Raganor feel a twinge of the pain he'd inflicted on Igraine. Lezay knew it.

"You are going to have to replace him," Lezay offered.

Montag felt a chill run down his spine.

"I don't mind you being our leader. Nor will the others. You have the right."

"Once I step forward, it can't be undone."

"So be it. Take the power, Montag. I'll back you."

"So I'll owe you?"

"Of course."

Montag crossed his arms, frowning deep in thought. "Do you have proof that Raganor hired Milano?"

"That he hired him, yes. That he specifically ordered him to kill Enric, no."

"I need that."

"I can't get that but from Raganor himself. You know that. If Milano was alive, it would be one thing. But Raganor isn't going to talk."

"He will eventually. He likes to brag."

"It could be years."

"Yes."

The two men eyed each other, the weight of the decision hanging in the air.

"I won't take on The Order until I'm sure he did it," Montag finally said, his tone firm.

"Your choice," Lezay shrugged with a rare solemnity. He let the silence hang a moment longer, testament to the gravity of the decision. Then like a candle being lit, his expression lightened into a cocky smile. "I'll wait two weeks. When the rest of the world starts petitioning you for her hand, think of me then." He turned out the door, as comfortable as if he owned the castle.

Montag threw a stack of parchments at the closed door, the pages fluttering to the ground like feathers of a stricken dove. Which was how Igraine must feel if any word Lezay said was true.

Chapter 46

"I'm grateful to you for coming, but we really are just fine." Igraine filled the wineglasses a little too enthusiastically and splashed some onto the table. She gritted her teeth in frustration. Though their visit was well-meaning, she was in no state to entertain the wives of Sirs Louis and Josse of Angoulême. Enric's friends had come to help, but as Igraine was quickly realizing, things had been well under control without them.

Lady Isabel steadied her hand and took the decanter from her. "Igraine, my dear, you are doing remarkably well for your circumstances." She filled the remaining glasses.

"How could any one of us do this alone indefinitely?" Lady Mary said. "You are managing an entire manor, raising an incredible daughter . . . but look at you, Lady Igraine. You are breaking yourself."

The ladies guided Igraine back to her seat. She looked at her hands as if they had failed her. It was more than spilling the wine. The bones beneath her tanned skin were more pronounced. She pressed those bony fingers against her face. She could feel it there too. She was literally turning into a skeleton of herself. A cough threatened from deep within her chest, and she hastily masked it by clearing her throat. It was the cold that sapped strength from her. The illness that had begun with the premature birth of her son would not relent.

"You don't have to do this to yourself." Isabel took her hand. "You are not a poor woman. You are nobility!"

"I didn't come with a dowry and even if I had, it would be long gone."

"You don't need one! You have your name. Your reputation."

"Widows remarry all the time," Mary pointed out. "You, of all of us, could have your pick of men." She smiled cheerfully and put an arm around Igraine. "You could *still* be the Lady of the Tournament."

Igraine rested her head on her hands. They did not understand. "I want Enric."

"I for one understand that sentiment completely," a third, gentle voice said from the doorway. The three ladies turned toward the elder woman, her long grey hair tied back into a tight chignon, one gnarled hand pulling her shawl tight around her shoulders as the other set down a fresh decanter of wine. Lady Levan joined them at the table, her body steadier and nimbler than her years should allow as she poured more wine for them all, despite their relatively full cups. She continued, "We have had several masses said for him. It still is not enough. I wish I could have been here with you sooner, my dear." She laid a hand on Igraine's, meeting her eyes.

Igraine held her fingers, her heart aching. The last she'd felt such motherly affection was when she'd said goodbye to Madame Brigitte. That thought made her homesick for the first time in years. "I'm just glad you came. This must be so hard for you both, being away. I wish Sir Levan could have come as well."

"Traveling gets harder every year. All those years of hitting the ground off rogue horses finally caught up with Enrique. But I'm here now." She squeezed Igraine's hand. "And I am glad."

"Any time you wish to travel with us, you are welcome," Isabel offered. "I know Josse plans to visit more often — to check up on Igraine. Enric was a good friend to him."

Lady Levan drank half her wine in one go and refilled the cup. "Lady Igraine, your friends do have a point. You are young. You could easily remarry into a good life."

Igraine groaned. She had in fact had several proposals already. She'd ignored them all. They were offensive, so soon after Enric's death. To the suitors credit, usually widows only pretended to miss the men their families had arranged for them to marry. Igraine's grief was still as raw as a blister during a long journey, though she kept pushing on as if she could hide the limp. "I'm too busy to even consider it." What she really needed was time. Another lifetime of time.

The three women rubbed her shoulders to console her.

"You had the love troubadours sing of." Mary sighed.

"You have a little girl to think of though," Lady Levan reminded her. Pursing her lips, she put it bluntly, "You will have to choose if you want her raised like a commoner, fighting for her way in the world as Enric did, or if you want her to grow up with the education and training of the nobility, much like yourself. There are advantages and disadvantages to both."

Igraine stiffened. "Is that why all three of you are asking me about this?"

"We love you," Lady Levan said gently. She took her hand. "Not making a decision *is* making a decision. Time has not stopped passing since Enric's death. Eleanor is now five years old. I brought her a little birthday present by the way, though it is late. No matter what you choose, there are decisions to make to secure that choice."

"You could take Eleanor to Lord Fougères, raise her in the castle. She'll feel right at home by the time she's grown," Isabel offered.

Mary cut in, "Lady Fougères is the most suspicious and jealous woman I have ever met. There is no way the Lady of the Tournament is going to reside under her roof. For Eleanor to live there, Igraine would have to yield her to the

Fougères. I don't think so. Igraine isn't dead! I still think she should remarry. Take your pick of men, Lady Igraine!"

"She's grieving. It's too soon," Isabel insisted. She hesitated. "Could they come to Angoulême with us?"

Mary winced. "As much as I would love to have them — it would be so much fun — our manor can't support another household. There are two of us already. Josse is trying to get out of Louis' way as it is. How could we take a third family group?"

"Get out of Louis' way? Is that how you consider it? Josse is the one—"

Igraine held up her hand and the ladies quieted. "No. It is hard, but we will be fine here. The crop this year is good. We have wine fermenting in the barrels that we can sell." She stopped as a cough racked her body. "I'm sorry. This illness just has me exhausted."

The ladies gave each other worried glances.

Igraine pushed ahead to distract them. "The manor will be prepared to produce more next year. We have enough to get by. I didn't marry for wealth, just happiness, and Eleanor and I have that here. She is the heir, and she will have to learn, as I, to be independent."

"But she won't have to be independent, Igraine. She is betrothed," said Mary.

Igraine sighed, avoiding the other woman's eyes. Mary herself had been betrothed at a young age and entered an arranged marriage as a teenager. She and Louis seemed to get along fine, but it was hard for Igraine to explain to her that they were an exception. She hoped for peace for her daughter, yet the dismal lack of contact with the Fougères since Enric's death was having her reconsider the betrothal. She hadn't liked it in the first place. Shouldn't Lord Fougères have reached out after the tournament? Josse had told her *he was there*.

Igraine set her resolve. "She will also have a means to manage herself, God forbid she need it." No, that was certain. Eleanor would have something to her name, not have her future based on her marriage. The girl was *not* going to go through what Igraine herself had.

Lady Levan watched her, her kind eyes taking in every subtle non-verbal cue. "So you do want her to be raised according to her station?"

Igraine hesitated, realizing that was what she had implied. As much as a commoner's life, with freedom away from the pressures of politics and power, appealed to Igraine, she was also acutely aware that a pretty girl fighting to put food on the table would have to face some terrible options. A noble woman would have doors opened to her by name alone. Enric had fought hard to give that to his daughter. Old blood, a title, his fame in the tournaments: these things had not been for himself, but for a reputation his family could fall back on. He'd earned himself his own manor and title. Igraine would give anything for Eleanor to hold onto it.

Except remarry. Just the thought of another man touching her made her skin crawl. Having tasted what it was to have true love, she was forever ruined from settling for anything less. If it existed for a second round, she knew it would take years to find it.

Lady Levan squeezed her hand. "It is a good decision. She's a capable girl. As are you. You have bright futures ahead of you."

Isabel took a deep breath. "How can we help?"

Igraine looked around at the three concerned faces. The tickle in her throat forced her into another coughing fit.

"I'll start by finding some honey, so you can get rid of that cough!" Lady Levan smiled as she rose and headed toward the kitchen.

"Really, Lady Igraine. If you need anything, let us know," Mary offered.

Igraine appreciated the sentiment but doubted how far Mary's generosity would stretch. She'd already said Igraine and Eleanor couldn't move to Angoulême. Igraine understood, but what more was there to offer help for? She had a hard time picturing Mary or Isabel picking grapes or herding sheep. "I will. Thank you both." Igraine pushed away from the table, having taken her fill of her friends' pitying looks. She stood at the window looking out over the fields, the sun splashing across what was left of the autumn leaves with golden hued rays. A copper horse grazed in the field peacefully. She frowned, her eyes narrowing on it. "Ladies, am I seeing things, or is there a chestnut horse in my field?"

Isabel looked out the window, brow furrowed with confusion. "Yes, there's a red horse."

"Lady Isabel, I don't own a chestnut horse." Igraine's heart pounded. It couldn't be. It simply couldn't. She pulled away from the window and headed to the door. Eleanor met her there, her face alive with excitement.

"Mama, Mama! Papa's red horse is back!"

"That's not possible, Eleanor."

"It is, I saw him! He has a white star and three stockings, and that scar on his leg from when he kicked the fence last year." The little girl bounced up and down with excitement.

Igraine charged out of the manor, her heart pounding. She walked up to the fence and stared at the creature, still covered in sweat from a hard ride from God-knows-where. The animal was lean and boney, grazing like he hadn't seen a blade of grass in weeks. He snorted at Igraine, eyeing her with the same challenge that had always greeted her. It was Enric's horse, Draca, all right. Igraine glanced around. Was Montag there?

A stableboy jogged up, his face pale and eyes wide. "My lady, I tried to stop him. I'm so sorry, I tried!"

"Stop who?"

"The man that stole your charger!"

The group of them turned toward the road, where a young man with dirty-blond hair was vaulting onto Igraine's bay mare. As he pulled the reins to spin the horse around, Igraine let out a whistle. The mare turned back to her. She ran, closing the distance, and the rider again pulled the horse around, kicking sharply. She whistled again. The horse fought the rider, now angrily shaking her head at the rough treatment. Igraine stopped in front of her horse, lifting her hand quietly. The panicked man desperately tried to force the horse away from her, and when it refused, Igraine took the reins. "Get. Off."

Josse and Louis came running from the cluster of cottages next to the manor, and the household came out brandishing pitchforks and hammers. Soon the young man was surrounded. His face paling, he finally slid to his feet.

"Who are you?" Igraine said furiously, handing her traumatized horse back to the stableboy. Her hand found the dagger that, as always, was on her belt, but she did not draw it. She breathed heavily, her weakened lungs struggling from the exertion. Fighting for the visage of strength, she stood straight and willed her heart steady.

The young man looked down his nose at her.

"I asked you a question," she stepped closer to him.

"It's the wrong question. A better one would be, 'who do I work for?'" Color returned to the man's face. His eyes flicked among the crowd surrounding him, calculating.

Igraine straightened, fury bubbling within her. "I know who you work for, you insolent thief. I do not ask 'wrong' questions. Now, you answer me, and we'll have a conversation. If I need to force the answers from you, I will have no trouble enlisting help to do so."

He eyed her up and down, seeming to make a decision. "Simon. Of Bavaria."

Igraine cracked a smile. "The princeling? How did you survive so long under my brother's tutelage?" It was an amazing feat indeed, as the young son of a prince was still a fresh and overwhelmed pupil when Igraine had last seen him at a tournament with Montag. She'd cautioned him to stay out of the way, thinking he wouldn't last more than a few months. He'd grown into himself quite a bit.

Simon frowned.

"Oh, you think I don't remember you? It's only been a few years, Simon. Must seem like an eternity under Montag's rule. Why aren't you a knight?" She cocked her head to the side.

"I will be in a week."

"Ah, I see. So this was the final test? To steal my horse?"

He was silent.

"Well, you failed. Now what? All those years of work for nothing? Montag has never knighted a squire. He only talks about it."

"He's going to knight me."

Igraine's eyebrows went up. The tickle in her throat returned, and she fought it back by clearing her throat. "As fascinating as this argument is, I have company. Take the chestnut back to Montag. Get off my estate." Igraine turned her back on him, making her way to the manor as the cough began to escape her lips.

Simon didn't move.

Josse appeared at Igraine's side. "I'm happy to deliver him to the duke, my lady," Josse offered, eyeing the young man with disgust. "Thieves usually lose an appendage."

Igraine got her cough under control and turned back.

The young man scuffed the dirt with his boot. "The task was only partly to steal your horse. I also have to tell him Enric is dead."

The three visiting ladies gasped. Igraine's eyes sparked with the Le Brun fire. "Does he care?"

Simon shrugged. "None of my business. If you want to keep your horse, I need a letter from you. To prove I was here. Then I'll be gone."

"If a letter would suffice, why didn't you ask?" Igraine gritted her teeth.

"Not a conversational person," the young man smirked.

Louis stepped forward, cracking his knuckles. Simon wasn't fazed. "My lady, with your permission?"

Igraine nodded once. "Secure him."

Louis and Josse stepped forward and held Simon without him protesting. Josse quickly disarmed him.

Simon smirked slightly as he let the men rough handle him. "All I need is a letter."

"What you need is a lesson," Josse hissed.

"No," Igraine said, holding up a finger. "Just secure him somewhere for a while."

That statement seemed to make Simon more nervous. "How long?"

"Does it matter?" Igraine smiled.

"I need to be back in nine days. I'm to be knighted."

"Oh, that *would* matter," Louis chuckled. He guided Simon away, shooting Igraine a wink. "Take your time, my lady. We'll interrogate him a while."

Igraine shook her head but smiled. She knew they wouldn't hurt the man, but he did deserve to be humbled a bit. She turned to the ladies, taking Eleanor's hand in her own. "Shall we?" She guided them back into the manor, stopping only once on the steps with another coughing fit.

"Mama?" Eleanor questioned. Her blue eyes were round with worry.

"I'll be fine, love. Run along and entertain our guests, so I can write to your uncle."

She secured herself in her chamber and drew out the ink. A tiny note would have to suffice. She had few words to say to Montag. For that brat of a squire's sake, she'd have to give him something to prove it was her. That was what Montag really wanted after all these years. He wouldn't ask if she was all right or if she needed anything. He would try to steal a horse to get his news that she was even alive. Well, she was. She would have thanked him for saving Enric from an instant death, but not after this stunt. Did she care how he was? Surely he was fine as always, or he wouldn't be testing his squires so close to an ordination.

She dipped the quill.

Burn the flesh to save the soul. For a while, she wrote. She smiled slightly at the change in words. Their father always said purge, as if there was something inherently wrong with them that must be cast out. Hopefully Montag would realize her new meaning. By cauterizing the wound, he had saved Enric for a little while at least. It just hadn't saved him entirely. He'd preserved Enric's life long enough for her to say goodbye, and for that she'd always be grateful. Hopefully he would understand, and take her gratitude with it, just as she noted his concern for her by this expedition to steal her horse.

She set the tiny parchment aside to dry and went to the window. Josse and Louis had Simon tied to the hitching post. The young squire sat on the ground, head back against the post. From the look of things, he hadn't said much, and by the way Louis and Josse were pacing, they were very frustrated. Igraine watched a few minutes longer as things appeared to escalate, at least on the part of Josse and Louis, then took up her parchment, rolled it, and returned outside.

The three men looked up at her as she approached.

"He hasn't said a bloody word," Josse said in frustration. "I'm happy to increase the pressure if you'll let me."

Igraine looked to Simon to gauge his reaction. There was none, just continued patience. He really must be Montag's prized pupil. She stood over him, waiting patiently until he met her eyes. He held the gaze. "Leave us, please, my lords."

"Lady Igraine . . ." Louis protested.

"Five minutes."

Josse and Louis stepped away. Igraine and Simon stayed locked in the stare down, Igraine tapping the tiny parchment against her palm. Simon's eyes shifted to it, then back to her face. She waited.

"What do you want?" Simon broke.

"Tell me what you want to know."

Simon hesitated a long moment. The tapping of the parchment filled the silence. "Who is Raganor?" His voice was surprisingly quiet.

Igraine inhaled. "When did you hear that name?"

"He and Sir Lezay utter it sometimes."

"And say what?"

"Who is he?"

"Raganor le Brun is my father."

Simon's brow furrowed. "I thought he was an enemy."

Igraine chuckled. Sarcasm laced her words as she asked, "What made you think that?"

Simon didn't hesitate. "Montag believes he hired Alberto Milano."

Igraine felt the wind leave her, hesitating a moment before falling into one of the worst coughing fits of the day. When she had again regained her breath, she looked at Simon, who was watching her with a curious intensity. Star pupil indeed. To only yield information when it got him better information. She narrowed her eyes. "Does he have any proof?"

"The lance was tipped with a Saracen point."

"Hard to get those in Aquitaine." Igraine stared at the dirt, her hands on her hips as thoughts swirled. She imagined the scene — a typical joust — and the surprise as a sharp point tore mail and flesh. "You were there. Do you think Milano did it intentionally?"

Simon thought. "You don't tip a lance without intention."

"Was Milano told to do it?"

"If he was, he took the wrong job. If he wasn't, embarrassment was an idiotic reason to die." Simon pointed his chin at Draca. "He couldn't ride that horse to save his life."

Simon watched Igraine. After a long moment of silence he shifted his weight, reminding her of his discomfort in being tied. She sighed and stooped to undo his ropes. He stood, rubbing his wrists. His demeaner did somehow bely more respect.

"Take your horse and go," Igraine said quietly, handing him the parchment.

Simon ducked away from her without so much as thanks. A minute later he emerged with the chestnut stallion fully tacked. As he readied to mount, Igraine called out, "Simon?" He hesitated. "Since you are only one of three people in this world that that horse has not tried to kill, don't kill him. He will serve you well in the years to come."

"Montag won't part with him."

Igraine smiled. "He already did. This is part of your test, princeling. That horse will be your ordination gift from him. Pace yourself better going back to Brunstein, or you'll be dragging a bridle behind you."

Simon nodded once and swung into the saddle.

"And Simon . . ." Igraine smirked as his attention riveted to her once again. "Next time you try to steal from me, I will not be so kind." She pulled aside a fold of her skirt to reveal the dagger. "And I have many allies." As if on cue, Josse and Louis emerged from the manor, their eyes widening and paces quickening as they noted the squire on the chestnut.

Simon turned away and galloped off, clods of dirt flying in a shower over them.

"Want us to go after him?" Josse said breathlessly.

"No," Igraine shook her head. "He is only a messenger." She turned back to her husband's friends, putting a hand on each of their shoulders. "Come, let's see what the cook came up with for dinner. You must be starving." As they entered the manor, Igraine glanced into the distance at the lone rider just as he turned out of sight. She had no doubt he would return to Montag with her message intact.

She wondered if Montag knew just how much worry his inadvertent message had caused. Raganor was involved with Enric's death? If so, then none of them were safe. Eleanor ran up to her, another big smile on her face. Igraine's heart clenched. Where was the safest place for her child?

"You were so brave!" Lady Isabel gushed a few minutes later.

"Why didn't you just let the men handle it?" Lady Mary asked, her tone a bit condescending.

"She's independent, ladies." Lady Levan put an arm around Igraine. She kissed her temple. "Enric would have been proud, my dear," she whispered in her ear.

Fatigue weakened Igraine's knees, and she leaned into Lady Levan for a moment before reaching for the wall to steady herself.

"Are you well, child?" Lady Levan asked.

"What a day!" Igraine said brightly. Though every muscle in her body suddenly ached, she would not let her guests see.

"Quite." Isabel smiled, oblivious. "Excitement seems to follow you."

Lady Levan still had her arm around her. "Come dear. Let's let you rest. You need to shake that cold."

Igraine shivered, but the cough stayed at bay. She let Lady Levan guide her up to her chamber, which felt rather oversized and cold now that Enric was not there to fill the space. Within the room, Lady Levan released her, looking around. She instinctively started tidying the space, collecting clothes, some of which were Enric's. Igraine just hadn't had the will to put them away. Igraine sat on the chest at the foot of the bed and watched without complaint. It needed to be done. They had to move on.

"Thank you," she whispered.

Lady Levan hesitated mid-bend as she reached for a shirt. She then retrieved it and gave it a shake. She made her way to Igraine and sat next to her, turning the fabric in her hands. She lifted it to her nose and closed her eyes, breathing deep. Her face looked crestfallen as she returned the item to her lap, hands absently folding it.

"You've lost a child," Igraine said softly. "It is I who should be helping you."

Lady Levan shook her head. "You lost a child, too."

"It's not the same."

"No. It's not. Just different." Lady Levan sighed. "You know, Enric had resigned himself that you would never leave your family. He told me he would rather stay a bachelor forever than marry anyone but you, even when it seemed certain you *would* marry another."

Despite her grief and fatigue, Igraine smiled. "Really?"

Lady Levan nodded. "I was rather angry at him. I wanted grandchildren, you see." Her face took on a faraway look. "But when I met you, I understood. And that is why I understand now why you don't want to remarry. You will never find what you had with Enric again."

They both stared at the floor.

"But, Igraine . . . you can still have something *different*."

"I don't know what that looks like."

"You are strong. You can run this place — or better — like it's second nature. You ran Brunstein, did you not?"

Igraine straightened. While Montag was building a name for himself and the family, the management of the huge castle had fallen to young Igraine. And it had thrived. "I did."

"And from what I hear, you did an excellent job." She hesitated. "I'm going to be brutally honest, Igraine. Mary and Isabel live like two cats at each other's throats. Though the brothers are your allies due to their loyalty to your husband, those two petty birds won't give you rest if you become indebted to them. And Enrique and I are old.

We never had enough to offer Enric, much less a lady like you—"

"You are so much to us."

"I appreciate that, dear, but I am a realist. And I also know Lady Mary was right that Lord Fougères' wife is a jealous woman. They may take Eleanor, but what use is that to you? That girl belongs to you, with you. You understand her fire when so many others would try to snuff it out."

"What are you saying? We are alone?" Igraine was acutely aware of that. How frustrating to be reminded. She wiped her hands on her skirts to hide her agitation.

"I'm saying you ran Brunstein exceptionally well. Perhaps you could do so again."

Igraine shifted as the silence fell over the room. "Go back to my brother?"

"Worth a try. Especially with Eleanor's betrothed there."

"It wasn't a happy place."

"I can't picture you being anywhere without friends." Lady Levan smiled gently and laid a hand on her shoulder.

Igraine thought of Madame Brigitte and the others, an ache of longing filling her heart. And Raoul — how big her little nephew must have grown.

"Mend the old wounds. For Eleanor's sake."

It certainly would be safer from Raganor there. Eleanor would love the castle. Still, they had made Levan Manor their home. Igraine had sewn the tapestries on the walls. Eleanor had her own hideaways. And the household — their friends — what would they do without them?

A thought struck her as suddenly as a bolt of lightning. "Lady Levan, what do you know about Enric's time in Jerusalem?"

"He was knighted of course."

"Do you know by whom?"

Lady Levan frowned, averting her eyes. "I know it was by your father." She inhaled slowly. "I don't know what happened over there, but Enric came home changed in more than title." She looked Igraine in the eye, a fire flashing deep within her blue gaze. "Today proved my suspicions — that you — and that little girl — need protection. It's simply not enough to be here alone."

Igraine abruptly stood and paced.

"I'm sorry to upset you. I'm sure there is another solution I'm not seeing. We could hire guards."

Igraine laughed. "No. You are right, as always. I just don't like it. I will think about it. At least I know my brother cares, if he's sending his squire to inquire about Enric. I wish he'd just come himself, but maybe he's not ready for that." She sighed. "He's a difficult man, Lady Levan. But he has done a lot for me. All I've done in return is abandon him for Enric."

"Blood runs thick, my dear." Lady Levan caught her fingers and squeezed. "I think that is where you learn to float."

Chapter 47

Montag nursed a cup of wine in his tower study, feet propped in front of the small fire. His papers lay neatly stacked on the table behind him, the latest message from The Order feeding the flames that flickered before him. Echoes of the feast down in the great hall reached his ears depending on the wind that occasionally whistled through the narrow windows of the tower. It was an ugly night, and little Simon wasn't home.

For now, Montag had managed to soothe the boy's parents, stringing a web of vague lies. Unable to maintain the farce in public, he'd retired quite early. They were offended. They would have to deal with it.

Perhaps he had underestimated the boy. He trusted that he would return, that his training was sufficient enough to carry him the long miles to retrieve a simple answer to a simple question. Montag let out an audible grunt, his eyes glassed as he stared at the flames. For all he knew,

Simon was dead. Montag wasn't looking forward to the morning. He finished off his wine and stood, stretching his shoulders. He'd been training the other squires hard. Perhaps too hard if he himself was feeling the exertion. He rolled his neck and shrugged the thought away. It was impossible to overprepare them.

He stood over his desk, wondering what work he could do. It was done. He rubbed his neck and briskly strode out of the room, down the spiral stair, and through the castle. He ignored those that greeted him, making his way to the gate. The hair on the back of his neck prickled. Simon would make it. He ordered his sentries to raise the gate, stepping forth as soon as the heavy metal cleared his height. The darkness enveloped him, the torches in the sconces behind him swallowed into a deep well of black as he stepped into the starless night. His ears strained, but the wind masked any sound but its howl. He knelt and touched the bare dirt of the road with a hand, brow furrowed as he felt for the vibration of hooves. He glanced up into the darkness and rose, watching expectantly. A few minutes later, a horse and rider cantered into view.

The sentries on the wall called him back, ready to shut the gate against the late-night visitor. But Montag ignored them. The rider slowed as he approached, halting before Montag, head tucked into his hood as his cloak swirled around him. The horse snorted impatiently, still eager to go, unaware that his journey was complete. Montag looked up at the man expectantly, nerves tingling, until finally the hood was lowered.

Simon glared at Montag with the exhausted, prideful gaze of an equal. Montag's lips curled into a wry smile of appreciation. Wordlessly Simon handed Montag a tiny bit of rolled parchment. Montag took it, eyeing Simon warily. His eyes flicked to the horse, smile fading to a frown as he noted Enric's chestnut. He had been very clear . . .

"He's dead," Simon said. "And Igraine was unwilling to part with her horse." He nodded his head at the note in Montag's hand. "You've got what you wanted. We set for tomorrow?"

"Yes," Montag admitted. As long as the note was in Igraine's hand, which it surely was, the boy deserved knighthood more than any other he'd trained. His squire boy was now a man if that look of calculating distain was any indication.

"Then I will go make my preparations." Simon pushed his horse ahead toward the gate, then hesitated. He turned back over his shoulder to say, "She's not well." He pursed his lips, considering his words. "Coughing. Weakness."

"How bad?"

Simon again hesitated.

"How bad?" Montag's voice rose, and he stepped up to the rider's leg.

"If she were my sister, and I had a care for her, I would go to her myself." The uncharacteristic quantity of words said much. Montag froze, a tingle of fear racing up his spine. He glanced down at the note in his hand. When he looked up again, Simon had ridden on through the gate. Montag quickly strode after him, waving at the sentries to lower the gate behind him. He paused under the first sconce he walked past and unfurled the parchment.

Burn the flesh to save the soul. For a while.

Montag looked around him, his heart pounding, but no one was watching. Simon had definitely completed his task. He stared at the words before him. Was it a thank you or a curse? He debated for a long minute, then decided it was irrelevant. He had to go see her after all. Simon's true message was worth far more than Montag had bargained for, and Simon knew it. He now owed the man something.

He could keep that damn horse.

Montag strode to the stables, mind listing the instructions that would need to be followed by his household if he was to make it out of Brunstein following the ordination tomorrow. And he *would* get away. He only had to be present for the ceremony, and then the festivities could carry on without him. After a long list of instructions was delivered to grooms, stablemaster, squires, and cook, Montag withdrew for a second time to his study.

He froze in place with his hand on the door handle as a familiar voice called his name.

"Rumor has it you're going to Aquitaine," Lezay's snide voice echoed.

"For an idiot, you have remarkable sources." Montag turned to face the man.

Lezay shrugged. "Can I come?"

"No."

"I'll be headed that way anyway, same as you." He smirked knowingly.

Montag thought of the parchment burned in the fire hours earlier. He leaned back against the wall with sudden exhaustion. He would have to take care of that matter first. At least it was along the way. He sighed. "If you keep your mouth shut we can travel together to the Bergfried. No further."

"We'll see," Lezay smiled and headed back down the spiraling stair.

Montag groaned and pushed open the door at his side. Never a moment of reprieve. Nor respite. And for now, all he wanted was rest, though he doubted it would stave off the worries that threatened along the edges of his consciousness.

Chapter 48

Igraine's hand shook as she penned the letter to her brother. All she could write was his name, then tears overwhelmed her. She pushed the parchment away, fearful she would ruin it. She looked out the window to her left at the child who played in the courtyard. Eleanor was pretending to fight some imaginary foe with a stick. The chickens were getting a good laugh at least. Igraine wiped her tears. She had to do this . . . for Eleanor's sake.

She picked up the quill, careful not to blot the ink. This would not be any quantity of writing, but what she had to say she did not want a monk to transcribe.

"Montag, my brother . . ." she mouthed as the quill scratched. She was tempted to write next "as your spy has likely informed you" but opted instead for the short and brutal "My husband is dead." She let out a shaky breath and dipped the quill. "I hoped to seek your forgiveness in person, but alas my body has other plans. I cannot travel—" She turned her head and coughed, groaning in frustration. "Please come soon, so that you may meet Enric's heir. I hope you are willing to act as guardian." No, that didn't seem to do justice to the gravity of the situation. She didn't cross out the lines, but squeezed onto the bottom of the small parchment, "Brother, I may not have much time. Forgive me." Hastily she signed it "Lady Igraine de Levan."

As she set down the quill, another racking cough shook her body. Her very bones ached. She hoped the letter was melodramatic. Perhaps it would bring Montag to Aquitaine, and their relationship could be repaired. She leaned back in her chair and closed her eyes, yielding to the weakness for a moment.

"Take that! And that!" The faint voice echoed through the window. Igraine smiled and looked out again. Eleanor's imaginary foe had been replaced by the manor blacksmith, a grandfatherly old man with a quick smile and easy humor. They were locked in a dramatic stick battle, which of course Eleanor was winning. The girl was fire itself. How would she fare away from everything she knew? Could Montag control her without having to quench her? Igraine flinched as Eleanor wacked the smith with her stick, forcing a loud "Ow!" out of him. He apparently was being a little too lenient in letting the girl win. Yes, she and Montag would have to have a long talk about how to temper that child's passion. Igraine could expect no less of a child of her own blood, let alone that of Enric's.

The smith let out another yelp and Igraine finally yelled out the window, "Eleanor, why don't you go ride your pony?"

The child looked up at the window, her face falling.

"What's wrong? I thought you loved riding your pony?"

Eleanor looked at the smith and mumbled.

"What did she say?" Igraine called.

The smith looked up at Igraine with a sad look. "She said the pony makes her miss her father."

The words cut into Igraine like a fresh blade wound. She leaned on the window frame for support as her knees weakened. Another coughing fit seized her. "Eleanor," she said weakly. "Come up here please. I want to talk to you, love." Eleanor threw her stick in the dirt and dragged her feet as she entered the manor. Igraine sank back into her chair as she waited for the child to climb the stairs.

It seemed an eternity and a moment before the little girl pushed open the heavy door. As usual, Igraine's heart caught in her throat as she noted the bright blue eyes. She was undeniably her father's daughter. "Eleanor, come here, child." Igraine opened her arms to her daughter, who climbed into them, pulling herself onto her lap. She snuggled her soft cheek against her mother's shoulder. Igraine held her tight, rocking her.

"I miss your papa, too, Eleanor."

"Why did he go away?"

"He didn't want to. Sometimes God . . . God just takes those he chooses. We have to trust that He has a better plan for them than we do."

"But Papa said he was going to teach me how to canter. And how to swordfight like him! Now who will?" Eleanor snuggled tighter into her mother's shoulder, sobs overcoming her.

Igraine wiped at her tears and kissed the top of the girl's head. "Oh, Eleanor . . . you will still learn those things I'm sure. You will find people to teach you. Even though the swordplay is hardly something fit for a young lady."

"But Papa said . . ."

"I know, I know. Your father just wanted to teach everything he knew to someone. You've done well in the short time we've had with him."

"He told me once you fought off a bad man."

"He did?" Igraine pulled back so she could look into Eleanor's tear-stained eyes. The girl nodded. "Hmmm." She set Eleanor on her feet and slowly rose, pausing as another coughing fit threatened but faded. "Come here, sweetheart." Taking Eleanor by the hand, Igraine led her to a heavy chest and knelt in front of it, leaning on the child as she lowered to her knees. Right on top was the familiar handle of her dagger. Smiling, she withdrew it, holding it on her lap. Eleanor's eyes grew wide.

"Mama!"

"This is mine, Eleanor." Igraine's fingers traced the seal of the crest and the graceful handle of the sheathed dagger. She pulled it from the scabbard and it sparkled in the light; it was sharp. She pointed out the crest to the awed little girl. "This was from your father . . . our family crest. The Levan crest. He had this made for me, as a wedding present." She slid the blade back to the safety of the sheath and handed it to Eleanor, handle first. "I want you to have it now. He'd want you to have it." Eleanor stared at the dagger like it was a priceless treasure, her hands gentle as if the offering was made of glass.

"Really, Mama? All mine?"

"Yes, love. Just be careful with it now." Igraine smiled, then shook with another long coughing fit.

Eleanor wrapped her arms around her. "Mama, what's wrong?"

Igraine waved her off. "My humors must be off. Don't worry, Eleanor. I'll be fine." She hesitated, then dug into the chest again. From its depths she pulled out a soft, thin chord. She frowned at it, then slid Enric's ring off her thumb. She held it up for Eleanor to see. Their eyes studied the delicate engraving on the pewter band. "This was your father's. As it was his father's and his father's. You are his heir, and he would want you to have this, too. It is too big for you now, but you'll grow into it." She slipped it onto the chord and tied it around Eleanor's neck. Eleanor held the ring in her hand with awe. Igraine smiled. "I don't think I need to tell you how important these two items are, Eleanor. I'm trusting you to take care of them."

"Mama, thank you." She threw her arms around Igraine's neck.

"Oh, sweetheart, I love you so much." She held her tight. Gently she released her and tucked a wisp of hair behind Eleanor's ear. "Now . . . I think there's a pony down in that barn that needs someone to ride her. Why don't you find Master Jorge and have him help you?"

Eleanor smiled brightly and nodded, bouncing from the room.

Igraine watched her go, then leaned wearily against the chest. "Enric, Enric . . . what can I do for her? If this is the last of my strength, how do I protect her?" She closed her eyes and slept, leaning there against the chest.

Hours later the maids found her. With worried glances they raised her to her feet and tucked her into her bed. "Letter . . ." Igraine pointed to her desk by the window. A maid picked up the folded note.

"Who to, my lady?"

"My brother . . . quickly." She sank into her pillows, her eyes again fluttering shut. She shivered as her fever returned.

The maid's eyebrows shot up. They knew only enough about Lady Igraine's tempestuous brother to fire all alarms if he was seen near the Levan manor. A few of the household had been there to witness Igraine's wild ride into Enric's arms. Now she wanted to contact him? Clutching the note like gold, the maid ran from the room and located the stable boy. The boy was young, but he would know how to find Montag. He would be able to ride all the way to Alsace, a kingdom away, and deliver a message to the Mephistopheles himself.

Chapter 49

December 14, 1179

Levan Manor, Aquitaine

The stench of death pervaded the room despite the cracked window. Montag swallowed and shifted his weight uncomfortably as he stood in the doorway. The maid that had led him upstairs silently withdrew back down the corridor. Steeling himself with a deep breath, he entered the room and softly closed the door behind him. The click of the latch made her stir.

"Eleanor?" she said breathlessly, reaching out for who she assumed was her daughter. Willing to nurture and protect even from her deathbed: that was Igraine.

Montag stepped softly up to her bed, kneeling beside her as much so she could see him as to steady his weakened knees. She had changed. His beautiful, graceful, fiery little sister was an emaciated, pale husk. Her hair lay matted and sweated against her head. Her eyes, once so sharp, now struggled to focus on him with a dim light. Even now, she let them flutter closed again.

"Ah, Montag. You came." Her voice was as weak as a breath.

Deftly, Montag took her boney hand.

"I was already on the road when I got your letter, Igraine. How long has this — Why didn't you send for me sooner?"

"What could you have done?"

"Protected you."

"From what, Montag? How do you protect someone from illness?" Igraine let out as raspy chuckle that ceased almost as soon as it started. It succeeded in tearing Montag's soul. "I am glad you came. You made good time."

Montag caressed her hand, still cradled in his own as if it was a bird. "My squire warned me. The letter made us ride faster."

Igraine seemed to rally at his words, her eyes peeling open to fix him in a steady gaze. "So you are willing to protect Enric's heir?"

Montag frowned but nodded. "It will be good for Raoul to grow up with his . . . cousin. They will grow to be allies. As Enric has no noble kin—"

"He does have kin. They would be good for her but Montag, you alone can keep her from Raganor." His eyes went wide. "Simon told me. I don't want him to get to her, too. And I can't endanger the others. They would never understand what they're up against."

"Igraine, on my life I swear I will protect your son. He will be raised as a noble and come into his titles. I will train him to knighthood. He will learn to hunt and ride and fight and govern."

Igraine was shaking her head. It was costing her so much energy. Why was she shaking her head?

"No, Montag. No son. But everything you say . . . will you do this for my daughter? My heir? My Eleanor?"

Montag stood and let his sister's hand fall back onto the bed. He'd made the terrible assumption that the second child had been born a boy. A second Levan *and Le Brun* heir. His eyes scanned her lean body. "I was told you were pregnant again."

"He died. Months ago." Her words were a whisper.

Montag felt that ache in his chest again. He rubbed it absently, before catching himself and stilling his hands. "He's killed you, you know," he said coldly. "If a rough childbed weakened you—"

"I don't have the energy to fight, brother."

"Good thing he's already dead, or I'd kill him." Guilt washed over Montag as he thought back to the aftermath of Alenor's childbed fever. Igraine's words, *How would you feel if that was me?*, rang loud in his ears. Now it *was* her, and the pregnancy and stress Enric had thrust upon her *did* make him feel something. Anger.

"Don't blame him. There is no one to blame. This just is. Montag, the love I had for Enric was a gift. Maybe you know love for your son . . . maybe not. It's different I know for me, with Eleanor. That love has its own power, but it is different. I hope you can love one day, like I loved Enric. Like I still love Enric. I cannot go to him, Montag, until I know our child will be cared for. I have tried to fight with all the strength I have left, but I feel it will not be enough. Now you have come back. Will you take care of Eleanor, Montag?"

He stared at her in horror.

"Do you think Raganor knows about Eleanor?"

Montag held his breath, then let it out in a whistle. "I don't know. You had her in the public eye. He has to know by now."

"When I'm gone . . ."

"Don't talk like that."

She held up a finger to silence him, trembling with the effort. "I don't know who else is capable of protecting her. Maybe Josse and Louis, but then they'd have to know about Father's crimes in order to understand the . . . gravity . . . of the situation. I'm not sure I want to tell them." She went quiet. "At this point, I don't have time to."

"Igraine . . ."

"Brother, will you protect her? Take her to Brunstein, where Father dares not tread. You are the only one he respects. If he could get to Enric from a distance, he can get to her. I could send her to Fougères maybe . . . but her betrothed is with you anyway. It would be good for her to get to know Edmond." Igraine abruptly shut her eyes, the stream of words having sapped what was left of her strength.

Montag shifted his weight, his knees starting to ache. He'd come for her, to take her back to Brunstein, to help her heal that she may remarry. Looking over her emaciated form, he was too late for that. And yet she wanted him to take the little girl? With that accursed name? "Why did you name her Eleanor?" he grumbled.

"Alenor was my friend. I wanted to honor her. Honor her bravery for loving you."

"She doesn't love me."

Igraine blinked her eyes open.

"Didn't . . ." Montag hastened.

"Montag . . ."

"Didn't," he insisted.

She relaxed, her eyes fluttering closed.

"He killed you. His vain tournaments — he killed you both."

"He took no risks other than those any other knight takes. You know that. You've been on the other end of the blade. Montag, it is better to love and live a full life in the light, even if it means dying early perhaps, than to live long empty years in darkness."

"Some of us have to live in darkness, so there's room in the light for the rest of you," he mumbled.

"The beauty of light is that it expands with each new flame you start. It's not too late for you, Montag. Love is not a sin. It is not weakness. It is strength." Igraine's eyes fixed him with another hard gaze, as hard as she could manage at least. They fluttered closed again. Her breath labored on. "Promise . . . me. Please take care of Eleanor."

Montag shifted uncomfortably on his knees, again clasping his sister's hand in his own. He laid his head on her bed. To an observer it was the perfect image of prayer. In Montag's mind, a thousand curses were being flung to God, to Enric . . . and even to himself. If he had only fought harder to pull her away from Enric's grasp! Then she would still be his beautiful sister, the Lady of the Tournament. He groaned.

A fragile voice whispered from the bed, the grating urgency despite weakness bringing the plea to his ears like thunder to an empty sky. "Please . . . Montag . . . promise me . . ."

"I will Igraine. I will." He didn't recognize his own voice, as it rasped the words through his emotion.

She breathed a sigh and seemed to sink deeper into her pillows.

With her eyes firmly closed, she whispered, "Will you forgive me?"

He furrowed his brow in confusion.

"For betraying the family to follow my heart. For not being there for you in your grief over Alenor. I know now how you must have felt—"

The pain in his chest flared hot as his pulse suddenly pounded as hard as it did in a fight.

She continued, "I regret not being there for you more, through all of it. With Father. I could have been a better sister."

"Stop," Montag rasped. Igraine opened her eyes, studying him with the most clarity she'd mustered thus far, then let them fall closed, the weight of the lids too great. The sound of her labored breathing hung in the air for several minutes. Montag fought his body, willing his lungs and heart to stop their race.

"Brother," she whispered so faintly he had to lean forward to hear her. "I forgive you. It's time you forgive yourself." When her lips stopped moving, she lay unnaturally still.

"Igraine?" Montag whispered. She did not respond, even when he shook her gently. He watched her chest rise and fall, her breath coming in irregular rhythm. He sat next to her, her frail hand in his own massive palm, and no matter what strength he prayed into her, she did not rally. As dawn's rays cut the sky early the next morning, Montag finally rose on stiff knees. He let go of her cold hand and wiped the feel of death off on his pants. He looked down

on the shell before him, then abruptly turned away, his mouth in a firm line of fury and pain.

The manor scurried into action as he strode through it. Maids burst into tears, realization dawning that their mistress was dead. The grooms jumped into action to ready horses, though they were uncertain if Montag would want to ride out or not. The cook pushed pots of water into the hearth before the kitchen boy had even built up the fire. There was fear and grief in everyone's eyes, for the beast of a man that roamed their home did not seem in a mind easy to tame. But it was not the household that Montag wanted to find. It was a child, a little girl he had seen only from a distance.

There before the hearth in the main hall, he found her. Slowly, the little five-year-old girl turned to face him, her face illuminated by the faint light of dawn shining through the manor windows. It lit her brown hair like a halo. Montag caught his breath, the stabbing knife in his guts twisting anew. She had certainly inherited Igraine's beauty, but with it, her father's dark hair and arrogantly angled features. Despite the dawn, she was already fully dressed, as the lady of the manor should be.

"My mother?" she asked in a small voice.

Montag shook his head, at a loss for words.

The child straightened her back and though she frowned, she did not shed a tear. "Would you like breakfast, Lord Montag?" she said carefully.

Montag shook his head, wondering what to make of her. Just what had Igraine trained this creature to be?

The little girl looked away, back toward the fire. "I'm not hungry either," she said quietly. She glanced up at him, suddenly nervous. "I'm not sure how to plan a funeral." She said it like a guilty confession, as if she knew this most important piece of her education was lacking.

Montag glared at her now, relishing in how she glanced away from him and her shoulders began to sag. *That's right, little daughter of Enric. You'll learn your place in this world like your father never did.* "We will bury her, and then we will leave."

"Leave?" The child's eyes grew wide.

"You're going to my castle in Alsace."

"Where's Alsace?"

"Where's . . ." Montag's eyebrows shot up. "They could teach you hospitality but they didn't teach you where your mother came from?"

"My father's family is from here, in Aquitaine." The girl chewed her lip. "Can we invite them to the funeral?"

"There is not going to be a funeral," Montag growled. "I need to get back."

"I can stay and run the manor until after the funeral. Just tell me how to find Alsace. I am a strong rider!"

Montag burst out laughing, only causing the girl to frown deeper.

"Fine. We will have a funeral. Send for your priest. Send for whoever you want." He turned on his heel. Breakfast might be good after all. At least a liquid breakfast consisting of strong ale.

"Uncle . . ." the little voice called.

He stopped.

"Did you love my mother?"

He stiffened as if struck. Hastily he turned and strode out of the hall. In the safety of the empty stairwell, he brushed wetness from his cheek. Ale. That's what he needed. A good ale.

Chapter 50

May 1199

Alec finished his part of the tale as they rode into Levan Manor's darkened courtyard. The moonlight overhead and the dim candlelight from the household's cottage windows illuminated the pain etched in Eleanor's face. Yet there was something else there, a spark in her eyes. Perhaps it was understanding.

Alec dismounted and held her horse's bridle. She made no move to get down from her horse, instead looking down at him with the regal posture of the knightess she was. He smiled a little to himself. If she wasn't his wife, he would have been intimidated.

She did not return his smile, her hands fidgeting with her reins, twisting the leather in her palms.

"I remember asking him that." Her voice was a breath on the wind, so faint that at first he thought he'd misheard.

Eleanor inhaled slowly, and Alec watched her pull herself together like a knight entering the tournament ring. She swung off the saddle and onto the ground, her

hand lingering on her horse's neck as she avoided meeting his eye. "I remember it much as you described. My early childhood was so perfect, Alec. My parents were the kind every child deserves and so few receive. I remember losing a little brother, though I never saw him. The day my father died I didn't realize what was going on, not entirely. I was so excited to see the knights. And when my mother passed—" She took a breath. "As you tell it, knowing how it all turned out, the story of my life is a tragedy. The bad men won."

Alec narrowed his eyes at her. "You think they won?"

"They survived didn't they?" She scoffed.

"Montag lived out his life surrounded by darkness, alone. I don't think he ever forgave himself for what he did to Alenor. He broke his own heart and was never able to love again. He kept your cousin at arm's length, never getting to experience the love between father and son. He lived in fear of his own father his whole life. Lezay may have lived on to do more damage, but in the end, he got his due." Alec's lips pressed into a firm line. Did Eleanor know the full extent of what had happened during the melee two years prior, the one in which Lezay had died? "The two of them survived longer than your parents, but what kind of existence is that, living alone in fear, mistrust, hatred?"

Alec put his finger under Eleanor's chin, forcing her to meet his eyes. "Your parents did not have long lives, but they had love, and they loved you. That foundation is what gave you the strength to be the wonderful, independent, kind-hearted woman that now stands before me. They are the victors here. And their victory lives on in you, because you have chosen to live in the light and not follow the darkness that pulled at you from all sides."

Tears glistened in her eyes, and he could not help but press his lips into hers. When he pulled away, her arms curled around his waist. He held her tight. "Eleanor, you saved me from the same darkness that ate Montag, did you know that?"

He felt her shake her head against his chest.

"I was in a bad place when we met. You don't know how deep my depravity was etched. You know what my intentions were as they pertained to you . . . and thankfully that is not what I got. That is because of the pure fire within you. Now these past few years with you, our son . . . it has changed me, Eleanor. This time with you has been such a gift."

She pulled away to look at him, her eyes shining with emotion. "You brought me into myself, Alec. Give yourself credit where it is due."

He smiled at her.

"I have one request as we go forward though."

A bubble of trepidation lodged in his gut.

"No more secrets." Eleanor shook her head, then met his eye with the fierce gaze of the warrior within her. "We are partners in this, Alec. And we are stronger together.

You learn something, particularly if it pertains to this grandfather that's appeared, I want to know."

He smiled down at her. "Fair enough."

She pressed a light kiss to his lips, but it was quickly interrupted by the sound of a door.

"Wait, no. Get back here!" a woman's voice said from the door of the manor.

Eleanor and Alec turned to see their approaching groom glance over his shoulder before turning back to the manor to help a maid restrain a toddler's escape through the open doorway. The little boy reached out his arms towards his parents, squealing in delight. The maid yielded to his wriggling body and placed him on his wobbly legs. With his fist clamped around her fingers, he toddled over towards them, not a trace of fear of the dark night, big horses, or the two figures that stood in the darkness of his courtyard evident.

Eleanor shot a smile up to Alec then knelt and spread her arms, her tiny son climbing into her lap and throwing his chubby little arms around her neck.

Alec watched the two of them and smiled. His heart swelled with joy and gratitude. This, this was living in the light. The risks taken by two lovers a generation ago had created this. Just what was in the works now?

About the Author

When J.A. Stein isn't dreaming up stories of centuries past, you can find her training horses like those in her stories. Or perhaps you won't find her at all, as she frequently disappears into America's stunning wilderness to chase adventure. She loves to read anything that has a plot and makes it a goal to write stories that can't be put down.

Reviews of this book are greatly appreciated and can be left on any retailer site, as well as Bookbub.com and Goodreads.com. The newsletter for this series includes bonus chapters, upcoming events, writing tips, and more. Please subscribe at www.authorjastein.com.

Looking for social media? You won't find it. Stein is a firm believer that time is better spent reading a book than a news feed. Then there is more time left over to experience your own story. That said, we'll pretend YouTube isn't social media. Check out @AuthorJAStein.

Acknowledgments

Despite all the hours we writers spend in silent isolation trying to put the thoughts in our heads onto paper, no one writes a book alone.

This book would still be hidden on a flash drive if it weren't for all the other individuals that offered their help and encouragement.

I owe a huge thank you to the awesome ladies on CritiqueMatch, Lindley, Emily, and Diane. Each of your unique perspectives brought out the shine in this story. Thank you for putting up with my silly mistakes while still keeping your feedback positive. Then there is my amazing editor Gail Delaney, who can comb through a massive manuscript and find all the spots where I've forgotten grammatical rules, among other things. I am so grateful for your attention to detail. Laura, my wonderful cover designer at Venom Co, thank you for being patient with me and bringing my vague ideas to life. I also owe thanks to my mom and my sister, who I can always count on to tell me if a story is ready to share with the world or not.

And Jake, though you don't read, thank you for listening to me brainstorm what my characters would and wouldn't do, and for all the nights I made you watch the TV muted.

To all the fans of *Knightess*, among which are the amazing ladies in the Orwigsburg Library Book Club, thank you for your support and encouragement. From you I get the confidence to actually tell people, "Hey, I wrote a book." I hope you enjoy this long awaited next installment. (And it didn't even take me 20 years!)

Also By J.A. Stein

Knightess is the epic medieval tale of Lady Eleanor de Levan, a woman running from her past, even if it means hiding her identity and pretending to be a commoner. She is content with her simple life, until Sir Alec Earnblaec discovers her secret. She is nobility, and she has a husband that wants her back. The delicate arrangement that ensues forces Eleanor to question how much her secret is worth, as Alec both builds up her confidence and challenges her resolve. Can she face her past in all its ugliness? Will she find the courage to face her fears, including her fear to love? The woman that emerges is no timid maid, as Alec assumed. She is a knightess, and she is strong.

The story continues with the grand finale of Eleanor's tale, *English Winter*. Once again, everything Eleanor has struggled to build, including her manor and her family, is threatened when her dark grandfather returns.

Is her and Alec's love strong enough to survive? Can she protect her son from a threat that knows no borders?

Perhaps the most intense novel of the series, *English Winter* will have you on the edge of your seat until the last page turns.

Also try *The Last Farm* and *Patch Town*, tales set near the author's hometown in Pennsylvania, each with a historical and romantic element.